THE SEA GLASS MURDERS

A Gold Coast Mystery

Timothy Cole

Pace Press
Fresno, California

Published by Pace Press
An imprint of Linden Publishing
2006 South Mary Street, Fresno, California 93721
(559) 233-6633 / (800) 345-4447
PacePress.com

book design by Andrea Reider
cover design by Tanja Prokop, www.bookcoverworld.com

Pace Press and colophon are trademarks of
Linden Publishing, Inc.

ISBN 978-0-941936-03-3

135798642

Printed in the United States of America
on acid-free paper.

This is a work of fiction. The names, places, characters, and incidents in this book are used fictitiously, and any resemblance to actual people, places, or events is coincidental.

Library of Congress Cataloging-in-Publication Data on file.

For Sarah Smedley, the love of my life

"Everything must be taken into account. If the fact will not fit the theory—let the theory go."

—Agatha Christie, *The Mysterious Affair at Styles*

Prologue

Dasha Petrov looked back on it later, after the dust had settled... after they'd removed the dead body from her living room.

This whole sordid business started with a scream in the night, she thought, a scream I never heard.

She had been sound asleep. She'd felt out of sorts and had taken a pill. Her sister Galina heard it. But because of Galina's stroke, the poor dear couldn't describe what she'd heard, and anyway, Dasha was snoring away, oblivious.

She had tried keeping Galina company in front of the fire—feeling the need to stay close. But Dasha had had a funny stomach, and those early shakes that would lead to fever. Wrapped up in an old quilt to ease the chills, it seemed to Dasha they were always huddled in front of a fire—first in that long-ago hovel in the Russian countryside, ice and snow blasting through the shutters, these days in their garden cottage along Connecticut's Gold Coast. When they were younger, there were campfires with schoolmates in the woods outside Prague, fires on the rocky shores of the Adriatic, fires in steel barrels with those wonderful American GIs far from home. There were the stubborn fires of the Berlin ruins, the catastrophic fires of the Pilsen bombardment, the comforting fires in the manor house at the end of the drive by the water. Her husband Constantine was alive and Seabreeze, their home, was in proper trim. Children put to bed, Dasha and Constantine would curl up in front of a cozy fire, sip a brandy, and tour the horizon.

Now it was just Dasha and Galina, situated agreeably in the guest quarters. Dasha's eldest son Boris had taken over the manor house. He and his family needed the space. She and

Galina had gladly removed themselves, slipping gently into their twilight. Galina had spent more than fifty years tending to the sick; Dasha was retired from the intelligence services of her adopted country—practiced at the theft of secrets. She looked back on her career with satisfaction. As with many émigrés, she loved America with unstinting devotion, having known intimately the dark heart of Nazi Germany, and a Soviet Russia bent on domination.

They had plenty of books and the Russian language newspaper. They were perfecting their borscht, indulging in a nightly vodka, and watching the news on television. Dasha's Soviet enemies would not soon forget the year 1989. There were nightly reports of the Red Army being driven back from its ill-conceived invasion of Afghanistan, graveyard of empires. And Gorbachev's campaign of glasnost was opening fresh lines of communication with the west. It was exciting. Sometimes Dasha would tell Galina stories about the old days and Galina would light up with the glow of remembrance. These days, the only way Galina could get in a word was by using her Russian Scrabble pieces, hastily arranged to ask a question—or issue a rejoinder. Galina would move the little squares to find just the right phrase, and Dasha would offer an encouraging response, plumbing the depths of her dwindling patience, knowing they'd have an eternity to speak once they reached the other side—as the scriptures promised.

But that night Dasha just wasn't herself. Maybe it was the cabbage rolls—*galuptsie*—their mother's recipe, from the time there was never enough to eat.

"*Spakuene noche, Galinka*," she'd said, employing the diminutive. "Not feeling well. Going off to take a pill."

Galina patted her younger sister on the hand and continued to gaze into the embers. The guesthouse had a great room with the fireplace and long table for dining. There was a smaller table for their Scrabble set in the corner window overlooking the garden. There was a galley kitchen accessed through a door at one end, and a greenhouse jutting off at an angle, where Constantine had propagated the spring plantings. Their bedrooms were in a little wing in the back. It was cozy, but suffered the same state of dilapidation as the rest of the once-thriving Seabreeze.

Dasha fast asleep, Galina stoking the fire with her one good hand, they would look back on this night and mark it down as the time when everything changed.

"It was a scream," insisted Galina with her Scrabble pieces.

She'd heard it coming from across the hedge, a female in distress—then male voices, agitated and urgent.

An emergency.

To Galina the nurse it seemed like her whole life had been one long emergency. First, the Paris hospital where she'd trained, then pressed into service with Patton's Third Army. After the German surrender she'd been hurled into the unspeakable calamity of Buchenwald and the typhus outbreak—then the emergency department of New York's Bellevue Hospital and the city's nightly avalanche of mayhem. She knew the sound of humanity stretched to the limit.

She tried to wake Dasha, but Dasha just snored away in drug-induced slumber.

Galina didn't dare go outside. Too windy and dark.

She went to the ancient rotary phone and dialed 911.

"What is the nature of your emergency?" asked the operator. Galina could only mumble, and the operator had the good sense to trace the call and alert the police. The night dispatcher radioed a patrol car and received an acknowledgment.

Galina waited in the great room watching the embers lose their glow. She didn't want to bother Boris. The police would arrive soon.

But the police never came that night. Galina never knew why.

Dasha's fever broke late the next day—after tea with lemon, honey, and a jigger of vodka. Galina tried to tell her about the scream, but Dasha just didn't understand.

"I know, Galina, dear. Sometimes I want to scream too," said Dasha. Soon, Galina would forget the scream in the night. She was usually pin sharp, but she was growing a little forgetful, especially when it came to recent events.

Later, after the pieces fell into place, it dawned on Dasha that the mess had started with a scream she'd never heard, and the unexpected arrival a few days later of the detective named DeFranco—with that beautiful red-haired girl.

That's when things really started to unravel, thought Dasha.

It was rare, in her retirement, to take in strangers. But she'd been both attracted and repelled when she saw them out on the beach. Curiosity overcame any initial reticence. She trusted her situational awareness, which had been tested under far more trying circumstances. She had a talent for calculating the distance and direction of any threat—in her gut, her peripheral vision, her nerve endings. When she saw the pair coming down the beach, she was naturally put on guard. She had legions of trusted friends—and a lifetime of enemies.

But she'd take the risk.

She remembered thinking…just like you, Dasha, to take the risk.

1

Discovery

Four days had gone by since Dasha Petrov's sister heard the commotion across the hedge. A squall had just passed over the collection of modest storefronts at Canal and Main, one of the outer enclaves of Westport, Connecticut—home to McMansions, fancy retail outlets, and gifted children. Rainwater flooded the greasy potholes in the parking lot behind the hardware store, and twilight was transitioning to a moonless night. Sergeant Anthony DeFranco exited the department's unmarked Ford Crown Victoria and approached the scene, red and white lights from a police cruiser pulsing against the trees. First responder Wendell McKurdy had taken the initiative of stringing crime scene tape around the green metal dumpster, where the hardware store stock boy had reported seeing a body.

Earlier that day the boy had inadvertently thrown away an envelope filled with receivables from the store's household accounts. The trash had been taken out to the dumpster, and the store owner produced a stepladder so the lad could climb in to recover the lost checks. The boy told McKurdy he'd dug down into the fetid waste and assorted swill to encounter the stiffened horror of what he thought at first was a mannequin or a blow-up doll—somebody's idea of a joke. But as he pulled away more refuse he realized the object was a formerly living human being. He'd scrambled back out over the side of the dumpster and down the ladder, fallen into the mud, and promptly convulsed in dry heaves. Pleas and cries brought his boss to the dumpster, and he too bore witness. The shaken youngster now sat in McKurdy's cruiser as DeFranco approached the scene.

He could smell it from twenty feet away. A thousand dead rats couldn't produce a smell like that. It was mixed with... What? Maybe ozone in the air? And something else. The last time he'd smelled a smell like that was in the far-off Republic of Vietnam. Death, of course. Unmistakable. Sweet, rotten, choking death. But napalm too? Jellied gasoline? Here?

He thought he'd left that smell for good in Southeast Asia.

There were protocols. First, any footprints near the dumpster would need to be photographed with a ruler for scale. The soles of the stock boy's shoes would also need to be photographed and archived; so too the soles of the hardware store owner. He spotted some prints in a muddy spot on the ground and swung his well-traveled Nikon into action. The flashgun filled the air with light. He walked around the big green box—Lord, that smell!—and spotted more footprints, one of which was deep enough to qualify for a stone casting. He knelt to take a closer look, took a photo, and marked the impression with a small flag.

At last he came up to the front of the dumpster, tiptoeing across a shallow puddle so as not to besmirch his Florsheims, and braced to peer inside. He took his Mini Maglite out of the pocket of his trench coat and twisted the lens.

This is why you get the big bucks, he told himself.

The lid to the dumpster was open, and right where the boy had pulled away some cardboard refuse—packaging for Weber grills and Duracell batteries and DeWalt drill drivers—was a blackened chunk of charred human flesh. It looked like lamb on a spit at the fireman's fair. The skin was split in places, and where it was split he could see the pinkish brown of the flesh underneath. The body had no head and no hands. Its arms were raised in supplication.

Headless? Why not? thought DeFranco. Let's really mess up an otherwise pleasant evening.

He glanced over his shoulder and was gratified to see a staffer from the medical examiner's office waft up behind him wearing a face mask and a one-piece plastic coverall.

Jones.

The last time DeFranco had seen Curtis Jones was six months before, covering an overturned church van on I-95, Sherwood Island exit. Four dead, three of them kids under ten. Two adults paralyzed from the neck down. It had been a long night.

Jones handed DeFranco a face mask and he put it on with care, linking arms with his fellow public servant. Jones was a crime-scene technologist, a diener in the argot of criminology, and his jurisdiction ranged all over Fairfield County—from the drug dens of Bridgeport to the stuffy old enclave of Greenwich, site of the Martha Moxley murder a decade earlier, when a Kennedy cousin had allegedly brained the poor thing with a six iron.

Jones ascended the stepladder and boosted himself over the edge and into the squalid hell. He extracted a penlight from a breast pocket and started his analysis.

"Female," Jones recited dispassionately. "Breasts have been burned clean off, but there's enough tissue left to offer a quick take. Need to confirm that back at the morgue. I don't see any genitalia but a body in this state is often of indeterminate sex. Not an African-American, but not white either. She's not burned from the knees down. Nice pedicure. Looks like a ring on the toe next to the big one on her left foot. We'll have to take a closer look."

Jones took out a magnifying glass and focused on the maggots embedded in the neck wound. "No blue bottle flies yet, pupae only," he said. "We'll want to get an entomologist on that. The maggots' growth rate will help establish the time of death."

DeFranco listened while Jones recited more observations. The neck wound was brown with rot but he could still see blood vessels, structures, and bone. Jones muttered something about serrations that might match up with the saw that had removed the victim's head.

"State CID will be here in a little while," said Jones. "Why not let them help me haul her out of here? They're going to want to take this over from the get-go."

"They already called," said DeFranco. "They tasked Westport PD to do at least an initial. They don't have the staff. Budget cuts."

"Whoa… Well, I'm telling you now," said Jones. "If this turns out to be one of those made-for-TV thrillers and you're on the witness stand, some smart son of a bitch might rip you a new one. Think F. Lee Bailey."

"Jones, what are you saying?" DeFranco's tone sharpened. He looked into the wizened African-American face of a man clearly his better when it came to life's ugly underside.

"I'm just saying you better get thy shit together at *your* crime scene. You own it," said Jones. "*60 Minutes* might come knocking. Let me get you a fresh suit out of my truck."

"Oh Jesus," said DeFranco, yearning for simpler days when he could put on his patrolman's uniform and march in the Memorial Day parade.

Why can't somebody else do this? he wondered, realizing just as quickly that the chief was too busy scheduling speeches at the Rotary Club, and the newbie McKurdy was barely competent to write traffic tickets. DeFranco was one of three members of Westport PD's so-called "detective bureau," and today he had the watch. His compadres in the unit were either off duty or out of town—one on vacation, one on bereavement leave following the death of his father. Otherwise, DeFranco would be functioning as a uniformed sergeant, serving as backup for those of lesser rank, like McKurdy, who, DeFranco noted, remained in his car to avoid dealing with the awful mess the stock boy had discovered.

The joys of seniority, DeFranco mused. Somehow the senior guy always had to get dirty, especially when things got out of hand. Sure, his seniority allowed for some flexibility when it came to duty assignments. Seniority helped when he took those moonlighting jobs at the Trumbull Mall, working security so he could help his son and daughter with tuition.

No, DeFranco told himself. You're it.

And he had to press on.

He accompanied Jones to the coroner's van and suited up, carefully folding his off-the-rack sports jacket and placing it on the front seat of the van. He kept his Colt .38 hammerless snub-nosed revolver, his "snubbie," on his hip, pulled on the coverall, and put a double layer of booties over his wingtip shoes. His long-deceased wife, Julie, would have understood that sometimes in life you had to climb into a dumpster with a corpse. But never with your good shoes.

He and Jones also double-layered their latex gloves, cinched up their hoods, donned goggles over their face masks, and otherwise girded for the intense unpleasantness that was about to ensue.

"She was dumped," said Jones. "Killed. Decapitated. Mutilated. Set on fire. All someplace else, then dropped here."

"Yeah, I get that," said DeFranco. "Otherwise, you'd have blood everywhere, and this whole dumpster would be torched."

"Looks like there was some effort to cover her up with trash," said Jones. "She's in pretty deep so she could make the trip to the transfer station without much bother."

"And from there to the compactor, to the truck, to the landfill. Sayonara," said DeFranco. "Still a good chance somebody would find her. Dumb not to put her in the ground."

He looked around the edges of the big metal box to see if any pieces of the body had come adrift during these exertions. The dumpster was the secondary—possibly tertiary—crime scene. He knew intrinsically that the location where this person met her demise would lead them to the killer.

Jones had a camera, too, and light from their camera-mounted flash units knifed through the gathering dark. Later, DeFranco noted how the photos didn't do justice to the horror of it. The pictures were flat and inhuman. The reality included the otherworldly stench, the oozing meat, and the sheer oddity of seeing well-pedicured feet protruding from the blackened torso.

Jones, bless him, climbed into the dumpster and probed around the deceased.

"Light sucks," he said. "And getting worse. This penlight isn't going to cut it. I've got a headlamp on the dash of the van. There's a body bag on a shelf. Eye level. Left side. Rack in the back. And get me that ball of polypro twine. I also need some evidence bags to tie around her feet and arms, and I guess that neck stub. It will hold the maggots in so we can get them into formaldehyde and measured."

DeFranco happily assumed the role of assistant, even though he knew Jones was a mere functionary too, chief assistant to the eminent medical examiner Dr. Samuel Goldberg. From prior dealings with the medical examiner's office, DeFranco knew that Goldberg, confined to a wheelchair due to childhood polio, rarely left his midtown Stamford morgue, where he could surround himself with the tools and chemicals and reference works of his bizarre but necessary trade. Goldberg sent forth Jones and crew to collect the sad remnants of humanity, a good portion of whom had departed this world unwillingly. DeFranco knew that Jones had an associate's degree in accounting and a certificate in criminal justice. At one point he said he wanted to be a cop. Now he was one of Goldberg's go-to crime scene investigators, having learned his craft at the knee of the great ME and through on-the-job training.

DeFranco was about to see Jones in action. He handed up the lamp. Jones put it on his head and explored around the corpse, starting at the feet and moving up the torso to the arms jutting forth.

"I'm looking for a weapon. Could be anything. Or a chemical stain. Or blood spatters. Or ligatures. Or wounding. Or a personal item like jewelry that could help identify this person." He used the word *person*, DeFranco reflected. He needed to remember that.

"We'll get that toe ring off back at the office and have a good look at it," Jones continued. "But for now the only thing I'm seeing is the faint outline of a tattoo on the left hip that remains unscorched. A butterfly? No, that's a hummingbird." The shape of any tattoos might be characteristic of an individual artist who could potentially help in identifying the victim.

"I am seeing bilateral scarring on the ankles from some kind of rope or twine. Was she trussed? But it's the skin pigmentation that's got me stumped. She's not black. And she's not white. I still say Middle Eastern...or Pakistani...maybe."

The stench now included a distinct note of human shit to add to the rotting meat and the sharply chemical aroma of gasoline... or was it diesel? DeFranco really tried not to throw up. But at last he couldn't bear it and walked well away from the dumpster, removed his mask and hurled his noonday lunch of tuna fish on rye onto the moistened asphalt. McKurdy, he was happy to see, was conveying the stock boy to the lad's parents, who were hustling him into a Mercedes sedan. DeFranco assumed they'd be making an appointment with a counselor so the poor kid could put the afternoon's trauma behind him. McKurdy wouldn't see his superior toss his cookies like a rank amateur.

Jones was rolling the body back and forth to get a glimpse underneath, ahhhing and hmmmming and seeming not to notice DeFranco's discomfort. Embarrassed, DeFranco thought Jones might be adopting an air. Jones would never throw up at a crime scene. Or if he had, no one would ever know.

"You're not the first person to get the heebie-jeebies, especially on one this bad," said Jones, not unkindly.

"Sorry," said DeFranco, feeling minuscule against the bulwark of Jones's experience.

"Okay. I don't think I see anything unusual here other than the corpse itself, which is highly unusual. No weapons. No stained clothing. No clothing period. No personal items like purses. No obvious entry or exit wounds apart from the decapitation. We'll get a closer look at that back at the lab. I'll bet we can capture some tool marks. I do see those unusual ankle scars. But for the rest, just a naked, burned-up body. It's going to be a bitch determining time of death. But there is obvious rigor, and we'll measure those maggot pupae. Dr. Goldberg won't like having the head missing. He likes to establish time of death by analyzing the vitreous humor of the eyeball. And sometimes burn victims can throw off time estimates." Jones was droning on, DeFranco observed, and he'd really need to nail all this down in a report.

"We'll need to put her in the body bag. Then you'll have to help me get her out of here. I am estimating about five feet five inches tall. Hard to tell without a head. We'll measure her femur when we get her on the table. That'll give us the height for sure. And I am estimating a weight of 110 pounds. Easy enough to manage. But it will take two of us. You up for that?"

"I s'pose," said DeFranco, trying to act game but nonchalant, as if hoisting the charred remains of dead females out of dumpsters was an everyday occurrence.

Jones performed the necessary work of laying the bag out next to the body. He tied the twine onto the woman's arms and around her torso, trussing the victim so her arms would fit into the bag. DeFranco watched, appalled, from outside the dumpster as the skin of the corpse seemed to melt into sheets and shift around the body like plates of semi-cooled lava.

"Come on up and help me get her in," ordered Jones. "Let's just hope she stays together."

He just wanted to get it over with, and, insensitive as it later seemed, he told himself it was like picking up the garbage from the yard after the raccoons had had their way. You had to just hold your nose and get on with it.

He climbed up the ladder, hoisted a leg over the side of the dumpster, and joined Jones in the fetid, stinking, sordid, disgraceful receptacle, final resting place of this formerly living human being.

"Do you want to take the head, so to speak, or the feet? You get the heavy end up there," asked Jones, offering DeFranco a choice.

DeFranco remained near the woman's upper torso; shifting to her lower half would only cause delay.

"This is fine," he said. "Let's get it over with."

"Hold her by the shoulders. Don't pull on an arm or it might come off," said Jones. "Believe me, it's happened. Just like a lamb shank falling off the bone."

The body bag was clean and sanitized and unzipped to its full length. She'd only take up half of it, thought DeFranco, recovered enough to settle his nerves and take in some detail. There was a sheet inside the bag to wrap around her before zipping her up. He knew the sheet was intended to capture and retain any stray trace objects that fell off the body between the dumpster and the autopsy table.

"Okay," said Jones. "On three. Pick her up and place her in gently. Don't try to slide her. The skin might come off her back. One. Two. Three." They lifted the corpse, which felt surprisingly light, and settled it into the bag. Jones zipped the bag closed and set about the task of tying twine to the handholds fore and aft. The idea, he said, was to get the body up on the lip, then gently lower it to the ground. They would climb out, move the body onto a gurney, move the gurney to the coroner's van, and Jones could get back to the office in Stamford in time to watch the rest of the pennant race for the American League East.

"It's Rocktober," he said, snatching some kind of normalcy from the daily insanity that had become his life. He told DeFranco wife number two had just divorced him because he wouldn't open up about his work.

"Last thing I want to talk about when I get home," said Jones. He told DeFranco home was an oasis, a safe harbor where he could forget the day's passing chaos. "I'm trying to get off the antidepressants."

"Sorry, man. If the taxpayers only knew," returned DeFranco in support, thinking of the way Julie had just *accepted* him the way he was—the screwy hours, the snotty, entitled, populace, the office climbers, the promises of promotion that never came. Always a chief on his way through Westport toward some loftier height, standing on the shoulders of the simple strivers like DeFranco, who weren't going anywhere.

Julie.

He missed her every day.

They climbed out of the dumpster, gave the contents a good look with their flashlights, and stood over the body bag at their feet. The cardboard she had been resting on was stained and wrinkled.

"I'm going to put that top layer of cardboard into some evidence bags," said Jones. "But there might be more underneath it."

"I'll figure out a way to empty the dumpster and sift through the contents," said DeFranco.

For now, all he wanted to do was get the body on its way to the morgue and start to secure the scene. He and Jones lifted her onto the gurney and Jones wheeled her to the van. Practiced at his craft, Jones shoved the gurney into the back of the vehicle and started removing his protective gear.

"Just stick your stuff in the bag in the back so I can put it in the incinerator when I get back to HQ," he told DeFranco. DeFranco complied, suddenly exhausted.

"You'll want to observe the autopsy, I suppose," said Jones. "We've got a bit of a backlog, but I am thinking around two p.m. tomorrow. Call in the morning to confirm."

"Just great," said DeFranco, his lack of enthusiasm palpable.

"The DA will need to be notified, of course, and I don't envy you having to paw through that dumpster."

"Yes. I've got a plan for that." DeFranco turned to McKurdy, who was standing stiffly next to his vehicle. The patrolman's pants' crease was a little too crisp, biceps too honed, badge and buckle too shined.

"McKurdy? A minute of your time if you're not too busy," said DeFranco, failing to conceal an acid tone. *Next time, let's see him get in the dumpster with the headless corpse.*

"Yes, sir," responded McKurdy.

"Buy a combination padlock from the hardware store here and secure the lid of the dumpster. Get a receipt. Set the combination at 06-02-45, my birthday. Then, call the sanitation department and have them send over a truck to pick it up. We need to inspect the contents and they need to take it over to the transfer station on the Sherwood Island Connector. Make sure it stays inside tonight and we'll dump it out tomorrow. We need an inside space with a concrete floor. Do you think you can do that?" asked DeFranco, retaining an edge he later reflected McKurdy didn't deserve. McKurdy, the low man, was just trying to do his job.

"Okay," McKurdy repeated back. "Secure the dumpster with a padlock...use the combination 06-02-45. Call Sanitation and have them remove the dumpster and store it overnight at the transfer station. The contents will be inspected in the morning."

"Mostly right," said DeFranco. "It has to be secured *inside* the building. Behind a locked door. Clear?" He was already thinking about the chain of custody for any evidence he might find inside the big green box.

"Crystal," said McKurdy, who turned on his heels and walked over to the hardware store. DeFranco set about the task of taking a casting of the footprint of interest, pouring in the quickset mix and waiting for it to harden.

Just then a van with a folded satellite antennae on top came roaring into the parking area behind the hardware store. A young woman got out of the right seat and ran over to DeFranco, who was leaning on the driver's side of Jones's vehicle.

"Tracy Taggart. News 12 Connecticut," said the woman, breathing hard and looking a little panicked.

He knew Tracy Taggart from watching her spot news reports on television, mostly town board meetings and track meets. Homicide was the big leagues for this small-town newshawk. She was prettier in person, thought DeFranco, hearing Julie scold him from the back of beyond.

"I will let you handle this one," said Jones. "My friend in the back has an appointment with the doctor." He started up the van, performed a K-turn, and left with the mysterious headless woman. DeFranco turned to the reporter before him.

"What would you like to know?" he asked her, knowing full well she wanted to know everything—and she wanted to know it now. He knew when he saw her reporting on the morrow it would be limited to the top gloss and drivel that had become the staple of television news. This was different, though. Incendiary. The gentle citizens of Westport, Connecticut, would not take kindly to a headless corpse in their fair town. Appearances. The nation was focused on the Iran-Contra scandal—the Watergate of the '80s—but he knew a headless corpse in sleepy, sylvan Westport would lead the news and make it to the top of the fold in the local papers. Maybe penetrate the bigger markets.

"Scanner indicated you've got a possible Signal 50," said the young woman. The news operations kept radio scanners crackling away throughout their day so they could overhear police and fire commands. The news media memorized the codes. A Signal 50 was a homicide.

DeFranco assessed the young lady and couldn't help noticing her red hair, cut in a bob, green eyes, smart, tailored suit, and black high heels utterly inappropriate for the grungy parking lot where they were standing. Miss Taggart didn't seem to mind.

The department's policies on press information were very clear: Give the press minimal information in the field; refer the newshounds to the public information officer back at the station (who, he knew, was a nine-to-fiver and therefore unavailable).

"Not a lot to say at this point," said DeFranco. "We have a victim of an apparent homicide. That's all we know." She'd heard "Signal 50," after all, so there was no point in denying Westport had been visited by the sordid spectre of murder.

"Male? Female? ID?" inquired Taggart.

"Unfortunately, we don't have an identification at this point," said DeFranco. Tracy Taggart's cameraman was now directly in his face and he knew he would be on TV first thing in the morning. He had to get this right—or face the chief, who was sort of prickly when it came to the image of the Westport Police Department.

"Gender? Age? Signs of a struggle? Obvious wounds?" pressed Taggart. DeFranco decided he would have to fill her in on the basics. It might upset a lot of people.

"Let me take it from the top," he told the news reporter. "Are we rolling?"

"We are now," said Taggart.

"My name is Sergeant Anthony DeFranco of the Westport Police Department Criminal Investigation Division."

He paused to make it easy for the videotape editor; he had done this kind of thing before, most recently with that awful church van rollover. For all his misgivings about the crime scene, he was comfortable in front of the camera.

"This evening at five p.m. we received a call from the proprietor of Crossroads Hardware Store at the corner of Main and Canal in Westport. He told dispatch that an employee had found a suspicious object in the dumpster behind the store. Dispatch sent the nearest officer to the scene. Patrolman Wendell McKurdy responded and he notified the detective branch when he discovered what appeared to be a homicide victim in the dumpster. At this time we have no identification, and the body has been removed to the medical examiner's office in Stamford for identification. An autopsy is being scheduled and will be conducted by Fairfield County medical examiner Dr. Samuel Goldberg."

Name. Rank. Serial Number. Credit where credit was due.

"Sergeant DeFranco, can you tell us anything about the victim?" asked Taggart, not unreasonably.

"Unfortunately, we do not have sufficient information at this time to properly ID the victim," said DeFranco. Could he get away with avoiding the fact they had a headless corpse on their hands? It would surely come out, probably sooner rather than later. The high school would be buzzing with it tomorrow when the stock boy related his improbable find to a rapt audience in the school cafeteria. From there it would be transmitted to dinner tables, then the commuter rails, then the boardrooms and barrooms of America's largest metropolis. The news was about to be released, thought DeFranco, and the police department would need to be perceived in peak form. Could he spare Westport this ghastly detail for at least a night? He had to admit, Chief Talbot wouldn't want the news of a headless corpse to get around.

"Could you give us a description?" asked Taggart. "Maybe it's a missing person. Maybe the community can lend a hand in identifying this individual."

"Well. We would prefer to make an ID, then notify the family through the proper channels. That's our policy." Yes, he told himself, fall back on "policy." Maybe we'll get away with it.

"Okay. Thanks, Sergeant DeFranco," said Taggart, turning to face the lens while DeFranco drifted away. "So there you have it. An unidentified body has been found in a dumpster on the back streets of Westport, the apparent victim of a homicide. This will certainly disturb the normally placid community on Connecticut's Gold Coast. We will add details as we learn more. For News 12 Connecticut, reporting from Westport, I'm Tracy Taggart…Stop."

"DeFranco!" Taggart called. Did he detect a fit of pique? The camera wasn't rolling, so he relaxed the knot in his gut. Reporters did that to him. They always wanted to know everything *right now*. And sometimes he and his colleagues just didn't have any answers. But DeFranco knew the bromides: "We are attempting to ascertain that." "The situation is under investigation." And his favorite, "Sorry, but that's of an evidentiary nature."

The attractive red-haired reporter—he had to be ten years her senior—came striding up to DeFranco to pepper him with more questions. He'd put up the normal barriers, if he could, but he also knew that bit about the missing head was futile. Taggart and her fellow travelers would know about it soon enough. And he didn't want to turn this reporter into an enemy.

"You have to give me something better than that," said Taggart, smiling, confronting him while the cameraman loitered at a distance to capture some B-roll. DeFranco appreciated that. He may have been comfortable in front of the camera, but he didn't like the lens right in his face.

The young lady was a vision, short red hair dancing in a light breeze, her smile a beacon.

"Come to the ME's office around two tomorrow afternoon. The autopsy should be finished by then. I will try to feed you what we've got." He didn't say that the charred, headless remains found in sleepy Westport would likely bring out the media in droves when that detail came to light, a fact that could sink vaunted Westport to a new, unseemly low.

"Okay, two o'clock ," said Taggart with a disarming smile. "But I know there's something you're not telling me, and I want you to give it to me first. I don't want to schlep over there for nothing." Behind that smile she was a little feisty.

He kind of liked that.

"I'll look for you," said DeFranco, smiling at the young lady, feeling something of an urge he thought long dormant.

The truck from the sanitation department arrived to remove the green dumpster and McKurdy followed it to the solid-waste transfer station to make sure DeFranco's instructions were followed. DeFranco looked around the area, crime scene tape down, rain misting through the light from the street lamps, Westport residents tucked in front of their televisions, kids doing homework. He took comfort as a peacekeeper that things were settling down and his little town would continue its delicate rhythms.

Time for some basic police work. He took out his flashlight and walked in outward concentric circles around the empty spot where the dumpster had been—looking for…anything. Cigarette butts. Coke cans. Slips of paper, receipts. Tire tracks were now all a confused mishmash, so he decided the casting of the one distinctive footprint would remain the best hope for linking the killer or killers to the place where the girl was dumped. He walked through the parking lot to a cluster of small houses along Main Street and started knocking on doors. After identifying himself, he asked about vehicles dropping things off in the dumpster behind the hardware store sometime in the early morning hours. The door of the first house was answered by a dad just loosening his tie. He hadn't seen anything but he'd ask his wife. DeFranco produced a card and moved to the next house.

An older gentleman in a threadbare cardigan pushing a walker came to the door. Early morning hours? He was up performing his usual nocturnal chores in the lavatory…but hear anything? Sorry. DeFranco left his card and pushed on to the next modest dwelling in one of Westport's less flashy neighborhoods. Same answer. Dry holes.

He drove away in the Crown Vic, back to the station to start his paperwork. He remembered Westport when there was a Gristedes Market and a family-owned bookstore right on Main Street. Now they called it the miracle half mile of Banana Republic and Brooks Brothers and Anne Taylor. He turned right on Parker Harding Plaza, drove by the Saugatuck River at low tide, past the construction project that would become a gleaming new library, and on to the public safety building on Jesup Street. It was mercifully quiet, a soft night, and with just a touch of chill to suggest the advent of fall. It was the kind of evening that signaled all's well, as the town criers once intoned. He seized on the contradiction.

There was a murderer in town.

2

Body of Secrets

DeFranco climbed the back stairs and made his way to his cubicle to start typing, knowing that the district attorney, a yet-to-be-determined defense counsel, the news media, the mandarins in the front office, all would be reading his account of the evening's business and forming judgments.

Why didn't he care?

He poured himself a small glass of Jack Daniels, neat, from the bottle he kept in a drawer. He knew he would have to keep an eye on his alcohol consumption. Julie was somewhere in the back of his mind raising an eyebrow. He only took one shorty to settle his nerves and focus on his composition.

Dispatch received a 911 call at approximately 4:55 p.m. this date regarding a suspicious object in a dumpster behind the Crossroads hardware store at Main Street and Canal. Patrolman Wendell McKurdy was on the Post Road in the vicinity of the Westport Playhouse and took the call...

DeFranco kept it short and sweet.

That's it, he told himself. Dry, brief, and boring.

He was dog-tired, unable to decide if he was fatigued following a long, tragic day—or tired to the marrow by life and loss, by the sheer dead weight of loneliness. Julie gone, the kids embarked on their own lives, he was mired and squeezed in a job that put him square in the middle between a clueless management and the sometimes self-involved demands of his fellow citizens. Sure, he loved his neighbors—and his adult softball league—but listening to neighbors hurl insults, or parents in denial about their booze-and pot-addled children, or the constant urban bickering that every town is heir to, left him fatigued and flummoxed. DeFranco loathed and loved the place of his birth.

He packed his briefcase, turned out the lights, and walked down the back stairs to his waiting Toyota Corolla. He had bought it used for his daughter, Angelica. Now in her freshman year at UConn, she didn't need a car. His own ride, a 1975 Jeep Cherokee, had died a lingering death. His son Sam was a senior at Connecticut College in New London, consigned to the Peter Pan bus when he wanted to come home to Westport.

He squeezed behind the wheel of the Toyota, moving his holster out of the way so his ancient revolver wouldn't jab him in the gut. He was old-school, no need for all that semi-auto, high-capacity folderol.

He drove to the Post Road, turned right, and made his way to Maple Avenue South and then to his beloved dead end, High Gate Road, last house on the left. He liked to catch a glimpse of the little house as he rounded the corner—that piece of trim of an upstairs dormer in need of paint. He loved the lines of the little house, the cobblestone chimney, and the bow-front window in the front living room. Deferred maintenance aside, it was their home, and very close to being paid for. Julie had picked out the modest stick-built Cape in 1965 and now it was the DeFranco base camp. It was just as important to the kids as it was to him, now that Julie was gone and the house was filled with memories.

Indeed, it was a repository for all the DeFranco family history— albums, certificates, a ribbon or two. His grandfather had arrived at Ellis Island in 1911 and immediately took a laborer's job digging out the roadbed and building the stone bridges and iron trestles that would become the New Haven Line. Granddad had stopped in Westport and started a little grocery down on Main Street, moonlighting as an auxiliary policeman. You could do that in those days. His own dad had been a Westport police officer, and that's how Anthony DeFranco had entered the family business. His dad had made it to lieutenant and had run the Criminal Investigation Division. It didn't look like Anthony would achieve this professional pinnacle. But he and Julie had been content to raise the kids on their little street—Brownies, Cub Scouts, Julie's stint as a second-grade teacher, until the breast cancer took her.

That last year was hell on earth. His wife, his lover, mother of his children—confessor—was wasting away in front of his eyes, finally unable to sit up and take nourishment. She died at home in his arms, the kids gripped by shock and tears. He had known death—in Vietnam up close and personal. But that last kiss on her pale brow, the last touch of her lifeless fingertips—the sight of his *friend* being zipped up in a bag and carted off—assailed him with a feeling of complete and utter futility.

A doer at heart, there was nothing he could do.

And that sense of helplessness would have driven him mad had it not been for Sam and Angelica. They didn't know that needing him so much right then was the support he required to remain upright when they wheeled Julie's casket into the church, where they sang her wonderful praises. And then, graveside, when they placed her gently in the earth.

DeFranco entered his empty house, finding as usual a visceral distaste in all that quiet. He took a shower to get the sights and smells of the dumpster out of his mind. Most of the time his evening ablutions were perfunctory at best, but tonight he took a long look in the mirror. He had his hair, that was something wasn't it? Black—salt-and-pepper at the temples. He put that on the positive side of the ledger. He had his mother's high cheeks and his father's dimpled chin. Okay, the broken nose was a bit of a story, earned fair and square sliding into second base. In his younger days people would say he looked like one of those Italian crooners—Bennett, Martin, Como. The free weights in the garage kept his upper body in some state of condition, and the thrice weekly run down to Southport Beach and back meant he could stave off most of the ills of advancing age. But God, he needed to start to live his life, especially after today's brush with death—and the prospect of getting to know a certain red-haired young lady.

Did he have a shot? And what would Julie think?

"Julie would tell me to go for it," he said out loud, laughing right along with her as, he was convinced, she watched her Tony from the beyond. But then he had his doubts, misgivings that arrived uninvited without Julie to keep him buoyed.

He got into his flannel pajamas for the first time since the weather had turned. He stretched out in bed and read that morning's edition of the *Westport News* detailing the fervent gnashing of the representative town meeting—zoning regs, boundary lines, cost overruns; the happy energies of soccer tournaments, a football team bound for "States!," the soaring arias of The Staples Players.

The innocence of his town scrolled across the pages.

And soon, DeFranco thought, a headless corpse.

3

Devil in the Details

The next morning DeFranco exchanged the tattered Corolla for the Crown Vic and drove to the solid waste transfer facility. He entered the building and found Patrolman Wendell McKurdy standing next to the same dumpster, wearing rubber swamp boots and a one-piece coverall. He had a leaf rake in one hand and he was wearing rubber latex gloves. He had taken the initiative of organizing a sanitation crew with the right machinery. They would tip the dumpster over and spill the contents onto the concrete floor.

"Good morning, Sergeant," said McKurdy. DeFranco sensed an air of expectation, as if McKurdy assumed his diligence deserved at least a thank you. DeFranco didn't believe in doling out compliments for people who were just doing their jobs. No one ever thanked *him* for just doing his job...except maybe Julie.

"Good morning, McKurdy," returned DeFranco. "Who are these fine gentlemen?"

"This is Ron Smith, morning supervisor of the Westport Sanitation Department, and Homer Bigsby. Homer is going to dump the contents of this dumpster wherever you want it," said McKurdy. "And Mr. Smith is going to supervise. Afterwards, Homer is going to scoop whatever you don't want to bag and tag and dump it into the hopper over there for disposal." With typical efficiency, Westport placed recyclables into various labeled receptacles, and placed the garbage and other effluvia into a giant compactor. It would be trucked away to become some other municipality's problem. Town property owners paid for this privilege, which showed up on their tax bill. It obviated the need for an unsightly landfill.

"Proceed, gentlemen," said DeFranco, feeling every bit the deck officer on a Navy ship, who must merely utter "Make it so" to set course and speed. DeFranco was prepared for the dreadfulness that was about to spill forth. Wearing old hunting boots and dungarees, he'd brought along a pitchfork so he could rummage through the trash. He wished Curtis Jones were here with his keen eye.

Homer Bigsby fired up a truck with forks and rolled slowly toward the dumpster. He deftly inserted big metal tines into the channels on the outside of the dumpster, but drove them in only an inch or two. He elevated the tines and the dumpster began to tip. Suddenly overcome by gravity, it clattered to the floor with a horrendous bang. With the contents of the dumpster thus disgorged, he prodded the dumpster in the other direction and it landed on its side a few feet away from the fetid pile that now lay at DeFranco's feet.

The problem, DeFranco now realized, was the material that had been on the bottom of the dumpster was now on top, and the refuse that had been closest to the corpse was now on the bottom. A lot of stirring and agitating would be needed to separate the garbage into something they could try to understand. The good news was that most of the trash was cardboard packaging belonging to the hardware store. This fact had not stopped certain citizens from availing themselves of the convenience of tossing household trash into the box. Each trash bag would have to be slit open, and DeFranco produced a jackknife from his pocket for this purpose. Supervisor Smith handed out a set of face masks to help deal with the stench.

Working at opposite ends of the pile, McKurdy and DeFranco raked away the refuse, separating and inspecting it.

DeFranco tried to channel Jones.

"We're looking for any personal effects, knives or sharp objects, saws in particular," said DeFranco. "Also, bloodstains or any obvious fluids or parts." McKurdy nodded in agreement.

DeFranco slit open white trash bags as he encountered them and used his pitchfork to paw through the detritus. Rotting food scraps, candy wrappers, dirty diapers, chicken bones—the accumulated leavings of society spilled forth onto the concrete floor while Bigsby and Smith whiled away on the sidelines. DeFranco mused that the elite of Westport generated the same kind of trash as his fellow plebeians, just more of it.

He stopped at a gold bracelet with the name Cheryl engraved on it, deciding it had probably been discarded by a spurned suitor, but he put it aside for later inspection.

Paper. Lots of it…with computer-generated notes, letters, and lists. He told McKurdy to be on the lookout. All of it would have to be read and preserved. The pair worked quietly and diligently and DeFranco was happy to have the help. Maybe McKurdy would deserve at least an "Attaboy" for their shared misery.

After an hour, DeFranco piped up. "We're getting down to where the body had rested. Flipping over those pieces of cardboard should show some fluid stains, maybe maggots." McKurdy started to carefully overturn some of the cardboard and, sure enough, there was a dark wrinkle where "she" had remained in repose. No maggots, thank God. DeFranco mentally flashed on those raised, blackened arms with no hands.

DeFranco and McKurdy pulled the cardboard away from the rest of the trash and put it aside. He would add it to the cardboard that Jones had removed and bagged the night before. There was a dark patch of something that looked like charred meat and DeFranco decided it was a piece of torched human skin. He picked it up with his gloved fingers and placed it in a Ziploc bag for the medical examiner. It might contain trace evidence.

"What's this?" he said aloud. He reached down and picked up an envelope that said *Receivables* on the outside. He'd carve out time to deliver the checks back to Canal and Main and make the hardware store owner's day.

He was beginning to worry about what he didn't see: no ID, no purse, no objects of adornment. DeFranco brought out a spray bottle of luminol, which glowed in the presence of bloodstains. After repeated attempts he could find no trace of blood. No drops, spatter, smudge, or samples for serology—missing elements that only added to the puzzle.

He and McKurdy pulled away the cardboard they thought would yield the most information and got down on all fours to inspect. DeFranco's heart skipped when he found what he thought might be a human pubic hair resting on a piece of cardboard…short, curly, and black. If the hair didn't belong to the victim, could it have come from the killer? He reached into his Lands' End cloth briefcase for a pair of tweezers and an empty plastic vial, and placed the hair inside it as if it were a piece of gold.

They were down to the last layer in the morning's archeological dig when McKurdy said, "Well, that was fun. Time for my shift."

"You're not on the clock?" asked DeFranco, his esteem for the young man beginning to nudge reluctantly upward.

"Nope, on my free time. Figured you'd need a hand," said McKurdy. "Glad to help if there's anything else you need."

"I think I've got it from here, but I'll keep that in mind. I'm headed to the ME's office with some of this stuff, then circling back to the station."

"Great. Keep me posted, boss," said McKurdy, turning on the heels of his green rubber boots and pulling the latex gloves off his hands.

Not the worst, thought DeFranco, nurturing a begrudging respect for the young police officer.

DeFranco stood in front of the rotting pile at his feet with hands on hips, trying to determine next steps, when Homer Bigsby provided the breakthrough they needed. "What's this?" he said, standing by the upturned dumpster with a flashlight in his hands. DeFranco walked over and looked inside the empty box. Bigsby's light reflected back five winks of colored light. DeFranco crouched down and entered the dumpster for the second time in twenty-four hours. He picked up the shining objects. Green. Brown. Clear. Red. And, yes, another green. They were roughly the size of a quarter, fifty-cent piece at most. Glass. But they were buffed and rounded, no sharp edges. They had turned white where they had been abraded the most. They were like little jewels.

"That's sea glass," said Bigsby. "My kids used to collect it at the beach and keep it in jars at home."

DeFranco was already spinning. Somebody had thrown the sea glass into the dumpster. It didn't walk itself inland two miles from the beach.

Significant?

He put the sea glass into another plastic bag and set up the task of bagging and tagging the relevant pieces of cardboard, the hair, the presumed chunk of flesh. It took him another hour to get the material photographed and preserved. Finally, DeFranco bid adieu to the trash heap and left Bigsby to scoop the stinking mess into the compactor. He extended business cards and courtesies to his fellow public servants. He used the employee restroom at the transfer station to get out of his jeans and back into business casual. He loaded his jeans and boots into the trunk of the Crown Vic with the rest of his trove and set off down I-95, destination Stamford and the county medical examiner's office.

The only predictable part of the morning was the sluggish traffic.

4

Protector Against Evil

DeFranco turned into the large open doors of the ME department's garage and parked. He saw Curtis Jones by a loading dock. Jones approached with his customary bonhomie, a little unsettling in the darkly serious surroundings of the medical examiner's compound.

"Hi, Tony," said Curtis affably. "We're ready to start."

"Oh swell," said DeFranco, his lack of enthusiasm barely concealed. He felt like he could let down his guard with Jones, who, after all, had seen DeFranco at his worst.

"Dr. Goldberg is intrigued with this one," said Jones.

"Help me with these evidence bags," said DeFranco. "The haul from this morning's sift through the dumpster."

They picked up their bundles—to be examined and then stowed in the ME'S evidence locker—and went toward the loading dock with Jones leading.

They made their way to an examining room and DeFranco remembered it well from the half dozen or so occasions he'd had to attend a postmortem, usually accidents or drownings or suicides, in his twenty-plus years on the force. He had attended one autopsy following a homicide, a domestic violence case, but he was there assisting another detective. The walls were tile and the fixtures were stainless steel. The floor—with a drain in the middle—was a dingy linoleum. An autopsy table was at the center of the room and it was really nothing more than a large tub, a stainless steel tray to hold the body, with channels down either side leading to a slop sink near the feet. The table had a raised platform with ramps leading up and down on either side. Of course, thought DeFranco—for the doctor's wheelchair. They approached the body bag on the table, and the doctor stormed into the room, driving his powered throne.

"Sergeant DeFranco!" shouted Dr. Goldberg, welcoming and familiar. DeFranco was amazed at the doctor's powers of recall.

"It has to be fifteen years ago," said Goldberg. "The case of the strangled housewife. You were assisting Detective Phipps. Hope he's enjoying retirement."

"Oh, I'm sure," returned DeFranco, still a little mystified at the good doctor's mental talents. The doctor, spine twisted and legs withered, manipulated the joy stick of his wheelchair and he mounted the ramp next to the table, settling in on the raised platform adjacent to the body bag. He wore a white coat and thick glasses. His balding pate was barely concealed by an elaborate comb-over.

"You've brought us an interesting one," said Goldberg. "Tell me a little bit about the scene."

"The victim was dropped into a dumpster behind a hardware store at Canal and Main in Westport. Obviously burned beyond recognition and leaving very little discernible trace evidence. Head and hands removed. The dumpster was not involved in the fire and there was no blood evidence. No way to get a sample, and no spatter. No outward signs of struggle or wounding with either gunshot, edged weapon, or punctures. They wanted to bury her in the trash pretty good."

"Yes, Curtis showed me the photographs and filled me in on most of it. But your perspective is important," said Dr. Goldberg. "Tell me about the environment. Did you notice anything peculiar around the box?"

"I canvased the neighborhood. No one heard anything unusual," said DeFranco. "Curtis might agree. The only unusual thing about the crime scene was how clean it was. There was a body. And that's it. Not a lot to go on."

"Well. First things first," said Goldberg. "It will be difficult but not impossible to establish time of death and, potentially, the identity of the victim if we're patient. Curtis, can you open the bag?" Dr. Goldberg turned to DeFranco. "Curtis is my eyes and ears—often even my hands," said Goldberg, smiling.

Curtis Jones beamed. He and another attendant pulled back the sheet inside the bag to reveal the headless corpse, now grayish black in the light of a sodium vapor lamp over the table.

"We couriered some of the killed maggot larvae to the state entomologist in Hartford. She established a gestation time of approximately four to six days to grow those maggots to their present size. Your hardware store employee discovered the body on October fifteenth, so that means this person died between the ninth and the eleventh. After she died, she lay on the ground somewhere—that's how she picked up the insect population—then she was moved. But if we assume she was placed in the dumpster sometime during the night of the fourteenth, you will want to query any neighbors as to anything they might have seen between twilight that night and dawn the next morning." DeFranco was taking notes.

Curtis and his helper got the body out of the bag and unwrapped it from the sheet, careful to note any skin, hair, or foreign objects that might have been left behind. She emerged, arms akimbo, and just as horrid. Curtis and his associate placed her on a body block to raise the chest and lower the shoulders, but her advanced state of rigor and decomposition offered the expected resistance.

"Curtis, you did your usual superb job preparing and transporting the victim," said Dr. Goldberg. Jones smiled in appreciation.

"Now, we have an approximation of time of death, and we know she died in a place other than where she was found. Let's try to establish an identity, and a manner and mechanism of death," said Goldberg over the lab's ventilation system, which was roaring away, removing a good portion of the reek that DeFranco had expected. "Curtis, please begin the postmortem with the classic Y-shaped incision from left and right clavicles to the bottom of the sternum, then down to the pubis. After that you can present the internal organs." Curtis Jones's talents extended to serving as Dr. Goldberg's hands as the foursome peered at the corpse, waiting for her to yield her secrets.

Jones, suited, gloved, and wearing a clear face mask, went to work with a large scalpel. DeFranco braced for the horror of it, but noted, except for those lovely feet, he might have been carving into a side of venison. He focused his attention on the doctor, trying to see the corpse through Goldberg's eyes.

"We'll go through a standard autopsy and then circle back to that neck wound. Curtis is laying open the victim's torso to expose the rib cage and sternum," said Goldberg. An overhead microphone recorded Dr. Goldberg's observations.

"He'll take his saw...very nice, Curtis...and cut through the ribs from the clavicle on each side down, then remove the entirety of the breastplate. That's it, Curtis. You're getting better all the time." DeFranco concentrated on the technicalities of the procedure, pushing aside the concept that this object had once been a living, breathing human being.

"We will remove the heart and lungs en masse, cutting the trachea just above the main bronchial branch," said Goldberg. "Structure is unremarkable, and there's an absence of lividity. Color is flat gray, caused no doubt by sudden, complete exsanguination. Meaning, Sergeant DeFranco, that the body was completely drained of blood, most likely prior to being burned. My hypothesis centers on the idea that the victim was killed, manner to be determined, then decapitated, before she was hung by the ankles. I am noting the ligature marks on each ankle made by thin wire or twine. Removing her hands assisted with the process of draining the body, and also, of course, robbed us of identifiable finger and palm prints."

"It's like he, or they, had all the time in the world," said DeFranco, the atoms of the case now arranging themselves into molecules.

"Quite so," said Goldberg. "Let's keep that in mind." Jones had exposed the heart and lungs. "The first thing I will note is general lack of any visceral fat or adiposis around the organs and the generally fine shape of the victim's coronary arteries. No signs of atherosclerosis, suggesting she's of a relatively young age. Early twenties I would guess, but we will refine that estimate when we perform a bone scan and measurement. Curtis, I am going to ask you to dissect the trachea and the upper lobe of the left lung," Goldberg directed while Jones complied.

"You see, there is very little soot or smoke inside the airway, suggesting the victim did not die from smoke inhalation, but was burned postmortem, no doubt to disguise her identity." DeFranco scribbled his notes. "Note the bronchi and alveolae are unremarkable, no signs of chronic obstructive pulmonary disorder, a tobacco habit, or scarring caused by pneumonia. She was very healthy, and she lived well, this one. That might be relevant when you try to figure out where she came from. It wasn't a back street, Sergeant. We will take tissue samples of her liver and send them out to toxicology and serology to get a clearer picture. We will want to know about any potential drug use, medications, or unusual blood typing.

"Curtis, you can remove and weigh the heart and lungs, and then we will turn our attention to the victim's other vital organs." Goldberg spoke to DeFranco while Curtis quietly worked. "Of course, Sergeant DeFranco, this will all be in my report, and as your investigation proceeds you will want to share any findings with the district attorney, Pers Mortensen. Mr. Mortensen will be taking this on personally."

The case was already starting to grow in size and shape. Then DeFranco remembered. Mortensen lived in Westport, big house near Compo Beach.

Reputation as a pain in the ass.

Jones had removed the stomach, liver, and pancreas, and was working on the intestines, placing each item on a scale and noting the weight for the microphone. The body's internal organs would be placed back in the corpse for burial or cremation based on the family's wishes...if DeFranco could find her family.

"Curtis, it's time to examine the victim's stomach contents," said Goldberg. Jones placed the stomach on a cutting board and sliced into it, the foursome leaning in to see.

"Practically empty, Doctor," said Jones. "I see some undigested… Looks like…sunflower seeds, maybe some walnut pieces and almond slivers…but not much."

"Okay, Curtis, check the contents of her colon," said Goldberg while Jones turned his attention to the victim's lower bowel.

"Not empty, but not full," said Jones.

"So she was starving?" asked DeFranco.

"Or being starved," returned Dr. Goldberg. "Curtis can you please check the ileum? And we'll want to note any transit." Then, turning to DeFranco, he said, "There is no real conclusion to be drawn. She may have been merely watching her weight. She might be a vegan. Or she might have been deprived access to food."

"A prisoner?" asked DeFranco.

"Or a kidnap victim," said Goldberg. "The toe ring suggests a nod toward the fashionable, and that pedicure looks recent—no chips or wearing—so her appearance might have been important to her. But she could have been suffering from an eating disorder. And that suggests a level of affluence."

"All of Westport enjoys some level of affluence, Doctor," said DeFranco.

"Of course, Sergeant," said Goldberg. "Just noting it for the record."

The medical examiner continued.

"So now," said Goldberg. "We get to the piece de resistance. The organs of reproduction and the genitalia… Curtis, tell us what you see."

"I see ovaries and fallopian tubes normal and unremarkable. But what's this, Doctor?" Goldberg and DeFranco turned toward the table. "Her uterus is slightly swollen and there is distinct scarring of the tissue surrounding the opening of the cervix."

"Oh my," said Goldberg. For the first time the doctor seemed truly surprised. "Curtis, I am going to ask you to try to dissect the uterus in situ. I don't like the look of the cervix."

Jones sliced into the victim's uterus, drew the tissue apart with a retractor, and allowed Dr. Goldberg to reach in with a gloved hand to probe inside. "No fetus. She wasn't pregnant. But this is fragmentary placental tissue. So I am hypothesizing that she *had* been pregnant. And the obvious wounding of the cervix suggests a forcible evacuation of the uterus using some kind of instrument…maybe a coat hanger or other wire. She was subjected to a curettage of the uterus without the benefit of dilation. An abortion in other words, and likely not in an up-to-date clinical setting. Curtis, we will need to retrieve tissue samples of any materials of conception for DNA analysis. And I would like to preserve the organs of reproduction for later examination. We might be able to match the scarring with any instruments Detective DeFranco finds in the course of his investigation."

Dr. Goldberg turned to DeFranco. "Establishing paternity will be difficult. Normally, the baby's DNA is a natural component of the mother's blood stream. But this mother has no blood. We can also attempt chorionic villus sampling by testing the uterine wall. But death and decomposition will naturally interfere with this process. Lastly, we can still attempt to obtain amniotic fluid for an amniocentesis, but again, the state of the corpse might make this impossible."

So it was on him, DeFranco thought, something inside him stirring to the challenge. What if it had been his own daughter on that table? There was a family somewhere that needed to know what had happened to their child.

"So that leaves several unanswered, or should I say, unexplained questions," said Dr. Goldberg. "Because we now seem to have more questions than we started with. Let's focus for a moment on the lower extremities, on the victim's pigmentation, possibly indicating her race, and on identifiable markings like those tattoos." DeFranco was being taken on a tour. He sensed his investigation—he was starting to own it—taking several intriguing turns.

"Curtis, would you mind removing that toe ring? Unfortunately you might have to clip the toe off to get at it." Jones found what appeared to be a cable cutter and removed the second, longer toe from her right foot. The ring came off and Jones picked it up with a tweezer, holding it up to a magnifier.

"Curtis, do you see any distinguishing characteristics?"

"It looks like fourteen-carat gold, solid, not plate, and there are tiny letters. Could be Korean, but it could be…Hindi?"

"Let me see," said Goldberg. "Not Sanskrit. Possibly Devanagari. Definitely South Asian. Detective DeFranco, I will have to consult a reference work back in my office."

"Certainly," said DeFranco, already in awe of the great doctor's powers.

"Curtis, we'll need a Polaroid of her tattoos. Tell me what you're seeing," said Goldberg.

"Looks like a bird. A hummingbird? On her left thigh," said Jones.

"Concealable by a bathing suit or out in the open for all to see?" asked Goldberg, turning to DeFranco. "That's relevant, Detective, because I have found that people who have secret tattoos also have a secret life—a beau, an independent streak, a bit rebellious—but are disinclined to step too close to the edge."

"No, this little bird is definitely within the boundaries of the panty line," said Jones.

"And now, Curtis. Let's travel back up to that neck. Or what's left of it." Goldberg pulled slightly back on his joystick and his wheelchair moved slowly backward along the length of the raised platform. DeFranco and Curtis's assistant moved in that direction.

"Tell me what you see, Curtis." Goldberg was taking pride in his colleague's abilities.

"I think her neck was sliced front to back with a large blade in one, possibly two cuts above the thyroid cartilage and below the hyoid bone. The blade sliced through the carotid artery and the jugular vein but was stopped by the disc between the C4 and C5 cervical vertebrae. At this point, whoever removed the victim's head used a saw. I am seeing tool marks in the external fascia. I want to get in closer with a camera, but I think we are seeing serrations no closer than two millimeters apart, which would suggest a wood saw, not a hacksaw," said Jones, finishing his discourse.

"And certainly not a bone saw," said Goldberg. "And that tells me they started cutting off her head, and when they met resistance picked up whatever fell to hand...in this case a wood saw."

"That means a wood shop, not a machine shop," said DeFranco.

"Possibly," said Goldberg.

"Wait a second," said Jones, leaning into the neck wound, wearing an eye magnifier. "There's a foreign object in her wind pipe."

All eyes turned.

Jones took a small needle-nose plier and deftly inserted it into the victim's trachea. He couldn't quite reach it, but they saw a wink of color reflected off the overhead lamp...red, rounded, and smooth.

Sea glass.

"Well, she was choked to death," said Goldberg, almost sadly, now that the manner and mechanism of death had been established. He'd been animated by the thrill of the chase, and now projected a note of empathy as the cause of the young woman's demise was clarified.

"How does sea glass wind up down a person's throat like that?" asked DeFranco.

"It's a safe bet she didn't swallow it," said Goldberg. "It was forced down her throat. She might have been drugged. Toxicology will help us there. But it could have happened during the course of an assault. And if that is the case, I think it's fair to say that the murderer suffered bite wounds on the left or right hands between the thumb and middle finger." Goldberg turned to Jones. "Curtis, we'll need to dust that object for a print, likely an index finger." He turned back to DeFranco.

"Find the person with that fingerprint who has those wounds, or perhaps scarring, and you've probably found your killer. The abortion confuses things. My hypothesis rests on the idea that the abortion was self-inflicted or performed by a second, untrained party, and it occurred at a time and place well removed from the murder. It foretells a relationship, perhaps with the killer, but perhaps not. The choking came later."

"Why the dumpster?" asked DeFranco. "If they had the time to put her in the dumpster, they probably had time to find a place to bury her."

"The murder and the preparation of the body was methodical up 'til that point," said Goldberg. "Placing the body in the dumpster suggests they were rushed at the last minute—about to be discovered?"

"Or they got sloppy," said DeFranco. "Same thing with the toe ring. Meticulous effort to conceal. But they missed the obvious. Why?"

"Speaks to the state of mind of the person or persons involved," said Goldberg. "Rushed. Distracted."

The words had hardly left his lips when the swinging double doors of the examining room swung wide and the massive form of State's Attorney Pers Mortensen entered the room, sweating, out of breath, graying blond hair tousled and tie askew.

"Why, Dr. Goldberg, did this postmortem examination take place without me or one of my assistants in attendance?" Mortensen bellowed. "And who," he said, looking at DeFranco, "is this?"

"Tony DeFranco, Westport PD." DeFranco coolly extended a hand, taking in the state's attorney from head to toe.

"Well, you're off this case," said Mortensen.

"On whose authority?" asked Dr. Goldberg.

"State CID is back on," said Mortensen. "Investigator Tamara Moriarty is on her way down from Hartford."

"I would be happy to meet the investigator," said DeFranco, "but I work for Chief Gerald Talbot of the Westport Police Department and the chief can let me know if I've been reassigned."

"In the meantime," said Dr. Goldberg, "the last time I checked, law enforcement is tasked to investigate and apprehend. The state's attorney is tasked to charge, arraign, present to a grand jury, and to try. As usual I am sure the investigating body will cooperate, but I don't quite understand the summary nature of this dismissal."

"It's above their pay grade," said Mortensen, aloof, unwilling to yield.

"Thanks," said DeFranco. "But until I hear from my chief I'll proceed with my discussions with the good doctor. If you hear from Inspector Moriarty, please send her my way and if my chief agrees, I will share my notes." Mortensen was turning a light shade of purple.

"Okay. We'll see," said Mortensen. "And we'll also see how you like being back out on patrol after I get done with you."

"You have no idea how happy that makes me," said DeFranco, the only snappy retort he could muster.

"Dr. Goldberg, I will expect to see your report and I will forward it to CID. There is no need to copy this man."

"Well," said Goldberg. "I will send my report to whomever I please."

"One question," said DeFranco. "Westport PD will be handling press liaison on this case. The cat's already out of the bag. News 12 Connecticut knows about the murder. They were at the scene yesterday. They'll soon know about the state of the victim when she was found. It will be all over town. We'll make sure we spell your name correctly, Mr. Mortensen."

"My office will be handling the press," said Mortensen. "Any release by you to the press, or release by Westport PD, will be actionable. I can have an injunction this afternoon. And Chief Talbot will be my first call when I leave here."

DeFranco doubted the chief would defer to Mortensen when it came to public relations surrounding his department. I mean, the man is spineless, thought DeFranco, but he won't cave in to Mortensen on that.

"I will follow standard procedures until my chief tells me otherwise," said DeFranco, turning to Dr. Goldberg. "Can we finish up in your office? Do you really think that inscription is Hindi?"

Goldberg looked happy to end this unpleasant brush with the prosecutor. "Follow me," said the doctor, spinning in his chair and heading for the doors.

"Lead on," said DeFranco, winking at Jones, who had remained standing over the headless corpse, scalpel in hand.

"Curtis, you know what to do," Goldberg called to his assistant. DeFranco saw Curtis freeze for half a beat, then reach for a small Igloo cooler on a nearby table.

DeFranco followed Goldberg down the tile-walled corridor with the bright fluorescent light. The doctor's wheelchair turned into an office and DeFranco followed him into this inner sanctum. As he expected, the doctor's office was a riot of books and papers, the urgent chaos of a busy man. Goldberg's personal environment said something about a person whose everyday task was to turn over rocks to find gems of truth.

"I never liked that man," said Goldberg. "A bully."

"Doesn't want his property values to go down," theorized DeFranco.

"Yes...well, let's see about that inscription," said Goldberg. He pulled a paperback off a shelf and flipped through the pages. "Yes. It's right here. Devanagari. The word on the ring is a paean to the Hindu goddess Kali."

"What does that mean, Doctor?"

"It says right here. *Kali* means protector against evil."

5

Strange Alliance

Tracy Taggart was sitting in the waiting room of the medical examiner's office, absently reading a *Stamford Advocate*. DeFranco was running late, but any unease he felt for keeping her waiting seemed to melt when she smiled at him—a warming glow framed by that pretty face and stunning red hair.

"Remember me?" said Tracy Taggart.

"You're unforgettable," said DeFranco, worrying he might have edged too close to a flirt. "Let's go get some coffee. Where's your car?"

"At a meter on the street."

"Let's leave it and take mine. I'll bring you back here," said DeFranco. She gathered her coat and a handbag and she preceded him out the door. They walked by her VW Golf and DeFranco gallantly produced four quarters to plug into the meter. "That should take the pressure off."

"Thanks," said Taggart, her smile unfailing. DeFranco did not necessarily consider himself to be an expert on the topic of women, but he surmised she'd had to contend with the usual pack of thoughtless youngsters who had tried to date her—smooth talkers who flashed money and wanted only one thing. Would she be interested in a more mature outlook?

He was getting ahead of himself.

They walked around the building and found DeFranco's department Crown Vic. He felt a little self-conscious his other ride was Angelica's downtrodden Corolla, but maybe that wouldn't matter. If he kept it professional, she'd never know. He walked her to the passenger side and opened the door, just as he liked to do for Julie. Tracy seemed touched.

He got behind the wheel and buckled in. "Let's swing over to Curley's on West Park," he said. "It's quiet."

"Anything is good for me," said Tracy. "I don't have to be at work for another couple of hours."

"I guess that means you're a night owl," said DeFranco.

"Low man on the totem pole," she said. "I work nights, holidays, weekends. I kind of like it. Puts me out of sync."

"What's wrong with being in sync?"

"Boring," she responded.

"They usually reserve the crappy duty assignments for the newbies. How long have you been at this?" he asked.

"I'm a late bloomer. I joined the Marine Corps out of high school and worked as a medical corpsman on a helicopter assault ship. My dad was a jarhead and I had no brothers. Lucky me. Semper fi. Then I got a scholarship to Syracuse and got my degree in broadcast journalism. So I'm the oldest rookie I know. What's your story, Detective?"

"I joined the police department when I got back from 'Nam in '67 and I've been on the force in Westport for twenty-two years. Sort of interested in doing something else now that my kids are grown," he told her.

"And your wife? What does she do?" DeFranco wondered if she was fishing, hoping to find out if he was available. "I'm a widower. Breast cancer," he answered matter-of-factly. He'd been asked the question so many times it no longer caused a squeezing in his throat.

"I'm so sorry," said Taggart in an apologetic tone. "Please accept my sympathies."

"That's okay. We have two wonderful kids in college and had some terrific years. So it's all good."

"My mom died of breast cancer two years ago," said Tracy. "I know what it's like to lose someone close." Grief, as usual, did its work to form a connection.

They pulled up to the diner and worked their way inside—cracked vinyl booths and fixed counter stools and the smell of grease.

"I love it," said Taggart. "Nice and gritty. The only thing we need are some hard hats on lunch break."

"Or some cops getting free doughnuts," said DeFranco.

"I bet you'd never take a free doughnut."

"Nope. Way too straight."

They took a booth and ordered coffee and Tracy Taggart cut right to the chase. "I cruised over to Oscar's Deli on Main Street in Westport this morning. Overheard some people talking. Looked like moms having coffee after dropping the kids at school. Sure enough, there's a buzz going around Westport. There's been a murder. And not just any murder. Mutilation. Burned corpse. Whole, horrible bit. Aren't you worried you need to get out in front of this? Calm people down? Tell them you're on it?"

She had him.

It hadn't taken her long.

DeFranco looked at her long and hard and thought about Mortensen, and about Chief Talbot (who, as usual, was absent without leave), and about Tamara Moriarty, inbound from state CID to save the day. He also thought about that poor, dead girl on the slab at Dr. Goldberg's office, who wanted nothing more than to have the goddess Kali deliver her from evil.

It was like a wave racing toward the shore, growing higher and gaining energy—about to break. He was also staring at the most beautiful ex-Marine he'd ever seen. Tracy Taggart was a part of the complex wheel that was starting to turn.

He had to make some calculations. Tracy wasn't going to go quietly. She wanted her story. And in a way she deserved it; no other media had responded to their Signal 50 on a rain-slicked night. There was no way he could put her off. He could tell her to go talk to Mortensen's office, but that would just delay the inevitable.

He also didn't like getting shoved around by the state's attorney.

He decided the people of Westport—his friends and neighbors, quarrelsome, petty, funny, often brilliant—had entrusted him with their protection. Of course, they needed to hear from their chief about what was happening in their town. And if Talbot didn't step up, they needed to hear from some responsible adult. So that left Tracy.

"Looks like you got your story," he said, toying with her.

"Not really. You've got a body. But I need a name. A weapon. A motive. And I need a killer. I'm going to get it anyway, Detective DeFranco. But I would like to get it faster and I would like to get it from you." Her remark bordered on the salacious. Wasn't this dance a bit like foreplay?

"Let me ask you a question," said DeFranco.

"Shoot."

"If someone told you you could have a Hershey bar now…but you could have a case of Hershey bars later if you were just a little patient, would you wait for the bigger payoff?"

"I might. As long as I could maybe have a taste of the Hershey bar now…kind of a sampler…and wait for the whole case later. I have a very demanding boss who wants it all and wants it now."

"Well, if I had to guess, I would say that the chief of the Westport Police Department is going to hold a news conference this afternoon or early evening—if a certain detective named DeFranco can find a certain chief named Talbot and get him on board. I would say it would be a good idea for you to be at that conference. If you trust me, and if you're patient, and if you are discreet—just for a while—I think you'll have the story of your life. But you have to tell me that you can keep confidences."

He was on the precipice. He was about to leap. He was about to put his career in the hands of a stranger.

And he didn't care.

He was, at least mentally, one foot out the door.

DeFranco started with the discovery of the body and the horrific mess inside the dumpster. Tracy appeared captivated, of course, hanging on his every utterance. Police usually communicated these sad events with dry pronouncements of name, age, address, and basic circumstance. It was all paint by numbers. But DeFranco was taking her *inside* the investigation, allowing her to see the very essence of the criminal inquiry into the sordid murder of a young woman.

And he told her everything. He couldn't help himself. And of course he had doubts. From the second or third sentence, he knew he'd gone too far. But she'd leaned in, she'd listened. And how long had it been since he'd had a woman in his life who would do that? Really listen. Well…not since Julie. There had been others, usually church ladies bearing casseroles. With each statement of fact he knew he'd dug his hole a little deeper.

Could he trust her?

He couldn't shake his misgivings, yet he forged ahead.

"This is what you can report," he said. "An employee of the hardware store at Main and Canal found on the evening of the fifteenth of October a burned, blackened corpse in the dumpster behind the business. The corpse had no head and no hands. It appears, following forensic examination, that the corpse is a young woman, possibly of South Asian extraction. There was no immediate way to ascertain her identity. The investigation is continuing."

"But of course there's more," said Tracy Taggart, finishing her coffee, raising a hand to ask the waiter for a second.

"Yes, there's more. These are the following salient, albeit unconnected, points," said DeFranco. "And these are the points I need to suppress for the time being. The killer or killers can't know what we know."

He knew information was power. There was limited supply and endless demand, putting him on the favorable side of the ledger. He was also banking on the idea that she would favor a long-term professional relationship—and having a source inside the police department would yield future dividends. Still, trust was always fragile. It could be broken in an instant.

He looked into her green eyes and plunged ahead, hope and regret in a sparring match.

Hope was winning. He would bring the young reporter in.

"The victim is young. She's fit. She has a toe ring that's engraved with Hindi letters to the goddess Kali. She's burned to a crisp, but there is no soot or smoke in her windpipe, meaning she died and was likely decapitated before she was set on fire..."

Tracy Taggart took in a breath.

"...and her hands were severed shortly after she was killed. How was she killed? She was choked to death. And how did that happen? She had a piece of sea glass, like this one, shoved down her throat." DeFranco produced one out of a pocket from the dumpster dive that morning.

Tracy looked away somewhere, off in the distance. She was trying to be the hard-bitten journalist but the inhumanity of what had befallen the girl in the dumpster hit her hard. DeFranco continued.

"Think about it. She's been asphyxiated. So now they've got to figure out what to do with her. That's when they come up with the idea to conceal the victim's identity. They cut off her head. Two quick slices at the front of her neck with a big knife...then a saw to get them through the disc between C4 and C5. But let's not stop there. Let's cut off her hands too. At the wrist. Maybe a chop from an axe would do. Not clear about that. The neck is hard enough to deal with. Then they hang her upside down 'til she bleeds out. Exsanguination, the ME called it."

Tracy was an ex-Marine, a medic, and she still found it hard to take. The next piece of information roused within her something beyond distaste...a deep-rooted anger.

"There's more," DeFranco continued. "Examination of the victim's organs of reproduction showed that she'd recently had an abortion. But the procedure was performed by an amateur with a coat hanger or some kind of crude tool. There is distinct scarring of the cervix. She had experienced severe pain and bleeding."

Taggart looked out the dirty window of the diner. Her world of TV brights on holiday feasts and high school sports and nor'easters and traffic tie-ups now seemed so decadently trivial. A young woman had been tortured and killed in Fairfield County, the summit of American abundance.

"Here's what you have to keep out for the time being. I know I'm repeating myself," said DeFranco. "You know nothing about the sea glass in her throat. You know nothing about the toe ring or the inscription. You know nothing about the pregnancy and the abortion. If those details get out I get fired and I wind up walking security at the Trumbull Mall for the rest of my life. And worse"—he grinned at Taggart—"you don't get your story."

"When can I report those details?" asked Tracy. DeFranco felt like she was buying into the bargain, but she didn't want this nondisclosure agreement to be in perpetuity.

"Give me a couple of weeks," said DeFranco. "I guarantee you'll get the story first. The killers are still out there. I need to bring them in. That job will be a lot harder if they know what we know."

"I get it," said Tracy. "I'm in. Two weeks. But one caveat. If I sense the competition getting all or part of this story—your information but from other sources—I will have to confirm the facts independent of you and run with what I have. I can't let my station get scooped."

"I get that. And I may need to extend that time a bit, a factor not unreasonably withheld." He'd read that phrase in a contract somewhere. It seemed to fit. "We'll need some close coordination."

"Let's shake on it," said Tracy, plunging her hand across the table. DeFranco took her smooth skin and light touch in his own beefy hand and their pact was struck.

"Now, give me your phone number and I'll have our media rep put you on the call list for the press conference that I cannot confirm will even take place," said DeFranco. "I need to get it organized, if I can."

"Okay," said Tracy. "I'm supposed to cover a Stamford City Council meeting but I think I can get somebody else to do that. Just let me know." She smiled at DeFranco and something warmed inside him.

But he realized the absurdity of that. He'd just made a deal with a member of the press.

DeFranco paid the check.

"Next one's on me," said Tracy, raising DeFranco's hope there might even be a "next one." He drove her back to her car and watched her in the rearview mirror as he drove away. He liked that smart trench coat and the felt fedora.

He drove to the entrance to I-95 and the faithful Crown Vic found the Westport police station. He walked up the back stairs to his cubicle and there, of course, was a note on his typewriter from the chief. "See me" was all it said.

So he put his briefcase down, kept his sport coat on, cruised by the coffeepot for his fifth cup of the day, and strolled casually to the chief's office at the front of the second floor. It had glass walls so the chief could see out, and everybody else could see in. The idea was to see and be seen—unless you were larking around with the local pols. The chief was wearing his usual white shirt, thin tie, sleeves rolled—bald head nodding up and down in agreement. DeFranco could see that roll of neck fat over the man's collar. Talbot needed to spend more time in the gym. He was talking to a woman.

Of course, thought DeFranco. Inspector Moriarty. Here to save the day. DeFranco knocked and the chief waved him in.

"Tony, this is Tamara Moriarty of the state criminal investigation division," said Chief Talbot. "Inspector Moriarty, Sergeant DeFranco." She wore a severe expression common to the typical overachiever, accentuated by a smart, button-down blue shirt, khaki slacks, black running shoes, and a huge .357 Magnum on her right hip designed to intimidate. Funny how duty weapons said something about a cop's personality.

What's the snubbie say about me? DeFranco thought.

"DeFranco has been handling the murder investigation on our end. DeFranco, Inspector Moriarty is taking over. I want you to give her everything you've got. We're holding a press conference at five p.m. today. I will lead that, then turn it over to the inspector here."

DeFranco was off the case. So be it. These things happen. He'd move on. Back to the cocoon he'd been living in. At least he'd had a nice cup of coffee with an attractive TV reporter.

"Not much to go on so far," said DeFranco, wishing to be cooperative, but somehow wanting to hold something in reserve.

He had trust issues.

"As the chief said, stock clerk found a burned, decapitated corpse with no hands in the dumpster behind the Crossroads Hardware Store yesterday afternoon. We have photos of shoe prints and a casting that may not belong to hardware store employees. The body had been bled completely out so there's no spatter at the scene where she was found. We believe she was killed and burned somewhere else, then dumped. Dr. Goldberg is working on his report."

"I know Goldberg," said Moriarty. "I'll call him." She seemed to dismiss DeFranco before he'd even left the room. She looked at the chief and smiled.

"Thanks, Tony. Nice job. You can go now."

You're an underling, DeFranco, he told himself. Face it.

He just had to get his kids through college, and then he'd be gone. He walked downstairs to the press rep's cubicle. Madge was well liked and malleable, the proper attributes for a press handler tasked with making the department shine before the public.

"Hi, Tony," said Madge. "What can I do you for?" He noticed she always fell back on the mildly flirtatious, the lubricant that helped move the gears in her division.

"You're having a press conference this afternoon to discuss the body we found," said DeFranco.

"Yepper. Making my calls now. *Westport News. Stamford Advocate. Bridgeport Post,*" said Madge cheerfully.

"Give this newbie at News 12 Connecticut a call." He handed Madge Tracy Taggart's name and phone number.

"But Bob Bannon handles police at News 12 Connecticut."

"You can call Bannon. But call Taggart too. She was at the scene last night. Nice kid. Could be the future. Let's get on her good side now." Like all good press agents, Madge knew she was in a battle of maneuver. It came down to building relationships.

"Okay. No problem. Dialing her now," said Madge. DeFranco felt a little duplicitous. He wanted to help Tracy, but not necessarily for the good of the department.

He wanted to see her again.

He spent the remainder of the afternoon listening to the parties in a landlord/tenant dispute, chasing down fingerprints off a fenced TV, and poring through the contents of a handbag found on Main Street, trying to ascertain the bag's rightful owner. He also found the time to call Missing Persons in Hartford, a state agency that collated data from all of Connecticut's townships. There was no record of a missing person in the state matching the description of a young, fit South Asian woman approximately five feet five inches tall and weighing approximately 110 pounds. His next query would have to be to the FBI if he hoped to find her, but for that he would have to inform his chief, and that of course would raise an eyebrow.

He was off the case.

A little before 5:00 p.m. DeFranco left his cubicle and went downstairs to the large room used for town events and official conclaves. Madge was overseeing the unfolding and deployment of steel chairs, and the TV crews were working on mounting lights and cameras. Chief Talbot and Inspector Moriarty were sitting on a small raised dais, joined by Pers Mortensen in all his weighty glory. They chatted amiably among themselves, looking up occasionally to watch the Fairfield County press corps enter the room.

There was the eager rookie from the *Bridgeport Post*, then the New Age sartorially suspect writer from the alternative weekly, then the haggard middle-aged stalwart from *The Westport News* who had been there and done that, wanting nothing more than to escape this ink-stained world. Then there was the aggressive striver Tracy Taggart, whose sheer good looks seemed to dominate the room. And where was Bob Bannon? Tracy obviously knew how to throw some elbows to get her competition out of the picture.

DeFranco approached the young reporter.

"I've been removed from the case," he said a little sadly.

"Well that's not good. What about our deal?" asked Tracy.

"We've got a two-week pact and I would appreciate it if you could honor that until things sort out. There are clearly aspects of the case we need to keep under wraps for a little while. Let's see what state CID has to say. I still may be helpful in the long run."

"Okay," said Tracy, still the dealmaker. "But if I get the details independent of you I will have to go with what I learn. I'll be respectful of what I can and can't say."

"That sounds fair," said DeFranco, who reminded himself he might be off the case but was still very much a cop. "Just remember. We have to hold back things only the killer knows. It's vital, and yes, there are lives at stake. Can I trust you?" DeFranco's look suggested this wasn't a game.

"I understand," said Tracy. "It's serious. And yes, you can trust me. But I also have a job to do. I'll keep you in the loop." They were in a verbal minuet.

More members of the press filtered into the room and Madge ultimately settled the motley group, thanked them for their attention, and welcomed Chief Gerald Talbot. The cameras started to roll, and nineteen-cent Bic pens began jotting notes.

"Thank you, everyone," Talbot began to drone. "As some of you may have heard, the victim of an apparent murder was found in a dumpster behind the Crossroads Hardware Store yesterday afternoon at approximately five p.m."

DeFranco audited the proceedings while standing in the back with McKurdy—with military haircut, uniform crisp and trim. He hung up on the word "apparent." There was nothing "apparent" about the headless corpse in the dumpster.

"Due to the gravity of this crime and the need to bring in more resources, we immediately called in State's Attorney Pers Mortensen and State CID Inspector Tamara Moriarty. They have kindly agreed to join us here today to fill us in on this unfortunate event, and to let us know the direction the investigation is taking. The probe is continuing, and there is much we either don't know or can't reveal at this time. But rest assured we have the best law enforcement assets in the state of Connecticut on this very important matter. People in the town of Westport can rest assured we will swiftly find, arrest, try, and convict the responsible parties. Tamara?"

Inspector Moriarty rose and DeFranco's first impression was "tough cookie." She now wore a windbreaker with CID printed on the back, and her badge had been moved around to the front near her belt buckle so she conveyed a look that said, "I'm the law." She wore her graying brunette hair straight to the shoulder with a bang that swept either side of her hawklike visage. Just standing there she commanded respect, and the room was utterly composed.

"Thank you, Chief Talbot, and thanks to every member of the Westport Police Department who has taken the investigation this far. Here is what we know. The decapitated body of the woman found in the dumpster yesterday is believed to be approximately twenty years old and of African American extraction."

DeFranco stood stock-still in the back of the room.

Right to acknowledge the state of the body, thought DeFranco. Whole town probably knows by now. Dead wrong about the woman's ethnicity. Where did that come from?

Tracy Taggart looked at him with just a hint of alarm. DeFranco returned her gaze and shook his head ever so slightly. They held the connection over this vague hint of collusion.

"Toxicology reports suggest the victim had heroin in her system, as well as THC, the chief intoxicant in marijuana."

Now alarm bells were ringing inside DeFranco's skull. That fact had not been confirmed. He tried to transmit a sense of calm to Tracy across the room. They were both poleaxed by what they were hearing. DeFranco tried not to let his amazement show. He ordered himself to keep cool, worried how Tracy was handling this gross case of misinformation.

"Present theory of this case rests on possible gang-related activity emanating from Bridgeport, or possibly New Haven. We believe the killers needed to find a way to dispose of the body and the dumpster presented itself. Clearly Westport and the dumpster are the secondary crime scenes, and we are working with police departments in local municipalities to get to the bottom of this tragedy and find the killers."

"Any questions?"

The old-timer from the *Westport News* wanted to know how the body was discovered and Moriarty restated the pattern of facts. A young African American reporter from the *Stamford Advocate* wanted to know how the police determined the victim's gang affiliations. Moriarty deflected, stating certain markings on the body, tattoos, were in the process of being evaluated but they appeared consistent with tattoos well-known to law enforcement. She was smooth, filling the air with words that meant nothing and went nowhere.

Tracy Taggart raised a hand. Moriarty chose to take her question. DeFranco braced himself.

"Do you know the exact cause of death? Did she die from her burns? Or was it gunshot or knife wounds? How about choking?" asked Tracy. She was leading Moriarty on.

"We believe she died of a drug overdose," said Moriarty. "Heroin…"

Tracy Taggart looked pleadingly at DeFranco, and DeFranco once again shook his head. *Don't go there. Not yet.* Tracy relaxed a bit and after two or three more perfunctory questions, the assembly started packing up to leave.

DeFranco made his way over to Taggart, who continued to sit in her folding chair, dumbfounded.

"Go do your stand-up. State the official position. Please. For now. Meet me at The Onion on Main Street in twenty minutes. I have to make a call. Something's not right," said DeFranco.

"You're telling me," said Taggart.

He left her and ran back upstairs to his cubicle to call the medical examiner's office. Dr. Goldberg wasn't in. He asked for Curtis Jones, who came on the line.

"Curtis," said DeFranco, not wishing to raise any alarms. "Did toxicology on our dumpster girl come back from Hartford?"

"It's supposed to be arriving any minute now," said Jones. "But I called a friend up there to get a preliminary. She might have had trace elements of Rohypnol in her liver—otherwise known as a roofie, the date-rape drug."

"Is that a friend you can trust?" asked DeFranco.

"Totally. What's up?"

"I need to see you. Alone."

"I get off work in an hour. How about Rory's on the Post Road, between Exit Twelve and Exit Thirteen."

"Great. Rory's. Seven o'clock. I finally get to buy you a beer. Something's come up."

DeFranco rang off and walked down the back stairs, around the front façade of headquarters, and headed for Main Street. He saw Talbot and Moriarty talking on the front steps of the public safety building. They were locked in discourse and didn't pay any attention to the man walking briskly with his coat collar turned up.

DeFranco found Tracy Taggart in the alleyway leading to The Onion—in a land of fancy restaurants, it was Westport's premier burger and beer joint. She was pacing and wringing her hands. She smiled when she saw him, illuminating a dark and chilly night.

"Well…this story just got a lot bigger," she said. "It's a cover-up."

"I didn't expect this," said DeFranco.

"Why would the state CID and the chief of police want to falsify what we know about the dumpster girl?" She looked into DeFranco's eyes, trying to find an answer.

"Something strange is going on," he said.

"No," said Tracy. "It's a conspiracy." He liked the way she got right to the point. She was clear and she was firm. Gutsy. But he was also on guard for the kind of hype he knew the media reveled in. In his contact with the press he knew they were prone to overreach.

"That's one way to describe it," said DeFranco. "That girl died of asphyxiation due to an intentionally obstructed windpipe. I saw it myself. They want us all to think this crime actually took place someplace else—a Bridgeport ghetto maybe. And the heroin overdose is bunk. Preliminary results indicate she had Rohypnol in her system."

"A roofie?" said Tracy. "That's the first thing that's made sense. There's been a scourge of that stuff in Fairfield County."

He was talking to a reporter about his own police department. He was betraying his chief—so why did *he* feel betrayed? Where were his loyalties? To the truth, he supposed, and now to this beautiful, albeit unlikely, confederate.

"Is your shift over?" DeFranco asked.

"My cameraman is transmitting back to the station. I need to call in. Then I'm free."

"Can you come with me to meet the tech from the ME? I just called him. We're going to Rory's on the Darien-Norwalk line."

"Can you give me a ride back to the station later?" Tracy asked. "I need to get my car."

"Sure," said DeFranco. "But you'll have to contend with my daughter's Corolla."

There. Cat out the bag.

"No Crown Vic? Bet the Corolla gets better mileage," she said.

Practical, thought DeFranco.

6

Betrayal

Rory's was a compact, intimate watering hole on the Post Road, a little larger than a hole in the wall, but not by much. The bar was full when DeFranco and Tracy arrived. They asked for a four-top in the back and Curtis Jones arrived just as they were getting settled. DeFranco remembered the ME tech with the apron, mask, and rubber gloves; he wasn't expecting the trim khakis, V-neck sweater, paisley tie, and buttoned-down Oxford shirt. Jones looked like a banker fresh off the Metro North commuter rail, not the dealer in death DeFranco had come to respect.

Tracy ordered a salad, DeFranco had a cheeseburger and Budweiser, and Jones went for the Chicken Marsala and a Sancerre. The subject turned to the girl in the dumpster. DeFranco could tell Tracy was leaping out of her skin—the thrill of the chase.

Keep cool, he willed her from the across the table.

"State CID inspector Tamara Moriarty has just told the world our victim was a young African American woman who had gang affiliations in Bridgeport or New Haven, based on her tattoos. The inspector said she died of an overdose of heroin, and also had THC in her system. She cited a toxicology report from the state lab in Hartford," said DeFranco. Tracy searched Curtis Jones's face for some flicker of understanding.

"Well, all that would be nice if it weren't total bullshit," said Jones. "I did manage to get my friend to fax me the tox study." He produced two quarter-folded fax pages from a back pocket. "Sure enough. Right here it says she died of a heroin overdose." Jones pointed out of the relevant passage on page two.

"Believe it?" asked DeFranco.

"I might," said Jones. "But I know she choked to death. And there's nothing in this report about asphyxia. That throws anything to the contrary out the window. And it doesn't jive with that verbal I received on Rohypnol. My guy in Hartford says he must have been confused. Weird."

"Can you retest her liver?" asked DeFranco.

"I could resample her," said Jones. "But the Finnazo Brothers crematorium in Port Chester picked her up an hour ago. We may not have a body to sample."

"Doesn't someone need to sign for a body when it's picked up?" asked Tracy.

"Usually," said Jones. "But this order was signed by the state's attorney's office."

Mortensen, thought DeFranco. Why?

"So here's a long-shot question," said Tracy. "Did you keep any tissue samples?"

"Dr. Goldberg always keeps certain samples on hand," said Jones. "So in this instance I have a piece of her liver, a piece of her lung, the cartilage of the trachea with the sea glass still lodged... Oh, and her uterus."

"Great," said DeFranco. "I can breathe again. Does anybody know you have those samples?"

"Not that I'm aware of," said Jones. "But it's hard to keep a thing like that secret for long."

"Is there any way you can retest those samples at an independent facility?" asked Tracy.

"I suppose so," said Jones. "Have to do some digging. I will have to bring in the ME. It's his department and it's my ass. I am not supposed to remove any materials."

"Law Enforcement 101," said DeFranco. "Preserving the chain of custody of any evidence."

"Have you ever seen a toxicology report get switched?" asked Tracy.

"Rare. Usually unintentional," replied Jones. "But it's a big department and things can happen. I just don't understand why the state's attorney had the body removed. I know the crematorium in Port Chester. Director is a friend of mine. I'll call him when I get back to the office."

"Yes," said DeFranco. "State wants us to think this a gang killing from out of town. Nothing to do with Westport. 'It's *those* people.'" Curtis Jones wore a pained expression and Tracy patted him on the shoulder.

"It's bullshit," she said, finding her inner Marine and neatly summarizing the evening. "But, gentlemen, I've got a story to produce and I need to move. What comes next?"

"You gave me two weeks," said DeFranco.

"I sure did, and believe me, we're going to need all of it to get this story straight." Curtis Jones looked at the unlikely duo seated across from him, and DeFranco thought he could read his mind. A cop and a reporter, actually collaborating?

"Okay, guys," said DeFranco. "We need a plan. Curtis, you're going to find a way to retest those samples. And you're going to see if you can get access to the girl in the dumpster. Tracy, you and I have an appointment on Compo Beach tomorrow morning. Bundle up. It's going to be chilly."

"I work Saturdays too. But if we start early I can cover all my bases," said Tracy. "And can you tell me why we're heading for the beach?"

"Looking for sea glass. Eight o'clock work?" asked DeFranco.

"You call that early?" Tracy responded. "At Parris Island we got up at the butt crack of dawn."

"Let's compromise and make it seven," said DeFranco, trying really hard not to like her.

7

Sea Glass

The next morning, DeFranco sat in Angelica's Corolla at Compo Beach, taking up a position near the twin cannons, still aimed out to sea to repulse invaders. Compo was Britain's D-Day beachhead during the Revolutionary War, when a contingent of redcoats came ashore to march on Danbury. Now, an orange flame gradually rose on the eastern horizon and the day emerged whole and clean. A building westerly wind pushed against the incoming combers, which sent curls of spindrift dancing in counterpoint to the oncoming waves. He remembered taking Julie to the cannons when they were young, before marriage and kids and day-in, day-out middle-class toil.

Julie liked the beach.

He took a last bite of a plain cruller, procured as he'd swung by Dunkin' Donuts. He grabbed his coffee and stepped out of the car to greet the new day. He wore the same construction boots he'd employed so well at the sanitation facility, a pair of blue jeans, a Navy peacoat, a ski cap, and some nice thick deerskin gloves he'd spoiled himself with the previous Christmas when no one had gotten him what he really wanted. The wind started to bite against his cheeks and he grabbed a scarf from the back seat so he could cover his face and keep up with the plan of the day... to scour the beach and figure out where one might find a good batch of sea glass. Not onesies and twosies, but a handful, because he figured whoever choked the girl in the dumpster had a good pile to choose from. Either that, or the killer was a collector, in which case he would know the best spots to find the little jewels.

Tracy Taggart's VW passed by the empty, off-season guard shack and sped toward DeFranco and his lone Corolla.

Girl's in a hurry, he thought, smiling. She pulled up at his feet.

"You could get a ticket, miss," he said.

"I would deserve it, Officer," said Tracy. "Seems like I'm always rushing somewhere."

"Ever get tired?"

"I allow myself to collapse on Sundays," she said. He watched her scamper out of her car and... Why was he always drawn to her footwear?

The high heels from the parking lot at the hardware store were replaced by pull-on Bean boots. And she'd remembered lipstick. And when he got up close to her he could smell some kind of perfume. Lavender. She grabbed her coffee and put her arm through his and he thought he'd faint dead away from this simple, innocent touch through all those layers of clothing. When was the last time a woman had reached out to him like that? Well... Julie of course, in the early days, before work and worry. Sure, Julie had consented to the primordial practice of procreation, even enjoyed it...but less and less.

He settled down.

"Our mission objective today is sea glass," said DeFranco. "And that means a lot of walking. We'll cover the sandy parts of Compo. Then we'll drive over to Sherwood Island State Park and have a look. Last, we'll go over by Frost Point and Beachside Avenue. A lot of those homes are private and it's hard to get around, but I've got a badge and a gun and that might impress even those people."

"Well, I'm not impressed," said Tracy. "I'm a certified Marine marksman with an M-16 and I'm qualified on an M-60 squad automatic weapon."

"Can't top that," said DeFranco. Even though he could. His Swift Boat had twin .50 cals fore and aft and enough small arms, grenades, and explosives to take out VC fortifications—and sympathizer hamlets...high on his list of things to forget.

They walked toward the beach and immediately started scanning the sand in front of them. DeFranco knew if they were going to find anything it would be at the surfline, where the water flattened the sand and hardened it, heavier rocks and pebbles dropping out of suspension near the water and the finer material progressing up the beach.

"What was your tool of choice in 'Nam?" asked Tracy innocently.

"A riverine patrol boat with big machine guns and six very pissed-off dudes."

"I know enough to let that go," said Tracy. "Daddy didn't like talking about Iwo Jima." DeFranco reminded himself that he'd shared those awful memories with only one other person and now even she was gone.

He had covered his tracks.

"What am I looking for, Detective DeFranco?" asked Tracy. He stopped to pull off his gloves and reach into his pocket for his shards of sea glass.

"The ones that have been in the water the least amount of time are these sharp ones. She had a smooth one in her throat, like this," he said, pointing to a rounded nugget that had a rich green color, and a white granulated effect around the edges.

"Do you remember the size?" asked Tracy.

"Imagine the dial of this Timex wristwatch," he said. "That was about it. It wouldn't take much to choke a person if it were shoved in far enough."

"But how do you get it down that far?"

"With extreme violence and brute force," said DeFranco, trying to imagine the very act. "That's why whoever did it probably got cut in the hand or hands going in. Only way."

"Let's walk," said Tracy, turning to the northeast and bundling herself against him to a point, he later believed, that went well beyond the professional. He insisted to himself that she just wanted to get out of the wind.

As the sun came up the waves marched ashore and the spindrift flashed in the new day's light, one thing became immediately apparent. There was very little sea glass littering the shores of Compo Beach. They walked back to their cars and agreed to keep Tracy's VW in the parking lot and jointly mount up using Angelica's Corolla. They covered the talking points on their way over to Sherwood Island—hometowns, old jobs, the craziness of the military. Tracy was a daughter of Indiana—a Hoosier reared on bratwurst and basketball. DeFranco was a hometown boy. When he was sent overseas by the United States Navy, every day he thought of Westport's shady streets and Long Island Sound lapping at her shores.

"Tell me about your kids," asked Tracy.

"Two of the best," said DeFranco. "Angelica is getting a degree in veterinary science. Wants to be a vet tech and maybe even go on to veterinary school if she can get in somewhere. Tough odds but she's very smart and very determined. Sam is sort of a scholar athlete still finding his way. He's reading all the great works at Conn College—Shakespeare, Proust, Henry James, Dickens— and he's a fierce forward on the soccer squad. He might be employable some day, but who the heck knows? Just a nice kid. I'll take that any day."

"I'd like to meet them," said Tracy—offering both thrill and a little dread in a single phrase. They pulled into the vast parking lot at Sherwood Island State Park, the only car on this crisp fall day, the wind rising. DeFranco had brought tide tables so they knew it was low water and coming in. They walked the full length of the state park beach, Tracy using him as a windbreak to his everlasting pleasure. They found some sea glass—greens, reds, and browns in various stages of abrasion. Not the mother lode that DeFranco was hoping for.

"Let's take a last shot at Beachside Avenue. Hard to access that beach but I know a way," said DeFranco.

Tracy stamped her feet and rubbed her gloved hands together in the passenger side of the Corolla while DeFranco drove down the Sherwood Island Connector to Nyala Farms, a pastoral scene of rolling hills and a massive nineteenth-century barn hiding a low-slung corporate headquarters, disparate worlds colliding. They drove down Green's Farms Road and turned onto Beachside Avenue, the epicenter of Connecticut's fabled Gold Coast. He turned into the little park at Burying Hill Beach and parked near the sea wall.

"Okay, Marine," he said. "Here's where the tough get going. It's a long walk all the way to Southport Beach, but we've come this far."

"Bring it on, baby," said Tracy. "It's a little cold but it's not the worst." Now she was killing him, every act of cheerful stoicism grappling his heart.

They clambered over the stones and DeFranco noted that even with a rising tide there was very little beach in places. They had to walk along the foundations of various walls built by the Beachside residents to hold back the sea. DeFranco had a passing awareness of the history of the place, and he'd even been called out to Beachside Avenue a time or two to roust out a prowler, or eject an old boyfriend under the watchful glower of a protective dad. Beachside Avenue was its own ecosystem, a cultural island of haves and have mores.

The mansard silhouette of the old J.C. Penney home hove into view, where the beach took a sharp right out to Frost Point. They trudged along, sticking to the mission, clambering over the stones, wet and sloppy with seaweed. The beach was pocked with big rocks, and manmade jetties jutting perpendicular to the seawall-hardened shoreline. The tide was cooperating and they could walk the beach unimpeded, but DeFranco could tell that, at high tide, the thin strip of sand would be unwalkable without getting wet. They came upon the Georgian manor, the Tudor reproduction, the Cotswoldian villa, then a pink behemoth that branched out right and left with giant wings. They could see huge windows and balconies and pergolas. It was someone's pride and joy.

That's when Tracy Taggart stopped, and two things struck DeFranco to his soul. At their feet lay a cornucopia of sea glass in every color imaginable and in every stage of wear—recent sharp ones, aged round ones. They weren't littering the beach in the thousands, but certainly in the hundreds. It was enough of a mother lode that he and Tracy regarded it as something of a success for their early morning gambol.

They also saw a lone figure staring out to sea, standing just beyond the eastern border of the pink mansion, on the far side of a rusty cyclone fence at odds with the grand, manicured landscaping characteristic of the neighborhood. It was an older woman, and she wore a green Barbour coat and Wellington boots. There was a beret on her gray head held in place with a fancy Hermes scarf. She was scanning the horizon, looking for something. She cut a majestic figure as she reached out with her gaze to embrace the wind and light. She turned and called them over to a little stairway that accessed the top of the seawall.

Looking back on it, DeFranco and Tracy decided their brush with death started right then, with an old woman waving them up those little stairs, and into the abyss.

8

Dasha

From atop the seawall Dasha Petrov could see the pencil-thin outline of Long Island twelve miles distant, and feel the first sharp chill of fall rolling off the water. She slung the binoculars from her neck by their fraying leather strap, and bent into the wind, leaning against her chestnut walking stick as one might lean against a friend.

She wore a weathered Barbour coat that had belonged to her husband. She still felt his arms around her when she put it on, and could smell his French cigarettes in the coat's padded lining. Constantine had also given her that chestnut stick, which she grasped with aging hands, knuckles swollen by the arthritis.

She wiggled her toes inside her Wellington boots and tightened the overhand knot of her Hermes scarf, which fastened her wool beret to her white hair. She reached into her coat's huge side pockets—the better for collecting samples of the local flora—and pulled out one of Constantine's cloth handkerchiefs. She daubed at her damnable runny nose, fearing for her lipstick.

She liked seeing the gulls and plovers scampering away from the wash. But she had a real fondness for waterfowl—for their migratory exertions. She too had ranged far and wide, often with the wind at her back, often not. Soon, the buffleheads and the canvasbacks would endure those slack gray days, snow swirling in. The Canada geese would make a mess of things, but, like her, they were survivors. The mallards reminded her of nature's fecundity and increase—mating pairs, together, against tide and time.

Constantine's binoculars—heavy Leupolds—felt strong and substantial in her hands. She adjusted her focus, scanning to the east, noting a skein of geese soaring over the wavetops. She turned to the west. Two people were rounding the point, coming in her direction, slipping on seaweed-covered rocks.

Coming to kill me at last? she thought at first as she peered through Constantine's binoculars. It was her guilty conscience visiting once again.

"I've been waiting for you," she said aloud...to the birds, to the wind, to the sound of the sea lapping against the shore. She said it to her long list of bygone adversaries, whose final sight of this earthly world was the penetrating radiance of Dasha Petrov's deep blue eyes.

She adjusted her focus.

After all, she'd been trained to observe. First by those anti-Soviet neophytes throwing ineffectual fodder back over the Slovak border to harass the Stalinists. Then the Prague partisans—rogues and highwaymen—but in a different league. Not the academics and choirboys of the anti-communist underground, but trained killers who despised the Germans and exulted in first blood following Hitler's annexation. The pair walking the beach weren't the summer snoops bent on spotting the potentates and kleptocrats at the peak of the food chain.

No. These two were head down, looking for something.

He was taller, dressed for the outing, so he was smart, knew how to prepare; she was matching him stride for stride, dressed for the weather, too. So they'd made a plan. He had on a watch cap and a peacoat, heavy jeans and calf-high construction boots, the kind with the steel toe, better to kick you in the shin. She was in a Maine plaid coat and a wool cap to hold down her red hair, cut short but peeking out of her hat and framing a pretty face.

Never underestimate a pretty face, Dasha thought. Kill you with a smile, or a dagger in the heart.

The girl was speaking, but the man kept his head down, always looking. Occasionally she put her arm through his and hid behind him out of the wind. So there was an attraction. Dasha knew the man felt a bit of a thrill when the woman touched him, even through all those clothes.

A woman could do that to a man.

They advanced along the beach, reaching down, picking up stones, throwing them back. So they weren't collectors. No bags, backpacks, or hampers. It wasn't a picnic. Police perhaps, but in plain clothes. The tall gent, possibly. But the way the woman nuzzled into him out the wind meant she couldn't be a fellow officer. Just tagging along—a girlfriend?—or was she just helping her tall, strapping acquaintance look for something along this stretch of what they called the Gold Coast? Regrettable term, actually. The place had pockets of real brilliance behind those tall walls and elaborate hedges, but also the rogues and rapscallions one finds around money. Pity there weren't more like Constantine.

A lion in the boardroom.

And a tiger in bed.

Dasha couldn't help thinking of being entwined with him upstairs, drinking in the view.

The two kept coming, and Dasha's curiosity was replaced by that telltale, long-ago flutter—when the police would stop you on the street and invite you to kindly get in the car. She flashed back to the day in Prague when she was hauled into Gestapo headquarters. *That* was a day to remember. They'd stripped her naked and inspected the labels and weave of her clothing. They examined the ink of her papers and peppered her with questions in German, trying to pierce her legend. But she had survived. There would be other brushes with authority. Hard. Soft. Push. Pull. That's the way these things went. She had an aversion to being confronted by police, understandable. But the older, rational Dasha—the Dasha of now—could not put that other life behind her. She quieted the nerves of the brazen girl who gently slipped back into her skirt under the evil watch of the SS fräuleins on guard.

Dasha watched them closely. The man wasn't keen on conversation. He paid scant attention to the winsome creature at his side, instead wanting to get on with it so they could get out of the cold. Then the girl stopped in her tracks and bent down to pick something up. She called the man over and the two of them knelt on the pebbles and sifted through the sand. They studied this little patch of beach, then extended their examination in a wider circle, looking up and down...pointing. Then they saw Dasha on the seawall, ready to start her morning tramp. Dasha sensed in their arrival the danger, and the opportunity, that always came with the unexpected.

She waved them over to the little stairs and took them all in. He had graying black hair, cropped short, a roman nose that had suffered some kind of insult—a sports injury, or a fist fight—a tall build and a forced smile. He was handsome, but also tired and vaguely tragic—beaten down, but bouncing back. The right girl could do that. A bit of attention and he'd be his old self. He approached Dasha and she eyed him warily—a homeowner protecting her domicile, but more than that. She'd once had to protect her life when confronted by strangers. She gripped her stick more firmly, feeling the chestnut knots and burls beneath pain-stricken fingers, twisting her hand around the top of the shaft and remembering the days when she could hold it with all her strength, and use it if she must.

As the man walked toward her he unbuttoned his peacoat, which blew open in the wind. His gold badge was on his belt and a revolver was nestled in a holster on his right hip.

Stand your ground, thought Dasha.

"Forgive the intrusion, ma'am," said the officer. "I would appreciate a few minutes of your time."

"How can I help you, young man?" asked Dasha imperiously. She looked him up and down. She was old, cranky, social filters gone. She wasn't impressed by this example of Westport's finest.

"My name is Anthony DeFranco of the Westport Police Department," he said. "And this is my...colleague...Tracy Taggart."

A hesitation, Dasha noted. He wasn't sure what to call the girl—and the girl looked familiar. She had seen her somewhere.

The gentleman would be expecting an air of superiority on the Gold Coast, and Dasha wouldn't disappoint.

Push him back, she thought. Knock him off stride.

"Don't the police usually come to the front door and knock? What are you doing on the beach?"

"We're investigating a serious crime and we believe it might be connected with your neighborhood," he said. He was brief, to the point...firm, yet polite. All of Dasha's previous experience with the police—on many continents—edged more toward the authoritarian. During the war they'd clap you in irons and ask questions later.

"Here's my card, ma'am," said the officer. Dasha took it from him and read *Sgt. Anthony DeFranco, Westport Police Department*, then the common saw, *To Protect and to Serve*. The sergeant had that command presence one might expect from someone responsible for public safety...but also an unmistakable ennui.

"And who is this?" asked Dasha, struggling to place the red-haired woman in the incongruous clothing and the pretty face. She belonged at the roulette tables in Monaco, on the arm of a count, not trudging along the beach like a common clamdigger.

"She's...assisting me," said DeFranco, hesitating again, wilting a bit under Dasha's disapproval.

Not sure what to call her, Sergeant? Dasha thought.

"Well, we're here," said Dasha. "How can I help you?"

"Like I said, we're investigating a serious crime," said DeFranco. "And we may have found some evidence. We would like to talk to you about that."

Dasha's powers of intuition were in full flower.

He's been beaten like a dog, thought Dasha. Lost love. Treachery in the ranks.

Today he was buoyed by the unexpected arrival of the mysterious red-haired girl. Dasha looked at the young woman's shining face and incandescent smile. The young thing had no idea of the power she held over the man standing awkwardly between these two forceful women—one retired from a long career, the other taking the stage.

"Noticed any unusual activity on the beach?" the sergeant asked.

"More canvasbacks than usual," said Dasha. "Always a good sign. What kinds of activities?"

"Strangers. Young people. Especially young ladies…young ladies with dark complexions?"

"The householders along the avenue troop up and down this beach almost daily, Sergeant. And I know them all," said Dasha. "We haven't had any strangers of the type you are describing."

"As I say—young, female, dark skin."

"Is she the perpetrator or the victim, Sergeant?" asked Dasha. "You'll have to be clear." At that, these two obstinate individuals, both convinced of their own impregnable rights, stared at each other, knowing one or the other would have to blink.

"Most definitely the victim, ma'am," said the sergeant at last, who looked into Dasha's deep blue eyes and communicated wordlessly they had arrived at a deadly serious moment.

It was Dasha's turn to hesitate. She'd spent her life delving into the deepest secrets of America's enemies. In so doing she'd uncovered the best and worst in people. A student of the human species, she'd plumbed the reasons some people would steal, cheat, betray—even kill. She sometimes wondered if her inquisitive nature would be her undoing. At the same time, she had long lamented a retirement that took her away from the grand struggles that had marked her career—even if, at times, they'd become her battlegrounds. All the better, she reflected. Confronting danger was when she felt most alive.

"Back to my cottage, then," Dasha directed. "I can offer you some coffee."

Bring them in, thought Dasha.

"We wouldn't want to intrude," said the woman, revealing a damning naivete. This was a police matter. The police rarely wondered if they were causing an imposition.

Who is she? Dasha asked herself.

"Let's get out of the wind," said Dasha firmly. "Then maybe I can finish my bird-watching. There's a male merganser in the neighborhood, a newcomer."

She led them across a clipped but browning, leaf-strewn lawn, by a sturdy but rusting cyclone fence, in front of a well-proportioned but less-than-grandiose wood frame house with gray shingle siding.

"I am Dasha," she said firmly in her unshakable Russian accent. "Dasha Petrov. Welcome to Seabreeze, our home. My son and his family live in the big house. They need the space. My sister and I live in the garden. Come back and let's get out of the cold. My sister had a stroke and she doesn't speak. She's lost use of an arm, but she can walk. And her mind is good." The old tradecraft was coming back. She reveled in the basic tools that drew in her targets.

What do they know? she asked herself.

Dasha led them past the side of the understated manor house, by a towering copper beach tree and a Japanese maple, down a rock-lined pathway flanked by pachysandra, toward a rough-hewn cottage that Hansel and Gretel might have found appealing. There was a little patio out front, smoke curling from the chimney, and a long greenhouse jutting off the house at an angle.

"Back in the old days this was a guest cottage, when my husband Constantine was alive. We'd start the early plantings in the hot house. It costs too much to heat now," said Dasha. "Come inside."

They entered a large triple-height great room with rafters, a river rock fireplace in the center of the far wall, a tattered couch, and side tables stacked with books and magazines. Newspapers in Cyrillic balanced on top of the pile. A stooped, graying figure in a shapeless smock was clearing the table one-handed—the woman's sister. The house was inhabited by an older set—overheated, a bit moldy, the faint whiff of just-cooked cabbage.

"This is my sister Galina. I'm sorry, but she's a little shy after her medical complaints," said Dasha, an understatement. Galina smiled and turned to a table in a corner to noodle over a Scrabble board.

"We adore Cyrillic Scrabble. Keeps us going," she said, a bit brighter, creating an imbalance in the exchange.

Pressure, then release, thought Dasha. Just the way you were trained.

"That, and Russian church on Sundays. Galina used to sing in the choir. Take off your coats. Take a seat by the fire. You must be freezing. Let's see about the coffee." Dasha continued to direct her unexpected guests by impulse. DeFranco and Tracy removed their outer garments. Dasha disappeared into a small galley kitchen off to the side and came back with a tray of cups and cakes.

"This is a beautiful place," said Tracy. "Have you lived here long?"

"My husband Constantine bought it in 1950, when the oil wells on Lake Maracaibo came in. He was a petroleum engineer. It was a grand place and spanking new, but then Constantine died and the taxes went up and up and, as you can see, we've had better days. But we've loved it. We try to keep up. It's been a real home after everything we've been through."

"Been through?" asked Tracy, probing.

"I don't want to bore you," said Dasha.

"No...we're interested," said Tracy, nudging DeFranco in the ribs. He nodded and smiled, then Dasha saw him looking at his watch.

Man's an upstart, she thought. He doesn't know who he's dealing with.

Dasha was well past caring. She had nothing to hide. Scenes from her long-ago life flashed then dissolved in cinematic panorama. Constantine always described his wife as formidable, a feature she could doff and don as circumstances required. Now, she felt an urge to tower over these two waifs.

"Well...there *was* the eviction by the Bolsheviks from our apartment in St. Petersburg, now Leningrad. I was very small but my sister remembers it well. Men came with rifles and bayonets. They pushed Father into a corner. That's all I remember."

Dasha struggled a bit as the next scene wheeled into view. "We went to our family dacha in Kaluga. Huge place—from my mother's side—and we lived there five years...in a caretaker's cottage near the stables. Smelled to high heaven."

She brightened, as memories forged when she was a young girl came more easily. "Our mother—can you imagine?—was raising us alone. Father was off with the White Army. She arranged passage to Latvia using forged passports. We rode for days in a cattle car. Father joined us in Riga. Then at last we went to Prague—eighteen happy years. Father got a job teaching Slavic languages. Then the Germans came."

Dasha's memories came more rapidly. "It was the thirties, mind you. We were overrun by the Wehrmacht and strafed by the Stukas. So we fled to Belgrade and hid in the cellars... until the Luftwaffe bombardment. Father was imprisoned by the Germans. Mother was taken in by friends in Vienna. My sister and I found refuge on the Dalmatian Coast. My sister loved the Adriatic. Then she went to Paris to train to be a nurse, and I made my way back to Prague to join the resistance." Galina smiled from her table in the corner. DeFranco and Tracy listened carefully as Dasha's history spilled forth.

Memories from that period came in a torrent. "At the close of the war the Soviets wanted nothing more than to crush Russian refugees like us. Such a confusing period. Galina had been working in Paris in '44 when the Americans came through. She wound up as a nurse in Patton's Third Army and followed the war all the way to Germany. Near the end of the war I walked west to get to the American lines. It was an awful time—shot at by American boys in their P-47s, held at gunpoint by Czech bandits, harassed by German deserters."

Dasha caught her breath as she recalled those dark days. "After that, a career with G2, American Army intelligence. From there, on to my beloved OSS, then the CIA...the early days. They liked the fact I spoke six languages, so I started out in linguistics. Interpreting and translating for the higher-ups. They learned to depend on me. It was a natural transition to what we called 'operations.' Dulles himself recruited me when I made a visit to Bern.

He had an appreciation for my work with the underground. The Soviets were siphoning off German technology and talent. We had our own program, Operation Paperclip, designed to identify and exfiltrate Hitler's rocket scientists. I was part of the team that brought in Werner Von Braun, who became the father of the American space program. To think he was killing Londoners with his odious V-2 missiles one year and was in Huntsville, Alabama, building American rockets the next.

"Galina had a tougher time after the fighting ended, trying to stop the sickness in the camps. She was the real hero. So many displaced people. But now look at her, poor thing."

"Good Lord," said Tracy under her breath, trying to navigate the twisting tributaries of this twentieth-century life.

"White Russians!" said Dasha. "Anti-communists. Thrown to the wolves. But we learned how to survive." They sipped their coffee and Dasha smiled at Detective DeFranco, trying to melt the icy distance she'd imposed out by the seawall. Tracy got up and gravitated toward a shelf filled with family photos that revealed a life of laughter and abundance, children in various stages, cocktail parties with elegant women in fur wraps, men in double-breasted suits. She tried to place the period by the lengths of the skirts and the widths of the lapels. She came to a photograph of a man in lederhosen.

"Is this your husband?" she asked innocently.

"Heavens no," shouted Dasha. "But he *was* my prize."

"Sorry for asking," said Tracy.

"It's quite all right, dear. In my work during the war and after, we practiced active measures. Basically it meant stopping the enemy from carrying out acts of war or espionage. Nazis. Soviets. East-Bloc Communists. Much later, crime lords and swindlers. Didn't matter. It was democracy's dirty work...and I was good at it.

DeFranco and Tracy leaned in to listen.

"I don't care who knows it now. I am too old and I am past caring. This one was special," she said, pointing at the photo. "There were others."

"Who was he?" asked Tracy.

"Reinhard Tristan Heydrich. SS *Gruppenführer*. Architect of the final solution. I seduced him and worked with Czech partisans, who attacked him as he drove toward a rendezvous with me. Operation Anthropoid. I was twenty-seven. He was thirty-eight, a true monster. He died of his wounds. Not a clean job. But we removed an archvillain.

"With Constantine, life became much more tranquil... and our three children are my joy. But I miss the cause. When Constantine died, I brought this photo out to mark those days. Galina objected at first. Didn't like being reminded of my past... activities."

Dasha turned to DeFranco. The sergeant had been swept along in the stream of Dasha's life. He looked a little less rumpled with his heavy coat off, a weight removed. Dasha saw a flicker of illumination behind those tired eyes.

He's been betrayed, Dasha thought.

"So tell me, Sergeant," asked Dasha, the hard edge gone, a lightness embroidering her tone. Dasha knew the man would try to please, get on her good side, speak too much and regret it later. She was, at heart, an interrogator, and knew her craft. The rubber hose, the hot lamp—the coercion. They were for amateurs. She would invite him in, bestow time and solace.

Isn't it what we're all looking for? she thought.

She looked at him reassuringly, and she could feel him soften.

"What did you find out on the beach?" she asked innocently. She was prepared for an abridged response one might expect from an officer of the law. Could she tease out more?

"There's been a murder," he began. "A kid found the deceased behind the hardware store on Canal."

"Terrible," said Dasha. "I saw it on television." Then, turning to Tracy Taggart she said, "I know you, young lady. You're with the news."

"News 12 Connecticut," said Tracy. Dasha looked down her nose, unimpressed.

DeFranco continued. "The body was found in a dumpster."

"We saw it on the television last night," said Dasha. "I suppose Westport is not immune." She meant it as an expression of comfort for a man charged with keeping the peace.

He took a breath and looked up toward the mantelpiece, seeming to visualize the scene. Dasha could tell investigating a murder was something of a rarity for this small-town sergeant. He lacked the blasé cynicism one might expect from police in the big city, where murder was a daily occurrence. She thought the man wasn't quite wide-eyed, but he *was* struck by a kind of wonder.

"Murder just doesn't happen here," DeFranco said. "Not in Westport, Connecticut."

9

Anatomy of Trust

"Perhaps we need to back up and start again. I've revealed to you my secrets," Dasha said, pointing to her Nazi target. "Why don't you tell me what's going on and maybe I can help you."

Dasha fixed DeFranco with a penetrating gaze. She sensed the officer of the law was about to open up, his inner struggle slowly changing to relief.

"There's something wrong with this investigation and I…we… are trying to figure it out."

"Miss—" began Dasha.

"Call me Tracy."

"Tracy, then. Your news piece said the murder took place elsewhere. A victim of gang violence and drugs. Then dumped in our little town."

"We have new information that casts doubt on that theory," said Tracy.

"We were also told the case is being investigated by state police," said Dasha. "You are with the local police, Detective. Do I have that right? Have you been removed from the case? Does the state police investigator know you're out combing the beach?" She had driven right to the heart of DeFranco's dilemma.

"Not exactly," said DeFranco.

Gone rogue have we? thought Dasha.

"Couldn't this get you fired?"

"Probably," said DeFranco. "But some things are more important."

Now it was Dasha's turn to feel relief. She'd survived epic back-stabbing and finger-pointing. Accusations and blame were standard fare in intelligence—cliques and infighting for breakfast, lunch, and dinner. But eventually they would all dine as one, raise a glass and live to fight another day—until the next fine mess. A piece of her ancient heart gave way to this trusting man. She sensed he was fighting against his by-the-book training. She needed to become his safe harbor, the way she handled all her assets.

Dasha was standing next to Galina and her Scrabble board. *Let him talk,* Galina wrote with the little wooden squares.

"A recap, Sergeant. Lay out the pieces," said Dasha. She would stick to facts. She wouldn't ask about his impressions or his assumptions or his views. Not yet. He was a man, after all, and a police officer at that. He wouldn't speculate. He'd keep his emotions in check.

"This is what we know," said DeFranco. "The state police investigator said the young woman in the dumpster died of a drug overdose. But the medical examiner's office determined she died of asphyxiation. She had a piece of sea glass shoved down her throat. Sea glass that looks an awful lot like the pile of sea glass out on that beach." He pointed south.

"The state police investigator stated the murder victim was African American. But we believe she was Hindu, or at least South Asian. She had a toe ring with an inscription to the goddess Kali.

"The state police investigator said they linked the tattoo on her thigh to gangs in either Bridgeport or New Haven. But her tattoo was nothing but a hummingbird. And there was a strange oily smell at the scene."

Dasha spoke. "So you have inconsistencies between the facts and the official statements."

Then Tracy weighed in. "Somebody's not telling the truth."

Dasha eyed the young woman, and Tracy felt an icy coolness from across the room. Dasha understood the sergeant's motivation. But she didn't entirely trust the overly attractive journalist who was likely bent on nothing more than personal advancement. Galina noticed the exchange and coughed to get Dasha's attention, compelling her to yield.

Galina, the big sister, could still do that.

"Yes, inconsistencies," said DeFranco.

"And you're going against your boss and your department and you two—an unlikely pair—are troubled by the same apparent case of misinformation, if not misconduct. You both want to know why, but for different reasons," said Dasha.

"She wants her story," said DeFranco, looking at his compatriot. "I want the story too. And I want to find and stop the people who did this."

"Come now, Officer DeFranco. The world will keep turning if this case never gets solved. It's just a girl. African American. Punjabi. What difference does it make?"

She was goading him, trying to elicit a reaction.

"Why upset the applecart?" she continued. "Somebody higher up wants this case to disappear. Why risk ruining your career?"

Mine the truth, just like always, Dasha thought. Bring it to the surface.

"I don't want to let down my town," said DeFranco.

"Bah," said Dasha. "You've been passed over too many times and you've ceased caring. This is personal."

She had him. They were in the presence of a master.

Tracy came to the rescue.

"There are obvious discrepancies," she said.

"You say the victim was choked by a piece of sea glass?" asked Dasha.

"Absolutely," said DeFranco. "I saw it lodged in her windpipe during the autopsy."

"And you are sure she didn't swallow it intentionally? An accident?" Dasha asked.

"Shoved in too far," said DeFranco.

"Do you have a sample?" Dasha asked.

"This was picked up in the dumpster where the girl was found," said DeFranco, showing the piece to Dasha.

"See how it's all worn smooth?" said Dasha. "It needs to be in the water a long time to get those edges like that. And you can tell which sea glass has been in the water the longest by how worn they are. This one is an old-timer. I would guess it takes ten or fifteen years to get it like that." She rolled the sea glass around in her hand as DeFranco and Tracy leaned in to listen.

"Choking with a piece of sea glass is not an act of a trained assassin," said Dasha, ruminating on what the crime revealed about the assailant. "A professional would use either a knife or a silenced small-caliber semi-automatic pistol, multiple shots to the head. No, this was an act that involved intimacy and emotion. Right up close. Belly to belly. Highly personal. The killer was mad and impetuous…not a thinker. That's not to say a case like this is always completely spontaneous. I remember a case in Berlin after the war. We were running a honey trap with a prostitute and a Soviet trade minister. Wanted to compromise him. We found her dead with a pfennig shoved down her throat. It was if to say, 'Here. You like money so much. Choke on it.' They were trying to send a message to the other harlots: cooperate with the Americans at your peril."

"She may have had the drug Rohypnol in her system," said Tracy. "Also called a date-rape drug."

"At least that's what's been alleged," said DeFranco. "The official word is a heroin overdose, but we just don't buy it."

"You need to know more about the girl," said Dasha. "Who was she?"

"We don't know," said Tracy. "Officer DeFranco has asked Missing Persons. No one matching the description of a young, slightly built Hindu woman has been entered into the Connecticut state missing persons system."

"And you've yet to ask the FBI?" asked Dasha.

"Correct. That's on the list of things to do. But I'm off the case," said DeFranco. "Limits my ability to maneuver."

"Well," said Dasha. "Your actions suggest you're most assuredly a part of this investigation."

"Let's just say I am making some private inquiries," he replied. Yes…a rogue, thought Dasha. Never good.

"Maybe she simply didn't want to be found," said Dasha. "Or the people in her life chose not to report her missing. This I can understand."

"What do you mean?" asked Tracy.

"You said she's Hindu?" asked Dasha.

"Appears so," said DeFranco. "Maybe Pakistani…in any event, likely the subcontinent."

Dasha walked over to Galina's Scrabble board. *Knows his geography*, Galina wrote.

"She comes from an insular family. That I can assure you," said Dasha. "And a family for whom honor and shame go hand in hand. Maybe she did something dishonorable and she was being shunned? She'd been abandoned…and therefore her family still thinks she's alive. Or, maybe the family can't go to the authorities because they're illegal. Not unusual. Or maybe *they* killed her. It wouldn't be the first time a daughter has gone off the rails. Cousins are brought in to kill wayward daughters all the time in some parts of the world."

DeFranco and Tracy recoiled.

"But how do you account for the sea glass?" he asked her.

"We all collect sea glass from the beach," said Dasha. "Especially this beach. Next door, there used to be a wooden catwalk with a gazebo at the end. Party after party, people would walk out and smash their bottles and glasses on the rocks. Year after year starting in the Roaring Twenties. A nor'easter took out the pier five years ago. Turned it into matchsticks. But the sea glass is still coming up on shore. Doesn't draw a connection to the murderer. Association is not causation. But it's an intriguing theory. And Lord knows we have enough scoundrels on this side of Beachside Avenue. Murder has never been out of the question on this street."

"What do you mean?" asked Tracy.

"We have dodgy investment bankers and thieving arbitrageurs and fading talk show hosts and bygone starlets. We have princes of the leveraged buyout, scurrilous landlords, and penny-ante quacks. We even have a pair of pornographers. I assure you, if crossed, any one of them might be capable of murder—except perhaps the talk show host. Lovely man, actually."

"So we have something to work with," said DeFranco.

"You have precisely nothing," said Dasha.

"Some things I failed to mention," said DeFranco. "The office of the state's attorney had the body removed from the ME's office and sent to a crematorium. We may not have a body anymore."

"Like I said. Smacks of a cover-up. Odd, but not evidence," said Dasha.

"And there is the issue of a recent, apparently nonprofessional, abortion—substantial cervical scarring caused by a rough tool of some kind. I am not sure if the investigators from the state are aware of that."

"A possible motive. Keep it tucked away. You have passion, intimacy, fear, certainly pain, and blood—lots of it. Not to mention the defilement of the body," said Dasha, ruminating. "What are your next steps, Sergeant?"

"Can you maintain confidences?" asked DeFranco.

"You can't be serious, Detective," said Dasha. "You don't get to be my age and not know how to keep certain delicate matters confidential."

"First step is to rescreen her internal organs and get the results on the record somehow," said DeFranco. "Second step is to start interviewing people in this neighborhood, people who spend time on the beach." He pointed south again, as if the thin strip of sand and rock was a forbidden land. In a way it was.

"I come back to your theory of the crime, Sergeant," said Dasha. "Use your imagination. What would it take to produce a corpse like the one you encountered in the dumpster two nights ago? Start there."

"Maybe we'll have more to go on later," said DeFranco. "Thanks very much for your help. Keep my card and call me if anything comes to mind."

"Don't worry," said Dasha, trying to soothe any ruffled feathers. "I'll be thinking of you. And you too, dear," she said, turning to Tracy. "I am sorry if I antagonized you. You two make quite a striking pair. As Constantine liked to say, sometimes it takes a double team to pull the wagon."

10

Instinct

They finished their coffee and left Dasha and Galina's little house in the garden. They walked down a long driveway through a gate by a seven-bay garage, and turned left down Beachside Avenue for the one-mile trek back to DeFranco's car at Burying Hill Beach.

"Do we trust her?" asked DeFranco.

"No," said Tracy, still a little burned. "Not yet anyway. I mean, we don't know anything about her."

"We know she had a license to kill."

"Can you believe that? What a character," said Tracy. "But does she tell the truth? And can she keep a secret? We just don't know. I mean, she could be in on it. The sea glass was found practically in front of her house."

"I don't think that means much," said DeFranco. "A lot of people along Beachside Avenue have access to that stretch of beach. She's an old woman past her prime."

"I guess rich people commit crimes too, don't they?" Tracy reflected.

"Certainly, but we're also looking at a cover-up. I don't see how Dasha could be involved with that. What's her motivation?" said DeFranco.

"Let's play along with Dasha for a while," said Tracy. "Assume easy access to a lot of sea glass makes a connection between Beachside Avenue and the killer—and that's a reach. Let's see what she comes up with. She knows the street. And God knows she's a resource."

They trudged back to the Corolla, and DeFranco set a course for Compo Beach and Tracy's VW. "Gotta get to work," she said.

"Thanks for a lovely morning." Then she surprised him with a light peck on the cheek. She leaned back in through the open door. "Keep me posted. Can I call you later?"

"Yep. I want to see where our body has gone. Maybe Curtis can run toxicology again." He gave Tracy his home number and his office number with extension.

"I'll do some digging," said Tracy. "I want to know more about Dasha Petrov. Oh, and just remember, Sergeant. You are off the case." She laughed, and left him utterly disarmed.

DeFranco lingered in the parking lot a moment, watching Tracy Taggart dash away in her little VW, off to move mountains. Her lavender perfume hung in the air.

You've got it bad, son, he told himself, thinking about their morning's forced march along the beaches of Westport. God, what a trouper.

He was delighted that a higher, well-earned rank allowed him to take the weekend off, and he meandered through Westport on his way to the ME's office in Stamford. He stopped at the public service building to glance through the previous evening's police reports. He noticed that Officer McKurdy and a new patrolman named Hughes, hired as a youth officer, had done an admirable job breaking up a teenage bacchanale.

Maybe we landed a good one this time, thought DeFranco. It's not that he was necessarily critical of his fellow officers of the law, but he had to admit the force was…uneven. He had to include himself in that assessment. He knew he wouldn't be doing this forever. He'd seen it before. Phipps was burnt to a crisp when he'd loaded up the RV and started heading west. The rest of the force was up and down. McKurdy could keep his belt buckle shined, but then he'd let his cruiser run out of fuel. Of course there was Gomez, a prince who coached middle school soccer and had literally taken a bullet in his Kevlar vest when he'd broken up an armed robbery at a Post Road liquor store, earning a citation. Between these extremes were the work-a-day cops who just wanted to put in their time. Increasingly, rising home prices drove Westport police and fire department officers north and east. DeFranco was grateful he and Julie had planted their flag well before the run-up in real estate.

He went by Oscar's Deli to order a coffee and a pastrami on rye to go. Then he walked a few steps north to have a chat with the clerk at the Remarkable Book Store, a friend from the summer softball league.

Softball.

Something they could all agree on. Cops. Firemen. Garage mechanics. Autoparts retailers. A couple of young lawyers and even a podiatrist. They all liked to don their cleats and head to the diamond, coolers of beer to slake their postgame thirst. Feeling the crack of bat against ball, watching it sail into the sky, smelling the fresh-cut grass and getting their pants dirty with desperate slides into home. They were all starting to deal with that muffin-top bulge, the bursitis in the hip, the knife-like sciatica. But quitting softball meant…quitting life.

He boarded Angelica's tattered Corolla with the intention of heading toward the medical examiner's office, but something in his gut urged him to head back toward Beachside Avenue. He needed another conversation with Dasha Petrov.

~

He pulled into the driveway and parked in front of the massive garage. He walked down the driveway and knocked gently on the cottage kitchen door, fearful he was interrupting someone's nap. Dasha came after the second knock, reading glasses perched on her nose and *Peterson's Field Guide to Birds* opened to the section on migratory pintails. She wore a smart tweed jacket and weekend khakis. Her lipstick had been restored with precision.

"Oh hello, Sergeant," said Dasha. "I expected you back, but not so soon."

"You jogged a few things loose," said DeFranco.

"I have a knack for that," she said, smiling, trying to offset their abrasive first encounter. "After you left I thought I saw a duck that frequents the Midwest. Fellow's off course."

"Maybe that was me," said DeFranco, laughing.

"No, Sergeant," said Dasha soothingly. "I feel you may have been off course for a while, but you have suddenly found your way."

"I've never been psychoanalyzed quite so much in one day."

"Just doing my job. You lost your voice somehow and now you're finding it again. Where's the redhead?"

"She had to go to work."

"Bit of a conflict consorting with the press, isn't it, Sergeant?"

"Probably," said DeFranco. Then, falling back on an available irony, he said, "There appears to be nothing *but* conflicts with this case. I'll take my chances with Tracy Taggart, especially over my own chief and the state's attorney."

"Excellent point," said Dasha. "You've got an orchestra seat to what might be a colossal deception."

"And—just to round things out—I'm turning to complete strangers for help," DeFranco added.

"Oh, we won't be strangers for long."

"I need a sounding board. Someone to share ideas. Somebody with experience," said DeFranco.

Dasha accepted without comment this cry for help. "I am not unacquainted with skullduggery, Sergeant. Had to sniff out clues to find a few traitors, or glean the intentions of the opposition. Even had to solve a few murders along the way, usually over-eager Soviet underlings removing our well-cultivated assets. Grisly stuff."

"I need a profile of who might have done this," said DeFranco.

"You said there was an oily smell at the scene. Ever smell acetylene? Maybe we need to look for a welder's kit," said Dasha. "You can haul one of those on the back of a truck."

"Let's focus on where the body was burned," said DeFranco. "You can't just torch a corpse in your backyard."

"Perhaps a place where burning happens all the time. There are burn pits in some industrial settings."

"Maybe someplace out of the way, but hidden in plain sight."

"Now you're using your imagination. Where would you go?"

"Fire department training center in Fairfield," said DeFranco. "And there's a heat-treating plant in Bridgeport that processes parts for Sikorsky. And there's a cinder block grill for frying chicken behind the Elks Lodge in Stratford."

"I'm a little skeptical, but it would be good to rule them out. Let me get my coat," said Dasha, stepping uninvited into DeFranco's investigation.

After a slight, awkward hesitation, DeFranco extended his arm. Dasha took it and they walked down the drive. She used her chestnut stick to point out the French lilacs Constantine had planted, and the decommissioned gas pump near the garage. "Pepé the gardener doubled as Constantine's chauffer when he went into the city, and Pepé's wife, Margarita, was our cook and nanny when the kids were growing. It's all gone to seed now. People tell me how grand it is and all I can see is the peeling paint."

They motored eastward along the shore through Southport, then intercepted I-95. DeFranco worried Dasha might object to the Corolla's geriatric suspension. "Sorry about these bumps," he said.

"Don't worry, Sergeant," said Dasha. "I spent time in the back of a half-track helping G2 sort out the mess along the Elbe. You haven't lived until you've slept under a tarp and awoken to powdered eggs and watered-down coffee. But it was a feast for those of us who hadn't eaten in a while. You were in the service?" she asked innocently.

"Navy. Vietnam. Swift Boat commander in the Delta," said DeFranco. His clipped response told Dasha he didn't want to talk about it, but she pressed on.

"I bet you've got some stories," she said. "I was in Indochina too, only they called the Viet Cong the Viet Minh back in those days. They were our allies against the Japanese, but we earned their emnity when we helped restore the French to Indochina. That's what caused the mess. Still, there was a job to do. Orders."

"It was long ago and far away," said DeFranco, obviously eager to change the subject. Dasha left it there, determined to circle back.

"Let's go to the Elks Lodge, then the heat-treating plant, then back west again," said DeFranco. "Could be a wild-goose chase."

"Goose chases and dead-ends. They are inevitable, Sergeant," said Dasha. "But we're like doctors. We have to rule things out." She didn't say their little sojourn had already met Dasha's goal. She wanted to get the sergeant alone, take his measure. Sometimes all that meant was a little idle conversation. She felt that telltale surge of adrenalin when an operation was getting traction and gaining speed. God help her, but she missed the game.

"So tell me, Sergeant," said Dasha as the tractor trailers whizzed by on the center lane. "You're putting a lot of stock in your sea glass theory."

"She choked to death on it," said DeFranco. "I saw it myself."

"But there are miles and miles of beaches along the Connecticut coast. There's sea glass everywhere. Why focus on Beachside Avenue?"

"No good reason. Other than the fact there seems to be a lot of it. I was hoping the ME could shed more light."

"But it takes time and space and privacy to mutilate and burn a human body," said Dasha. "It takes a fairly substantial vehicle like an open pickup truck to haul a smoldering corpse to a dumpster, and no small physical ability to heft it over the lip and drop it inside. Place and people, Officer DeFranco. Did it take two? Or one large person? And if that could be determined, can we move toward an assumption of the physical description of the assailants? And why the dumpster in the first place? Why not just bury it? The murderer would have to know the body would be discovered at some point, if not at the location of the dumpster itself, then certainly at the transfer station, or the landfill where Westport's upscale trash eventually winds up. The assailants didn't care if they were discovered, suggesting a certain hubris. Or a certain panic. Were the killers pressed for time? Or overconfident? Or on the run? Or was he, or they, trying to send a message?"

"At this point it's just hard to say," said DeFranco. "There was an effort to conceal it. But if it had been buried, we wouldn't be having this conversation. Maybe it was a screwup."

"Conjecture, Officer," challenged Dasha, her tone changing, sharper now. "A piece of the puzzle, perhaps. But solving a puzzle requires context, a framework, and most of all a theory. We have the time and place of the discovery. It's clear the girl wasn't murdered there, so there must be another crime scene where the act, then the dismemberment and fire, took place. Where can you imagine those places might be? What is your *theory?*"

"Let me get to that," said DeFranco, now on the defensive. He knew if it were the chief asking these questions he'd backpedal to a safe corner—nods and ahems and "I'll have to get back to you." When Dasha probed he felt challenged yet supported, as if she too were in the thick of it.

"All right, Mrs. Petrov—"

"Oh please, call me Dasha."

"All right then, Dasha," said DeFranco. "Why sea glass? And why Beachside Avenue? Like you said, the place has its cast of characters. I come back to a theory, as you like to call it. Consider your low-rent murder in Father Panik Village in Bridgeport. Probably a drug deal gone wrong. Perp would drop the body and leave it in the street and hoof it out of there. Period. Your nice middle-class murder would probably be accompanied by some kind of domestic disturbance. Dad strangles mom right in the kitchen and one of the kids calls 911. Your Beachside Avenue murder is a whole different league. Space. Time. Tools. Industrial-strength effort to conceal. Head and hands gone. Burned to a crisp. It's big. Just like the avenue. Too bad they got sloppy with that toe ring."

"Well, Sergeant. We can't always depend on sloppiness in our adversaries, can we? But when it happens, we have to be ready to strike. I remember targeting a kingpin in the *Ustashe*, the Croatian fascists. I was dancing with him at the Kavana Café in

Dubrovnik in 1941. I put a pill in his brandy and lured him to the parapets surrounding the old city. I baited him into making an inappropriate advance and I pushed him off onto the rocks. He got sloppy."

"So you're a killer too, Dasha."

"Oh yes, Sergeant. But always for God and country. You have to be on the side of right."

"That's where it gets sticky," said DeFranco. "Who's to say?"

Self-doubt, thought Dasha. A point of inflection...

"Those who win the war write the history," said Dasha. "And I was determined to win."

"Well, I wouldn't call Vietnam a win," said DeFranco. "In fact, it wasn't even a draw. I don't know why we were over there."

A forbidden topic, she thought. But he needs to talk about it.

"You have to put Vietnam in context with our struggle against the Soviets and the Chinese. And that war is still being waged, Sergeant. We may win it yet. It's too bad our little sideshow caused so much damage. To them and to us. I adore the Vietnamese and I'd go back to Saigon in a minute."

"Beautiful people," said DeFranco. "And yes, we caused a lot of damage. It was more than just a little sideshow."

So that's it, she thought. An atrocity.

"Plenty of blame to go around, Sergeant. Their side. Our side. Best to let it go."

"Easier said than done."

They arrived at the Elks Lodge and found the grill in the back. Twenty-five feet long and six wide, it had a homemade metal rack on top that was clean but corroded. They walked to the rectangular cinder block pit and quickly surmised it hadn't been used to burn any poor murder victims. The benevolent order of Elks had shoveled out the ash and left it in some semblance of order.

They found the heat-treating plant, and DeFranco's badge elicited a tour from a shift foreman. It was a Dickensian scene of a dirt floor and dark spaces lit by open flames tended by sweat-drenched men. They were annealing fasteners for high-tech helicopters—Bronze-Age techniques brought forward across the centuries.

"I think we're looking for black marks, hair, skin," said Dasha. They came up dry.

They drove over to the Fairfield County fire-training center, and it was closed for the weekend, affording them a chance to drive around the structures. The county had built a four-story cinder block tower so budding firemen could learn how to haul hoses up staircases and rescue mannequins from simulated smoke inhalation. They found a firepit and were disappointed to see how clean the fire department had left it. Scorch marks, yes, but no telltale signs of grilled animal matter.

"Like I said," observed DeFranco, "a wild-goose chase."

"No, Sergeant. Now you know. No lingering doubts. You've done your due diligence. You can check off those boxes. But I have to ask you something. Why are you so hard on yourself?"

"What gives you that idea?"

"You have a lot coming at you, and you want to get it all down and get it right. You feel it's all on you."

"Isn't it?" asked DeFranco. "A woman has been killed. The people who are supposed to solve this crime are trying to cover it up. It's *not* right." Dasha knew she was now addressing the former navy commander, responsible to men and mission—not part of the get-along, go-along rank-and-file putting in time.

"There are risks, Sergeant," said Dasha. "You are going against the grain." She knew she was needling him. "You are putting yourself in the crosshairs."

"I don't have a lot to lose," said DeFranco. "And somebody has to fix it."

"Righting old wrongs, Sergeant?"

"You're trying to psychoanalyze me again, Dasha." He laughed. "I couldn't sleep at night knowing I didn't do my best...for her. For the girl in the dumpster."

"What's next?"

"I'm off to the ME."

"And I need to check on Galina," said Dasha.

"You take very good care of her," said DeFranco in a show of deference.

"She's been my anchor since...forever," said Dasha. "And it almost wasn't so. When she joined Patton's march across Europe, she knit the bones and sewed up the wounds of the young GIs. I was stranded in the east, trying to outrun the Red Army. After the Nazi capitulation we left little notes in all the churches trying to find each other. I signed mine Boris the Goat after our little kid in Kaluga. She was Galinka. We found each other in a displaced persons camp outside Munich, and we've been together ever since. She held my life together when I was off fighting my wars."

"That's the way I feel about this place, for better or worse," said DeFranco. "Westport held me together."

"That's a nice way of expressing it."

"It can be a little close-minded and prickly. But it's home."

"Is that why you can't let the case go? You need to tidy up the place?"

"Hadn't thought of it that way, but I guess you're right."

"We're of a like mind, then, Sergeant. I also found my work rather cleansing."

"As long as you've got a clear field of fire and the wrong people don't get hurt," said DeFranco.

Collateral damage, then? she thought.

"Okay, Sergeant. More stories later. Please tell me what you learn today, and let me add this. The TV reporter could be trouble." Dasha knew she was taking a risk.

"I know," said DeFranco somberly.

"Best to build in some distance, Sergeant. You might be moving too fast. You don't know her."

"What do you mean?" he asked, finding a rare bit of jest. "I met her two days ago." They both laughed, but Dasha turned to him as he idled the Corolla in her driveway.

"She's in it for herself," said Dasha. "Be very wary of a manipulation. She senses a weakness, Sergeant. You're single?"

"A widower."

"Okay, then. My spouse died long ago," said Dasha. "The lone-liness never ends. Do you want her help? Or do you want her to fill a need?"

"You're asking tough questions, Dasha," said DeFranco. "I thought this was about the girl in the dumpster?"

"To help that girl in the dumpster she needs a champion. And that's you, Sergeant. You have to be at your level best. Let's hope Tracy Taggart isn't trying to get in your way for her own ends— or the ends of her employer. Her boss may take the story away from her if she's not careful. And any allegiance she has toward you will immediately dissolve. I know how these things work."

"Right now I find her very helpful—and for some reason, I find trusting complete strangers easier than trusting my own department."

"Yes. The officials seem to have gone off the rails. You have a point. You and I don't know each other very well. But I believe you'll find I can be trusted."

"Forgive me, Dasha, but that remains to be seen."

"Yes, Sergeant. Some skepticism. A wary, watchful eye. Nurture that. I've yet to win you over. But I will. You'll see."

~

He came around to open her door and he watched her walk with surprising energy up the driveway. He exited the avenue and drove to the interstate, heading west for Stamford. He kept the car in the center lane and maintained the speed limit, letting traffic flow around him. He used the time to think about where everything seemed to be headed—and of course he thought about Tracy. He conceded making a deal with a reporter wasn't his brightest move. She'd told him she'd need to pursue the story independently, now that he was off the case. Would she follow those instincts? Or would she heed his wish to shield informa-tion from the killers—for the girl in the dumpster. He had no idea which way Tracy Taggart would turn.

Stamford was in the midst of a building boom with a new railroad station and more financial office complexes—Fidelity, Chase, Merrill Lynch. He loped over the side streets to the public buildings that included the medical examiner's office. He parked and walked into the compound, struck immediately by the sight of an idling ambulance, lights flashing, back door open. He went inside and found milling personnel wearing the standard white coats, aprons—and pained expressions. He approached a uniformed Stamford city police officer and produced his badge and ID. In the middle of this assemblage sat Dr. Goldberg in his powered wheelchair, head down, hugging himself and rocking slowly back and forth.

DeFranco approached him, and put his hand on his shoulder. The doctor looked up into his eyes, tears streaming.

"Haven't you heard?"

"Heard what?" asked DeFranco.

"Curtis Jones is dead."

11

Organs of Deceit

The information hit DeFranco like a baseball bat, and caused a strange heat to braise the skin between his eyes. His breath quickened after a first, sudden intake. Then the information settled over his frontal cortex, covering and infusing everything in his brain. He couldn't find the words, until he finally stammered something vaguely coherent.

"When? How?" he said to the doctor, still rocking in his chair.

"He was hanging by the neck in a closet off the lab," said Goldberg. "Used his own belt. He left a note."

"Does Curtis have family?" asked DeFranco, remembering Jones had mentioned antidepressants.

"A son from his first marriage. He's only eighteen. My secretary called him. He's on his way over."

"Can we go somewhere to talk?" DeFranco asked the medical examiner.

"Can it wait, Sergeant?" asked Goldberg.

"I'm afraid not, Doctor. I'm sorry."

Goldberg turned to a woman at this side. "I will be in my office. Send Alan Jones to me at once when he arrives." Then he turned back to DeFranco. "That's Curtis's son. He's a wonderful young man. Like his father. I don't know what to say to him."

Goldberg manipulated the joystick of his wheelchair and it turned in place to slowly glide down the hall. DeFranco walked behind him. They found Goldberg's office and the doctor managed to maneuver through the blizzard of books and papers drifting inside.

"Such a loss…" he muttered, voice trailing off. "Now I know what families go through when they've lost a loved one. And the loved one winds up here."

"Will there be a postmortem?" asked DeFranco.

"Haven't thought that far. I will probably bring in a colleague from New Haven. I won't be able to bear it. I never thought I would say that. After all, death is our business. But Curtis was like a son to me. I loved him. I taught him everything. Such a great heart and mind."

"May I see the note?" asked DeFranco.

Goldberg handed him a white sheet of typing paper with text generated from a word processor. Back in the day, you'd see typescript from a Royal or an Olivetti that had smudged, irregular characters. But with the advent of the personal computer, the type was clean and neat, hammered out by an infallible strike-on printer.

First, I want to say how sorry I am, read the note. *I know this act lets a lot of people down. But I just can't continue to work day in and day out in a place that deals so closely with death and loss. I'm tired of it. And like my grandmother used to say at the prospect of dying, "I'm going home."*

It was signed Curtis Jones with a large *CJ* in handwritten caps next to Curtis's name. The note was soulless and impersonal. Anyone could have written it.

"Tell me how he was found," asked DeFranco.

"Cleaning crew," responded the doctor.

"You said he was hanging?"

"That's what they said," said Goldberg, looking at DeFranco, wheels starting to turn through the pall of shock and grief.

"Was his neck snapped? Had he dropped? Or was he just choked?" asked DeFranco.

"We'll find out in the postmortem," said Goldberg. "I will want you to be there. He liked you."

"If you want me," said DeFranco, just as Dr. Goldberg's assistant knocked, then entered the room.

"Dr. Goldberg, Alan Jones is here," she said.

"Oh God. It falls to me," said Goldberg. "How many times have I treated tending to the living like just another chore so I could get back to the lab and the real work?" Goldberg's voice trailed away and he looked out the window and beyond.

"Well, I have a responsibility to Curtis. Please excuse me, Detective." The doctor motored out of the room, his shriveled form shrunk even further by the weight of what he was about to do. His assistant remained behind. DeFranco had wanted to talk to him about the crematorium. Curtis Jones's son came first.

"Are you Detective DeFranco?" she asked.

"Yes."

"I have a package for you at the front desk. Please swing by when you leave." She left the room, leaving DeFranco alone in the doctor's disordered sanctum. Was the man's space and surroundings a bit like his busy mind? So much to know. So much to absorb. So much to learn to gain a truth that came in fragments and strands and, at last, human failings.

DeFranco walked toward the front of the building to get his package and to leave this awful place, at least for a while, to retreat to his little dead end, maybe watch some football. How about a beer? But he had to contact Tracy, tell her about Curtis once her shift was over. When would that be?

You've got it bad, thought DeFranco.

He stopped by the assistant's desk. She handed him an Igloo cooler secured with red *Evidence—Do Not Remove* tape. Also taped to the top was a piece of paper with the words *Anthony DeFranco, Westport PD* written in Magic Marker. He pulled up the folding handle and left the building, walking down the street to re-enter the ME's office parking lot from the rear. The wind had died down, but now a gray overcast turned everything flat and dull.

He found Angelica's Corolla and noted that the ambulance had left the premises. The deceased, after all, had been dead on arrival. No need to transport the remains to the medical examiner. In fact, in many ways, Curtis Jones *was* the medical examiner, a man who loved shedding light in dark places.

He hesitated. The sanctity of the evidence deserved respect. But then he thought of the downward spiral this case was taking. He breached the evidence tape with his car key and took a quick look inside, instantly recognizing the need to leave the compound and find some privacy. He drove to the railroad station parking lot on the south side of the newly constructed Steward B. McKinney terminal, driving up the intertwining ramps to the top deck. He shut off the Corolla and turned his attention to the cooler sitting on the seat beside him. A handwritten note from Curtis Jones came out first.

Hi Tony. Something may have come up and I won't be able to get to these today. I found a lab in White Plains that can handle the matter privately. Good to get it out of Connecticut, I think. Lab-Right Corp. Talk to Mike. No news from the Finnazo cremato-rium until they open Monday. Let's catch up then. Curtis.

Certainly doesn't sound like a man about to kill himself, thought DeFranco. He pulled out the contents of the cooler. First came a jar with a notation. *Jane Doe. Westport 101589. Uterus removed 101689. Dr. S. X. Goldberg presiding.* Then in small type *Preserved with six parts water, three parts ethyl alcohol, one part formalin.*

Then came a jar with the same identification marked *Liver Sample.* Then a smaller jar marked *Lung Sample.* Another one was marked *Trachea Sample.* The jars were also sealed with evidence tape. He spent some time with the trachea jar. If he turned it just right and gave it a shake, he could see the sea glass embedded in the flare of the girl's windpipe.

He put the trachea jar under the seat of the Corolla. He wanted to show the sea glass to Dasha. The liver was the important one for toxicology, Curtis had said. He put the rest of the contents back in the cooler and decided he would drive it to Lab-Right on Monday morning before his shift.

He put the cooler on the right front seat and left the garage, tracing the usual route back to Westport. He got back to his little Cape as the light was waning. He trudged up the porch stairs, holding the cooler in his left hand, and with his right worked the key into the lock of the kitchen door.

Something moved to his left, a shape, a form, maybe just a shadow. He stopped and stared into the backyard as the twilight now made a rapid fall with the coolness of the coming evening. He looked back on it later. He had the cooler in his left hand, key in his right hand, absorbed by the idea of getting into the house, to finish this terrible day. He wanted to surround himself with the comforts and familiarities of home. He looked to his left, put the cooler down on the concrete floor of the little porch, pulled his coat away from his holster with the elbow of his strong hand, and moved his right hand down to palm the handle of the little snubbie on his hip.

He felt a sudden sharp pain in the back of his head. All he could see was a fierce white light and then stars streaking across black. He grabbed the railing and tried to get his bearings. Then a second blow came, a roundhouse from the left from some kind of a blunt object—not a fist, but something hard and moving fast, a truncheon or a blackjack, not wood, maybe leather. It struck over his left eye. It made a weird sound. Not a crack. More of a thump. That's when he fell on his back, to the fleeting sound of retreating footsteps on the gravel driveway.

The next thing he knew, he was looking into the worried face of Tracy Taggart, who said, "Jesus, Tony. Are you all right? What happened?"

12

Tracy

It was past midnight. He was on the couch in his living room, a bit too much of a bachelor pad, he thought, for a first visit by the one and only Tracy Taggart. But then the pain shot through his head, front to back, and there was blood on the front of his shirt. It was coming back to him. He couldn't see out of his left eye, which felt like it was swollen shut.

"How did I get here?" he asked Tracy, who was a vision, really, in her smart dress and tasteful makeup. She'd obviously just come from work. "And how the heck did you find me?"

"I looked up your address in the phone book," said Tracy. "And you gave me your phone number this morning. I called, and when you didn't answer I decided to drive over. Found you an hour ago on the back stoop. Frozen and bleeding. But you were breathing and sort of half conscious, so I got you to your feet and got you inside. I stopped the bleeding, for the most part, thanks to some Marine Corps training, and then decided packing you off to the hospital would just annoy you—neck's not broken. So I'm your nurse. I've got the wound over your eye closed with a butterfly, and I've got a gauze pad and a head bandage for that bump on the back of your head. Looks worse than it is. I'm icing it down with a bag of frozen peas, and I've got some Advil ready for pain. I've got the blood contained with some dish towels but I really would like to get you out of that shirt."

"You're the most beautiful thing I've ever seen," said DeFranco, uncaring.

"Well…you're a little delusional, but that's obviously just the head injury talking."

"There was a small Igloo cooler," said DeFranco. "Did you see it?"

"Nope."

"Oh hell," said DeFranco. Then he remembered Curtis. He looked straight at Tracy—a look that suggested she pay close attention.

"Curtis is dead," he said flatly. "Official word is suicide. They found him hanged inside a closet at the ME's office."

Out of his good eye, he could see the color drain from Tracy Taggart's face and her eyes grow wide. "The dumpster victim's vital organs for the new tox screening were in that cooler. He left it for me before he died, or—"

"Let me finish," said Tracy. "Before he was killed."

"It never ceases to amaze me. We just had dinner with the man, and now he's gone," said DeFranco in a faraway voice.

That was death for you. People just disappear. Except for the ones you've killed yourself. They lay there right in front of you, all limp, mangled, and twisted.

Tracy paced the room, wringing her hands. DeFranco could tell Curtis's death was hitting her hard. He watched her work through the combinations. Curtis was on the trail of the dumpster killer. So were he and Tracy. That made them targets, too. How would the introduction of Dasha Petrov influence this deadly mix? DeFranco listened while Tracy searched for answers.

"I got some more information on Dasha Petrov," said Tracy at last. "I think she's legit."

She'd arrived at the office before her shift started, and her first assignment wasn't for an hour. She turned to the station's Lexus-Nexus terminal and typed in *Petrov*.

"Constantine Petrov came up in the first reference. He was born in Siberia. Father was an officer in the White Army and his parents were on the run from the Bolsheviks. They wound up in Harbin, China, in the great Russian diaspora following the end of the Russian Revolution. First the Czar abdicated. Then the Czar and his family were murdered. Budding democratic movements led by Kerensky were stamped out. A military coup attempt led by a Czarist general named Kornilov died on the vine. Petrov grew up speaking Russian at home and Mandarin in the streets. Smart as a whip, he came to the attention of Royal Dutch Shell executives who arranged admission to MIT for his engineering studies. He went back to China and led several Shell expeditions to tap resources in the region. He came to the unwanted attention of the Japanese, and finally fled to Australia for the duration. He was a civilian contractor assigned to General MacArthur's staff. A wizard at logistics, especially moving fuel for the American war machine. He went back to China after the war, then to South America—Venezuela's Lake Maracaibo—always chasing the oil. He married the former Dasha Sokolov and they moved to Beachside Avenue to raise their three children.

"Dasha's curriculum vitae was harder to glean. She'd mentioned Heydrich, and I found numerous references to the assassination of Hitler's lieutenant on a Prague backstreet in May of 1942. The shooters were part of a Czech hit team dropped in by the British. They'd used a young woman as bait for their trap. Very little is known about her, but Heydrich was on his way to see her when he was injured. He later died of infection.

"Dasha also mentioned Allen Dulles and Bern. Dulles ran Allied intelligence for the Office of Strategic Services out of an OSS safe house in Switzerland. After the war the Allies scoured Germany to find the scientists responsible for Hitler's rocket program. They grabbed Werner Von Braun, who became father of the American space agency. Finding Hitler's scientists was called Operation Paperclip. I found a photograph of Von Braun and some of his associates about to board a train, surrounded by American soldiers and others in plain clothes. A young woman was in the photograph. I'm sure it was Dasha Sokolov, who became Mrs. Constantine Petrov."

"So she really is a spy," said DeFranco.

"I found a history of the early CIA. Missions in West Germany, the East Bloc, Yugoslavia. There are references to the agency tapping into the multilingual skills of Russian and Czech expats.

Females in particular. They had a special talent for exposing and compromising the opposition. No names of course. But Dasha wasn't just making it up. They even had a name for them, The Ravens."

Tracy helped DeFranco sit up and gave him some water. He swung his legs off the couch and planted his feet on the floor. His head didn't bother him as much as having no working left eye.

"That box had dumpster girl's liver sample, lung sample, and uterus," said DeFranco. "Curtis left it for me...before they found him. He was worried it wouldn't make it to another lab. Looks like he was right."

"Jesus," said Tracy. "What now?"

"Go out to my car and get the small jar out from under the driver's side seat. That's her thyroid cartilage and trachea with the sea glass embedded. I took it out of the cooler because I wanted to show it to you and Dasha," said DeFranco.

"Genius," said Tracy.

"Blind luck," said DeFranco.

She returned with the jar.

"Put it in the freezer behind the ice cube trays," said DeFranco. "Tomorrow's another day. Sunday, in fact. Your day of rest."

"I prowled around Angelica's room and found a flannel nightie. Do you mind if I stay here tonight? I don't want to leave you. Purely professional, you understand."

"No problem," said DeFranco, delighted to have Tracy Taggart under his roof.

"Just don't get any funny ideas."

"I'm actually flattered you would think I'd have any funny ideas in my condition," said DeFranco.

"Well, guys like you have been known to rally," said Tracy, her smile lighting up the room. "And we haven't even had a date yet."

"Let's please get around to that, shall we?" DeFranco's flirt instincts were born anew...after how long?

Tracy helped him to his feet, then checked the door locks and doused the lights. "That wimpy .38 the only gun you have in the house?" she asked innocently.

"Remington 870 pump-action riot gun with a pistol grip in the master closet," said DeFranco. "Double-O buckshot on the top shelf."

"That will be helpful," said Tracy. "Just so you know, my Kimber .45 is in my purse and tonight I'll have it under my pillow."

"...so there's no funny stuff," said DeFranco. "I hope you have a permit for that thing."

"Of course," said Tracy. "Dad taught me to shoot and wouldn't let me come to the Northeast without it."

"I need to meet this guy," said DeFranco.

She took his arm around her shoulder and guided him up the stairs, which took longer than he expected. She got him into the master and removed his bloody shirt. She took away the frozen peas and rechecked his head bandage. Julie would have approved of the way she put a couple of bath towels down on the pillow to absorb any overnight seepage. He was a little surprised, but grateful, when she unbuckled his pants and let them fall to the floor. As he stood there in his paisley boxers, he thought, Why worry? She's a trained nurse, for the love of Pete.

Then she sat him back, yanked off his socks, swung his legs up, and got him under the covers. "There's a glass of water on the bedside stand and a couple of Advils in case you get any serious pain in the night."

He smiled and watched her go over to the master closet to find the Remington. She brought it out, controlled the muzzle and her trigger finger like a true Marine, found the slide release on the trigger guard, and opened the breach to determine the status of the weapon. Unloaded. She found the box of shells and put six in the tube and one in the chamber before racking the slide closed.

Girl's ready, thought DeFranco.

She went to his bedside to turn out the light. "Sleep tight, DeFranco," she said, giving him a sisterly peck on the cheek before exiting the room. "I'll leave the door ajar. Just let me know if you need anything."

"I'll be okay," he said. Thanks Tracy Taggart, he thought. You're really something.

~

Tracy went to Angelica's room, put the shotgun in a corner, put her Kimber on the bedside table, and got into her borrowed nightie. She managed to find a new toothbrush still in the wrapper and did her necessaries before returning to the bedroom. She turned out the light and before she settled in, she looked out the window. A single street lamp cast a cone of light halfway down High Gate Road. She saw the red taillights of a nondescript dark sedan come on, then a wisp of exhaust, and finally headlights drilling through the night before the car eased gently down the road.

"We know you're watching…whoever you are," she said aloud before turning to Angelica's double bed with the pink comforter.

13

Human Contact

For Constantine, Dasha was a woman of action—never one to stand still, always planning her next move against enemies foreign and domestic—or formulating a Seabreeze dinner party for a dozen Petrov intimates.

Those were the days, reflected Dasha, Margarita in the kitchen, Pepé in a white coat serving canapés, kids banished upstairs, friends in full banter, cocktails in hand. They always boasted an ambassador or two, but preferred the chiefs of mission between assignments, seasoned diplomats with ears to the ground. Henry and Claire Luce liked to show up, always bearing roses and caviar. So too came the Henry Cabot Lodges, soon to take up their new post in Saigon; Smith Richardson of Vicks; a stray Vanderbilt, old man Bedford. They all came. Evenings at the Petrov salon would only conclude in the wee hours, with empty shot glasses from Constantine's vodka toasts hurled into the fire.

"Briggs Cunningham always arrived at the wheel of an exotic sports car, Galina," said Dasha. "Now there was a bon vivant. He was perfectly comfortable besting the field at Watkins Glen—or winning the America's Cup."

Dasha and Galina sat before the smoky embers, absorbing the nightly news on the television, intrigued by more murmurings from a Soviet Union in transition.

"Gorbachev is really trying to make a difference," said Dasha. "I knew him, Galina…Moscow State University 1954. Dashing young lawyer. I was under questionable cover. But that's a story for another day."

Galina responded with her one good hand whirling over the Scrabble board.

Doomed, she wrote in Russian.

"Galina, why so pessimistic?"

Of course Dasha missed their conversations, which had begun decades ago under blankets in the bed they shared in Kaluga, a frosty wind off the steppes rattling the panes. Now Dasha would have to do with one-word responses, and occasionally, if pressed, a full string of disjointed phrases that she always interpreted correctly. At this point, they could read each others' minds.

Apparatchiks, Galina wrote.

"Yes, the bureaucracy. He'll be crushed under the wheel of the Soviet system. But he has star power," said Dasha. "And don't discount the power of the media. Wide dissemination of opposing thoughts may upend things in our favor. They are talking about a Sky Bridge connecting television audiences. That's one way to expose their putrefied system."

You're relentless, wrote Galina.

"Yes dear," said Dasha. "I'm doomed to carry on the fight."

The policeman and the girl?

"I knew you'd bring it up," said Dasha. "Yes, he's handsome. That chiseled Italian look. But he's a peculiar one. And I'm dubious of the reporter's intentions."

Galina moved her hand around the board with near youthful dexterity. *He's confused.*

"Yes, Galina, confused," said Dasha. "He was on a recruiting mission. He is looking for help—against the treachery in his department, the perplexity of the case, the urgent need to apprehend the killer. He can't turn to colleagues in the police department. His trust has been abused. Somehow he felt comfortable turning to us. Any port in a storm, as Constantine liked to say."

The girl? wrote Galina.

"Yes, we'll see what becomes of her, won't we?" said Dasha. "The first hint of competition for her story will knock her off balance. What do they say? Seldom does a plan survive first contact with the enemy. Same holds true for competition in the media. She thinks cozying up to the sergeant grants her an exclusive. She's not the only enterprising journalist intrigued by the case of the headless girl. Let's see how fast she abandons her pact with the sergeant when she, or especially her boss, senses a bit of challenge."

Sea glass?

"It's more than just a theory, Galina. What else can he go on?"

Immigration?

"Yes of course, you're right, Galina. If she's foreign born and just visiting, she had to have come through Immigration. But there's a logic to all this. If she's young, she'll have congregated with those her own age, perhaps her own nationality. Relationships, Galina. Everything—all of history—is founded on human contact."

14

Plan of Action

DeFranco awoke the next morning as the first tentacles of light stole into the master. His left eye was partially open, a good sign, and he was happy the pain from that bump on the back of his head was moderating. He was also happy that ace TV reporter Tracy Taggart was nuzzling into his chest, one arm across his body, with a distinct but delicate snore emanating from her slightly parted lips.

Just enjoy it, DeFranco, he told himself sternly. And no funny stuff.

He had no idea how or when she got there.

He drank in the scent of her hair and felt the smooth skin under Angelica's flannel nightshirt. She pushed her hips into him and he was scared to move a muscle lest she break away. At last she awoke, slowly, then spoke in a whisper. "House is freezing. Don't get the wrong idea."

"It's okay. It's Sunday. Go back to sleep," said DeFranco.

And she did. He lay there just listening to her breathe.

Finally, she stirred close to nine o'clock in the morning, practically the middle of the afternoon for these two go-getters.

"I'll make coffee," said DeFranco, sliding toward the other side of the bed. Julie's side, he mused. He thought Julie would like Tracy.

Then Tracy remembered where she was and sat up straight. "Tony, your head. Can you see?"

"Swelling is down and pain is manageable," said DeFranco, amused she'd progressed from the businesslike "DeFranco" to the familiar "Tony." It had only taken a bash on the head.

"Let me see," said Tracy, taking him by the hand. He sat on the edge of the bed and she got up on her knees to inspect. "Nasty lump. It's oozing a little. I think I need to shave around there and close it up with another butterfly. Do you have a scissors and an electric razor? Don't worry. I won't butcher you."

"Yes on both counts," said DeFranco. "Medicine cabinet. I'll put the coffee on and meet you back here in five." He wobbled a bit getting to his feet and was out the door. He noticed the shotgun resting upright in a corner, chamber closed. It was loaded. He went downstairs to the kitchen, started coffee, rummaged in the refrigerator for some bacon, and prepared to slice up a leftover baked potato for some home fries. Least he could do was make the girl a nice breakfast. When things were underway, he went into the freezer and pulled out the jar with the trachea floating serenely. It looked like the remnants of something you might find in a butcher shop, from a pig or a calf perhaps, a striated tube with a flare at the top forming the cartilage of the thyroid. In the middle of the trachea was the pressed-in sea glass, just as green and polished as the day it was found.

"At least it's something," he said aloud, wincing at the loss of her other body parts. Curtis Jones would find that more than disappointing. Those objects might have been the reason the man had lost his life. He put the jar back in the freezer.

Safe-deposit box. First thing Monday morning, he counseled sternly.

He finished fixing breakfast, loaded two plates and poured two cups, put it all on a tray, and walked back upstairs, his gait a spritely shuffle. His head hurt but there was a beautiful woman in his bed, and that supplied a certain motivation. When he got back in the bedroom Tracy was sacked out on her stomach— it was Sunday after all. So he put the victuals on a dresser and started to creep toward the bathroom when she piped up. "You're a dream for letting me sleep."

"I brought you breakfast, but I can just as easily let you sleep for a while," said DeFranco.

"No," she said. "I don't know how long it's been since a man cooked me breakfast, so I want to savor it." She rolled over, brought her knees up to her chest, and covered herself. DeFranco set the tray on the bed so they could both partake a bit more elegantly. Tracy's red hair was tousled and unruly, and her nightie was unbuttoned a bit so he could see the cleft and swell of her breasts.

"Let me scarf this down. Then I'll work on your noggin," she said.

"Take your sweet time," said DeFranco. "We've got some planning to consider." He tried to be nonchalant. He felt his personality split decisively between the sex-charged teen ever lurking in his soul, and the prudent family man with a princess for a daughter and Julie's loyal and loving husband. He was both thrilled and frightened—so he focused intently on safer ground. The obvious energy and intellect of journalist Tracy Taggart.

"It starts with answering this," said Tracy. "Who would want to club you in the head and steal the primary evidence in the case of the headless corpse?"

"Somebody connected with Curtis," said DeFranco. "The package came from his office. They knew it was there. They knew I took it."

"You were probably a half step in front of them," said Tracy.

"Who are these people?" asked DeFranco, eager for Tracy's take.

"Curtis was connected to…everybody," said Tracy. "The state's attorney, the ME, the state CID cops, the dead girl, and through her to the killer. Curtis was in the middle."

"And so are we," said DeFranco. "Maybe if you're smart you'll go back to your apartment. Where?"

"Stamford. Long Ridge Road."

"Right. Go back to your apartment on Long Ridge Road with your nice Kimber .45 and let me handle this. I don't want you to get hurt," said DeFranco.

"Noble of you," said Tracy. "But I'm pretty sure they know I'm here."

"Why?"

She told him about the car idling in the street the night before. Her VW was in the driveway. It wouldn't take much to run the plates.

"Let's take a flyer and see what Dasha Petrov thinks," said Tracy. "We can show her the sea glass. It might jog something. Let's go with the idea there's a connection with Beachside Avenue. It's all we've got. We have to start somewhere."

DeFranco recounted his meandering drive with Dasha to all the known burn pits the day before. "And we've got Curtis's postmortem," he said. "That might yield something."

"We can always circle back to that," said Tracy. "Let me get your head bandaged, find you a ball cap to wear. Then we can head out."

"Dasha and her sister are probably at church," said DeFranco. "No use rushing."

Tracy and DeFranco compromised with a leisurely morning of coffee refills, the Sunday papers, chitchat—and DeFranco's once-suppressed recollection of how comforting it could be to have someone share your life. He didn't want the morning to end, and yet he refused to believe it was a beginning. He just felt a kinship with the beautiful Marine, who was, at that moment, puzzling over whether to hide the riot gun in the trunk of the Corolla, or put it on the back seat, where she could get at it if she needed it.

Always thinking three moves down the chessboard, thought DeFranco.

At 2:00 p.m. they drove away from High Gate Road, the dumpster girl's trachea ensconced in the evidence jar, itself in a paper bag at Tracy's feet. She was alert for nondescript sedans and only saw children playing hopscotch in a driveway—the rest of Westport's gentle citizens no doubt tucked in for an afternoon of pro football in front of their television sets. They drove down Beachside Avenue and pulled into the drive with the seven-bay garage. They parked the car, locked the shotgun in the trunk, locked the doors, and carried the bag down the driveway to Dasha and Galina's little cottage. Smoke drifted from the chimney, signaling someone was home.

DeFranco knocked on the kitchen door and soon Dasha appeared in her tweed jacket, now with her Hermes neck scarf. She wore gold hoops and had applied her lipstick with precision. That guy in Dubrovnik didn't stand a chance, thought DeFranco.

"I was hoping you'd come back," she said. "And what in the name of God happened to your face?"

"I wish I could say I slipped in the tub," said DeFranco.

"Oh my. Sounds like a story. Please come in. We just got back from church." Galina loitered in the background, a ghost, then left the room. "Take a good nap, Galina, darling," said Dasha to her sister as Galina disappeared. She turned to her guests. "She's been out of sorts. Memory troubles. She gets frustrated."

"Poor dear," said Tracy, reflecting on her Hoosier elders who'd arrived at a similar crossroads.

"Who would like some cake?" asked Dasha. "It came from the bake sale."

"I'll take some," said DeFranco, but Tracy demurred.

"So what's the news?"

"Someone clubbed him over the head when he was trying to get into his house last night," said Tracy. "He had a package from the medical examiner's office containing the dead girl's liver and other body parts. Tony—Detective DeFranco—was going to take them to a lab Monday morning to have the toxicology screen repeated. The body parts were stolen."

"Come sit by the fire," said Dasha. "Let me try to process this."

They followed her to the couch.

DeFranco explained. "I went to the ME's office yesterday to speak with one of the medical examiner's principal assistants. His name was Curtis Jones. He was at the dumpster where the girl was found and he helped the ME perform the postmortem. Curtis was found dead yesterday. Hanged in a closet off the ME's lab. They're saying it's a suicide. He left a note. I have my doubts."

"Oh my," said Dasha, absorbing the weight of it.

"Before I left, an assistant at the medical examiner's gave me a cooler. It was from Curtis. It had the girl's body parts for retesting. Curtis and I had discussed taking the girl's samples to an independent lab. A note from Curtis inside the box suggested I take it out of state. The jars inside the cooler contained the dead girl's liver, her uterus, a piece of her lung…and this." He produced the jar with the trachea floating in it. "I kept this out to show you and Tracy. The person who hit me took the rest of the samples, but didn't get this one."

"May I see it?" asked Dasha. DeFranco handed it to her and Dasha held it up close. She peered down the airway and saw the piece of sea glass winking back.

She smiled.

"Two people are dead because of this little piece of glass," she said reflectively. "Counting the assault on you, that's three individuals who've met with some kind of violence. Did you say your friend at the medical examiner's office left a suicide note?"

"I read it," said DeFranco. "Weird and impersonal. Anyone could have slapped it together. I think Curtis had been having a rough time—second marriage ending, antidepressants in the picture—but I'm skeptical Curtis would have taken his own life. He was invested in this case."

"Trust those instincts, Detective," said Dasha. "But you still need evidence. It's fortunate you kept this piece. I doubt it would be very effective for lab testing though."

"Why not?" asked Tracy. DeFranco already knew the answer, but he let Dasha continue.

"For DNA analysis, this body part would certainly work," said Dasha. "But you'll need a known DNA sample from the dead girl so a comparison can be made. For tox screening it would have been better to have her liver, which absorbs blood and processes waste."

"Oh hell," said Tracy, deflated.

"But, my dear, you can use this for bait. For your trap."

"Trap?" asked Tracy.

"Identify a person to whom you discretely and directly convey a piece of information," said Dasha. "See where and how that information re-emerges. You can't involve an underling. If you drop your information too low in the chain of command, you won't know how high the conspiracy goes."

"But what do we tell them?" asked DeFranco. "What's the best way to get it out?"

"You want them to know they were unsuccessful in taking *all* the girl's body parts. You want them to know you have information that contradicts their official findings," said Dasha. "You want to drop a nugget and see if it elicits a reaction. Start at the top. The higher you go, the deeper and more pervasive the conspiracy. If releasing the information fails to cause a reaction, go down a step. Put the information into the chain. Where it comes out is where you'll find the cover-up. And where you find the cover-up, you'll find the girl's killer. If your friend at the ME's office was murdered, you'll likely find his killer too. It might be one in the same."

"So we'll poke the beast," said DeFranco. "Somebody could get hurt."

"Kind of funny coming from you, with your eye practically shut," said Tracy. "Somebody has already gotten hurt. And Curtis got himself killed."

"Actually I was thinking of you," said DeFranco.

"I know how to take care of myself," said Tracy. "That lump on your head suggests you might need help in that department."

Girl's got a bit of a bite, thought DeFranco. It dawned on him that snapping back might mean she cared.

"You're both in it up to your necks and you need to have a plan," said Dasha. "But you just can't shout it from the rooftops. Your targets will run to earth. Right now they think they have *all* the young girl's body parts, and they're probably breathing a sigh of relief. But we can hope they might get sloppy." She looked at DeFranco, forging a shared connection. "Can we presume they don't know about the trachea?" asked Dasha.

"No idea," said DeFranco. "But when they find out, it's a fair bet they'll try to get this evidence. And that means they'll come for us."

"You need to be ready," said Dasha. "Establish a safe place. Make it secure."

"You've done this before?" said Tracy.

"Many times. Especially when I worked counterintelligence, trying to capture this nation's traitors," said Dasha. "The Soviets were relentless, of course. We'd leave a piece of information in the wrong place to see who in our organization would pick it up. Then we'd see how it would emerge on the other side. Classic. Our traitor would transmit the details and if the opposition pursued the lead, we knew we had our man…or woman, as it turned out. We broke some moles that way…and of course a few eggs. It didn't always work."

"Try, try again?" said Tracy.

"Oh, in that game we never quit," said Dasha. "We tried to turn their diplomats and their commissars and their generals. They tried to penetrate our hierarchy. A grand game."

"Anybody ever get hurt?" said DeFranco, returning to the theme.

"Of course," said Dasha. "Usually the unprepared." He reflected on that when Tracy went to the heart of the matter.

"Do you think there's a connection between these deaths, Beachside Avenue, and all the sea glass we found out there?"

"The evidence is flimsy and circumstantial," said Dasha.

It was DeFranco's turn.

"You're right, Dasha. The killer needed space and time," he said. "And the place where the corpse was dumped was remarkable for what wasn't there. Clothing, wounds from bullets or edged weapons. It's all missing. And to burn a body you need accelerant and time. Nobody to bother you."

"I still like simple and obvious," said Tracy. "She died with sea glass in her throat. We have a pile of the stuff right out on the beach. There's a connection." Dasha smiled at Tracy. She saw something of herself, perhaps.

"Can we begin there?" Dasha asked. There was a quiet confidence in her tone. "I only have a hypothesis. A hypothesis that needs to be tested."

"Let's hear it," said DeFranco.

"First, the dead girl must have a name," said Dasha. "And if she has a name there has to be a record of her coming through Immigration. And if she came through Immigration there's likely a photograph of her that can be circulated, or an address for her destination in the States. Tell me. What was the name the medical examiner found on her toe ring?"

"Obvious," said Tracy. "The goddess Kali. Maybe her parents named her Kali."

"Precisely," said Dasha. "Detective DeFranco. I am sure you have a way to contact Immigration at Kennedy. Find out if a young Indian girl arrived in this country, alone, maybe two months ago, but perhaps more recently. First name Kali."

"Long shot," said DeFranco. "Definitely worth a try."

"Let's continue. The victim is young. There is no missing person's file that matches her description, which means she has no family and perhaps only tenuous connections. She's just passing through. Perhaps a student or someone on tour. She's on the move so her family isn't worried they haven't heard from her," said Dasha.

"But the ME said she may have been killed a week ago," said Tracy. "Surely someone would have noticed her missing and raised an alarm."

"Not if her family lives elsewhere," said Dasha. "Not just Punjab, perhaps, but Kashmir or Goa or Jaipur or Darjeeling. Countless other places the poor thing may have come from, with the subcontinent teeming with multiple millions of people. She's *not* missing…not yet. She's on holiday."

"I see your point," said DeFranco. "But she didn't just land at international arrivals and decide Westport looked like a nice place to visit. There must have been some kind of connection. Maybe an invitation."

"Yes. Quite right," said Dasha, moving along. "Now, Kali's young. She's pretty. She's just arrived in America and she's filled with enthusiasm. She's coming to meet…friends. She's probably not high school age. She's a bit older. And I don't think we're talking about a foreign exchange student. Foreign exchange students are tightly controlled by host parents and the schools. We've had one or two here over the years. It's not regimented but sponsors are certainly paying attention.

"No, she's met someone abroad, someone her own age, someone well-to-do, someone who's extended an invitation to visit anytime. 'We've got a big place. Plenty of room. Lots of fun,'" said Dasha.

"Beachside Avenue," said Tracy. "Party central."

"Now complete the picture," said Dasha. "She got pregnant by her Beachside Avenue host while the young man was in India taking his grand tour. That's where they met. But now the young man has gone back home. She's shocked and dismayed. He's told her to drop in anytime. There's an open door. Let's assume she's among the well-born. She's got enough money to fly halfway around the world. She likely had access to birth control. But for whatever reason, she gets pregnant over there and the panic starts. She, or her sex partner, wants to get rid of it. Hence the mangled abortion. Maybe she was forced."

"Like you said," interrupted DeFranco. "It's just a hypothesis."

"Simplify it," said Tracy, already several steps out front. "She's chasing him down. She wants a commitment. Now the guy is motivated to end the relationship. Maybe end her."

"My dear," said Dasha. "You'd make a lovely spy. Bottom line... She's here. She's pregnant. And trying to figure out what to do. We need a household on this street where the young lady might have associates. Same age or close. Plenty of money. Overindulged. Lots of foreign travel and budding resumés."

"Any candidates?" asked Tracy.

"Three," said Dasha. "Sure, this street has its fair share of misanthropes. We have the swanky property developer who owns row upon row of tenement slums. We've got the cigarette machine entrepreneur. We've got the mergers-and-acquisitions king who's under federal indictment for selling his clients' secrets. Believe me, they're all here. But only three households have older college-age children who might have befriended Kali, welcomed her in—before things veered off course."

"We'll need names," said DeFranco. "It's worth trying to track down."

"The Rosewigs to the left." Dasha waved her hand somewhere toward the east. "He's a film producer. Two kids. A bit older. Recently out of college. Stanford, I think, and the other one went to Columbia. I hear bellowing over the fence from time to time so there might be some domestic troubles. Where there's smoke there might be fire.

"The Angus McCarran family next door to the right. More money than God. Mr. McCarran owns a finance company called a hedge fund and they trade in something called derivatives. I haven't the slightest idea what those are, but you can check. Two kids. Older daughter and a younger son. They went to Greens Farms Academy down the street and then got accepted to the Ivies. Judging from the music blasting over the hedge on the weekends in the summer, I would say wild parties aren't out of the question.

"Five doors that way," Dasha continued, "there's a casino tycoon named Leipzig. Four kids. Late high school, early college or thereabouts. Two have been in and out of jail for the usual juvenile offenses: driving while intoxicated, minor drug possession, shoplifting."

"Doesn't make them murderers," said Tracy.

"No. But if you believe in the broken windows theory of policing," said DeFranco, "their offenses just get bigger if they haven't brushed up against the law at some point. They might have pushed their limits."

"Combine the usual youthful chicanery with absentee parents and too much money," said Dasha. "It can be a bad mix."

"Throw in a sense of entitlement," said Tracy. "The law doesn't apply to them. They are the princelings and they are destined to rule the earth. They can't get slowed down by a pregnant Indian girl. They have worlds to save. And of course they are smart enough to pull off the perfect crime."

"Go look up the case of Leopold and Loeb," said Dasha. "Chicago society murders in the twenties. Ghastly. Bright kids who went wrong."

"You two are getting ahead of yourselves," said DeFranco.

"It's a hypothesis," said Dasha. "You begin with what's plausible. If this hypothesis doesn't work, we move on to the next one."

"You make it sound easy," he said.

"Easy?" asked Tracy. "You call this easy? Your eye is practically shut, Tony. They wanted you silenced."

"I just wonder who 'they' is, that's all," said DeFranco.

"And one more thing," said Dasha. "Think of the manner and mechanism of Kali's death: Bleeding from a botched abortion. Choked to death. Dismembered and mutilated. Then burned. How does all that happen?"

"Jesus," said Tracy. "Lord of the Flies."

15

Body of Evidence

Tracy and DeFranco left the cottage carrying the little sack with the girl's trachea, trying to decide next steps.

"Let's get your car and you can follow me to the ME," said DeFranco. "They may have finished Curtis's postmortem. Then I can escort you home."

"Well, if you escort me home I can certainly make you dinner," said Tracy.

"Deal," said DeFranco. "But you realize this will lead to an endless cycle of gifts, gestures, and reciprocal acts of appreciation. Back and forth. Who knows where it will lead?"

"Let's keep it a mystery for now," said Tracy. "We've got enough on our plate."

"Including a quick stop at the police station so I can grab the dumpster crime scene photos," said DeFranco. "They have to be back from the lab by now. They're probably in Chief Talbot's mail slot to be forwarded to state's CID. He won't miss them for a couple of days."

"Careful, DeFranco," said Tracy, nudging him in the ribs. "You don't want to give them an excuse to fire you. Isn't that pilfering?"

"Not pilfering," he returned. "Borrowing."

Later, as DeFranco drove west on I-95, keeping Tracy Taggart's VW in his rearview mirror, his overriding concern was keeping the dumpster girl's evidence safe. Although he wasn't sure his adversaries knew the trachea even existed, he couldn't take a chance on losing the only piece of evidence they had beyond Kali's toe ring. So he decided to put it in his Lands' End briefcase and carry it with him at all times. Just looking at the briefcase on the seat next to him made him nervous.

The next point was also clear. The little Colt hammerless he'd worn every day for more than twenty years was woefully inadequate for self-protection. And the Remington 12-gauge was impossible to conceal and, frankly, dangerous to haul around in the trunk of Angelica's car. He needed some additional firepower, and he was a little jealous of Tracy's Kimber.

Time for that Glock, an expensive notion he'd always resisted.

Lastly, and perhaps more problematic, were some lingering questions. Where was their safe zone? Where could he and Tracy circle the wagons? The place where they could fall back in case their effort to poke the beast actually yielded the desired effect. From prior experience in far-off Vietnam he knew it was often necessary to draw fire in order to refine targeting. Dasha had proposed a modified version of the same concept. But you needed a place to hunker down.

Then, an uncomfortable realization hit him like a thunderclap. He was winging it, defying sensible police procedure—notifications, team building, backups, and most of all a chain of command. He was working on hit-or-miss impulse. Curtis's death only deepened DeFranco's near bottomless feelings of distrust.

They pulled into the ME's parking lot, quite late on a Sunday afternoon, and walked through the loading dock to the morgue. The examining room was dark, and DeFranco hoped that he'd missed Curtis's autopsy; a written report would suffice. But Dr. Goldberg had wanted him there, so seeking out the ME would close the loop. He and Tracy walked toward the doctor's office, where a light shone into the hallway. DeFranco knocked and Goldberg invited them in.

The doctor was staring off someplace, disengaged. He was reduced in stature even further, and DeFranco thought he looked almost like a poor handicapped child, waiting for help from an unkind world.

"Dr. Goldberg," said DeFranco. "This is a colleague, Tracy Taggart. She and I are working on finding out who killed the girl. We're hoping we can help Curtis's family too."

"Oh yes," said Goldberg, turning in his chair. "What in God's name happened to your face, Sergeant DeFranco?" It was now a vivid purple with mustard accents.

"Well, Doctor…Curtis probably broke a dozen regulations and forwarded our dumpster girl's body parts to me for independent testing. He wanted to get away from the state system. Those parts were stolen from me and I was mugged."

Goldberg's face registered surprise, morphing into enlightenment. "If Curtis wanted to get you those body parts, he probably had a very good reason."

DeFranco decided not to mention the trachea. He felt he could trust the medical examiner, but he didn't want to expose Goldberg to potential harm. It began to seem like too much information could be lethal.

Goldberg returned to the matter at hand. "You missed the pathologist from New Haven. Competent. Thorough. Respectful. And filled with confusion."

"What happened?" asked DeFranco.

"He believes Curtis was murdered," said Goldberg. DeFranco and Tracy somehow weren't surprised.

"How so?" asked DeFranco. Tracy listened carefully.

"His pharynx was crushed, but his neck was not broken. Didn't you ask if he'd been dropped? No evidence of that. Cervical vertebrae all intact but the carotid artery was ruptured, suggesting a crushing injury, along with asphyxia. And there was a dirty footprint on Curtis's back. The examiner thought whoever did this put Curtis's belt around his neck, put him facedown, and held him there with his foot while he choked him to death. Then he picked Curtis off the floor and tied the belt to a coat hook inside the closet to make it look like he killed himself. Amateurish, really. Had to know we'd figure it out pretty quickly."

"Curtis isn't heavy, but it would take a big man to hang him up like that," said DeFranco. "Do you have a photo of the footprint?"

"It's just come from the dark room," said Goldberg, handing a package to DeFranco. Reluctantly, DeFranco opened the envelope and photos of his friend Curtis spilled out. Curtis hanging by the neck. A close-up of Curtis's throat with the belt digging in. Examining room shots showing Curtis's neck opened wide so you could see his voicebox and a dissected vascular structure. DeFranco was more curious than sad. He handed the photos to Tracy, and she seemed to absorb the visual information without emotion.

DeFranco turned to the photo of the footprint on Curtis's back. It was clearly delineated, lots of crisscrossed treadlines like you'd see with an athletic shoe, nothing formal. And there was very little wear, except for a smooth patch near the outside of the right foot near the little toe.

"What's this wear point mean to you, Doctor?" asked DeFranco.

Goldberg took a look. "The person who owns that shoe suffers from supination of the arch. Meaning he walks on the outside of his foot, probably on both sides but sometimes it's limited to one side, especially if it's the result of an injury."

DeFranco took the photos from the dumpster crime scene and flipped through them one by one—until he came to the footprint in mud.

"We took a casting of this one," said DeFranco. "It's back in the evidence locker at Westport PD." He added "I hope" under his breath.

He laid both photos side by side. The footprint in the mud had the same deep crisscrossed treadlines, and the same wear point on the outside. "Doctor, do you believe the same shoe made both of these prints?" asked DeFranco.

Goldberg brought his glasses down toward his nose and lifted the prints up close.

"Tell me precisely where this print came from," said Goldberg.

"On one side of the dumpster behind the hardware store at Main and Canal, where we found the headless girl," said DeFranco.

"The shoe that made that impression was the same shoe that stood on Curtis's back while the life was being choked out of him," said Goldberg drily.

The doctor's decided to come back to work, thought DeFranco.

"Detective, you're pursuing a multiple murderer."

16

Stalker

DeFranco gripped his Lands' End briefcase a bit more firmly as he and Tracy left the ME's office. They got back to their cars, still shaken by Goldberg's revelation.

"My place," said Tracy. "I'll put together dinner. I don't feel like going out."

"Me neither," said DeFranco.

"No use in trying to ditch whoever it is we're trying to ditch," said Tracy. "They already know where I live."

They left the ME's parking area with Tracy leading. DeFranco watched for a tail and chose several candidates in the early evening traffic, all traveling at a steady pace, but no stand-out vehicles jockeying for position. Just plain-Jane sedans moving sedately toward Long Ridge Road. Tracy led him toward a three-story condo with indoor parking and he followed dutifully, parking next to her.

"I'd feel a lot better if that shotgun were up in my condo having dinner with us," said Tracy. DeFranco fetched the beast out of the Corolla's trunk and carried it nonchalantly to the garage door leading to the elevator lobby, hoping he wouldn't scare any of Tracy's neighbors. They made it into Tracy's modest abode without running into anyone, and DeFranco propped the Remington in a corner, glad it was available.

He looked around Tracy's home. Tasteful. Understated. Orderly.

"It's not much," she said as she rummaged in the freezer. "But it'll do until I get promoted to the executive suite, which will happen probably never."

"I don't know," said DeFranco. "I've watched Tracy Taggart, ace reporter. I think you're headed for stardom."

"If we don't wind up like Curtis first," she said grimly. "Like a drink?"

"Jack Daniels?" asked DeFranco.

"Old Grand-Dad do?"

"It's not Tennessee sipping whiskey but I like it," said DeFranco. And she even likes bourbon, he thought.

Tracy pulled some frozen spinach and a frozen lasagna out of the freezer and popped them in the microwave. "I never have time to shop, so this frozen stuff will have to keep us alive," she said.

"I'm not complaining," said DeFranco. Tracy set the table and took a minute to look out her front window to the street.

"Curtis murdered by the same person who put Kali in the dumpster. You bopped on the head and Kali's tissue samples taken. This is shaping up into a nightmare," said Tracy. "When can I stop playing investigator and start doing my job as a journalist?"

"Soon," said DeFranco. "I don't think you've got a story unless we can identify who's at the center of all this."

"I don't know. We've got connected murders. The situation has changed, Tony," said Tracy.

He looked at her...hard...and he was not unsympathetic. "I know you're under pressure and it's probably killing you, but do you see the importance of holding back information? The killer can't know what we know."

"I understand that. But can you work with me?" asked Tracy.

"How so?" asked DeFranco. He was growing nervous.

"I have to at least get Curtis's alleged suicide on the record. Unnatural death of a medical examiner staffer is news. At least I'll feel like I'm not completely abdicating my duties."

"Works for me," said DeFranco. "As long as you confine it to the official statement from the ME's office, but we can't link Curtis to the dumpster girl. Not yet."

"Okay, Tony. I'll go along with that. We made a deal. But that deal was predicated on different information. The story is changing. I'm just saying we may need to adjust our under-standing as things evolve."

She's persuasive, thought DeFranco.

"If my boss finds out I'm holding back, there will be hell to pay. I could lose my job," said Tracy.

"Funny you should say that," said DeFranco. "When my chief finds out I've been digging around through back channels, I could lose my job too. I'll be working security."

"And I'll be right along with you selling ladies' cosmetics," said Tracy. They both laughed.

"Do you think Dasha's theory has any merit?" she asked.

"It's real sketchy," said DeFranco. "But one thing is for sure. When they find out we have Kali's trachea with the sea glass inside, there will be a shitstorm, and we'll have to figure out how to get out of the way."

"Get out of the way? Or stand our ground?" asked Tracy. "Tony, do you see that car across the street? Plain blue sedan. Maybe a Chevy. I think that's the car I saw on High Gate Road in front of your house last night." DeFranco joined her at the window and saw the vehicle idling on the road, lights off, a single person on the driver's side.

"Under most circumstances I'd go tap on the window and ask to see some ID. Maybe look at his shoes. But as long as we have Kali's evidence unsecured in my briefcase I don't think we can risk it. We don't know how many are out there."

He couldn't lose the last piece of the girl, discarded like so much trash.

"I see it shaping up like this: I'll bunk on your couch tonight, then get Kali's windpipe secured at my bank vault in the morning. I need to call the crematorium in Port Chester and find out where her body is, and I need to call Immigration. I also need to call my friend Lenny, Westport PD armorer, and upgrade my personal gear."

"'Bout time," said Tracy.

"Then I think we should follow Dasha's advice and let my fellow officers of the law know what we've got. I'll start with

Talbot and see if he leaks. If he's able to contain himself, I'll move on to Mortensen. I predict he'll have some kind of hemorrhage, and if the dogs get unleashed we know we've got our man."

"I don't think Mortensen's the guy with the worn-out athletic shoes," said Tracy. "Too high up. But he might be getting help from a contractor."

"Agree he's getting some help," said DeFranco. "But Tamara Moriarty was spewing such a river of BS at the press conference she's got to be involved somehow—unless she was somehow duped. I just can't figure out how to link Mortensen and Moriarty to the victim, and if Dasha's correct, to the Beachside Avenue crowd."

"Key will be what you learn from Immigration," said Tracy. "If they've got a Kali coming in through Kennedy and she gave them a local address, game over."

"Maybe game over. But not set and match," said DeFranco. "There are a lot of loose ends. Even if we learn there's a Kali coming into this country in the right time frame, we still have to link that person to the deceased."

"Well," said Tracy. "We've got Kali's DNA in your briefcase. We just need to contact her family to get DNA that matches."

"Stray hairs from a brush would do it," said DeFranco, contemplating the challenge. "What time is your shift tomorrow?"

"I go in at two and finish at eleven, assuming it's quiet," said Tracy. "If anything breaks loose it could go longer. That's the nature of the beast."

"Just like cops' hours," said DeFranco. "Sometimes you have to go all night. I have to be in at noon and I'll be at it into the evening. Can we keep in touch?"

"I'd like that," said Tracy.

DeFranco did the dishes while Tracy flipped through the channels. She spent some time with her own station to come up to speed on interviews with county officials and school pageants and automobile accidents. Her weekend colleagues were keeping pace with the usual fodder.

She was after bigger game.

She went into the kitchen while DeFranco was putting away the dishes.

"Time to take a look at your wounds," she said.

"Nurse Tracy, I presume," said DeFranco, sitting down at the kitchen table so she could take a look at the top of his head.

"Swelling's down and the wound is closing up okay. No more seepage. And it looks like your eye is opening and closing properly, but it's a beautiful shade of purple. What are you going to tell your coworkers at the station?"

"Slipped on a bar of soap," said DeFranco. "Ran into a door. I don't know. The usual."

"I'll change your butterflies in the morning," said Tracy. Then she pulled up a chair and looked DeFranco in the eye. "I crawled into bed with you last night because I was cold. But I want to sleep with you tonight because I'm scared. I need you to hold me. I'm not ready to go beyond that just yet." DeFranco hung on the phrase "just yet." "But I feel like I'm getting closer to you and I just don't want to rush it. When it comes to things like this, I like to go slow. Is that okay with you?"

"Perfectly," said DeFranco, who leaned across and kissed her on the cheek.

Good things come to those who wait, he told himself. He was scared too. But he wasn't sure what scared him more, unseen hands at work killing people in his jurisdiction, or getting too close, then losing, this brave, beautiful woman.

17

Hide the Corpse

"Time to get busy," DeFranco muttered as the light inside Tracy's bedroom made the subtle shift from black to gray. Tracy was using his chest like a pillow and purring softly. He drank in her scent and delighted in the feeling of her leg draped over his, flesh to flesh. There was nothing in the world like the feeling of two people wrapped around each other in a warm bed. Feeling close and connected had overtaken that randy boy who once greeted him in the mirror.

He carefully extricated himself from Tracy's embrace and made his way toward the shower, letting her sleep. He found the requisite toiletries, then got back into his clothes from yesterday, hating to wear the same socks two days in a row. He stopped at the window on his way to make coffee. The blue sedan was still in place, but the driver was gone. That could only mean the driver was home in his own bed and they had been concerned for nothing…or the driver was right outside Tracy's door.

"Checking on our friend?" said Tracy, coming up behind him, wearing a shortie terrycloth robe. DeFranco tried to focus on their situational awareness, but couldn't help notice the lovely skin below her neck, and those long legs.

Keep it professional, he thought.

"Car's there but the driver isn't," he said, drawn to her tousled red hair. "He's either taking a pee break, or he's not our man—or he's right outside our door. Pick one."

"Fourth choice," said Tracy. "He might have friends. I don't like this, Tony. I think I'm going to play hooky today so we can be each other's backup. I just don't know where this is headed."

"Maybe you can call it research," said DeFranco.

"It's not research if I'm not on assignment...yet," said Tracy. "For now it's a sick day. So what are our plans?"

"I want to find dumpster girl, so first stop will be Finnazo Brothers in Port Chester. Then I want to introduce you to my friend Lenny," said DeFranco.

"Any friend of yours is a friend of mine," said Tracy. "Let me get dressed."

He took out Tracy's *Yellow Pages* directory on the hope that the Finnazo Brothers funeral parlor and crematorium in Port Chester, New York, might be listed. There it was. Corner of King Street and Parkway Drive near Lyon Park. He wrote down the address.

Tracy re-emerged, ready for the day. The dress and heels gave way to jeans, sneakers, a heavy fisherman's sweater, and a windbreaker—day-off attire. She still looked ravishing. She ate a banana and had some cottage cheese. He settled on a couple of scrambled eggs. They put their coffees in two travel cups and headed out the door, DeFranco carrying the Lands' End briefcase with the girl's trachea, and, of course, the Remington, once again hoping he wouldn't alarm Tracy's neighbors. Tracy didn't want any members of her television audience to recognize her, so she tried for something incognito with a ball cap and sunglasses. DeFranco thought it might even work.

"Bring your Kimber," said DeFranco. Tracy slipped it into a quick-access compartment of her purse, courtesy of her Marine dad, and slung it over her shoulder.

"Feel better now?" she asked, toying with him.

They climbed into Angelica's Corolla and traced a route back to the interstate. The air was chillier and the sky grayer, signaling the onset of winter. Retirement to a double-wide trailer outside Naples now looked positively delightful. Kids grown. Professional accomplishments in the rearview mirror. Maybe a gold watch. A do-nothing security job to bring in a little cash.

Only now there was a person named Tracy in his life.

You're getting way ahead of yourself, DeFranco, he reminded himself.

They exited the interstate at Byram on Greenwich's western flank and crossed over the bridge into Port Chester, stopping at a service station to ask for directions to King Street. He made his way there and pulled up in front of number 454, an enormous Victorian house with Finnazo Brothers Funeral Home on a sign out front. DeFranco didn't want the briefcase to get out of his sight, so he held onto it as they walked up to the front door and rang the bell. A portly, balding man sporting a mustache and wearing a black suit opened the door. DeFranco produced his badge.

"Good morning, sir. Anthony DeFranco. Westport, Connecticut Police. And this is my colleague Miss Taggart. Can I ask you a few questions?"

"Of course," said the little man, almost as if DeFranco had been expected. Making contact with the police was not uncommon in the funeral business. "Please come in. My name is Simms. I've worked for the Finnazo brothers for thirty years."

"This will be brief," said DeFranco. "I was informed by Curtis Jones at the Fairfield County medical examiner's office that you picked up a body two days ago under a request by State's Attorney Pers Mortensen. It was slated for cremation."

"That's correct," said Simms. "We brought the deceased back here for preparation. But then there was a change."

"A change?" asked DeFranco.

"An investigator from Connecticut came with another order, also signed by Mortensen, requesting the body be released for more analysis. She and two officers put the deceased in an aluminum travel casket and put it in the back of their van. Said they needed to move it back to a lab in Hartford."

"She?" asked DeFranco.

"Yes. I have the paperwork in the next room. Excuse me. She signed the release documents." He came back with the carbon copy of a form headed *Release and Disposition*. Lots of lines and boxes to be ticked off. Signed at the bottom by one Tamara Moriarty, Connecticut State CID.

We're playing a game of find the corpse, thought DeFranco. "This helps a lot. Can I have a photocopy of this?"

"Of course," said Simms. "I'll be right back." He disappeared into his little office.

"They're panicking," said Tracy under her breath. "They're not sure what the hell to do."

Simms came back with the copy, which DeFranco inserted in his briefcase.

I'm coming for you Moriarty, he said silently to himself.

"What are the usual rules for handling a situation like this?" asked Tracy. "I mean, who issues the death certificate? If there's no family, who's in charge of accepting the remains?"

"In most cases when there's a death from natural causes, the funeral home is empowered to prepare the death certificate and file it with the town clerk," said Simms. "The town clerk can issue copies and record the death with vital statistics. But when there is a suspicious death, the authorities have the right to keep the remains during the course of an investigation. The coroner gets involved and sometimes there's an inquest. We thought it a little unusual to have the body released to us so soon. And also a little strange to receive an order for cremation. Normally these things take more time. There's usually family involved. It's also unusual to have such a sudden change in plans."

"I take it no family had been contacted," said DeFranco.

"The police didn't mention the deceased had a family. Told us no one had accepted the body, so they were in charge," said Simms.

"Did the investigator say where the body was going?" asked Tracy.

"I would presume the state authorities would be in communication with you on that," said Simms, looking down his nose.

"Bit of confusion," said DeFranco. "Trying to clear it up."

"But to answer your question. No. Where the body was transported was not shared with us. We just needed a signed receipt."

"Thanks," said DeFranco. "Last question. Did you have a look at the body before it was removed?"

"We examine all the bodies that come into our care," said Simms.

"Notice anything unusual?" asked Tracy.

"The person was obviously the victim of unnatural circumstances," said Simms. "No head. No hands. Advanced rigor and decomposition. A toe missing. And a piece of flesh missing from her thigh. Clearly a police matter. Frankly we were glad to see her go."

"Thanks," said DeFranco. "We'll be leaving." They turned and walked toward the front door of the funeral parlor, both in quiet turmoil.

"Chunk missing out of her thigh?" asked Tracy, incredulous, when they were out on the sidewalk.

"They were after her tattoo," said DeFranco. "They're trying to erase the girl from the face of the earth."

They drove eastbound on the interstate and took the exit for the Route 7 extension. They got off at the second exit and made their way to a commercial building in a small industrial park off Main Street. DeFranco drove around to the farthest building. It had a large roll-up door for vehicles and a smaller side door. The small door had a sign over it that read Leonard Loughlin Specialty Company. He knocked twice and Lenny answered. Full beard. Farmer John dungarees. Dirty hands with grime under the fingernails. Distinct odor of Hoppe's gun oil.

Lenny was a professional armorer for several local police departments and he spent his days filing, lubing, and cleaning weapons for law enforcement up and down the coast. He knew all the cops. And the police respected Lenny, unkempt and disheveled, as potentially the one element that stood between life and death in a gunfight. If you were forced to draw your duty weapon you wanted to ensure beyond the shadow of a doubt it would perform as advertised. No feed failures, ejection problems, accuracy issues. Your service piece had to be perfect.

"I remember you," said Lenny. "But it's not like you come around here often."

"Never needed to," said DeFranco. "My little Colt is just part of my wardrobe now after all these years. But I'm looking for an upgrade. Lenny, this is my friend Miss Taggart."

"How do you do," said Tracy, extending a hand.

"I would shake your hand, ma'am," said Lenny. "But let's not and say we did. I've got grease up to my elbows. You say you're looking for an upgrade? Does that mean something or someone has given you a reason to upgrade? I have to ask."

"Past due," said DeFranco. "Need to get with the times."

"Individuals in your line of work have been known to equip themselves for private activities on the side," said Lenny, turning to Tracy. "Sorry, ma'am, but I am known for being a bit blunt. Cops come in here all the time pissed off at an ex-wife or skinflint brother-in-law or no-good two-timing fellow officer. You guys are under a lot of stress and you're not all lily-white." Tracy and DeFranco were coming to realize that.

"Westport's a little too sleepy for that sort of thing," said DeFranco. "I just think it's time to up my game. There's a new century coming."

Lenny led them deeper into his shop. They were surrounded by gun racks and safes, and there was a small indoor range with massive steel backstops to prevent projectiles from passing through walls and leaving the building. Shotguns. AR-15s. Sniper rifles with massive optics. Shelves filled with semi-automatic pistols.

"That hammerless snubbie is only going to stop someone if you knick an artery going in, or break a bone. Not much of a wound channel." Lenny was getting technical.

"A .45 has a lot of energy but you have to get pretty close to hit anything with it. Pain in the ass to carry. Too heavy, and profile is all wrong. It was really meant for a leg holster. Most guys carry it cocked and locked because of the grip safety and the thumb safety, but it's a practice I don't advocate if you have to carry it concealed—unless you can carry it in your purse," he said, turning to Tracy with a smile.

"Let's start with the basics. Moving to a semi-automatic or sticking with a revolver? Both have advantages. Semi-auto has more firepower but a revolver is simpler, and the bullets stay with the gun. You snag your semi-auto magazine on a piece of clothing, it falls out of the gun and your ass is grass."

"Excellent point," said DeFranco. "But I think it's time to move to a semi-auto. I operated a SIG in the Navy."

"SIG? Not a Colt .45? You in special forces?" Lenny was going to a place DeFranco seldom visited.

"Swift Boats in the Delta," said DeFranco.

"No way," said Lenny. "You fuckers were hard-core." Then turning to Tracy he said, "Sorry, ma'am."

"She's an ex-Marine and she's got a Kimber .45 in her purse," said DeFranco.

"Excuse me," said Lenny. "Didn't realize I was in the presence of a jarhead."

"Nurse on a helicopter assault ship. But I'm qualified with a lot of the tools of the trade," said Tracy confidently.

"I knew I liked you when you walked in the door," said Lenny.

"Okay, you guys," said DeFranco. "We can have a meeting of the mutual admiration society another time. Let's get back to business."

"I think you need to move with the times," said Lenny. "Relegate your snubbie to backup status with an ankle holster and get yourself a Glock 17, standard frame size, chambered for 9-millimeter Parabellum."

"Capacity?" asked DeFranco.

"Seventeen rounds in the standard frame size," said Lenny.

"What about the controls?"

"Simple is better, especially when speed is important. Glock has a trigger safety, which is probably sufficient. But if you're concerned, keep the chamber clear until you're in the threat zone and rack one in as necessary."

"What's your preferred carry rig?" asked DeFranco.

"If you're going to wear a sport coat, then a shoulder harness will do," said Lenny. "It will let you carry a couple of extra magazines. It means you'll have to cross draw from your weak side, but for most people that's not a problem. It's just a little slower."

"Sold," said DeFranco.

"Let's try it out," said Lenny, leading DeFranco and Tracy to his firing range. He put a target on a binder clip attached to a chain and ran it out seven yards. He loaded DeFranco's magazine, then handed him the Glock grip first with the chamber open and the magazine removed. DeFranco stepped to the firing line, keeping the muzzle pointed downrange. Lenny handed him a loaded magazine and DeFranco slid it into the magazine well and released the slide. He watched a round move smartly into the chamber, aimed the pistol at the target, and squeezed off a round. The gun bucked in his hand, but the recoil was more than manageable. His little snub-nosed revolver kicked harder. He fired ten more rounds in rapid fire into the target and Lenny handed him a second loaded magazine.

"Close the action on an empty chamber, then put the magazine in. Get used to charging the weapon with the slide," said Lenny. "Safer for carry."

DeFranco pointed the Glock downrange, racked the slide, and brought it up to a firing position. He fired ten more rounds, correcting a tendency to shoot low and right.

"Need some work on your follow-up shots," said Lenny.

DeFranco emptied the magazine, working on small improvements.

"Come back when you have some time and you can use the range," said Lenny.

"Mind if I exercise my Kimber?" asked Tracy.

"Let me get you a fresh target," said Larry, rummaging in a pile and coming up with a clean sheet. He ran it out and Tracy stepped to the firing line and pulled her Kimber out of her purse. She kept the muzzle pointed safely downrange, flicked off the thumb safety, and fired off three clean rounds, drilling the bull's-eye.

"I see why you keep her around, Sergeant," said Lenny.

"She can be pretty stimulating," said DeFranco.

"All right, you two," said Tracy. "What kind of body armor do you carry?"

"You can go with a lightweight Kevlar vest if you're moving around a lot, in and out of a car for instance," said Lenny. "But the tactical guys like a vest that includes a pocket for a ceramic trauma plate. Protects your center mass."

"I guess I like that," said DeFranco. "Let me try on a couple. Do they come in ladies' sizes?"

"Yep," said Lenny, looking at DeFranco sideways.

They settled on the heavy-duty style. But he also bought two Kevlar vests for lighter duty and everyday wear.

"Last but not least," said DeFranco. "We need a 12-gauge pump riot gun. I like the Remington 870 with a pistol grip. And some double-ought buckshot."

"Nice," said Lenny. "Can't go wrong there. Eight boxes enough?"

"Yep. And throw in eight boxes of 9-millimeter Parabellum, and eight boxes of .45 ACP for my colleague here."

"I like her already," said Lenny.

DeFranco had a zero balance on his Citibank card and he knew this was going to be expensive. 2,829 dollars in fact. He worried a little bit about his kids' tuition, deciding it would be a bigger worry if he weren't around to pay it.

"You charging this to your department?" asked Lenny.

"No, this will be on my own account," said DeFranco. Lenny eyed him warily but started toting up the order.

"You're on official business, right? So I can waive the background check?" said Lenny, leading the question.

"Uh, yeah. Appreciate that," said DeFranco. It was nice doing business with a professional. "Last thing, add a couple of these tactical carry vests for ammo and other accessories. Men's large and women's medium. We're going to need some pockets. And I need a couple of bandoliers for the shotgun shells."

With the trunk of the Corolla loaded, DeFranco drove down the Post Road past Stew Leonard's to get to his branch of People's Trust bank, where he kept a safe-deposit box. He carried the Lands' End briefcase in with Tracy at his side, arranged to go into the vault, and deposited Kali's trachea in the family box with insurance documents, the kids' social security cards, and other papers. He took a last look at the sea glass inside the trachea, floating in formalin, and felt a sense of relief he was finally able to secure the last vestige of the headless girl.

She was real.

But he wasn't finished.

They drove to a self-storage center on the Westport-Southport line and opened an account on a small walk-in space accessible twenty-four seven from outside. Sixty-five dollars a month for six months, payable in advance. There was a nice beefy padlock and a shelf inside. They carried their morning's purchases into the storage locker, placed them carefully, taking time to fill the bandoliers with shotgun shells, then rolled the door down and snapped the lock shut. It was something of an arsenal, DeFranco supposed, and far superior to the meager firepower he possessed that morning. Now he and Tracy each had matching shotguns. He had something to throw back in their direction when they came.

And, more and more, he knew they'd come.

"Well, we got a lot done and it's only noon," said Tracy. "Let me buy you a hot dog at Swanky Franks off Exit Fourteen and you can run me home to get my car. I've just made a miraculous recovery and I think I should probably get to work."

When the time came to part, DeFranco was sad to turn the Corolla around and head back toward the immense uncertainties ahead.

18

Competition

Tracy Taggart found it impossible to be fastidious in her tiny cubicle off the studio. Newspapers, notepads, maps, histories—all the tools of her general assignment beat were spread across her desk in a horizontal system that defied any particular order. But she knew where she could find the things she needed—if she could just get the Styrofoam coffee cups out of the way.

Her job didn't offer too much time for reflection, but she couldn't get the case of the headless girl—or Tony DeFranco—out of her mind. She had a burning desire to get what she knew on-air, and she also knew that her standing with the sergeant, complicated by personal feelings just emerging, handcuffed her to a purgatory clearly of her own making. She had heard the old hands say it was so much easier when you just did the job without personal relationships.

That's when Bob Bannon walked past, stopped on his polished penny loafers, and leaned into her tiny domain. While her feelings toward DeFranco were decidedly mixed, her feelings toward Bannon were perfectly clear. From the crisp crease of his Brooks Brothers khakis to his gold-buttoned blue blazer and club tie, she beheld him with a cool aversion. He was too slick, too composed, too self-involved, too confident. That ungainly pass he'd made at the last office function sealed it. And he was the police reporter. She knew he wasn't happy when she took over the dumpster murder in Westport.

"Taggart, you're going to do just one press conference on that dead black girl in the dumpster and let it go at that?" he said, eyebrows raised.

"I'm working it from another angle," she responded without making eye contact, picking up that morning's *Times* and opening it to the Op-Ed right in his face.

"Why not some interviews with the youth officers in Bridgeport and New Haven? Get a feel for the gang scene around here? Just trying to help," said Bannon.

"Appreciate it," said Tracy coolly.

"There's bar talk the *Bridgeport Post* is questioning the gang theory. They've got reporters on the ground who are pretty plugged in. No gangs they know of have any connection to a dead girl. Your story covering that angle?"

"Bob, I've got it," said Tracy firmly.

"Well, you better let Hank know," said Bannon. "I'm hearing he'd like to see more energy on this story." Hank was their take-no-prisoners news director.

"Bob, I've got plenty of energy, thanks. I'm a little busy here."

"Don't say I didn't warn you," said Bannon, clearly trying to elicit the desired mix of self-doubt and anxiety in a felllow colleague, all part of the newsroom politics.

Tracy Taggart now came to that moral crossroads that many a young, aggressive journalist eventually had to face: stick with your deal, on the *chance* of a better story down the road, or go with what you've got and maybe make management happy *for the time being.* She could drop Tony as a source and go around him to get most of the story anyway. He as much suggested it when he told her he was off the case. She could get Goldberg to open up about the sea glass, and trace it to the beach, any beach, for the first piece. She could localize it to Beachside Avenue later on, which remained only a theory. She wouldn't technically violate her pact with DeFranco.

She left her cubicle and marched toward Hank the News Director's closed door—and stood with arm raised, ready to knock. Then she remembered that good, hardworking man with whom she'd shaken hands back in Curley's Diner.

She had given her word. Like a Marine.

And she reminded herself that anything she released now might make the killer go to ground, lost to kill again.

She went back to her cubicle and got ready for that evening's assignments.

19

Firepower

Ten years ago he liked to work days so he could get home and have a family supper and help the kids with homework, maybe go to ball practice when the weather turned nice. Now that the kids were grown and out of the house he preferred the late shift. It was better to work right through the evening hours, take a nip from the bottle of Jack Daniels he kept in his desk, and head straight to bed when he got home close to midnight. Best not to think about things, just lumber along and play down the clock.

So now it was three in the afternoon, morning errands accomplished, and he was getting ready to head out the door of his little house on High Gate. He put on his new shoulder holster, glad the leather wasn't too stiff. He loaded a full magazine into his new Glock 17, keeping the chamber empty, and put the pistol in the holster under his left armpit. There was provision for two more magazines under his right armpit, which gave him a capacity of fifty-one rounds of 9-millimeter Parabellum. With his Colt hammerless in the ankle holster, he had fifty-seven rounds of firepower—giving him cold comfort. He knew in his heart guns weren't the answer.

He knotted his tie and put on his sport coat. Yes, his weapon was concealed…but just. Standing in front of the mirror, he could see the butt of the grip winking out at him when his coat was open, and the bulge was unmistakable with his blazer buttoned. He'd have to get a new sport jacket, a little fuller in the chest.

He put on a lined trench coat against the chill and wet he knew was waiting on the other side of the kitchen door. Doors and windows locked, he left his house knowing it would take a determined twelve-year-old exactly ten seconds to get inside. He fired up Angelica's Corolla and headed for work, parking next to the department's Crown Vic, his love—speed, space, nice trunk, a real battlewagon.

If he needed it.

He climbed the back stairs and went to his cubicle. There was a stack of police reports from over the weekend that would need a follow up: an attempted break-in at a jewelry store on the Post Road; vandalism at the high school; an assault complaint from the Greek restaurant near the Sherwood Island Connector, kitchen staff going after each other with knives, sending one to Norwalk Hospital.

Any one of the three would require a personal visit, he thought, which would afford him an excuse to get out of the office and swing by Beachside Avenue for a follow-up.

In ten minutes he found himself knocking on Dasha and Galina's familiar door, and he was glad to receive Dasha's beaming smile.

Most people would run for the hills, he thought. She leans right in. He was still a little wary of this aging spymaster.

"I've been waiting for you," she said.

"How did you know I would be over?" asked DeFranco.

"Your investigation is entering a critical phase," she said, her smile gone. "I sensed you have the wisdom to proceed with caution, especially when it comes to the psychology of your targets. These things need the utmost consideration."

"You said targets plural," said DeFranco.

"Yes," returned Dasha, patting the couch and bidding DeFranco to sit next to her. She'd just lit a fire. "You will want to understand the source and nature of the betrayal. Christ had his Judas. And this is not an exercise that relies on cold facts, because there aren't any yet, except for the dead girl, and perhaps your sea glass. This is the part where nuance and subtlety come into play, the ability to read minds. And follow your instincts."

"I have never been very good at reading minds," said DeFranco. Julie would be able to attest to that.

"Men rarely are," said Dasha. "It's not your fault. You only see black-and-white. You have two speeds, fast and slow. Only two directions, forward and reverse. Women notice the shades of gray. We look into the eyes and the faces of people so we can understand the truth behind the facade. We look for the subtext and the understated."

"Is this what they call a woman's intuition?" asked DeFranco.

"Perhaps," said Dasha. "But we always proceed from certain unassailable assumptions. A person who is cold will seek warmth. A person who is hungry will need food and drink. A crying child does not wish to feel abandoned, needs to be comforted. A killer is fully aware of his guilt. That self-awareness can't be masked by words or deeds. It will always be written on his face."

"You seem confident," said DeFranco.

"Not confident. Just experienced. Do you read Shakespeare?"

"A long time ago," he said.

"And likely for a school assignment," said Dasha. "It's not the same thing. You need to read it for enjoyment. But also as a window on the soul."

"What do you mean?"

"Everyone is familiar with the phrase 'The play's the thing...'" said Dasha. "But a student of Shakespeare would be able to complete the sentence. '...wherein I'll catch the conscience of the King.' Fewer still would be familiar with the phrases that precede it: 'I'll have these players play something like the murder of my father before mine uncle. I'll observe his looks. I'll tent him to the quick. And if he but blench I'll know my course.' The play within a play is intended to expose the killer, who Hamlet knows will not remain unaffected when he sees his own act of murder played out onstage. He will react. Hamlet will see it on his face. And Hamlet's suspicions will gel into action."

"I've seen it in the interrogation room," said DeFranco. "Confront the accused with reality and they soon collapse. Unless they are very good. Or they've got a good lawyer."

"You read it in their faces, don't you?" said Dasha.

"If you're open to it," said DeFranco. That's where he needed some coaching, he would admit.

"The same thing can be found in Julius Caesar. 'Yon Cassius has a lean and hungry look.' Or, 'The angry spot doth glow on Caesar's brow. Calpurnia's cheek is pale, and Cicero looks with such ferret and such fiery eyes...' Their emotions are written all over their faces." Dasha was reciting from memory. She grew in DeFranco's estimation.

"And you are wise to know your limitations," said Dasha. "Iago exploits Othello because the poor man is far too literal. He can't see between the lines, or around corners. He's handicapped, like all males of the species, sorry to say. Please don't take offense. But he's also overconfident. That's ultimately his undoing. He can't conceive he might be wrong."

"But you would admit men can be useful in a full frontal assault," said DeFranco. He thought about what it's like to be on the business end of a 12-gauge shotgun. For close-in work, as he learned in the Delta.

"As long as your flanks are protected," said Dasha, countering. She paused a moment. "You will want to exclude your chief from the conspiracy."

"Yes. But there's a part of me that would enjoy watching him swing in the wind."

"Perhaps you'll get that opportunity," said Dasha. "But do you think he's capable of hiding a crime like the case of the headless corpse?"

DeFranco reflected. The man was narrow-minded, self-involved, a shirker, given to tantrums, and always looking like he'd rather be somewhere else. The golf course. A fancy dinner. A trip to Tampa in the teeth of winter when the town needed its chief to be on duty. Being a party to a conspiracy would simply take too much energy.

"Yes," said DeFranco. "He couldn't plan it—or wouldn't. But hide it? Yes."

"Confront him," said Dasha. "State explicitly the disparities between Moriarty's theory of the crime, her official statement, against what you know to be true. The girl didn't die of a heroin overdose. Someone fiddled with the toxicology report. She was choked to death, likely a crime of passion. Likely sparked by her inadvertent pregnancy. Tell him you have the sea glass. Don't reveal its whereabouts. Just tell him it's safe. If he's part of the conspiracy, someone will try to stop you. You'll soon know. That welt over your eye will be nothing compared to what they'll bring."

"How do you think he'll react?" asked DeFranco.

"Interesting question," said Dasha. "I have observed the guilty ones grow quiet. They avert their gaze. Cheeks become slightly flushed and you can see their eyelids blink, not excessively, but pronounced. The innocent get loud, effervescent, giving a full voice to wrath and indignation. Talbot will likely threaten, but ultimately he'll become an ally. If he's innocent."

"But I'm off the case," said DeFranco.

"You'll hear that very clearly at the beginning of your interview. But that feature of the case will be dropped toward the end of your conversation. You and Talbot will join forces. But only if he's *not* a party to the conspiracy."

Dasha could see the future.

"Not sure I want him on my side," said DeFranco.

"If he's innocent, give your chief something to do to keep him occupied," said Dasha. "Those of us in the lower ranks call it upward babysitting."

"Immigration," said DeFranco. "He can try to find out when Kali came into the country. Her full name. Again, only if he's not a part of it."

"Good for starters," said Dasha. "He might even help you confront the state's attorney. But I would keep him well away from Tracy. He won't understand the nature of your relationship with the TV reporter. It's out of bounds, Sergeant. I take it there's no way you can disassociate from her at this point?"

"No," said DeFranco firmly. "I've gotten her in too deep, and now she's in danger. We're being watched."

She paused to reflect. "That's interesting," she said. "A problem but also an opportunity."

"How so?"

"More bait for your trap."

"Not sure I like that idea," said DeFranco, a pained expression suggesting feelings for the girl.

"I see you're involved with her," said Dasha. "Or am I mistaken?"

"No. Not involved. But interested, I guess."

"Ah yes," said Dasha, reading his mind perfectly. He was a man after all.

"We've been thrown together into this situation. I don't want her to get hurt," said DeFranco.

"Of course not," said Dasha. "Can I assume you are prepared?"

"If you mean can we protect ourselves, the answer is yes."

"Don't be overly confident," counseled Dasha. "There are no guarantees in a gunfight. I was fighting the communists in French Indochina in 1950. I nearly lost my leg and my life because I was overconfident."

"You've certainly been around," said DeFranco. He'd had his own moments of fear and violence in Southeast Asia.

"Yes. Thank God Constantine rescued me. Gave me a home. A man of great caring and patience."

"I appreciate your time, ma'am," said DeFranco.

"You can call me Dasha," she said. "We're brothers and sisters in arms now."

"Yes. We are," said DeFranco, taking her hand.

20

The Chief

He left Beachside Avenue and made his follow-up appointments to address the petty crime that every town is heir to. Toward sunset he made his way back to the public safety building and dropped his briefcase in his cubicle. He removed his sport coat and walked with purpose toward the chief's lair. He saw Talbot leaning back in his chair, watching a golf tournament on the small television he kept for monitoring the local news. His feet were up, and DeFranco saw his protuberant belly and that unwholesome neck-roll—not that DeFranco was a saint in that department. Observing Talbot's state of decline only reinforced DeFranco's urge to make more use of his time in the gym. DeFranco knocked and Talbot waved him in.

"Fuck happened to your face?" asked the chief. "And why all the hardware? You know we like to keep a low profile."

"Self-protection," said DeFranco. "I was assaulted at my home Saturday night."

"What?" Talbot's initial shock suggested he didn't know about the bang on the head DeFranco had received. Did he know about the missing body parts?

"It has to do with our dumpster girl, our headless corpse," said DeFranco.

"You're off that case," said Talbot, getting exercised, as Dasha had predicted.

"No, chief. I'm in it hip-deep," said DeFranco. Talbot was turning a shade of purple, bright with anger.

"Goddamnit, DeFranco," Talbot screamed. "We don't want any part of that fucking case. That shit landed on us from Bridgeport or New Haven. State CID said so."

"Get comfortable, Chief," said DeFranco. "Let me tell you what really went down." Talbot seemed to acquiesce to DeFranco's calm, deliberate statement. The chief softened, thought DeFranco, but his cheeks retained a hint of color.

"Mortensen wanted me off the case. Moriarty stated in the news conference the girl died of a heroin overdose. She's an African American. Her tattoo is gang related. But the ME found the actual cause of death. The girl was choked with a piece of sea glass shoved down her throat. She did not die of a heroin overdose. A tech at the state tox lab told the ME's office she had Rohypnol in her system, the date-rape drug. My contact at the ME's office was in the process of retesting her internal organs to verify that—when *he* was murdered. Strangled. Shoeprint at the scene of *his* murder matched a shoeprint at the dumpster. He managed to get the girl's tissue samples to me so they can be rescreened independently to check on the overdose theory. Those body parts were stolen Saturday night. Taken off me, and I was clubbed unconscious. Her liver. Piece of her lung. Her uterus. They're missing. Two people are dead, Chief."

"Holy crap," said Talbot. DeFranco tried to read the look on his face. It registered real surprise. How much did he know?

"Mortensen and Moriarty are trying to cover something up," said DeFranco. Talbot looked him straight in the eye, then blinked. Twice.

"They ordered the body removed to a crematorium in Port Chester. I went there this morning. Moriarty came back to the crematorium and took the body somewhere. Signed a receipt for it. I've got a photocopy. Don't worry. It's safe." DeFranco had no intention of turning it over. Talbot's jaw grew slack.

DeFranco continued. "Funeral director had a look at the corpse before it left," said DeFranco. "That tattoo that Moriarty said was a gang symbol? It was just a hummingbird. I saw it with my own eyes. But the body came in to the funeral parlor with the tattoo carved out."

"They're hiding something," said Talbot, under his breath, perhaps a little too swiftly.

"There's more," said DeFranco. "The girl wore a toe ring. ME figured out the Hindi inscription on it. It has a reference to the goddess Kali. We think the girl's first name might be Kali."

"Good guess. Impossible to verify," said the chief. He was pushing back, thought DeFranco.

Just then, News 12 Connecticut was starting to broadcast on the little television in Talbot's office. DeFranco got sidetracked, waiting for Tracy Taggart to come on air.

He turned to the chief and regained focus.

"I have a theory the girl was visiting someone in Westport," said DeFranco. "She arrived at Kennedy a month or so prior to her murder. She was pregnant, or became pregnant soon after her arrival. She was forced to have an abortion according to the ME, who saw evidence of trauma on the girl's organs of reproduction."

"Oh Jesus," said Talbot.

A motive.

Just then, DeFranco noticed Tracy Taggart coming on-air. She was transmitting live from the scene of a 7-Eleven stickup in Stamford. He turned back to the chief.

"Like you said, I'm off the case. But I'm telling you now, for the good of this department, I am calling Customs and Border Patrol at Kennedy and will see if a woman named Kali arrived from South Asia some time in mid-September. Approximately five foot three or five foot five, approximately 110 pounds. I need her full name. I need to know where she came from. Next of kin. And I need an address where she was headed in the States. They ask for that on the Immigration card inbound travelers are supposed to fill out."

"I get it," said the chief, a bit absently. DeFranco watched Tracy on the TV, barely hearing his commander.

DeFranco stopped dead and watched.

Behind Tracy was the same blue sedan—it was a Chevrolet Impala—with a man standing next to the trunk, his back slightly turned. He was wearing a ball cap. Collar turned up against the chill. He was looking over his shoulder, right at Tracy Taggart.

DeFranco turned cold. He turned back to face the chief.

"What else do you have, DeFranco?" said Talbot.

"The guy who took her tissue samples from me missed one," said DeFranco, his gaze drilling directly into Talbot's brain. "I've got the dead girl's trachea with the sea glass pushed in." Talbot's mouth was wide open now, with no sound coming out. "If I'm right, that sea glass will have a print off the killer's right index finger. I'm in the process of getting that evaluated independently."

Is this what they mean when they say dumbfounded? thought DeFranco.

DeFranco stared at the TV, willing Tracy to somehow stay with her camera crew, get into the van, get back to the TV station where he could call her.

Was it live or was she on tape? It didn't matter. She needed to get somewhere safe.

Now.

He looked at the chief.

He had priorities.

DeFranco left Talbot's office and hurried back to his cubicle to collect his things. As he left, Talbot was getting loud but DeFranco couldn't understand a word.

He took the keys to the department's Crown Vic and raced down the back stairs.

First stop, the self-storage facility. When he got there he put on his body armor over his T-shirt and put his shirt and tactical vest over that. He put Tracy's gear, the extra shotgun, and the ammunition in the trunk of the big Ford.

Next stop, home. He needed to grab some clothes and a shaving kit. He was going to operate out of Miss Taggart's apartment for a while. And if not there, anywhere.

He needed to protect her.

He turned into High Gate Road and rounded the corner, coming to that spot in the road where he could always catch that first glimpse of his little house.

Tonight was different.

Sheets of flame were coming out of the second-story dormers, and the living room was glowing orange behind the bowfront window. He rolled down the car window and could hear the fire crackling as it consumed his home. His life. He got on the Crown Vic's radio to put in a call to Westport Fire Department.

"Talbot, you lying, stinking fuck," said DeFranco.

The chief had to be involved, he insisted to himself.

He got out of the car and strode up to his front stoop. The house was on fire, but that was the least of his worries.

As he stood watching an ominous orange glow build inside his living room, a tall, rugged individual in jeans and a windbreaker, wearing black driving gloves and a ski mask, came rushing out of the house wielding DeFranco's prized aluminum softball bat. Thrusting it out like a lance, he jabbed DeFranco in the gut and knocked him back onto his front lawn. Wind gone, his head once again the recipient of a worrying smack, he opened his eyes to see the man standing over him, bat raised. DeFranco twisted out of the way as the bat came down, whizzing past an ear and grazing his shoulder. The man threw the bat away and ran down High Gate Road, into the misty night, just as DeFranco's neighbors started coming out of their houses to watch the fire. Two men rushed over to help DeFranco to his feet.

His house.

Base camp. Headquarters. Oasis.

Could he save it?

Have you ever been able to save anything? he thought.

"Stay back," he told his neighbors. He ran inside. Fire was creeping up the walls, and the curtains in the living room were now involved. He saw pictures of Julie and the kids crinkling black in their frames. Scrapbooks and albums were burning on a bookshelf. His favorite chair was alight, and the television screen was cracked and smoking. He got down on his hands and knees and tried to make it to the kitchen, to the fire extinguisher on the wall next to the stove. The fire, heat, and smoke were too much. He retreated back into the living room, and found the open front door. He got out five seconds before an explosion blew out the windows and raised the roof, which collapsed into the attic.

The gas line?

The back of DeFranco's windbreaker was on fire so he stopped, dropped, and rolled like they teach the kids in grammar school. The back of his hair was singed and that pain in his side felt like a cracked rib. He lay on the wet grass and looked up at the stars and heard the far-off sound of sirens mixed with the crackling roar of his life turning into ash that rose into a cobalt, moonless night.

How did I get here? he asked himself. And now where do I go?

One thing dominated his mind. Where was Tracy Taggart?

21

Numbers Game

It was two days before the unfortunate fire on High Gate Road, and Angus McCarran was indulging in what he liked to call his reward, a well-deserved bit of respite after a life creating wealth for himself and others. In his frantic, pell-mell existence, it was the one moment of leisure he allowed himself. Strict instructions to family and staff he was not to be disturbed. He was sealed up in the master bedroom of his home on Beachside Avenue, facing seaward behind floor-to-ceiling glass doors. With the catlike creep of dawn, there seemed on this gray day a complete blending of sea and sky, no horizon to delineate where the water ended and the sky began—just enough fog to erase the far shore of northern Long Island. He lay in his California king with the pillow-top mattress, and if he elevated his neck twelve degrees he could see nothing but gray translucence as another day emerged.

He was floating in three dimensions, airborne, his sensory perceptions removed so that all he could think about were the beautiful numbers that swirled in perfect symmetry throughout his brain. He didn't think about his needy wife of twenty-five years, at that moment decamped to their Park Avenue apartment. Nor his daughter, the equestrienne, living in Wellington, Florida. She would get to the Olympics, by God, if she had to spend his every last dime. Nor John, his hope, who was waiting to hear from Wharton.

He was alone. Floating.

But he knew he'd have to arise at some point. He would have to adjourn the drift and swirl of his consciousness—put aside those numbers parading through his mind—and set about the tasks he'd initiated long ago, when he was just a fresh-faced newcomer at Goldman. Despite instructions from higher-ups, he'd never been the buy-and-hold type. He was after bigger game. He identified four or five issues known for their volatility and took massive positions, betting on the correct side of minor swings that amassed ever larger sums. That led to something he designed called flash trading, where algorithms of his own devising would spot prospects and buy and sell gargantuan positions instantaneously. Money flowed into the firm. He was noticed. He was flattered by senior staff. He received their emoluments—and plotted his escape.

He established McCarran Holdings and expanded his reach, creating the myriad formulae that foretold how the needles might move. Two percentage points here and there were enough to fill his coffers and lead to other ventures. He purchased at cents on the dollar downtrodden steel mills and rustbelt refineries so he could break them up and sell off the bits. He determined ways to skirt the environmental impacts and exploit the tax abatements, then vanish with the proceeds.

After that came an interest in trophy real estate—Manhattan landmarks, and LA industrial lots, and pristine mountain preserves and whole Hawaiian islands. Then came futures contracts, commodities windfalls, and that marvel of financial legerdemain, the derivative. Calls. Puts. Options. The money cascaded into his accounts. In fact, he liked to remind himself, he made money in his sleep when you considered the far-flung holdings in the McCarran empire, flags planted on multiple continents and in practically every time zone.

"The first billion is always the hardest," he'd once told his son John, then just twelve years old, hoping to inspire the young man. But early flickers of worry for the boy had blossomed into serious concern. John turned out to be a bit of a dawdler, indifferent at school, cruel toward other children, socially inept, his only real talent manipulating friends with money or favors.

He pushed thoughts of his troubled son away and prepared to heave himself out of bed, then onto his exercise bike while he watched the news. After that, the five-headed shower, then off to breakfast and an orderly day of watching markets on the seven computer monitors in his home office. He'd keep in touch with associates and partners and various minions back at the McCarran Building in lower Manhattan. In his infrequent idle moments he would research the acquisition of another antique Ferrari, and book a yacht charter for his heedless wife's sixtieth birthday. He would somehow get around to discussing the weekend's menu plans with his cook and housekeeper Glennis. And he'd check in with his butler, handler, mechanic, and factotum, Robert, about their latest project to get son John onto a firmer path.

It was such a bother. He had gotten the boy into Princeton by the skin of his teeth. Dreadful high school grades and middling SATs were offset by that princely donation to the Institute for Advanced Studies. It was to honor Einstein, he told friends and colleagues, but it was really a bribe to get his son properly situated in the Ivy League. In his freshman and sophomore years there was no avoiding the fact that the boy had gone overboard, winding up in the local clink for drunkenness and brawling. During John's junior year in Paris, he'd had to pay off the gendarmerie on Rue de Oberkampf. The lad's quarrel with the hashish dealer had come to a head. That little incident only took some time and money, and Robert's unique persuasive skills.

Internships weren't a problem. There were enough firms on Wall Street trying to curry favor with McCarran that finding a slot for young John at Kidder Peabody or Drexel Burnham or some other hot M&A shop was a simple matter of picking up the phone. But even those plum assignments would somehow get spoiled when John made inappropriate advances toward the women in the wire room, or wound up in bed with the daughter of an important Saudi client. Angus would send Robert in to fix things and the young man would be once again set on a proper path.

Today young John, now a senior, was sleeping off a hangover at the family's Beachside Avenue home, having driven up two days previously to attend a barn-burner party at Yale. His classes and exams back at Princeton could wait, of course, because, after all, he had priorities. Angus McCarran slipped by the young man's door and heard murmurings within, assuming some young lady—a Yale conquest?—would be appearing in the kitchen, famished and disheveled, wearing a borrowed robe. He padded down the floating double helix staircase in his Brooks Brothers slippers, glided through the living room and into the den, his book-lined lair with fireplace and leather couches and computer screens adding the right balance of utility and comfort.

He pushed a button under the edge of his desk and Glennis silently appeared in the doorway wearing her official livery, a gray smock with a white apron. On the family retainer for twenty years, Glennis was an African American church lady, and McCarran thought she might have been pretty once. These days, lines were forming around her lips and there were bags under her eyes. She and Robert lived in separate apartments in the servants' quarters atop the carriage house. Across the street, McCarran kept a garage for his stable of prized Ferraris and lesser though significant English motorcars.

"Good morning, Glennis," said McCarran politely. He always wanted to treat the staff cordially, a badge of honor and some-thing of a counterweight to the curt indifference his children showed.

"Good morning, Mr. McCarran," said Glennis. They'd dispensed with the curtsy long ago, a formality Mrs. McCarran still insisted on when Glennis was in her presence.

"Just some scrambled eggs and cinnamon toast and coffee if you please," said McCarran. "And let's try to be nice to John and his guest whenever they wake up."

"Certainly, sir," said Glennis.

"Do you have any idea when John heads back to Princeton?" asked McCarran.

"I have no idea about Master John's plans," said Glennis. As always, Glennis conveyed a certain coolness when it came to matters pertaining to young McCarran.

"I guess it will unfold in the usual way," said McCarran with a wan smile of resignation. John would leave a trail of dirty laundry and demand extra cash while dropping off his latest credit card bill. The Jaguar his parents had given him would need fixing and could he please take the antique MG? McCarran saw it coming.

"Can you send in Robert?"

"Right away," said Glennis. "He's in the back office." McCarran kept an office for servants off the kitchen where they could use the phone or personal computer on official business and keep notes, owner's manuals, and files to run the house.

McCarran turned to the stream of data that marched right to left across his computer screens—stock valuations, currency shifts, government reports on jobs and GDP, bond prices, a screen devoted to breaking business news—his constant companions.

Robert came into the room, wordlessly correct in the presence of his employer. An ex-Navy SEAL and once a key figure in US State Department security, Robert remained tall and strapping despite having arrived at the twilight of an energetic career. He was a few days past fifty, close-cropped salt-and-pepper hair, arms like tree trunks, and a narrow waist. He was tough, loyal, and discreet. McCarran paid him handsomely, direct deposits to an account in the Caymans. McCarran had heard rumors about Robert's abrupt release from the military—something about human rights violations or extrajudicial killings. But didn't that make him more valuable? The man was a mercenary, and that's what McCarran's business and personal life sometimes called for.

"Any word on your cleanup detail?" McCarran asked. Robert didn't like to communicate too much information, even to his boss.

"It's going as well as can be expected," said Robert. "But that contractor continues to be a disappointment."

"We can't afford too many disappointments."

"He came highly recommended," said Robert. "But he's been a half step too late or out of line."

"It's been a mess right from the start, Robert," said McCarran. He watched the man's face and could tell Robert didn't like this characterization. McCarran knew Robert was all about control.

"Best to concentrate on what's going right," said Robert. "We're making progress on recovering all the evidence. And the payments have cleared."

"Too many people involved," said McCarran. "I don't like it. Have we paid off the right officials?"

"We've got the local police and the state police covered—at the top. The story they've put out stands up pretty well."

"I don't worry about the story standing up. Will *they* stand up?" asked McCarran.

"There's always a risk," said Robert.

"Well, your job is to mitigate risk."

"I wouldn't worry too much about our officials. And the story is dying down. Local press seems to have let it go. But I don't like that girl from the TV news. She's too close to the detective. He's off the case, but he's been nosing around. Bears watching."

"I'm still nervous about the chief of police. He loves to take our money. But he'll fold like a cheap suit. Same thing with that woman in the state police. Not to be trusted," said McCarran.

"We have our cutout," said Robert. "They're being paid by our third party."

"I trust *him* least of all," said McCarran. "Doesn't know a damn thing about the importance of containment. Never has."

"Well…one step at a time," said Robert.

"You'll have to take over personally, Robert," said McCarran, his voice tinged with frustration. "And disengage from the contractor. Step in."

McCarran wanted to say, "That's why I pay you," but he held his tongue.

22

Telltale Video

As DeFranco drove westbound on I-95, he thought of the kids, of course, their cast-offs, treasures, sports gear, photos. Angelica liked to keep a diary, dating back to when she was five. Sam had a lot of books he loved. Of course, their little house was where he and Julie had made a life—and now it was gone.

He was angry.

They're trying to get to the sea glass in the dead girl's throat, and Moriarty's signature on that receipt, thought DeFranco. So why not burn the whole thing down?

"Fuck," he exclaimed into the Crown Vic's voluminous interior, realizing this Old English expletive wouldn't bring his house back. Or stop the madness that was beginning to close in. Talbot was clearly involved, but who was the big guy with the baseball bat?

He'd brought Tracy into this mess.

Okay. She'd wanted her story. But she hadn't signed up for this kind of mayhem. He had to find her and it was only 10:00 p.m. He figured she'd be finishing up her shift at News 12 Connecticut, so that's where he aimed the car, now his battle-wagon. News 12 Connecticut was located on Cross Street near Hoyt in downtown Norwalk. He headed there and cruised to a halt in the visitor's space, on the lookout for their ubiquitous Chevrolet. Ammunition and long arms locked in the trunk, he walked toward the front entrance, looking for their watcher—the man in the ball cap.

No such luck, DeFranco told himself, imagining the thrashing he'd deliver to Tracy's stalker, quite possibly the individual who had taken away the DeFranco family home—maybe Curtis Jones's life.

He walked in, presented his ID and badge to the security guard, and asked for Tracy. The guard gave him directions back to the newsroom. For all the crisp, clean relief of the television screen, News 12 Connecticut behind the scenes was actually a bit of a pit—a warren of little editing rooms, a conference area with over-turned Styrofoam coffee cups and stacks of printed matter, soulless cubicles with typewriters and phones, eager personnel beavering away to finalize the eleven o'clock broadcast. The anchors were setting up in a large room in front of huge television cameras on wheels, teleprompters spooling up to feed them the evening news. DeFranco noticed a floor-to-ceiling green screen slightly off stage, surmising it was somehow used to communicate the weather.

He saw her dash around a desk with a sheaf of papers in hand, slurping at a coffee cup and gesturing to an acolyte in jeans, sneakers, and a headset. Tracy wore her red suit and those black high heels. Her hair was combed and brushed to perfection and she had a pair of tasteful hoops adorning each ear. She'd just reapplied her lipstick.

Something rippled across DeFranco's heart.

He had no home. And he wasn't sure he had her. But he knew he had to take very good care of this person. She saw him and she smiled, sending out a lifeline that drew him near.

"You're safe," said DeFranco.

"Of course," she responded. "What's wrong?"

"Talbot's in on it," said DeFranco. "Mortensen. Moriarty. Place is rotten."

"How do you know?" asked Tracy.

"I interviewed the chief, told him about the sea glass in the girl's throat and the copy of the receipt we received today at the funeral parlor. I told him I had her trachea with the sea glass. I think he leapt to the conclusion the body part and the document were hidden in my house. My house is now burned to the ground, Tracy. They're after me. I have a strong suspicion they're after you too. You were broadcasting from a bodega stickup this evening. Guy with the Chevy was in the background. I saw him on your six o'clock stand-up."

"Oh my God, Tony. That was a tape from late yesterday. Couldn't get it in last night's broadcast so we ran it today. We saw that Chevy at your house, then later at my apartment. They know I'm on this story. Do you think they'd risk messing with a TV reporter? I mean, that's just crazy."

"Whole thing is crazy," said DeFranco, agitation open and revealed. "When are you off work?"

"I have one news piece to read at the anchor desk, a toddler on life support after a hit-and-run. After that I'm free."

"I need you to spool up your last four or five assignments. B-roll too. Our man in the plain blue Chevy has been watching you. Need to see if your cameraman has a shot of a license plate," said DeFranco.

"Watching me?" Tracy was incredulous. And suddenly determined. "Tony, I have to take this to my boss. The station has to know what's going on."

"It's okay with me," said DeFranco. "But if your boss has any sense he won't want to run anything until there's an arrest. Right now we've got a lot of dots and they aren't even close to getting connected."

"The story is *about* the dots, Tony. We can get them out there and connect them later. It may even smoke the killers out in the open."

"I'm coming around to your way of thinking," said DeFranco, still shaken by the night's conflagration.

"I'm not sure we should go back to my place," said Tracy.

"I've got an idea on that but you'll have to tap into your inner Marine," said DeFranco, smiling for the first time that day.

"Swell. As long as there's a shower."

"You won't be disappointed."

23

Tale of the Tape

He stood offstage and watched her read the teleprompter. A heart-rending tale of a little boy and a driver wanted for vehicular assault. If the boy died it would be manslaughter. Her last line was a call for donations. Her gaze locked on the camera and DeFranco envisioned all of Fairfield County reaching for its collective wallet.

When she was finished she led him to an editing room. She closed the door and DeFranco removed his vest, showing off his new Glock hardware.

"Somehow I am feeling more comfortable, Detective DeFranco," she said when she observed his added firepower. "I've got some tapes from the last three days. This might take a while."

She booted the plastic videotape cartridges into the editing machine and fast-forwarded. She and DeFranco were glossing over the B-roll, establishing shots of street signs and landmarks, storefronts and meeting rooms, the inside of the remote van, and headshots of Tracy Taggart laughing with the camera crew, putting aside for a moment the stresses of the past few days.

She and DeFranco were looking for a blue car, a man in a ball cap, off to the side, a fender, a trunk lid…some kind of connection. And then they found it. It was from a stand-up in front of the bodega that had been held up at gunpoint. Tracy was speaking into the camera, holding her microphone. The light was failing and the air was subdued in a gray mist. The same blue Chevy was at the curb behind her. You could see the front of the car, the driver low and dark behind the wheel.

"Can you zoom in on that plate?" asked DeFranco, sitting up straight.

"I'm not the best at this but I can do the basics," said Tracy. She manipulated a joystick to position a cursor and twisted a dial, and the front bumper and grille of the Chevrolet grew to fill the screen. They couldn't make out the license plate.

"Let's try more tapes," said Tracy. "We've got time."

She ran back through a week of television output: Tracy at a warehouse fire. Tracy at a street fair. Tracy at Westchester Airport for a small-plane mishap. Tracy at Shippan Point waiting for a nor'easter. They spotted the Chevy in three out of five of her most recent stand-ups.

"No joy identifying the car or the driver," said DeFranco.

"Let's try one more," said Tracy, unwilling to give up. They went back to Moriarty's original news conference and Tracy's stand-up in front of the Westport Public Safety Building. The Chevy was there, parked on Jesup Street. No driver, but if you zoomed in you got a full frontal shot of the Chevy's grille. Tracy fiddled with the controls and suddenly a license plate popped into view and filled the monitor.

"Oh hell," said DeFranco. "A Georgia plate. Most of it's covered with mud. Trying to hide something? Third digit is a three and last character in the string is a G."

"Is that something we can work with?" asked Tracy.

"Yes. But like everything, it will take time," said DeFranco. "Probably a lot of cars fall into that category."

"But we can narrow it down by make and model," said Tracy.

"You're thinking like a detective."

"Well," said Tracy. "It's high time I started thinking like a journalist. I've got to get something on the air about all this, Tony."

"Interesting problem," said DeFranco. "All you've got are some unsupported allegations, gross inconsistencies, and a lot of he-said-she-said."

"We caught Moriarty in a lie about the girl's tattoo," said Tracy. "And we've got some inconsistencies in the tox screening. There's also the single footprint found at two murder scenes, Tony. For God's sake." She was upset with their arrangement. He could see her point.

"Tracy, we'll definitely need to shine a bright light on all this when the time comes. But if the story breaks too soon, we'll lose the killer. He'll go to ground, might even kill again."

She's a racehorse and she can't wait to bust out of the gate, he thought.

"Tony, I get it. But it's not easy."

"You'll get my full support when the time comes, but right now we need to refute the heroin theory if we can. And we have to try to run down that license plate. Not to mention giving our dumpster girl back her name."

"Okay. Look—I keep some clothes in a locker here in case I have to go out in the boonies on assignment. And I have a toilet kit. I'm going to pack a bag and we can get out of here. But let's cruise by my place and see if our friend is there."

"Good idea," said DeFranco. "I'd like to have a chat with that guy."

24

Close Encounter

Tracy settled in the front seat of the cruiser and allowed herself to stretch out. "I see why you like this thing," she said when they were halfway to her apartment. "You can really relax and breathe."

"I hate those little Japanese skateboards," said DeFranco. "But sometimes in life we have to drive what we have to drive."

"So now you're a philosopher," said Tracy and they both laughed, their momentary amusement suspended when they rolled closer to Tracy's condo.

The blue Chevy was parked right outside.

"Time to get tactical," said DeFranco. He knew he was winging it again. After the interview with Talbot, after the fire, he didn't really care any more. "I'll let you out here and give you time to get up close to the vehicle on the other side of the street. Watch my back. Stay out of sight. You have your Kimber?"

"Right in my bag," said Tracy a little gravely.

"You might want to get it into the pocket of your overcoat," suggested DeFranco. "Cocked and locked?"

"Always," said Tracy. "Daddy wouldn't want me to carry it any other way."

"Fine. But can we get you out of those heels?"

"Hang on. I've got a pair of Nikes in my duffel." She rummaged in the back seat and came up with running shoes, hoisting each leg up to put them on. "Okay. Off I go."

"Just hang back in the shadows and keep an eye on that car," said DeFranco. Tracy looked at him in a way that suggested she cared more than a little. "That gun of yours is for defense only. Got it?"

"Don't get hurt." She smiled.

"I'll be fine," said DeFranco, not exactly sure if he would be. He still felt that swelling black welt on the side of his face.

He got out of the Crown Vic, pushed the electric key lock, and surveyed the scene. Everything was quiet. No passersby and very little local traffic. It was past everyone's bedtime.

He walked closer to the Chevy and noticed the driver missing from behind the wheel, raising the hackles on the back of his neck. If the driver wasn't in the car, then the driver was out of the car—and that meant the driver could be anywhere. He stopped to look around, crossing his strong hand across his chest to remove the Glock from the holster. He pushed the handgun in front of him at the apex of an isosceles triangle formed by his forearms. He was worried about what might be behind him, and off to the sides. He'd been outflanked before. He couldn't let that happen again.

He wanted to get a closer look at the license plates on the Chevy so he could fill in the blanks. He knelt down by the rear of the vehicle and reholstered the Glock. He ran his hand across the plate. Through a thick layer of mud DeFranco discerned Georgia plate 423-AMG. Peachtree County. It was the same car from the videotape.

Tracy's stalker.

"Long way from home," DeFranco muttered under his breath.

He produced the Mini Maglite from his vest and stepped around the side of the vehicle to shine it inside the car. Back seat was clear. He tried the door. It was locked.

He was trying to plan next steps when he heard feet running up behind him. He turned and ducked just in time to avoid the swing of what looked like a leather truncheon whip past his ear.

Then he had one of those split-second moments that felt like an hour.

Do I shoot the bastard right here, or try to take him in? he thought.

He knew he was within his rights to stop the assault, and he knew if he shoved the Glock into the man's gut and fired his attacker would go down permanently. Threat stopped.

Could he kill him? The last time he'd killed anyone was long ago and far away.

So he froze.

He felt the wind from the truncheon on his face as it swung past from the other direction. The man was off balance, so DeFranco punched him with his strong hand, fingers gripped around the Maglite to give his fist more heft. DeFranco's fist gouged into the attacker's gut and cracked a rib. The man bent in half and went down on the ground, exhaling in pain. That gave DeFranco a second to deliver a kick to the man's midsection, which cracked a rib on the other side. DeFranco got a good look at him this time. Black jeans, black gloves, black leather jacket, a ski mask. Same guy who had attacked him at his house that evening? DeFranco wasn't sure; he seemed of slighter build.

He didn't see the man's left foot kick out. DeFranco tripped on the attacker's leg and went down in the gutter on his back. The man let out a gust of air and an audible wince and got to his feet. The last thing DeFranco saw was his assailant's backside as he ran, limping, down the street.

After that, Tracy Taggart's beautiful face filled his view and asked for the second time, "Tony, are you all right?"

"Fine, except for my pride."

"Man just assaulted a police officer," said Tracy, looking a little flabbergasted. "He doesn't know how close he came to getting shot."

"I just didn't feel like it," said DeFranco. "Too much paperwork."

There was something else that stopped him, a promise he'd made to himself. It was forged in the Delta. His team had taken fire and returned it, hitting the wrong people. And DeFranco had stopped killing right then and there. He figured it would take a lot to get him to pull the trigger now—a threat to Tracy Taggart chief among them.

One thought nagged him. Could I follow through if our backs were against the wall?

"Let's get out of here," said Tracy. "He's still out there."

"Good idea," said DeFranco. "But let's slow this dude down a bit." He reached into his tactical vest and pulled out a heavy Leatherman folding toolkit with a knife, then methodically slashed all four of the Chevy's tires. He used the tool's Phillip's head screwdriver to remove the vehicle's license plates. Lastly, he wrote down the VIN number stamped behind the windshield, smashed the passenger side window, and reached into the glove box to find the registration. It was empty, not even an owner's manual. "Well, he's not going to use this thing tonight, and we'll get a bead on who owns it tomorrow. Georgia? Who knew?"

"So where are you taking me, Detective DeFranco?" asked Tracy. He swore it sounded like a flirt.

"I hope you like boats," he returned.

25

Hunkering Down

He remembered what he liked about late fall in a boatyard. Sure it was cold, but it was also quiet. They pulled into Norwalk Cove Marina near Calf Pasture Beach and drove silently down the alley formed by sailboats and powerboats put up for the winter, covered and decommissioned until spring. Row after row, the boats propped up on their metal stands were more than enough to hide the Crown Vic from the casual observer as they made their way toward Dock C, Slip 12 West.

DeFranco positioned the car between two old sailboats—a Bristol and a C&C—on stands. He aimed the car out the ingress, and unloaded Tracy's duffel, the shotguns, the ammo, her body armor, and the other accoutrements of their involuntary sideline.

"Can't wait to see what you've got in mind," said Tracy.

"Uncle Guillermo's Grand Banks 42," said DeFranco. "Old bugger can't stand paying the haul-out fees each winter, so he alternates. This is the year he's keeping her in the water. It'll just take a few minutes to fire up the space heaters and make it livable."

They walked down the dock toward a lonely trawler floating proud against the onslaught of the coming winter.

"There's a bubbler in case it ices in, and full shore power, plus some propane and fresh water. Guillo keeps the bilge heated so the tanks and water lines don't freeze. It'll be kind of cozy," said DeFranco. "Besides, I don't have any place to go."

The thought pained him.

"Well, my friend," said Tracy. "You can always bunk with me, but under the circumstances I'm glad I'm not home either. I really don't like being watched."

They stepped aboard the big trawler's teak side decks, ducked through the sliding hatch by the wheel in the center salon, and dropped their gear. DeFranco crouched by the electrical panel and started throwing switches on the AC side. Master on, outlets, hot water, battery charger. Then the DC panel, cabin lights, fresh water pumps. He turned on two small space heaters and then attended to the seacocks for the head intakes fore and aft. Tracy drew the curtains and inspected the larder. Canned vegetables. Pasta. A jar of tomato sauce. A small brick of parmesan cheese and a grater. An unopened bottle of pinot noir. Enough to keep the wolves from the door. Tony left the cabin to turn on the propane tanks in a locker on deck and when he came back in, Tracy was in the aft cabin inspecting the sleeping arrangements.

"I can take the forward stateroom if you'd like your privacy," he said gallantly.

"Well," said Tracy. "I'm still cold and I'm still scared. But more than that right now I just want you to hold me. That guy had me spooked."

She dropped her duffel on the double berth and walked toward DeFranco. She put her arms around his neck and looked into his bruised face. She lightly kissed the bump, and he made a sudden intake of breath, sensing a peculiar but unmistakable blending of pleasure and pain. She dropped any pretense of holding back. She worked her lips around to his waiting mouth and kissed him slowly.

She held him around the waist and looked into his eyes. "Thank you, Tony, for looking out for me," she said.

"I think we're looking out for each other," said Tony. He meant it in more ways than one—but he didn't want to drive her away with excess sentimentality. It had been a very long time since he'd been with a woman—in any sense. She put her head on his shoulder and squeezed him for all he was worth. He drank in her scent, and became entwined in the very idea of her. He'd been walking across an emotional desert, and he'd found his oasis.

"How about some food," she finally said, breaking free.

DeFranco, speechless, could only nod in agreement.

They both liked the fact they were alone—no need for periodic trips to the window to peek behind the drapes and check for watchers. The wind howled outside the boat's cabin, and flecks from a light snow flashed in the moonlight. Guillermo had a stash of candles. The pinot noir went down smoothly and the pasta was not disagreeable. Tony told her stories about Uncle Guillermo, who'd had four wives, and wanted to be a big-shot Mafioso but wound up running a deli in Bridgeport. He'd won the Grand Banks in a poker game. Guillermo didn't spend a lot of time aboard the boat—*Paisano*—so Tony and his kids kept her exercised.

Tracy sipped her wine and laughed in all the right spots and threw out her bright, shining smile. She told him about the bizarre stories she'd covered: the man who ran down the street in his boxers pursued by his knife-wielding wife; the bank robber who apologized to customers for inconveniencing their day; the dog that saved the child from crossing in front of the city bus; the man who was brought to the ER by a hooker after he'd suffered a heart attack. Thinking he was on his deathbed, he confessed to his wife he'd been cheating on her for thirty years. Of course he made a full recovery and when he got home, his wife shot him.

"Dead?" asked DeFranco, incredulous.

"Nope. A .22 round in the behind. But the guy got the point and they lived happily ever after," said Tracy, laughing. "Don't let me go on. We'll be here all night. I don't want you to get tired of me."

"That would be impossible," he said. He liked her at any time of the day or night, but he especially liked her by candlelight.

You've got it bad, DeFranco, shouted a voice in the back of his head. He turned down the volume.

It was past midnight and Tony started cleaning up. Before he washed the dishes he showed Tracy how to operate the commode in the aft-cabin head—flip a lever, work the pump handle to fill, pump again to discharge. It was one of those sacred intricacies of dwelling afloat. You either adapted or recoiled. Tracy adapted. He performed his own ablutions in the forward head and when he went aft he found Tracy under the comforter of the big double berth. He stripped to his skivvies, turned out the light, and joined her.

When she gravitated in his direction he quickly discerned she was in her flannel pajamas, warm to the touch. She kissed him and looked into his eyes, then patted his cheek and rolled away to face the teak cabin liner. The adult Tony, the Tony with two grown children who'd had a long-term love in his life, acknowledged that physical intimacy under the threat of violence, with a murderer on the loose, was nothing short of preposterous. But the misguided boy dwelling within wanted her body and soul then and there. He knew a tap of the brakes might prolong their relationship, and he was loath to rush things and thus drive her away. He was content to drink in the lavender scent of her hair, and listen to her softly purring. He spent the remainder of the night sifting through the details of the case of the headless corpse, and how to keep them both safe. When he finally did get to sleep, the first particles of dawn were already infiltrating their floating hideaway.

26

Seeds of a Cover-up

They both awoke around ten o'clock in the morning, grateful they'd chosen to work the night shifts at their respective trades and therefore had their mornings free.

DeFranco wondered aloud whether or not he still had a job. Failing to remove himself from the case of the headless corpse might give Talbot grounds for dismissal.

"But I am sure he'd rather have you in the department where he can watch you than outside the department where you can cause him serious damage," suggested Tracy. "I mean, isn't your next stop the FBI?"

"Could be," said DeFranco. "Man's a louse and an idiot."

"But you can't believe he's the mastermind," said Tracy. "Does he have that kind of juice? I think he's just doing someone else's bidding. It's likely he doesn't even know what's going on."

"I think you're right," said DeFranco. "He's covering for somebody. Mortensen, Moriarty, the killers." He used the plural because he was by no means certain they were dealing with an individual assailant. "I've presented a lot of this to him already, then I ran out when I saw that guy on TV at your stand-up. The chief and I are by no means finished."

"You can go to work like nothing has happened," Tracy said. "Okay. Your house has been torched. It will elicit some sympathy, or at least it should. When and if Talbot confronts you, mention your next call will be to the arson investigators. After that maybe the Feds. I mean the corpse was transported across state lines. Doesn't that make it a federal matter? Not to mention corruption. Tell him you suspect the person who burned down your house was probably trying to destroy evidence in the dumpster murder. That's obstruction. Your talk with Talbot and losing your home is just too close to not be connected, Tony. The arsonist could be the killer, or Curtis's murderer. You're not accusing him of anything—yet. Just keeping him informed. As daddy used to say, 'He'll shit green.'"

They both laughed at the color commentary of an ex-Marine.

"I need to meet that guy," said DeFranco.

"Oh you will," said Tracy, giving him hope, at the same time causing him to gird against disappointment.

He was in deep.

"Let's get some breakfast and I'll run you to your car," said DeFranco.

"Good plan," said Tracy. "But I need to swing by my apartment and get some things."

They went about their morning and when it came time to drive up to Tracy's condo, they swung by the place where they'd left the damaged Chevy the night before. DeFranco half expected to see the vehicle's frame up on blocks, wheels missing, hood up, engine dismantled—a victim of a little moonlight auto salvage. Either that or the city had hauled it away, making the task of closer examination easier.

The Chevrolet was gone. DeFranco called the Stamford impound facility when they got to Tracy's apartment, but there was no report of a blue Chevy Impala brought in the previous evening with the VIN number DeFranco recited.

No parking tickets. No night-shift reports. The busted Chevy— and their stalker—had vanished.

27

Danger This Close

Robert was in danger. He knew it in his bones. The last time he'd sensed trouble this close was Grenada, with the Cuban militia surrounding his position and the only way out a rooftop extraction by a passing Blackhawk. His contractor had lost his vehicle in a dust-up with the so-called detective. The girl reporter was in on it. His simple instructions were to case the girl's Stamford condo, report on their movements until he could find a way to compromise her—all it would take would be a word or two to the station owner from a high-placed principal. She'd be off the story and on her way to Podunk. But the detective had bested his guy in a straight-up fight—cracked ribs. Worse, the car was on a side street in Stamford with tires slashed. He'd have to use the flatbed McCarran used for his Ferrari collection.

That's how Robert—steely-eyed commando—found himself on the darkened streets of Stamford, Connecticut, at midnight, cranking the hapless Chevy onto the back of his boss's truck. All he needed was to have the truck's plates made by a local cop or a pissed-off neighbor. It was bad enough the Chevy's plates were gone. The car was registered to an obscure Chinese import/export company registered in Macao—only traceable with lots of time and no small ingenuity.

The cable winch dragged the vehicle up the ramp and Robert chained it down. Next stop, LaJoie Salvage in Norwalk. Three crisp hundred-dollar bills to his friend Shaquille would see the car inserted in the crusher that night.

So what are the priorities?

He ticked through his list as he drove eastbound on I-95 toward the Norwalk exit.

First, confirm Moriarty's receipt for the corpse and the girl's remaining body parts were lost in the High Gate Road fire.

He'd needed to act fast to get that done. A call from Talbot to Mortensen to McCarran and he was rolling out the door. It helped that the cop's house on High Gate Road was only a mile away. He tried to make it look like a bad wire in a lamp. The broken gas line behind the stove helped things along. But he couldn't assume the evidence had burned up in the fire. He hadn't expected to see the cop, but he'd taken care of him. He'd have to make a more permanent job of it later.

The real puzzle was the reporter. Why wasn't she getting all this on-air? Didn't she feel like she had enough to go on? Yes, there was the potential for big charges against big people. She had to get it right. Maybe that's why she was holding back.

He had to stop her. Only way to keep her off the air was some good old-fashioned persuasion. Maybe a knife to that pretty face? End her TV career for good.

The next errand was his own escape. He had a Panamanian passport. He needed to shift funds from the Royal Bank of Scotland's Georgetown branch on Grand Cayman over to Banco Popular in Panama City. He also had his reserve fund in the wings—gold bullion, diamonds, cash, bearer bonds. More than enough to disappear for a while. Take a little trip down to Pedasi on the Pacific Coast. He could work on his surfing skills at Playa Venao.

McCarran could figure out the rest it on his own. Robert had tried. Johnny would be all right. He was too stoned and drunk the night the Indian girl died.

But that other guy.

Mean little fucker.

It was time to end it.

If he could.

Bail out if he couldn't.

He still needed to work some angles.

All of the links to the McCarran family would have to be cut. That was his job. Any person or piece of evidence would need to be scrubbed clean. That included the money-hungry chief of police and the bimbo from the state police. And the contractors. Both of them. He needed them now. But he'd get around to finishing them off too. He couldn't tolerate ineptitude. That left the TV reporter and the detective. He had to get to them before they found the link to their cutout. Busy, busy.

Who was next on his list?

"Moriarty," he said out loud.

28

Curtis Steps Up

Curtis Jones was reaching out from the grave.

DeFranco sat in his cubicle at the public safety building, having dropped Tracy off at her television station. He assumed Talbot would be making an appearance to ask him to collect his things. He would be escorted from the building. Gross insubordination. Fired for cause. DeFranco had been meddling in the case against direct orders.

DeFranco frankly didn't care about the job, although he conceded he'd miss it. No, but there were forces at work that had placed him and Tracy directly in the line of fire. Job one now was to protect her. In order to achieve that goal he had to get to the bottom of the case of the headless corpse, and the possible link to Curtis Jones's murder. There was a clear, linear path and he had to find it.

Then came the letter.

Sitting on the middle of his desk was a number 10 envelope postmarked *Stamford* the day Curtis died. The return address was the ME's office with Curtis Jones's name penned with care underneath it. DeFranco's name and the address of the Westport PD was sketched across the body of the envelope, and the first thing DeFranco did was compare the handwriting with Curtis's "suicide note." The note had been typewritten and the signature was an infantile *CJ*. The envelope before him had Curtis's name written out in full—in a hand that wasn't quite tight, but meticulous and certainly confident.

He slit the envelope, opened it, and held his breath.

He pulled out a letter and an index card.

He was looking at the killer's fingerprint.

Dear Tony, wrote Curtis. *I'm usually not the paranoid type but I am getting a vibe here that the case of our dumpster girl is ruffling some serious feathers. Closed doors. State's attorney nosing around. I am preparing a package for you to get rescreened. It's better that you handle it that so it gets done right. I will leave you instructions. But I also wanted to send you the enclosed under separate cover. I removed the sea glass from the girl's throat and dusted it for fingerprints. I got a solid hit on what might be the right index finger of the person who pushed it down her throat. I wanted to catch that before I put the sea glass back in her trachea and preserved it in formalin. This way you'll have a print you can work with. Please knock on my door when you get to the office. In the meantime, I am mailing this to you so it's got a postmark with date stamp and it doesn't somehow get lost. Talk soon. Curtis.*

DeFranco looked down at a white index card with a piece of clear tape on it. Under the tape were the characteristic whorls of a single fingerprint. Curtis's envelope, note, and contents were so overwhelmingly significant DeFranco didn't waste a second putting his next plan into action. He gathered up his things and went down to the parking lot. He had overstayed his welcome with the Crown Vic—no use adding grand theft auto to his list of sins—so he found Angelica's forlorn Corolla and drove over to his People's Trust branch. He negotiated entry to the safe and placed the fingerprint next to the girl's trachea in his safe-deposit box. He jumped back in the Corolla and made his way back to the office.

It was time to call Customs and Immigration—and to check in with Westport's chief of police.

"God, I hope he's pissing in his pants," he muttered aloud as he swung the Corolla into the officer's lot back at the public safety building.

29

Good Hunting

Dasha Petrov sensed a familiar, bygone thrill.

The hunt was on, and like any good intelligence agent, she wanted to pay close attention to her cover.

It had been a full day since she'd heard from DeFranco or the red-haired girl, but there was no reason she couldn't do a little digging on her own. The weather had turned colder, and leaves from the copper beech trees were fluttering down. On these brisk fall days she liked to bundle up Galina and install her on the lawn with a rake to keep her busy, albeit one-handed. Galina loved making a contribution, however meager. Dasha dressed them both in layers—down vests underneath their field coats. Satisfied Galina was safe and happy, she marched across the lawn of their fine, weathered house, pinnacle of Constantine's pride. It was their castle, after all, and it was now the home of their progeny. God above, she hoped they wouldn't see her starting off again on one of her beach treks. She was suffocating from all their loving kindness, always fretting about her cholesterol or her blood pressure, and those little mental slips everyone is heir to.

She had work to do.

She was pursuing her hobby of identifying sea birds and migratory fowl, the same cover she'd assumed for years. There was an advantage in consistency. Often she'd tramp the Audubon Conservatory on the north side of the street, looking for wrens or bluebirds. People on Beachside Avenue had gotten used to the sight of Dasha Petrov with her binoculars—on the beach, on the street, sometimes on the seawalls or private properties lining the avenue.

She was a harmless, even comforting, sight.

Nice thing about growing old is that no one pays attention to you anymore, she thought. Better yet if you act a little daft, early onset or whatever they call it.

These days she sensed her son and daughter-in-law eyeing her a bit more closely, looking for signs of enfeeblement. But Dasha was sharp and fit, determined to prove them wrong.

After a lifetime of espionage, she was also a font of secrets, including one she'd shared with only Galina. Concealed at the top of her chestnut stick was an eight-inch knife blade inserted into a camouflaged scabbard formed by the rest of the stick below. It had a double razor-sharp edge shaped in a long triangle intended to cause the most havoc going in or coming out. As her trainers in the CIA often said, to kill with a knife meant opening the floodgates of blood.

Being a birder allowed her to blend in with the environment. She wasn't being nosy, merely engaging in an innocent intellectual pastime—even though she did sometimes inadvertently train her binoculars on uproarious dinner parties, or family spats, or illicit couples in flagrante.

She left Galina and set out for the beach to begin her standard reconnoiter, this time with purpose. She walked east, her target the Leipzig residence. Leipzig senior was the gambling tycoon, owner of a jai alai fronton in Bridgeport, with televised horse and dog racing, food courts, a bar and grill, even a babysitting service and playground—making it more convenient to separate people from their money. Leipzig was under some kind of cloud according to *The Bridgeport Post*, something about inappropriate contact with the state gambling commissioner. An enterprising reporter had observed them together in first class on a flight to Vegas.

Just a thug, thought Dasha when she'd read the news.

The Leipzigs, the Rosewigs, the McCarrans all had late school-age or early college-age offspring. They all fit the loose profile she'd contrived for her hypothesis. The nice thing about the Leipzig clan? Their patriarch already had one foot in jail. Maybe the little Leipzigs hadn't fallen too far from tree?

Dasha had seen it happen, entitled children pushing an envelope that only seemed to expand with the easy availability of cash and time. Certainly one could find a criminal element among the lower classes, she mused. In those cases, stealing (or worse) was a matter of survival. You might find more innocents in the middle classes—toeing the line, after all, is what got them there. But in high society, misbehavior was a God-given right—a form of entertainment, with dad always on hand to make bail or get the charges dropped.

Two of the Leipzig kids—a boy and a girl—were attending Green's Farms Academy at the western end of Beachside Avenue. Two older Leipzig boys were in college, one having barely made it into the state school at Storrs, the other at BU.

A party school, sniffed Dasha.

And oh yes…the Leipzig kids had already touched the hot stove of law and order. The younger girl had been arrested for shoplifting mascara from the local Rite Aid. The number-two child at UConn had had a succession of DUIs. His driver's license was hanging by a thread. There was already talk on the street about installing the reprobate in rehab.

Dasha needed to get inside each of her three target domiciles, so she decided to accelerate her standard practice of staying in touch with the help. When the principal target of an operation was hard to penetrate, it was better to cozy up to the periphery. So she'd made bird-watching dates with the live-in staff along the street—a harmless, scatterbrained old woman literally out for a lark. Not that bird-watching was a compelling interest among the domestics on Beachside Avenue, but Dasha always seemed to make it interesting. She asked questions, really listened, always concerned. The key, Dasha found, was to turn the conversation back to family.

So, from time to time, it wasn't unusual to see Dasha chatting with Consuela, the Leipzig's cook and housekeeper. And on those days when Consuela's food preparation might be a bit taxing—a party in the offing, or a seasonal soiree—Consuela would invite Dasha into the Leipzig kitchen for a cup of tea so they could converse about the birds they had seen, or the changing of the seasons—more often, the social dynamic of their exalted avenue. On this particular day Dasha mounted the Leipzig's seawall at their usual hour and Consuela waved her back to the kitchen.

"Come in, Dasha," said Consuela. "The family is gone but I have to prepare for a party on Saturday. Canapés. Desserts. The lot."

Dasha scurried along and soon found herself warming her hands around a mug of Constant Comment off the Leipzig scullery. Their initial topic, a passing flight of swans, followed by the encouraging re-emergence of canvasbacks—and the vexing problem of visiting Canada geese, their barrage of droppings left behind to show for it.

"And how are the children getting along?" Dasha asked, dispensing with preliminaries. Her voice was low but not conspiratorial. She was *concerned*. The Leipzig offspring had had to bear so much. Consuela rolled her eyes and emitted a long-suffering sigh.

"*Dios mio*," said Consuela. "The younger ones are failing in school and getting in trouble. The parents are fit to be tied. The kids don't listen to their father anymore. He has his own problems, you know."

"Yes, I read the papers."

"The older two are keeping their noses clean but they aren't doing well in school either, which causes their mother a great deal of worry."

"What kind of friends do they keep?" asked Dasha, arriving at her carefully planned point of inflection.

"Oh, the normal ones," said Consuela. "Some are nice. Others I am not so sure."

"Do the older kids travel? Getting out and seeing the world sometimes offers a clear eye, a new perspective."

"Oh no. They go back and forth between college and home."

"Any foreign friends over? I am a little biased because I was raised in Europe during some tough times. It's a fine way to see how the other half lives."

"Couldn't agree more, coming from Mexico. It wasn't always easy. But no. These kids are American through and through. For better or worse."

"The kids spend any time with other kids on the street? After all, sometimes these connections can lead to good things, some constructive relationships."

"They know the McCarran boy, John…used to play together when they were little. But not so much anymore. He went to that fancy school in Princeton. They used to see the Rosewig kids, but they're away at school too. No, I think the kids are all going their own way."

"A little sad," said Dasha. "Lots of nice ties on this street if you are open to them. I raised my three on Beachside Avenue. They're not the worst."

They prattled on. Dasha wanted to know about Consuela's sister in Guadalajara, and that nephew headed for law school—the leavening that baked in their friendship. Dasha looked for an opening to take her leave. She didn't get the sense the Leipzig progeny were up to murder. Her instincts as an interrogator were on the lookout for hushed, pregnant silence, trembling lips—the truth violently suppressed, struggling to break free.

With Consuela it was just the usual dirty laundry.

Dasha extracted herself with her consummate grace and walked down the street toward the Rosewigs. Their domestic was a Peruvian named Daisy. The kids were a bit more settled. But the parents had somehow found themselves on the precipice of divorce.

"Such a nice couple," said Dasha in sympathy.

"They are wonderful as individuals," said Daisy thoughtfully. "But they just can't be together."

"So sad."

Daisy's voice dropped an octave and she glanced from side to side. "You know, I think she's seeing someone."

"An affair?" asked Dasha, feigning incredulity. Affairs were her stock and trade, mother's milk to those of her profession.

"She's visiting the hairdresser twice a week and her nails and toes are always polished. She sings to herself. Two or three days a week she leaves the house before noon and comes back after two. She has a glow."

"Oh, the glow," said Dasha, all knowing. Women could reap deep meaning from trace evidence and conjecture, discerning in these bare fragments a towering truth.

"Do you think he suspects?"

"Oh no," said Daisy. "Too busy with his work."

There you had it, thought Dasha.

At least Constantine could balance life and work. A beautiful dancer. A wizard in bed. A titan in the boardroom.

She patted the handle of her chestnut stick.

Dasha made an elegant retreat and slipped next door to check on Galina. The poor dear was a bit cold so Dasha led her into their cottage and placed her before a wonderful fire with a nice chicken soup. She then scooped up a book on loan from Glennis, the housekeeper next door. She had borrowed it with the intention of returning it at some propitious moment—an excuse to turn up unannounced.

She could tell during their brief encounters over the years that Angus McCarran had little regard for the Petrovs residing to his east. White Russians weren't the up-and-coming demographic he preferred, and the Petrov residence was, frankly, a bit tattered— peeling paint and rusty cyclone fencing and missing shingles. He made a point of directing his gardener to clip both sides of their shared hedge, a neighborly gesture the Petrovs appreciated. But this trifling gift also kept his own property in its customary state of trim.

Before the McCarrans had arrived on the street, the previous owners had installed a little door in the hedge, and McCarran kept it functioning in deference to tradition. That's how Dasha gained entry to the sprawling McCarran compound, always impressed with the perfect McCarran lawn and the nicely edged McCarran walkways and the mirthful McCarran topiaries prancing across the landscape.

"Money, money, money," Dasha muttered as she made her way toward the kitchen door.

She rang the bell and Glennis answered after a single ring. She wore her gray maid's uniform with a white apron, dishwashing gloves on each hand, and a fleck of soap suds clinging to her graying hair.

"Hello, Glennis," said Dasha, exuding her standard charm.

"Nice to see you," said Glennis, a bit cool to Dasha's trained ear.

"I brought back your homeopathy book. Very interesting. I think my sister might benefit from some of these ideas. I thought the chapter on arnica was especially good."

Dasha noted puffy eyes and an ashen pallor. Glennis had also lost some weight in the month since Dasha had last seen her. Her smock hung loosely from her thinning shoulders.

"Darling, you don't look too well," said Dasha.

"I'm fine," said Glennis, clipped and self-conscious. Dasha waited for an invitation to enter. She hesitated on the stoop and Glennis said at last, "Some tea?"

"Well, just for a minute. I don't want to leave Galina for too long. Poor dear."

Glennis led her through a vestibule, a mudroom, a passageway flanked by bathrooms, an office, coat closets, and at last into the vast McCarran kitchen. There was a cobblestone fireplace, a bar setup, and a conversation area in front of a huge television set. The McCarran food prep was first class: ovens, dishwashers, compactors—able to handle the most intimate meal or the grandest catered affair.

Glennis found a teakettle and fired up the range. She took Dasha's coat and led her to the couch. Dasha could tell birdwatching was the furthest thing from Glennis's mind.

Open slowly, she counseled herself. Let her talk.

"We're getting a lot of activity at the bird feeder," Dasha told Glennis, who had joined her on the divan.

"That's nice," Glennis said. "That woodpecker I told you about last time hasn't come back." The McCarran's housekeeper was opening up a bit. Dasha could tell she'd been aching for human contact.

"No, they're very territorial. He probably lives in the Audubon and only pops over for a visit. Have you seen any of those black-poll warblers we saw last time?"

"Dozens," said Glennis, warming to the pleasant distraction of simple companionship.

"Aren't they wonderful?" said Dasha. "Come over to our feeder and you'll see more."

"I'll try," said Glennis. "I don't seem to be getting much of a break these days."

"Official duties?"

"Mr. McCarran has been spending a lot of his time in the country. Mrs. McCarran has remained in the city."

Another breach? thought Dasha. "I hope everything's okay," she told Glennis earnestly.

"I think it's just the stresses caused by son John," Glennis confessed.

"Having difficulty finding his footing?" asked Dasha. "It's not uncommon with some young people."

"I think it's a bit more serious than that. Crazy friends. Lots of parties. Doing poorly at school. I overheard his father speaking with a psychologist. He thinks his behavior is manic. Please don't tell anyone."

"You know I'm a tomb. Wouldn't dream of telling a soul," said Dasha. "I hear loud music across the fence from time to time. Has the young lord been entertaining?"

Glennis sagged at the recollection. "Out on the beach. Before the weather turned. It was terrible. Drinking whiskey right out of the bottle. Smoking marijuana. Boys and girls drunk and disorderly."

"Anyone get hurt?" asked Dasha, driving the point like a nail. Glennis looked down and away, a subtle sign of anxiety that caused Dasha's heart to soar.

"Yes," she said weakly, a weight removed.

"How serious?" asked Dasha.

"I'm not sure," said Glennis, wringing out a handkerchief, delighted to be telling someone, anyone, about that awful night. "A girl just disappeared. I saw John and one of his friends carry her up from the beach and over the lawn. She was unconscious, like a rag. They were trying to get her to the back of the property by the carriage house."

"Do you know who it was?" Dasha asked, understanding the delicacy of the moment, her softness freeing Glennis to convey the hard truth.

"One of John's girlfriends," said Glennis. Dasha could tell Glennis wanted to work in some distance between herself and the mysterious girl.

"He met her in India when he went out there on a summer tour. He invited her to the States. She seemed nice." Dasha's hypothesis was finding firmer ground.

"Do you remember her name?" asked Dasha.

"No. He never introduced us, and I never asked her name. Didn't want to. They come and go. I don't like getting attached. But I did come to know her."

Odd, thought Dasha. Glennis had come to know her, but not know her.

"John doesn't like me...hasn't since I came here when he was a little boy. I made him pick up his toys."

Ah, the beknighted scion, thought Dasha. "How long was she a guest?"

"A week, ten days. It was pleasant at first. Then they'd had some words. Then it became...awkward." Glennis was holding something back. Something pivotal.

"Then their wild party," said Dasha.

"Most of the kids had already left. It was just John, and that other boy."

Glennis—sweating, on the verge of tears—nodded toward Dasha, her confidante. She'd been yearning to tell someone the truth. Then she froze, a look of terror on her face.

She looked past Dasha to the entranceway.

Dasha turned around and saw Robert, McCarran's handyman. Tall, angular, muscles bulging, the man was stock-still, fixing Glennis in a menacing gaze.

The most useful implement in Dasha's toolbox was the frail, slightly batty exterior she could assume on demand.

"Oh my," she piped up as Robert's huge, rangy form glided into the McCarran kitchen. "Where are my manners? I am Dasha Petrov, your neighbor next door." She struggled out of her seat on the couch and advanced toward the glowering man now dominating the room. He seemed to look past the old woman who had invaded their home and continued to fix Glennis in a look of unquenched venom. Dasha appraised the man and took his measure in the fleeting moments she had available. A blank expression, military haircut, older, something of a sag in the features of his face, especially on each side of his mouth, frown lines.

Dead eyes.

Dasha maneuvered herself between the man and Glennis, holding her chestnut stick. She put out her hand, and he took it reluctantly, attempting to uphold civilities despite an awkwardness cleaving the air.

"Robert," said the man. "I work with Mr. McCarran."

"Yes, I am surprised we haven't met. Glennis and I are old bird-watching friends. I was just returning a book she loaned me. My sister had a stroke and I am studying homeopathy as a way to perk her up a bit." Robert glanced at the coffee table and saw the volume resting on a corner. That security alert consuming his brain quieted, but only slightly.

"That's nice," he said without enthusiasm. "Glennis, can we speak?" Glennis looked down and away. Dasha knew the look of fright. She had seen it often, even felt it a time or two.

"Yes, I must really be leaving," Dasha said. Then, attempting to shelter Glennis in the only way she knew, she continued, "Glennis darling. I am going to call you later. When you have a free moment I really do wish you'd come over and take a look at our bird feeder. I am having difficulty getting the seed mixed just right."

Robert needed to know the neighbor lady would be looking after Glennis. The two women had a connection, and if the connection were to break, it would call unwanted attention to the McCarran household.

Dasha smiled and waved and worked her way toward the door. "I will call you, Glennis. We can get together. How about tomorrow?"

She made her way back through the hedge and found Galina asleep on the couch in front of the fire, a book and her glasses on her lap.

After what Galina had seen, after what she'd lived through, her sister was safe, and Dasha intended to keep it that way.

30

The Power of a Name

What was her name?

Everyone had one. It was your label, your brand, your badge. It was the simple, grand device that differentiated, yet bound, all the peoples of the earth.

DeFranco was seized by the idea of giving the victim back her name. His wife gone, his house burned and flattened, his kids at school and oblivious, soon to be shocked and shattered. The least he could do was to find the name of the dead girl at the center of this.

He got back from the safe-deposit box and made it upstairs to his cubicle, heart racing.

He needed to work the phones and started dialing. The department really did need to upgrade from the old rotary dialers to the new push-buttons.

For anyone, even a small-town police officer, confronting the federal bureaucracy could be daunting. He'd start with Customs and Border Protection headquarters in DC, then see if he could find a CBP number for the primary local gateway, John F. Kennedy International Airport. Down in the stack of numbers was the relevant listing, with sublistings for day supervisors, night supervisors, and public affairs.

He dialed the day supervisor, got an agent on the first ring, and identified himself.

"Police inquiry?" said the young woman on the other end of the line. "You'll need to speak to my supervisor. Please hold." It was as he'd expected—a bureaucratic shuffle. He needed to be patient as he hacked through the thicket.

"Officer Jankowski," grumbled the next voice on the line.

"Sir, this is Detective Anthony DeFranco of the Westport Connecticut Police criminal investigation branch. I am looking for a person who came through Immigration between two and six weeks ago. She is a possible homicide victim. First name Kali, K-A-L-I. No last name. Possibly arriving from India, Pakistan, or South Asia. Approximately 110 pounds. Five foot four, five foot five."

"Hold it," said Jankowski, unable to conceal his exasperation. "I need to find a pen. Our system is down. As soon as it comes back online I can check. You say Kali and South Asia is all you have?"

"That is correct."

"Can you hold or do you want me to call you?"

"I can hold."

"Might take a while."

"Not going anywhere. This is the most important thing on my desk," said DeFranco.

He went on hold and listened to scratchy Muzak and doodled on a pad.

Jankowski came back on. "Bunch of records to go through here and I am being dragged off to a meeting. Let me fool with this some more and get back to you."

"Here is my direct line," said DeFranco, wondering if he would even have a direct line in the building when Talbot got finished with him. "But let me have *your* line also and I will call you by, say, five p.m. if I haven't heard from you." Jankowski gave him a number and extension, then rang off.

DeFranco's phone rang almost immediately. It was the arson investigator—a contractor who worked for several municipalities.

"Harris," the man said. "I think we ought to meet at the scene." He sounded worried. DeFranco grabbed his trench coat and found the keys to the Crown Vic on the communal hook used for official vehicles. The car was free, a simple comforting luxury in this time of concerted stress. He hadn't been back to High Gate Road since the night of the fire.

Harris was there when he arrived. His house was reduced to blackened sticks protruding from the ground at odd angles, the bones of a corpse, with a spindly brick chimney piercing the sky. After a career in public safety, he was used to the heavy sadness caused by calamity's aftermath. But the emotion of seeing their base camp, their oasis, reduced to this sorry state took him by surprise.

What was that squeezing in his chest that came unbidden? The sudden heavy breathing? Were those tears clouding his eyes?

The last time he cried was when he and the kids laid poor Julie in the ground, so he was surprised at this sudden visitation by his own humanity.

Harris came down to the road, hand extended, and DeFranco took it meekly. DeFranco had to look away. He wiped his face on his coat sleeve and Harris, having experienced this reaction, was kind enough to turn back toward the catastrophe and the business at hand. DeFranco slowly approached the hideous mess. The second floor had collapsed onto the first, but the first floor had not descended into the basement, so they could walk on the subfloor.

"I've been all over this so I think it's safe," said Harris.

DeFranco tried to speak but nothing came out. He tried to recognize where the rooms had been, where they'd put their Christmas tree, hung their pictures. The blackened box of the television set was in a far corner. Somewhere near the back were the remains of their kitchen, appliances scorched and ruined.

"Arson," said Harris. "And a professional job of it too." DeFranco listened absently.

What would he tell the kids?

"I think it was a spark from a purposely overloaded wall outlet that caught a curtain on fire. Here's a piece of it. Smell that?" He held it up to his nose. "That's some kind of kerosene or lantern fuel. Whoever did this didn't splash it around. They soaked it in."

DeFranco was starting to pay attention.

"But what really set this off was over here," said Harris. He walked across the debris to what had been the kitchen. The gas range was standing in the middle of the floor, walls around it gone.

"Right here you can see where somebody took a channel lock and unscrewed the gas line. See where that brass flange is all scratched? That's a quick, dirty job of popping off the line and filling the house with gas. It was fully involved when the company arrived. She went quick."

DeFranco looked at the range, the flange, his daughter's burned field hockey stick, his son's blackened baseball mitt. They'd been in a closet near the back door.

He wanted to vomit and got himself to the driveway before bending over and losing his breakfast. Harris looked away. DeFranco's job as a father was to protect his kids, his home. He'd failed.

DeFranco came back up on the foundation and gathered himself.

"I'll need photos," he said casually. "Have to match the grooves on that fixture with the tool that made them."

"Already on it," said Harris.

"And I'll need you to remove that part and put it in the evidence locker at Westport PD."

"No sweat, but I have to ask you something."

"Shoot."

"Do you have any enemies?"

"I didn't before a few days ago," said DeFranco.

31

Safe Harbor

After his regrettable hour on High Gate Road, he spent the rest of the day aboard *Paisano*, reading a book, trying not to think. He couldn't go back to the office. At 8:00 p.m. he went to a Kohl's department store to stock up on some clothing, buying a small duffel to put it in. At 10:00 p.m. he drove the Crown Vic to Norwalk and News 12 Connecticut, waiting patiently next to Tracy Taggart's VW until her shift was through. He didn't want to disturb her while she worked. She came out of the building around 11:30, warily at first, then brightening at the sight of DeFranco leaning against the fender of her car.

He really looked at her, noticing everything. She wore black boots with two-inch heels, a sophisticated camel overcoat, and a wide-brim hat. Her smile was a brilliant white on this drizzly night—and he was astonished this smart, attractive high achiever was walking briskly in his direction.

How did he get so lucky?

"God, I am so glad you're here," she said.

"I really don't want to let you out of my sight," said DeFranco.

"Tony, we've both got jobs," said Tracy, protesting. "It's impractical."

"I don't want anything to happen."

"I think I've shown you I can take care of myself."

"No question, but it looks like we're taking care of each other," he said.

"I don't usually go this fast."

"How fast do you usually go?" he asked, then kicked himself.

"I've had a handful of boyfriends. I'm not a kid anymore. Guys I've been with aren't really interested in who I am," she said.

"You're a man of substance, Tony. And let's say I'm growing very fond of you." He was waiting for a "but…" and decided to get out in front of it.

"But we have to get real, Tracy," he interjected. "We've been thrown into an intense situation. Let's get ourselves through this and then see what happens."

She smiled at him, relieved, and took his hand. "When this is over, do you think we'll have anything left to talk about?"

"Sure hope so," said DeFranco. "But let's not sweat it until we have to. In the meantime, I've grown to depend on you. And oh, I love sleeping with you."

She laughed. "We're a lot alike, then."

"So do you want to go back to *Paisano* tonight. It's your call. Whatever you decide, I just want you to feel comfortable and safe."

"I love *Paisano*," said Tracy, kissing his cheek.

32

Fired for Cause

Interesting that his usual pile of papers, notes, and scraps were all gone—even his illicit bottle of Jack Daniels. That's how they'll get me, thought DeFranco. Drinking on the job. He still had a typewriter and a phone, a local phone directory, and reference books for contacting state and federal law enforcement.

At least that wheel's turning, thought DeFranco, just as he felt the overheated presence of Chief Talbot over his left shoulder.

"DeFranco," said Talbot. "My office. Now."

Showtime, thought DeFranco, as he followed the corpulent form of Talbot through the warren of cubicles toward the front of the building and the chief's glass-walled domain. DeFranco stopped at the coffeepot en route just to add a tincture of civil disobedience.

"Alcohol in the office, Tony? You know that's against regulations," said Talbot.

"Is that what I'm being charged with?" asked DeFranco quietly.

"Among other things."

"I presume you've got a bill of particulars I can respond to."

"It's being assembled. For now the booze is enough to get your badge and gun and ask you to leave the building."

"I presume you've checked all the other desk drawers out there," said DeFranco, knowing full well there were shorties and flasks and other paraphernalia in the desks and lockers among the ranks.

"I have," said Talbot, "and your bottle of Jack Daniels is the only one I found." DeFranco had to hand it him; Talbot was an infighter.

"Good to know. Next call will be my lawyer and my union representative," said DeFranco.

"Suit yourself, asshole."

"I'm going to have a busy afternoon," said DeFranco. "I've got Immigration calling me back with the name of the dead girl in the dumpster. Then I'll be meeting with the FBI in New Haven. We'll be talking about corruption in this department. I'll be fitting in News 12 Connecticut to start laying out the real story of the headless girl. Now that I'm a civilian I will be able to exercise my First Amendment rights more freely. The first selectman and the representative town meeting will be interested in your personal role in this. You're covering up for somebody. Oh, and don't forget. I've still got the girl's trachea. It's got the sea glass pushed inside it. That's what choked her to death."

Talbot's jaw dropped.

"I've also got a clean print of the right index finger of the person who shoved it down the girl's throat. It refutes everything Moriarty told us. I've got the dead girl's DNA. We'll get a match when we find her next of kin. Customs and Immigration will be helping me with that. I'm going after Moriarty and Mortensen and anyone else involved."

Talbot grew quiet. DeFranco thought it was the look of self-assuredness slowly leaking out of the chief's overly confident balloon. But the chief just needed a brief pause to find his voice.

"Where is that evidence?" shouted Talbot. "It needs to be secured in the evidence locker and the state's attorney needs to be informed."

"It's secure," said DeFranco. "The state's attorney is tainted. So's state CID. The fingerprint is going to the FBI, along with the girl's trachea. As soon as I get a name from Immigration I'll make my notifications."

"You'll be impersonating an officer," said Talbot. "I'll add that to the charges. Badge and gun. On my desk now. You're fired." Talbot had summoned some inner reserve.

DeFranco smiled. He unbuckled his ankle holster with the snubbie tucked in and laid it on the chief's desk. He took off his shoulder rig with the new Glock, put it alongside, and placed his ID and badge next to his service weapons. The snubbie was an old friend and he'd hate to see it go, but parting with the new Glock was painful.

"You don't have a permit to carry a gun in the state of Connecticut," said Talbot. "I catch you with a gun I'll add weapons charges. We're already up to evidence tampering and obstruction."

"You're the chief," said DeFranco. "Just know that Curtis Jones at the ME's office was murdered trying to protect the evidence of the headless girl. Whoever killed her killed him too. I've got evidence of one killer at both murder scenes. They're making a list, Chief. I'm on it. So are you. Anybody connected with this case—and the cover-up."

"Fuck you, DeFranco," said the chief, the color starting to drain from his face. There was a knock on the door and Madge from public affairs stuck her head in. She seemed a bit flustered.

"Chief. Hartford is on the line. It's about Inspector Moriarty. Something awful has happened."

33

Moriarty

She liked working late. The daytime hours were always filled with meetings, paperwork, endless decisions. At night she could put her head down and wade through the avalanche of material heading her way in a time of budget constraints and diminishing resources. She'd lost two assistants in the latest round of layoffs, so it fell to her to make sure the five investigations on her desk maintained forward motion.

There was the string of bank robberies surrounding New London; the child molester, as yet uncaught, near New Haven; the embezzlement case in Greenwich; the discovery of skeletal remains in the Litchfield woods…and that dumpster girl down in Westport.

That investigation was going nowhere, she was glad to note. She got the impression Mortensen preferred it that way. Mortensen had supplied the narrative and she'd gone along with it. Who's to say the girl wasn't a victim of gang violence? And the tox report *was* inconclusive. Now that she had the body away from Goldberg and in the state morgue things would cool down. She could take her time. It would probably blow over. She had to concede it was very gracious of Mortensen to make sure her son's second semester at Babson was paid for. No quid pro quo, mind you, but a wonderful gesture from a fellow public servant. She would let the investigation ride along for a while, and would rely on Talbot to keep that detective (DeFranco?) under control.

It was dark out and she could tell the brisk cadence associated with the twelfth floor, home of the brass, had dialed back to a more nocturnal rhythm. Around 8:00 p.m., the office grew blessedly silent. She could sip her decaf tea and read her reports and prepare the memoranda she would fax to field offices on the morrow. Her estranged husband was out on the road, quietly getting himself stewed in the darkened lounge of some nondescript Holiday Inn. Served her right for marrying a high school jock, whose ambition only rose as high as the low bar of itinerant salesman. She would really need to get around to filing for divorce. But then she thought about her son in college, and how deferring this plan until graduation might be the better option.

She was thus ruminating on life and work and disappointment when she looked up from her desk and saw two uniformed police officers come quietly through the door. Her assistant had left at 5:01. She looked at her watch. It was 8:15 p.m. and the rest of the floor was still.

"Can I help you?" she asked the first cop in. In that fleeting instant she relied on her police instincts, initially honed as a Hartford patrolman. Number One was six feet tall, standard blue uniform with tie, wearing body armor under his duty shirt. She couldn't see a municipality patch on his shoulder unless he turned sideways, but he wore a full utility belt, including a holstered semiauto pistol, probably a Glock, magazine pouches, a Taser, a radio linked up to a microphone clipped to an epaulet. Number Two looked the same, a bit shorter maybe. Anyway, these officers of the law obviously had no trouble getting through security in the lobby.

"Are you Inspector Tamara Moriarty?" asked Number One.

The instant she said yes, Number Two withdrew his Taser, snapped the cartridge with high-voltage wires and penetrators on the muzzle, and fired it at close range into Moriarty's upper torso. Two probes flew out from the cartridge and struck her in the upper chest and the quad muscle of her left leg. She'd been tased before, in training, so she wasn't surprised by the instantaneous convulsions the Taser produced. But she was overwhelmed at how her throat closed, and how the scream she was trying to manage came out as a choking *zeeeee* sound as her legs and arms flailed involuntarily in her leather chair. Her eyes were wide open and she knew precisely what was happening to her, even though she was completely paralyzed.

Number One removed her large-frame Smith & Wesson revolver from her waistband holster and unclipped her badge, laying them both on her desk. He took an envelope out of his shirt pocket and laid it next to her badge and gun.

On the outside of the envelope was typed *To My Family*.

Number Two turned off the Taser and she slumped in her chair. Her eyes closed tightly and she caught her breath. "Who the fuck are you," she managed through clenched teeth.

"We represent some friends of yours," said Number One. "They want you to sign this release so we can dispose of the body you brought in—the dumpster girl from Westport." The cop produced a document, put a pen in her hand, and moved her hand over to the paper.

"What is this?" she asked weakly.

"We need her back," said Number Two. "Sign here. You've got ten seconds or I tase you again." Moriarty thought of her son and her responsibilities. She didn't care about the goddamn girl in the dumpster. She followed Number One's index finger and found the right field on the release form.

She signed her name.

She sensed Number Two behind her opening the window. She could feel an October wind come through—cold but quiet, not enough to disturb the papers on her desk. Number One extracted the two electrodes from Moriarty's torso and upper leg.

Both the uniformed officers reached under Moriarty's shoulders, picked her up out of her chair and dragged her to the open window. She tried to move her legs and arms or just scream but the only thing she could do was keep her eyes wide open and perceive every second of her last living moments as they sat her down on the window sill, then casually, wordlessly, pushed her off.

The last thing she saw as she sailed downward with the chest-squeezing force of gravity were two clean-cut white faces watching her go. The last mortal image lodged in Tamara Moriarty's brain—before she landed on the roof of a parked Connecticut State Police cruiser—were the words *Westport Police Department, To Protect and to Serve* on Number One's shoulder patch.

34

Conspiracy

Talbot was on the phone, his swivel chair turned away from DeFranco, who sat opposite, drumming his fingers on the desk. He listened to the chief's side of the conversation.

"Hmm. Jumped out her office window? Last night? Left a note? She'd just signed a morgue release for our homicide victim? Body picked up by two of *my* officers? Names? They must have signed for it. What do you mean you can't read it? Unintelligible?"

That got DeFranco's attention. The dumpster girl was once again in transit, this time at the hands of two uniformed Westport police officers?

Talbot turned his chair back toward DeFranco. His face was drawn, the color drained. DeFranco saw the man's dilemma. He represented nothing more than dissension in the ranks. But now the chief might have outright criminals on his payroll. Disloyalty and betrayal had infiltrated the department. "Don't tell me," said DeFranco. "Moriarty killed herself and left a note. Just like Curtis Jones. Anybody connected with this case is on a list, Chief."

"No evidence she *didn't* kill herself," said Talbot.

"We'll need to see that pathology report," said DeFranco.

"It's being faxed over now."

"I'm telling you, anybody can write a fucking suicide note," said DeFranco, disgusted.

"Take your guns and badge, DeFranco," said Talbot. "I'm putting you back to work. We need to know who picked up that body, and where they took it."

DeFranco estimated he'd been fired for approximately twenty minutes. "Couldn't agree more," he said. "But she's probably in a fresh hole somewhere between here and Hartford."

"I want to know who was off-duty yesterday and might have had time to drive up there. I want to know what vehicle they used. I want to know if there's a connection between the missing cadaver and Tamara Moriarty's death."

"You're going to call Mortensen?" asked DeFranco.

"I'll get to the fucking state's attorney," said Talbot.

The man looked flustered and mortified, thought DeFranco. The chief's in on it. Dasha was right. You can see it in his face. He's been paid to look the other way.

The chief elevated his burgeoning girth out of his chair and put on his blazer and Burberry trench coat over that. He stalked away from his office and DeFranco looked out the chief's window to see him storm to his coveted black Cadillac DeVille positioned in the chief's special parking place at the front of the building. Talbot backed out and drove down Jesup Street. DeFranco turned away and started to walk toward his cubicle. He picked up his guns and badge before he left the chief's lair, failing to notice the green Dodge Ram pickup truck falling into formation behind the chief's retreating Cadillac.

35

Rajastan

Immigration could wait. He needed to speak to Tracy. He dialed her number at the TV station and learned she was out on assignment. Her stalker was still out there. He needed to hear her voice.

Then the phone rang and Jankowski from Immigration came on the line.

"Detective DeFranco?"

"Yes?"

"We have an Indian female, first name Kali, last name Patel, clearing Immigration at Kennedy on September thirtieth," said the CBP officer.

"Thanks very much," said DeFranco, senses tuned. "Did her inbound Immigration card give her home address and her destination in the US?"

"Yes and no," said Jankowski. "Prepare to copy."

"Hold on." DeFranco grabbed a pad and pen from Officer McKurdy's cubicle next door. "I'm back."

"Okay. Here we go. Kali Patel, 278 Azad Marg Road, Jaipur, Rajastan."

"Do you have a phone number for this residence?" asked DeFranco, heart racing.

"Stand by," said Jankowski. "Plus 91 141 222 0206."

"Last question," said DeFranco. "Did she put a local contact down on her Immigration card?"

"Not specific," said Jankowski. "She just put down Connecticut and the screener at the desk just waved her through. Sometimes we get busy."

DeFranco was deflated. "Thanks, Officer. Appreciate it."

"Crap," muttered DeFranco. It was as creative an expletive he could muster at the moment.

The phone rang again, and in an instant he was speaking to Tracy Taggart. She was a bit out of breath, but tangibly alive.

"Her name *was* Kali," said DeFranco. "I just got off the phone with Immigration."

"Dasha was right," said Tracy, extending credit to their collaborator.

"I've got an address and phone number in Jaipur. I need to make a notification and get a sample for DNA analysis."

"I don't envy you that call," said Tracy. The significance of this responsibility reminded Tracy that a police officer's burden needed to be respected. But she also had a job to do. "Tony, I need to get something on the air about all this."

"Yes. It's time," said DeFranco. "But let's talk about it. We need to smoke out who caused this. We need a plan."

36

Tag

The truck was following too close, thought Talbot, as he raced his Cadillac down Long Lots Road. He was heading home to use the phone. He didn't want to use the phone at the office. He needed to speak with Mortensen about just what the hell was going on. Their plan was falling apart. But a pickup truck was right on his tail, matching his speed. The chief pressed harder on the accelerator and the truck just kept coming.

He tried going slower. Maybe the truck would pass. The truck slowed down too; now it was just inches from the Cadillac's bumper. That's when he saw what was coming, and he cursed his own fateful stupidity.

The truck moved into the opposite lane, then turned back toward the Cadillac's left rear fender. The truck accelerated and struck the rear of the chief's car from left to right, inducing the Cadillac to spin. The chief had seen the technique before in a seminar on offensive driving. In a high-speed chase, the last resort to stop a vehicle was to force the car being pursued into a spin. It was a police tactic. The driver of the truck knew the drill.

The Cadillac started veering left, tires screeching, belching rubber. The chief lost control and the vehicle exited the road, sliding backward down an embankment and coming to rest against a large maple tree. He was dazed, and a small rivulet of blood was working its way down his left cheek.

The Cadillac was aimed back up the embankment. He saw a tall man approach. The man had a hammer in one hand and a bottle of something in the other. He walked over to the chief's side of the vehicle. Talbot fumbled for his service weapon on his right hip, a Smith & Wesson .38 he rarely fired.

The man didn't say a word. He opened up the driver's side door of the Cadillac, unfastened Talbot's seat belt, and grabbed the chief by the tie. He pulled him half out of the vehicle.

The last thing Chief Talbot saw was the man's upraised arm, hammer in hand. Then cut to black. The man hit the chief in the head a second time. Then a third. Each time he struck the chief there was a spray of blood. He wanted to make sure the chief was dead, not satisfied until blood and brain poured down Talbot's stunned, speechless face. Then the man grabbed the back of Talbot's head and smashed it forward against the steering wheel. He did it again and again, leaving blood and brain and causing the wheel to crack.

Pleased with his work, the man took the bottle of Stolichnaya, opened it and pocketed the cap. He poured vodka down the chief's throat, and splashed it on his clothes for good measure. He put the cap back on and threw the bottle on the passenger side of the Cadillac. There was more gore on the end of the hammer and the man wiped it on the steering wheel.

Hammer still in hand, he walked back up the embankment to his waiting truck and threw the hammer in a plastic bag in the truck bed. He'd clean it later.

Now he needed to get back to the garage and tidy up. And he needed to get rid of the truck. Shaquille would be busy tonight.

And where were the detective and the TV reporter?

They were next.

37

Time and Space

Dasha had needed a day and a night to collect herself and to process. God she hated growing old. The meeting in the McCarran kitchen with Glennis had sparked a new, distinct line of inquiry. And while she was sad her friend had brushed against this new peril, she knew her investigation was now on a clearer path. That was the problem with assets in the field. They got themselves into trouble and sometimes got hurt. But you couldn't let their travails deter you from the mission.

She grabbed a Pentax 35-millimeter camera with a 50–100 zoom lens and loaded it with a roll of Tri-X black-and-white film, pained fingers managing the sprocket and advancing the film lever. It was now late afternoon. The light was fading, but she knew if she pushed the ASA she might be able to capture the images she needed. She walked out of the driveway, directly across Beachside Avenue, and found the path that entered the dense conifers of the Audubon Society arboretum. She knew it well. Walk straight north fifty yards, then straight west three hundred yards. That should put her directly behind the McCarran garage holding the potentate's rare car collection. It was directly across the street from the McCarran carriage house that abutted the avenue. The building was removed from the street and set back behind some dense forsythia. She'd glimpsed it from the road, of course, but out on her bird-watching treks she'd also observed the facility from the side and rear.

What did Glennis say? They'd carried the girl to the back of the property. She was limp like a rag.

Standing among the trees, her flashy Hermes scarf in a pocket and her Barbour coat blending into the greenery, she brought her binoculars up to study the back of the garage. It was a large, stoutly built structure with roll-up doors on either end. There were gas pumps in the back next to a concrete pad used for washing and detailing vehicles. There was a frame on wheels with a chain fall in the middle for extracting engines and other heavy parts. Two large gas bottles—one for oxygen, one for acetylene— were attached to a cutting torch one might need to separate a rusty exhaust pipe.

She needed to get closer.

She watched the building for a minute or so and noted the lack of activity. She walked out of the woods and moved with purpose toward the back of the garage, swinging her Pentax up and shooting the scene, cursing the low light and hoping she could document something of the space for DeFranco. There were two twisted coat hangers on the hooks of the engine puller, a blackened scorch mark on the concrete off to the side, roughly six feet long and three feet wide. She photographed it, noting flecks of gristle clinging to the concrete—like chunks of blackened bacon left over in a pan. She would need to get a sample of that.

She smelled the end of the cutting torch, trying to distinguish the odor of acetylene from the rest of the normal grease and grime you'd expect in a garage. She looked into the drain in the center of the concrete pad, trying to figure out where the runoff went—determining that it likely flowed into a septic field or similar impoundment.

She knew she needed to work quickly. She tried a side door next to the giant roll-up door. It was unlocked and she crept inside, knowing she was leaving the safety of her cover—a demented old woman out to watch the birds. She was crossing into the danger zone. An unlocked door usually meant someone would be back soon.

In the waning light she saw a dozen or so canvas-covered shapes—the McCarran collection, of course. She cursed the fact she hadn't had time to mount her flashgun. She would need to come back. She went to a workbench along one wall, with tools mounted on a pegboard. They'd been around awhile. Most of them were dirty, well used, even rusty. Wrenches. Socket sets. A channel lock. Several types of hammers.

Two implements stood out. A wood saw. Clean and shiny. And a hatchet, polished and sharpened. They weren't new, but they'd been brightened up. She took a photograph. A hammer was missing from its silhouette on the pegboard.

She poked around in a trash can with her stick. She got down on her hands and knees. She needed to look under the tool bench. She was trying to find the unwanted, the discarded, the abandoned...anything.

"God, the *light*," she fumed.

There, off behind a leg of the workbench, was a clump of black, human hair. She picked it up and put it in a pocket of her coat.

She heard a vehicle on gravel and she moved toward the door. The beam of a single headlight reached from the driveway into the Audubon conifers to her left. She walked outside and turned right toward the corner of the garage, propelled by a dormant energy suddenly released. A green pickup truck came up to the concrete pad just as she disappeared around the building. She peeked around the corner and saw the left front headlight of the truck hanging by a wire. The right front fender was dented. There was black paint on the truck's chrome bumper.

Robert.

He exited the vehicle and slammed the door, furious. He picked a plastic bag out of the truck bed and placed it near the drain in the middle of the concrete pad. Then he uncoiled a garden hose, stripped off his clothing, and walked naked over to the side of the building. He found a barrel, threw in his clothes and some broken lumber, poured in some gasoline from a can and set it alight. The fire illuminated the peculiar scene of Robert, naked and glistening, as he turned on the tap to the garden hose.

A strong one, thought Dasha. He'll be tough to take down when the time comes.

Robert stood in the gathering chill over the drain, hosing himself off. He spent time cleaning the mud off his athletic shoes. Then he opened the plastic bag and washed the hammer.

Out, damn spot! thought Dasha, summoning Lady Macbeth as she breathed in the cool air of dusk.

Then Robert did something so puzzling she took in a sudden, involuntary breath. He got into the pickup to start it. And while the fire in the barrel roared away, he opened the doors and trained the hose inside—seats, overhead, dash, lingering a bit over the steering wheel. Water went in one side of the cockpit and out the other. He stood there, apparently satisfied, then went into the garage. Dasha heard him clattering around and watched him re-emerge—dressed in jeans and a fleece jacket. He put a mountain bike in the back of the truck, shut off the lights, and drove the pickup away from the McCarran garage.

Someone died violently tonight, thought Dasha, little realizing it wasn't a single victim.

It was two. And over two days.

She walked quietly back into the forest, Constantine's chestnut stick reaching out, planting itself firmly in the ground, showing her the way.

38

Probe

DeFranco was at his desk reading Tamara Moriarty's faxed autopsy report. It was the extent of her injuries that amazed him. Back broken in three places. Spinal chord severed at the cervical vertebrae. The malleolus of the tibia and fibula sheered off, causing twin compound ankle fractures. Internal injuries, including a collapsed and bleeding spleen, dissected aorta, ruptured liver.

All of this damage had happened in a millisecond. Massive. Complete. Instantly fatal.

The photographs coming through the high-speed printer didn't do justice to the circumstances. The first picture showed Inspector Moriarty lying in repose on the dented roof of the cruiser, the light bar cracked and broken under her neck. Her ankles were at right angles to her legs and her back was twisted.

The expression on her face was strange, thought DeFranco.

Awareness.

Not bewildered or puzzled. She looked enlightened.

The photos kept coming, including an autopsy shot showing Moriarty on a slab, naked, those sightless eyes somehow cognizant. Her torso was misshapen and it was hard to look at her leg bones protruding from her ankles.

But what caught DeFranco's eye were the perfect marks on Moriarty's abdomen and upper leg—two raw dots that looked like she'd been pricked by an ice pick. Something mechanical—a tool, a probe—had caused those marks. He put the fax copies in a file, not quite able to get the sight of Tamara Moriarty out of his mind.

39

Scene of the Crime

He had to hand it to Madge.

When the call came in about the fatal auto accident on Long Lots Road—a Signal 60 in local police parlance—she started working the phones to capture the essentials. She knew the media would be calling, looking for answers. He overheard Madge gamely pursue the particulars with the EMTs, the fire department rescue company—at last the investigating officer. DeFranco had been carrying the Moriarty file back to the chief's office. He wanted to share it with Talbot when he came back to the station.

That's when DeFranco heard a stifled scream and the sound of shock and emotion catch in Madge's throat.

"Oh no," she cried. DeFranco watched her hang up the phone and look for someone, anyone, with whom she could share the awful news. It was if she needed to expel the information as soon as she'd absorbed it. It was too big to contain.

"It's Chief Talbot," said Madge, looking into DeFranco's eyes. "He's been in an accident. They think he's dead."

It's not like there was any love lost for the man, thought DeFranco. But he never wished him dead.

"Who's on the scene?" he asked Madge.

"McKurdy and Hughes."

"Okay. I'm going out there." DeFranco walked over to the radio room and told dispatch to call the team and have them secure the scene. "If the chief is DOA, I don't want him moved until I get there."

"Roger," said the sergeant on duty, who conveyed DeFranco's directive to the patrolmen.

DeFranco went upstairs to get his coat, taking a second to fasten his snubbie to his ankle and slip into his new shoulder rig for the Glock. And where the hell was his camera? He found it in a cupboard over his desk. He found some boxes of Kodak Ektachrome, adequate for night work, and his flashgun. He checked it to make sure the batteries were fresh.

He drove the Crown Vic out to Long Lots Road and soon saw the familiar sight of flashing red and blue lights, traffic slowed to a crawl, and officers of the law milling around, keeping the press at bay. DeFranco saw the satellite van for News 12 Connecticut and hoped his "colleague" would be on hand. Cops and reporters. They always seemed to rendezvous at someone else's misfortune. He saw her, of course, and his heart took a little leap before he collected himself and returned to business. She was talking to an EMT when DeFranco approached.

"Hi," he said simply.

Tracy turned. The smile that normally greeted him was gone. A man was dead just down the embankment.

"Bad day," she returned. "When can we talk?"

"It's going to be a long night."

"I've got two hours before Danny, my cameraman, and I have to upload for the eleven o'clock."

"It will be at least that long, but I will try to get you something you can use. Then there's the rest of it we need to cover. Did you hear about Moriarty?"

"Don't tell me," said Tracy.

"She's dead. Apparent suicide last night. Went out her twelfth-story office window. Now Talbot," said DeFranco.

"You used the word 'apparent.' Do you think Moriarty was murdered?"

"Can't say. But Jones, Moriarty, Talbot—all connected to Kali. All dead. It can't be a coincidence."

"Could this auto accident *not* be an accident?"

"Won't know until I take a closer look," said DeFranco. "One thing for sure. We need to get your story straight about Kali and we need to get it on the air. It might be the only way you and I stay alive."

"Jesus, Tony. This is huge."

"I know. Let me take a look at what we've got here. Give you something for tonight. Then work on the bigger picture in the morning."

"We have to find Dasha," said Tracy.

"Hate to say it. But you're right. Let me go down the embankment and see about the chief. I'll be right back."

DeFranco walked down the road, a solitary man in a trench coat with a job to do. The gaggle of press and civilians parted the way, and after a brief chat with McKurdy, DeFranco stepped over a broken guardrail, alone.

The trunk of Chief Talbot's prized Cadillac was butted up against a tree. Damage to the vehicle appeared superficial—just the scrapes you'd expect after smashing through a few saplings. DeFranco skidded down to the open driver's side door and tried to take in the scene as a whole before breaking it down.

What would Curtis do? he asked himself. There was a time a few days ago when he recoiled from the ugly underside, leaving Curtis to do the dirty work. Now he was in it up to his neck. He had to do his job, and also protect Tracy. He knew which task was more important, but in truth, both objectives had now become one.

He flicked on his Mini Maglite and the horrible end of Chief Talbot flashed in front of his eyes. The chief's forehead was… God, just *bashed* in, with blood and telltale gray matter everywhere. There was a spray of blood and gore on the steering wheel and on the car's cloth ceiling liner. The smell of vodka drifted upward and DeFranco saw the half-consumed liter bottle on the passenger side. He knew the chief enjoyed a cocktail or two, but he wasn't one to drink and drive—or swill and drive in this case.

Already things weren't adding up.

It was the sheer violence of the chief's head injuries that both appalled and fascinated DeFranco. To crack a skull like that would take tremendous force, and the lack of damage to the vehicle suggested the energy that caused the head wounds wasn't consistent with the energy of the crash.

He looked around the car. Other than the stove-in trunk lid pushed against the tree, the vehicle was potentially driveable. If the chief had smacked his head against the steering wheel, you'd expect the front of the car to be smashed in all the way up to the windshield pillars.

He didn't like the look of that left rear quarter panel. It was pushed in almost delicately, and there was green paint streaking across the dent.

This vehicle had been involved in a collision, he quickly concluded. He went to work with his Nikon.

He went back up to the cockpit. Why wasn't the chief wearing his seat belt? He leaned in with his flashlight to get a better look at the chief's battered face. The stench of vodka was overwhelming. The chief's mouth was open and there were pools of unswallowed alcohol. DeFranco shined his light on the utterly ghastly crack across the Chief's forehead and saw first one, then another, half-inch round circles in the center of the fissure where the man's blood and brains were erupting.

"What the hell caused that?" said DeFranco out loud to himself.

"Caused what, sir?" said McKurdy, who had drifted into the scene behind him.

"Careful where you step, McKurdy. Go up to the Crown Vic and get the dental stone to make a shoe cast, and the dust kit. Is the ME here yet?"

"Yes, they're waiting up on the road," said the junior officer.

"Send them down with a body bag and a gurney. Also, call a wrecker and arrange to have the vehicle towed back to the station on Jesup." DeFranco rattled off instructions, a bit more patient with the patrolman now that he was more confident with his crime scene protocols.

"You think this is more than just an accident?" asked McKurdy.

"Not sure yet. I'll want Dr. Goldberg's opinion." No use in raising an alarm, thought DeFranco.

"Of course," said McKurdy, who scrambled back up the embankment.

DeFranco needed to go back up to the road to fulfill his obligation to News 12 Connecticut. He found Tracy and pulled her away.

"Chief Talbot is about as dead as you can get," he said, grabbing Tracy's elbow as she took in an extra breath.

"Did he just run off the road?" she asked.

"That will be my official position. Tonight. Subject to change… when I know more. But, Tracy, I am going to tell you something, and again I have to ask you to keep this quiet. For one more night. I promise. I think he was pushed off the road. And I think whoever did that smashed his face in with a hammer." Tracy's lower lip started to quiver, but she quickly composed herself.

"God, Tony. Another one?"

"Please trust me, Tracy. It will work out okay. But I need to get the guy who did this, and I need you to help me. We can't spook him."

Two nights ago he thought Tracy might abandon their pact, run around him to report the real story of the headless girl. But tonight she looked DeFranco right in the eye and said, "We have to get him, Tony. We have to. We're next."

"Here's what I suggest," said DeFranco. "You and Danny get some B-roll. You can shoot down the embankment while the ME team works, but I would appreciate it if you would refrain from photographing the deceased."

"Only decent thing to do," she said.

"When you get your B-roll, do your stand-up here. You can report Chief Gerald Talbot died from injuries sustained in a one-vehicle accident on Long Lots Road. I have to give the ME crew some instructions, then get back to the station and make my calls. I need to get the chaplain and speak to the chief's wife, in person. Come to the building when you're done out here and I'll give you an interview. It'll be an exclusive. You can upload from there."

"I'm on it," said Tracy, her expression downcast and serious.

DeFranco knew it was difficult for her to put her journalistic duties on hold.

"Don't worry," he said. "You'll be able to start working on your piece very soon—probably within twenty-four hours. And you'll have all of it."

"Just don't let me get scooped, Tony. Please. The chief of police has just been murdered."

"I know this is hard, Tracy," he said. "But we've got to get the people who did this. I think they are capable and well funded. And they're an extreme flight risk. Wherever they go, they'll kill again. We have to stop them."

40

Broad Shoulders

Madge was too upset to talk to the press, so DeFranco became the defacto public affairs department that night. His first job was to notify next of kin and that went as dismally as he predicted. The department's official chaplain was an unctuous pleaser, the Right Reverend James Burroughs, whose real income derived from counseling young married suburbanites on the verge of divorce. DeFranco picked him up and they drove wordlessly to the Talbot residence, bypassing the mess on Long Lots Road. Mrs. Talbot had been busy making the chief's dinner when the front doorbell rang, and she answered it with a dish towel over her shoulder. Gray, frumpy, looking forward to the chief's well-subsidized retirement, she answered the door with a beaming smile that vanished at the sight of DeFranco and the chaplain, both of whom she knew from departmental gatherings.

"Can I help you?" she asked, somehow knowing with wild, tear-flooded eyes the real reason for their visit. It went downhill from there and DeFranco managed to get the Talbot's neighbors on scene to help the missus manage the remainder of the worst night of her life.

He drove Burroughs back to his rectory and made it back to the station to find Tracy and her cameraman waiting patiently.

"Took longer than I expected," said DeFranco.

"We're good. We've got most of it uploaded and I've got an editing team ready to catch this interview and splice it in. We'll make the eleven o'clock with time to spare."

DeFranco was pleased. Westport needed to hear from the voice of authority about a catastrophe that involved all of them.

It would get worse in coming days when he intended to convey the real nature of Chief Talbot's demise.

"Let's go inside and find a decent backdrop," said DeFranco, suddenly concerned about appearances. He was representing the department.

They went into the foyer where the desk sergeant greeted the public. A wooden bench, a state flag, and Old Glory occupied the background. Tracy set up the shot, a three-quarters front view of DeFranco's head and shoulders with space for the chyron, Danny shooting obliquely from the left.

"Just look at me," said Tracy softly. "State your name and rank, and give us the basics. Then I'll ask some questions."

"Roger."

"We're rolling and recording," said Danny.

"My name is Sergeant Anthony DeFranco of the Westport Police Department."

Pause.

"Our town suffered a tragedy this evening when Westport Police Chief Gerald Talbot was fatally injured in a single-vehicle auto accident on Long Lots Road. We are investigating the cause of the accident, and will have a follow-up in the next couple of days.

"I know I join many residents of our community in extending our sympathies to the Talbot family. I know that Chief Talbot's wife, Jane, and his two children, Susan and Kathy, are devastated at this loss, and they can count on the support of this department—and all of Westport—in the coming difficult days.

"Chief Talbot was our chief and our leader. But he was also our inspiration, our friend, and at critical times, our guiding light. He pursued his duties with energy, fairness, drive, and distinction.

"He will be missed. It will behoove all of us in the department to perform our duties a little bit harder in the coming days and weeks, the way Chief Talbot would have wanted."

That sort of wraps it up, thought DeFranco as he continued to look into the camera lens.

He would leave out the bits about the venality, the self-interest, the bullying—possibly even accessory to murder if his suspicions held.

"Sergeant DeFranco, that was a moving tribute," said Tracy Taggart. "Can you tell us any more about why Chief Talbot's personal vehicle might have left the road?"

"We're looking into every angle. It's possible some wet leaves caused his car to lose traction. We'll have more on that as it becomes available."

"Can you elaborate on the injuries the chief sustained in the accident?" asked Tracy, not unreasonably. DeFranco didn't really want to go there. But he realized Tracy needed to ask the question.

"The preliminary investigation suggests head injuries. Fairfield County Medical Examiner Dr. Samuel Goldberg will be investigating the extent of the injuries and we hope we'll be getting that report soon," said DeFranco. Just kick it down the road, he thought.

"Thanks, Sergeant DeFranco," said Tracy. Then turning to the camera she continued, "A sad night in Westport as the town comes to grips with the death of Chief Gerald Talbot in a freak auto accident. Reporting from Westport, I'm Tracy Taggart. News 12 Connecticut."

The klieg lights dimmed and Danny ran the equipment out to the van for the upload. Tracy lingered behind.

"Anything more on what really happened?" she asked DeFranco.

"Well, like I said at the scene, he was run off the road by a vehicle with green paint. And he was beaten to death with a hammer."

"Tony," said Tracy, looking into his eyes, "I'm not doing my job here. The man was murdered and I just reported he died in an auto accident."

"I know. You're going to get that story. But we need a little more time. But there's more. Weird marks on Moriarty's body—almost like a cattle prod."

"Ice pick?" asked Tracy innocently.

"We'll know soon enough," said DeFranco.

41

Forensics

He awoke aboard *Paisano* thinking he was home in his own bed and remembering, with some discomfort, he was actually aboard a forty-two foot trawler gently rocking in a building wind.

Reality surged in like the tide.

His home of almost a quarter century was charred black and knocked flat, an unshakable truth mollified by the flannel-clad body of Tracy Taggart draped at his side. He took comfort in the simple sound of her breathing. She touched every part of him, and he vowed to stop and eliminate any threat that even came close to her. Home was now an abstraction. It was life or death, just like the Delta, and if you didn't lean into the mission, then prepare to be devoured. He had fellow sailors who'd lost their edge. It led to fear, and worse, hesitation. Hesitation at the very instant raw instinct, quick judgment, and rapid reaction were the needed attributes.

He was quite ready to kill for her—a sensation he thought he'd left in Southeast Asia.

They awoke famished and freezing and decided to repair immediately to Penny's Diner on East Avenue, stoke up on omelets and coffee, then set about their day.

They arrived at Tracy's apartment—sensitized to the possibility of watchers—took a shower, and tidied up. She was early for work so they went together to the ME's headquarters.

They found Dr. Goldberg holding fast against the avalanche of paper inside his office.

"I wondered when you'd get here, Detective DeFranco," boomed Dr. Goldberg, recovered, but only mildly, from the loss of Curtis Jones. "And Miss Taggart. You are getting an exclusive inside look at the underbelly of police work. It's not neat, simple, or clean, but it's often triumphant."

"Detective DeFranco has opened my eyes to a lot of things," said Tracy.

"The importance of determination, for one," said Goldberg, tossing DeFranco a rare accolade he hadn't sought and didn't need.

"To be honest, the case feels like it's chasing us. I wish it were the other way around," said DeFranco. "I presume you've had a chance to come up to speed on Chief Talbot?"

"Oh yes," said Goldberg. "Finished with him an hour ago and my associates are just closing things up. Definitely murdered. Head battered with a cheap Stanley hammer you could buy at Home Depot for six dollars. Amateurish attempt to make it look like a DUI. His blood alcohol was .01—probably from a single pilsner at lunch. That shoe casting we took at the scene of the accident was not conclusive. We think it's the same brand but it's not an exact match from the dumpster or from Curtis. Detective DeFranco, will you be the investigating officer?"

"Until the first selectman decides on a new chief and the new chief decides how he or she wishes to deploy me," said DeFranco. "Can I presume the states attorney has been informed of the results of the postmortem?"

"He has. He's been uncharacteristically quiet," said Dr. Goldberg.

"Okay," said DeFranco. "If you could fax your report to my office I would be grateful. Miss Taggart and I need to keep moving."

They left the doctor and drove to News 12 Connecticut. Tracy was early, but she knew the station manager—her boss's boss—and the news director would be in.

"This is your story," said DeFranco. "I can cool my heels in the waiting room."

"I need you with me, Tony. Do you mind?"

"Only if you think I can help."

Tracy knocked on the news director's door. Hank was short, balding, crooked teeth—having spent a lifetime behind the scenes making things happen while his more telegenic colleagues went before the camera. But Hank was intense, and seemed delighted that Tracy Taggart's relations with the local police meant Sergeant DeFranco had accompanied her to a story pitch. Hank was old-school. He liked, insisted on, sourcing from credible authorities.

Hank stopped her after Tracy recounted the discrepancies between the erroneous Mortensen/Moriarty description of events and the actualities before them. Hank called in his super-visor the station manager—"Jameson," he said to DeFranco, extending a hand—to listen to Tracy Taggart's gothic tale unfold, and she hadn't even gotten started. The ethnicity of the victim, her alleged nationality according to Immigration, the confusion over the tox screening, and the hint that a date-rape drug might have been found in her system. DeFranco added a nugget about the telltale shoe print at the dumpster, also imprinted on Curtis Jones's back. The same shoe might have been at the Talbot acci-dent, but it wasn't clear.

DeFranco contributed what he knew about Tamara Moriarty's "suicide," the puzzle piece of those two small penetration wounds on her upper torso and left leg, the bizarre connection between Kali's removal from the state morgue by two uniformed Westport police officers, one, it seemed, with poor handwriting.

Tracy lingered over the body of the dead girl. The body parts extracted by the medical examiner's office—the sea glass embedded in Kali's throat that potentially led to Beachside Avenue.

"And let's not forget," said DeFranco, by now the elder statesman. "We haven't made a positive ID of our Kali yet. We need to get a positive DNA match between the dead woman and a DNA sample procured from her family, if we can."

"How long will that take?" asked an impatient Hank.

Jameson apparently wanted to take up a position on more defensive ground. "We might need to bring in the station's lawyers," he said.

DeFranco saw an opening that might give him more time to determine the dumpster girl's identity. "That'll take a while," he said. "I can use that time to nail down the DNA evidence. That connection has to be rock-solid, and I don't feel it's there yet."

"We need to charter a helicopter," said Hank, on the edge of his seat. "We need to pan over the whole fucking street." Jameson appraised his news director coolly.

Tracy wrapped the story around the murder of Chief Gerald Talbot, as stated unequivocally by the medical examiner that very morning. DeFranco layered in the details of the hammer blows, the nearly pristine automobile, the collision with the green-painted vehicle. He suggested an interview with Dr. Goldberg to lend some authority to the recitation of Talbot's fatal injuries.

"I need a crew and I need a little time this morning with our Beachside Avenue source," said Tracy.

"We've got to move, move, move," said Hank. "And we need to bust in on the state's attorney in his office. Can we pull this together for the six o'clock? Follow-up at eleven?"

"Tough," Tracy stated. "We need to think about giving it at least another day." She was with DeFranco in wanting the story to gel, for the dots to connect. "But I'll keep you advised if I can push that up."

"Who else is on this story?" interjected Jameson. "Is there really a chance we'll get scooped?"

"Unlikely," said Tracy. "But I understand we're in a bit of a race. Newspaper in Bridgeport is interested in the gang angle. They don't think it holds water." She thanked her nemesis Bannon for that bit of intel. It threw Hank a lifeline with management. He was right to push, but pushing could put them in legal jeopardy with any number of well-funded Beachside Avenue highbrows.

"If I may," said DeFranco. "Actual charges, an arrest, would help protect the station. Like Tracy said. It will take time."

Jameson finally came up to his full height. "Tracy. Wonderful job. And thank you, Sergeant. It's an important piece and we are going to pursue it with everything we have. But it's a bit prema-ture. The four of us are on the executive team to oversee this story. Information about the case of the headless corpse doesn't leave this room."

Management was retreating, while the reporting ranks wanted to race to the finish line. The tension was familiar. Tracy Taggart grew reflective, and brought some needed news judgment to the disparate pattern of facts.

"Gentlemen," she began. "We've got more than enough to go forward with a news piece right now. We're within our rights to cover an ongoing investigation, despite the fact we have no suspects and no arrests. Emphasis on the plural! We begin with three deaths—two murders verified by the ME, one suicide that's under a cloud when you consider the removal of the headless girl. Kali connects all three. Let's pull the piece together around what we know and what we can verify, then bring in Kali as the common denominator."

DeFranco admired the logic, and even Jameson lowered his defenses. Hank pulled in his horns. He'd be able to go after the Beachside Avenue crowd, which is what he seemed to be advocating, but likely in a follow-up.

"But we still need time," said Tracy. "We need Danny and an editor to put together some B-roll. The ME's office, the spot behind the hardware store in Westport, the chief's accident scene. And I would push for a schlep up to Hartford to get state CID headquarters."

"We can get that in the can," said Hank.

"Sergeant DeFranco and I have some more interviews. Then I'll need to start writing," said Tracy. "If you can have someone else cover me today I'll get busy." DeFranco was amazed the elliptical conversation he'd just witnessed ultimately found a clear avenue. Tracy Taggart's story was a go.

"We'll give you whatever you need," said Jameson, supplying some needed ballast to steady the ship.

42

Notifications

It was the middle of the night in Jaipur, but DeFranco knew if it had been his daughter he wouldn't want the caller to respect any time zones. It was every parent's nightmare, and he was about to visit it upon complete strangers a world away. But he was connected to these people and he had to go about this terrible task correctly. They would want to *know*, he decided, an understanding that arose from the depths of his heart. He was giving them the truth, and that simple fact gave him the steel to dial the phone.

A man answered.

"Is this the Patel residence?" asked DeFranco, little realizing that Patel, like Smith or Jones, was a common appellation on the subcontinent.

"Are you certain you have the right Patel?" answered the man in English, lingua franca of the Raj.

"I believe so," said DeFranco. "I am trying to reach the home of Kali Patel. My name is Anthony DeFranco. I am a police officer in Westport, Connecticut. In the United States. Have you had any contact with Kali Patel?"

"She is my daughter," said the man.

"Have you spoken to her recently?" asked DeFranco. He had to get this right. If Kali had checked in since October 15, then wrong Kali, wrong Patel, wrong girl, and they would need to start over.

"She flew to the States on September twenty-ninth. I haven't spoken to her since we dropped her at the airport. Why? Is there something wrong?" DeFranco braced.

"Unfortunately, sir, we have found a deceased woman who may have been a Kali Patel. We are seeking confirmation."

"Deceased?" the man croaked on the other end of the line. DeFranco heard sudden female keening in the background. Kali's mother?

"Yes, sir, I'm afraid so," said DeFranco. "But we are still working on identifying the remains. Did your daughter have a ring on her toe with an inscription of the word 'Kali'?"

"Yes," the man stammered. Inside DeFranco's brain, one more piece of the puzzle moved into position.

"Did she have a tattoo on her hip in the shape of a hummingbird?"

"I am not aware that my daughter had a tattoo like that, but she adored hummingbirds. It sounds like something she might do. She has a mind of her own," said Patel. Like dads everywhere, dads in India were usually the last to know.

"Can you tell me who your daughter was coming to visit in the States?" he asked

"It was a college student. In Connecticut. I don't know his name. Kali said they had struck up an acquaintance when the boy was traveling here earlier this past summer. She wanted to visit him in the States. Her mother and I didn't want her go to. She can be a little willful."

"Sir, I am very sorry to have to communicate this terrible news to you and your family. But I need help in identifying the remains," said DeFranco.

"How did this happen?" asked the man.

"We believe she died of unnatural causes," said DeFranco.

"Killed?" asked the man, his voice guttural and wracking. New keening, louder, came through the scratchy line. "How?"

"We are in the middle of our investigation. As soon as I learn more I would be glad to share what I have. Right now I need two things." DeFranco heard the man crying on the other end of the line.

"I will try," said Mr. Patel. "I am a physician. I have resources here."

"That's good to know," said DeFranco. "We need to try to match your daughter's DNA with samples we've taken here. Can you see if she left any hair or other bodily tissues or fluids in your home? Hair from a brush would likely work. Also, saliva from a cup, discarded chewing gum...anything." Did he want to bring up the fact Kali had been pregnant?

He'd wait.

"I will see to it," said Dr. Patel, now fully awake.

"I need the materials as rapidly as possible. DHL might be a likely carrier. Is there a DHL in your area?"

"Yes, I see them all the time at the hospital where I work."

DeFranco gave Dr. Patel the address of the police station on Jesup Street. The crying in the background had slowed from a scream to a heaving sob.

"We would also like to have any notes or mementos your daughter may have exchanged with anyone in Connecticut," said DeFranco. "We are still trying to identify her assailant."

"I understand," said Dr. Patel. "Where is my daughter right now?" DeFranco had braced for that.

He had to lie. He had no idea of Kali Patel's whereabouts, a detail that appalled him.

"The last word I had on that was that she's in a Connecticut state morgue, if in fact it's your daughter," said DeFranco. "That's why we need DNA evidence."

"If she was killed, how did it happen?" Dr. Patel pressed.

"It's still part of an ongoing investigation and I am unable to tell you the exact nature, time, or location of her death," said DeFranco, knowing how lame he sounded. His statement was technically true. He knew where Kali had been found, but not where she'd been killed. "Here is my telephone number, Dr. Patel. You can call me anytime. And I will certainly contact you, sir, when I know more. Thanks in advance for your cooperation. I hate having to bring you news like this. I pledge to get you more information as soon as I have it."

He had to get off the phone. But Dr. Patel wanted to talk. Kali was their joy—attentive and successful in school, she was going to follow her father to med school, wanted to help everyone. She was really looking forward to the trip her father and mother didn't want her to take.

Each detail caused DeFranco new agony.

Finally he pried himself loose from the receiver as gracefully as possible and sat in his cubicle staring into space, cursing Talbot for taking away his Jack Daniels.

43

Forever a Spy

Dasha was putting another log on the fire, having settled Galina—still in her robe—before their beloved Cyrillic Scrabble set. The doorbell rang and Dasha padded through the kitchen and out to the back door to find DeFranco and Tracy Taggart standing in a misting rain.

"Come in and get dry by the fire," said Dasha. "I just put a coffeepot on. It will be ready in a moment."

"We hope this isn't an inconvenience," said Tracy.

"Heavens no," said Dasha. "I have been waiting for you. There are some meaningful developments in our case."

"I like the words 'our case,' Dasha," said DeFranco.

"Well, after today, I hope you'll see we're on the same team," she said. Coffee cups full, a cake from a church bake sale plated and sliced, fire crackling, Dasha Petrov related her tale of sleuthing along Beachside Avenue.

She updated her hypothesis. Was there a connection between the young female victim and, potentially, people the victim's own age living in the place where sea glass—the kind used to choke her to death—was found to be so abundant?

"I've been conducting acts of espionage on this street from the moment I arrived in 1950," said Dasha. "I'm a bird-watcher, you see, and this simple avocation allows me to indulge in flagrant, tawdry prying wherever I go. The ability to walk unmolested with binoculars gives me a fine tool for digging into private lives. You can think ill of me if you want. Spying, my dears, is what I do."

"I'm not one to throw stones," said Tracy the rising journalist.

"No complaints from the neighbors means no complaints from me," said DeFranco, officer of the law.

"My first task was to rule out potential suspects," said Dasha. "The Leipzig offspring are a total mess. Father with one foot in jail, kids failing in school, petty thievery and drunkenness. But I'm an interrogator and didn't detect anything from my inside source that would lead me to believe any of the Leipzigs capable of death and dismemberment."

"You've got an inside source?" asked DeFranco.

"You're my handler so I can tell you, but it can't go anywhere else. All the domestic staff on the street are in my network," said Dasha. "Little happens in any of these houses without me knowing about it. Don't hate me. It's just the way I live—and survive."

"Nothing wrong with gathering some good intel," said DeFranco.

"Having eliminated the Leipzigs, I penetrated the Rosewigs and came up dry," said Dasha. "Oh there's plenty of drama, but nothing that bears on our case."

"Okay, it's my turn," said Tracy. "The girl in the dumpster *was* named Kali. Or at least Immigration confirmed a Kali coming into this country and traveling to Connecticut at the end of September. Absolute confirmation won't happen unless we can get a DNA match." Dasha smiled as she thought about the handful of black hair in the Ziploc bag.

"Sergeant," said Dasha. "I presume you're prepared to reach out to the dead girl's family in India? We need fingernail clippings, hair strands…anything." She wondered if it would match the hair she had in her bedside table.

"I called the parents of the girl named Kali Patel who came through customs on September thirtieth. It went about as well as you would expect—meaning…terrible. But after her father collected himself he pledged to try to find some of the girl's DNA evidence in their home and have it shipped over here. DHL could have the materials here in a day. If they exist. Then there's processing time."

Tracy brought Dasha up to speed on the apparent suicide of Tamara Moriarty, the peculiar markings on her body, the disappearance of Kali's corpse at the hands of two uniformed but unidentified Westport police officers. And finally the death of Chief Talbot the previous evening.

"Curtis Jones. Tamara Moriarty. Chief Gerald Talbot. They all have a connection to the dead girl," said DeFranco. "Someone attempted to disguise their deaths with suicide notes or by staging an accident. The ME saw through that. And the footprints at the dumpster and Curtis Jones's murder scene point conclusively to a common killer. The shoe prints from the Talbot scene are not as clear. Same brand of footwear, but not necessarily the exact same shoe."

"Tell me," said Dasha. "Did you find any green paint on the chief's car?"

"How did you know?" asked DeFranco.

"And did he die from head injuries sustained from blows from a hammer?"

"Right again," said DeFranco. "The ME confirmed it."

"And two penetration wounds on the suicide…what's her name? Moriarty? How deep?" Dasha asked.

"Not very," said DeFranco. "Look like pinpricks. Hard to make out with the extensive injuries she suffered when she finally landed."

"Ice picks go in at least four inches," said Dasha. "She died in a police department, Sergeant. Plenty of weapons about. Why not a Taser? Was there a high wound and a low wound, aligned vertically?"

"Yes," said DeFranco. "And Tasers normally strike twelve to eighteen inches apart above and below the beltline."

Dasha tossed off these theories like you'd assemble words on a Scrabble set. And her probability of success was remarkable.

"I'll start from the beginning," said Dasha. "There are holes that need to be filled in, but this, I believe, is where we are. We've got a rough idea of where Kali died, but we're not sure who killed her. And we have the complication of these other deaths. Makes me wonder who's next."

A hard rain was now beating against the windows of the little cottage, and Dasha got up to put another log on the fire. She remained in front of the fireplace, wringing her hands together and pacing as she thought through the dots.

"She's young. She's well-to-do. She's met a young man, an American, in India, and she's decided to follow him back to the States. She may or may not be pregnant at this stage. But she shows up next door, looking for young John McCarran. The lad is enrolled in school in Princeton...but it seems as though he's not too pressed by classes and exams because he has a lot of free time. Not the first undergraduate to take more than the prescribed four years to get through.

"There's a party on the beach, and according to Glennis, my source inside the McCarran household, there's an incident, a disturbance, that results in John and another lad carrying the unconscious, possibly lifeless, form of our Kali up from the beach and back somewhere toward the carriage house. McCarran has another garage for his car collection across the street. But that comes later.

"Whatever happened on the beach isn't clear. But someone pushed sea glass down the girl's throat, choking her."

DeFranco interrupted. "I've got that person's fingerprint on an index card in my safe-deposit box, courtesy of Curtis Jones." DeFranco explained the arrival of the note and index card.

Dasha looked at him and smiled. "They panic, carry her away, and call Robert, McCarran's handyman. We'll need to know more about him. Robert shoos them away and handles things on his own.

"Robert takes her behind the garage, cuts off her head and hands, and strings her up by her ankles using an engine hoist. I've seen it. He empties her blood over a drain, then burns the body with a cutting torch. I also saw where that happened."

"I need to consult an attorney on whether I have probable cause for a search warrant," said DeFranco. "I'll have to go through Mortensen—and that's probably a nonstarter. But there's certainly reason to invite Robert to the station for questioning."

"Sounds like you're asking him to tea, Sergeant," said Dasha. "The man is highly dangerous. My undercover operation shows he used a saw and a hatchet."

"That jives with Curtis's original postmortem of the girl in the dumpster," said DeFranco.

"And a hammer on poor Chief Talbot," added Tracy.

"I saw that too," said Dasha. "Suffice it to say I observed the raptor in its natural habitat. And then there's this." She walked into a bedroom and brought out the Ziploc bag containing black human hair. "I think it belongs to the dead girl."

"Probably inadmissible if it was found without a search warrant," said DeFranco.

"A detail," said Dasha. "We're trying to stop a murderer, Detective."

DeFranco would still need evidence he could present in court.

"We'll have it tested," said DeFranco, surmising his ally Dasha was probably guilty of breaking and entering.

"What about the pregnancy?" asked Tracy. "And worse, the mangled abortion?"

"My source inside the household will likely be able to shed more light on that," said Dasha. "She's my next target. And it's still not clear who murdered Kali. It might have been the feckless John. It could have been someone else. But Robert was tasked with the clean-up."

"And he's made a bigger mess," said DeFranco.

"The suspects in the girl's murder can now be safely linked to the McCarran household," said Dasha. "Son John, Kali's lover. Perhaps the errand runner, Robert."

"So the trick now is to make a case and make it stick," said DeFranco. "I'll need to go around the state's attorney, who was part of the initial coverup. And not get anybody hurt in the process."

"You're at a crossroads, Sergeant," said Dasha. "Robert had confederates inside your own department. Arrest him now and possibly lose the traitors? Or wait a day and see what happens when Tracy's story comes out?"

"I'll probably regret this decision," said DeFranco. "Let's wait."

44

Hail to the Chief

"Thanks, Dasha. I have to get back to HQ," DeFranco said, turning to Tracy and finishing his coffee.

"And I have to get to the station and start writing. I'll need to interview you, Sergeant. Where will I be able to find you?" she asked.

"I'll be hunkered down at HQ and I'll leave word if I leave. Can you do the same?"

"Sure. My car is in Stamford. Can I borrow the Corolla?" asked Tracy.

"It's been feeling neglected. Here are the keys. Watch your back."

They drove to the police station on Jesup Street and Tracy drove off in Angelica's little car.

And I need to speak to the kids, thought DeFranco. Their house was gone, for Christ's sake. He'd been caught up in events—and enraptured by Tracy Taggart. He'd neglected his own children. Sorry, Julie, he appealed to his long-dead wife, there's a lot on my plate.

He dropped by his cubicle and removed his sport coat, then ventured toward Talbot's domain. He found the first selectman sitting in the chief's chair, flanked by three citizens DeFranco barely knew from articles he'd read in the *Westport News*. They were members of the representative town meeting. Also in attendance was the town attorney, Ken Bernhard, who began the discussion:

"Sergeant DeFranco. Forgive the intrusion. We know you're busy," he said. "Without divulging any evidence, can you bring us up to speed on the status of the investigation into the chief's auto accident?"

"Simple question with no simple answer," said DeFranco. "The medical examiner told me this morning he thinks the chief was murdered." There was a collective gasp from the little assembly of town fathers, accompanied by flushed cheeks, wide eyes, slack jaws. DeFranco was more attuned to human reactions, something he'd learned at Dasha's knee. "But I need to back way up. Westport now has a serial killer, with confederates who may have penetrated the police department."

Stunned silence.

He ran through the particulars: the headless girl, the official dissembling (saving Mortensen as a bonus for later), the bogus suicide of Curtis Jones, and the apparent defenestration of the state investigator, possibly at the hands of two Westport police officers. Those two had also probably absconded with the wandering corpse of Kali Patel. He described in vivid detail the chief's disproportionate head injuries. He left out the McCarran connection, fearing one of the meeting participants might have a relationship with the mighty avenue. He also chose to remain silent on the subject of News 12 Connecticut, whose intrepid reporter was no doubt at that moment banging away on the story of her brief but spectacular career.

The first selectman spoke first. "We'll want to avoid any discredit to the town."

Leave it to the *bürghermeisters* to think of appearances first, thought DeFranco.

"Well, the real story of the headless corpse will get out soon," said DeFranco. "I know for a fact News 12 Connecticut is making inquiries." He'd leave out his singular role in helping shape Tracy Taggart's upcoming piece. "One thing is for sure. When they come with cameras we can do nothing but tell the truth. The story will blow over faster. We've had enough collusion and cover-up." The little group nodded in agreement, even the first selectman, who glanced toward the town attorney for a nod of approval.

"Well," said the first selectman. "We were very pleased at the way you represented the department and the town in your interview after the chief's accident. It was classy, and the town handled the news well. We came here today to let you know we are making you interim chief of police. We'll settle on a permanent chief when the dust settles. But right now we need a leader, Sergeant DeFranco. And you're it."

"Not sure how I feel about that," said DeFranco. He saw the double-wide in Naples slipping away. "But I'll give it my best shot."

First task: Who were the traitors?

45

Tour de Force

DeFranco had to hand it to her. She knew how to get things done, aided in no small measure by Danny's day of foraging for B-roll and Hank's persuasive talents in procuring a Bell Jet Ranger from a charter outfit in White Plains.

She didn't make the six o'clock news, but Hank and Jameson held out for the eleven, and they scheduled news slots the next day for follow-up. DeFranco met her at the television station and marveled at her presence on-air when she wrapped up with a steely-eyed summation at the anchor's desk.

The piece opened with Tracy Taggart walking down the beach on the seawall side of Beachside Avenue. She was, more or less, in front of the McCarran residence.

"Death came to sleepy, well-to-do Westport last week, when the headless body of a young woman was found in a dumpster behind the Crossroads Hardware Store at Canal and Main."

The piece then cut to the previous week's footage of the scene of the crime.

"The official pronouncement from the state's attorney and the state's Criminal Investigation Division focused on a drug-fueled gang war—far removed from upscale Westport, pride of the Connecticut Gold Coast. But an exclusive News 12 Connecticut investigation has revealed the fallacy of the state's interpretation of how the woman met her fate—and also learned that three more individuals connected with the case have died under suspicious circumstances."

Here the piece cut to B-roll of Moriarty at the first press conference, Moriarty's office, Moriarty on the roof of the state police cruiser, Moriarty in a body bag being transported on a gurney to a waiting coroner's van. The B-roll continued with shots of Curtis Jones, and shots from Chief Talbot's "auto accident." The camera came back to Tracy Taggart on the beach, the wind fluttering her hair as she looked into the camera and formed unbreakable connections with her viewers. She had everyone's attention, including the CNN bureau in New York, the assignment editor of *The New York Times*, a police reporter from *USA Today*, and the news director of News 4 New York, who were all scheduling trips up to Fairfield County at first light.

The story of the headless corpse was breaking on a national scale.

"Fairfield County Medical Examiner Dr. Samuel Goldberg has confirmed to News 12 Connecticut that crime scene investigator Curtis Jones was murdered last Saturday. Jones worked the scene the night the headless corpse was discovered. He was found hanged in a closet at the medical examiner's office with a bogus suicide note. A footprint at the Jones murder scene matched a footprint at the Westport dumpster where the corpse was found, linking the two crime scenes a day apart and fifteen miles away.

"Motive for Inspector Jones's murder? He was trying to retest the murder victim's blood to punch holes in the official theory that the girl died of a heroin overdose.

"State CID investigator Tamara Moriarty, who first advanced the theory that the headless corpse was a gangland killing, was also found dead, an apparent suicide, now under its own cloud of suspicion. Today, the medical examiner confirmed that the single-vehicle accident claiming the life of Westport Police Chief Gerald Talbot was a murder. Cause of death, massive head wounds from an assault with a hammer."

The piece cut to an interview with the medical examiner, filling in the details of cause of death.

"What connects these tragedies? The headless girl in the dumpster, and…"

The camera followed Tracy as she bent down to pick something up off the beach.

"A little piece of sea glass…just like this."

Here the camera cut to an interview with Acting Westport Police Chief Anthony DeFranco in the chief's office at the Westport Police department.

"Chief DeFranco," opened Tracy while two cameras recorded the interview. "Who was the headless woman in the Westport dumpster?"

"We are in the midst of confirming the decedent's identity. But I can tell you what we believe so far. She is alleged to have been a foreign national visiting friends in Fairfield County."

Tracy pressed on. "State CID investigator Tamara Moriarty, in a press conference in this building last week, said the body was that of an African American woman who was a victim of gang violence," said Tracy to add context. "Moriarty said she died of a heroin overdose and was then dumped here. But now you are saying the victim is likely from another country, and may have been visiting Westport?"

"That is the focus of our investigation," said DeFranco. "The body had certain distinguishing characteristics, which we were able to investigate with the help of the medical examiner."

"Chief, Investigator Moriarty said the victim died of a heroin overdose. Is that correct?"

"No, that is not correct. At the outset, medical examiner technologist Curtis Jones and the medical examiner believed the victim had Rohypnol, the date-rape drug, in her system. The medical examiner also found a piece of sea glass, which you sometimes find on the beach, lodged in the victim's throat. The victim was asphyxiated."

The camera cut to a piece of sea glass in Chief DeFranco's hand.

"So Investigator Moriarty lied?" asked Tracy Taggart.

"I can't accuse Investigator Moriarty of lying until I have more facts," said DeFranco. "But Moriarty and State's Attorney Pers Mortensen had the medical examiner's preliminary finding the day after the body was found and before they made their announcement about suspected gang-related activity."

There. DeFranco had exposed the fraud.

"What can you tell us about the victim?" asked Tracy.

"We believe she lived in India and she was visiting a local family. That's all I can say until we can run down DNA evidence and make the right notifications."

"But then, Chief DeFranco"—Tracy bored in for effect—"things started to go wrong for many people associated with this case."

"Yes," said DeFranco, town fathers be damned.

46

Threat Level

Robert listened to Chief DeFranco's interview in the carriage house apartment. Not usually given to fear, he sat bolt upright in his T-shirt and underwear and planted his feet firmly on the floor. He normally took a passive interest in the television news, especially the local channels. This time he was riveted and his normally imperturbable heart was racing. He got quickly dressed in jeans, a dark jacket, and a ski cap, pulled on his backup pair of athletic shoes—throwing his Adidases into the closet—and hoofed it across the street to the garage.

He ran to the back, past the commercial van he'd procured the previous evening from his friend Shaquille, and proceeded into the garage to equip for the evening. A shovel. Rope. Night-vision binoculars. Heavy-duty gloves. An FNH double-action semi-auto pistol in 9 millimeter and his prize, an H&K MP5 in suppressed full-auto, firing 9-millimeter Parabellum. It had a red-dot sighting system and a thirty-round magazine.

He locked the door, loaded the van, and drove quietly away, heading for Norwalk and News 12 Connecticut. Maybe he'd get his chance. Maybe he wouldn't. But right now he needed to know what he was up against, and he needed to be prepared.

47

Trail of Blood

DeFranco looked at Tracy from offstage and tried to judge how Westport would react when the town learned the true extent of the damage. He couldn't flinch, and, remembering the smoking embers of his home on High Gate Road, he knew he and his family were also victims. The whole town had been victimized, in fact.

And it had to stop.

Tracy Taggart was on-screen, continuing her taped interview with the new chief of the Westport Police Department.

"My colleague Curtis Jones was murdered," said DeFranco. "There is evidence found at the scene of his death that matches evidence found at the dumpster where the girl was found."

"And what about Tamara Moriarty?" asked Tracy quietly.

"She was also an apparent suicide, but there's evidence emerging to suggest she was murdered. Wounds on the body inconsistent with how she died."

"Can you elaborate?" asked Tracy. DeFranco knew she was just doing her job.

"I can't at this time. It's of an evidentiary nature." He was pleased Tracy didn't bring up the Westport Police officers who were at the scene of the crime in Hartford. He had nothing to add until he learned more. It was as if she was tuned in to what he could say and what he couldn't say.

"So that brings us to Chief Talbot," said Tracy, whose understatement drew in her viewers. "How is he connected to the case of the headless corpse?"

"The chief was connected only circumstantially at this point. Further investigation will reveal more. But all we know is that the girl was found on his watch. And we also know his death is highly suspicious."

"Suspicious?" asked Tracy. "How so?"

"The medical examiner believes the chief did not die of wounds suffered in the car accident. He believes the chief died because of an assault that happened immediately after his auto accident."

DeFranco could almost feel Westport reeling.

"An assault?" asked Tracy. "What were the circumstances?"

DeFranco flinched but he expected the question.

"The medical examiner believes the chief was beaten to death with a hammer." Tracy paused for effect.

"Chief, do you think all these deaths are connected?" asked Tracy.

"Yes I do. And our investigation will pursue the facts wherever they lead. We have evidence of the dead girl's death by choking— the actual sea glass—and thanks to investigator Jones, we have a fingerprint of her killer."

"Any suspects at this time?" asked Tracy. DeFranco knew he needed to punt until he could get a competent prosecutor on the case.

"We have several leads we're following," he said.

The camera cut to Tracy Taggart barging into the office of State's Attorney Pers Mortensen followed by Danny the tireless cameraman. There were shots of Mortensen pushing them away, with his hand in front of the camera lens.

"Following our interview with Chief DeFranco in Westport we tried to interview Pers Mortensen, but as you can see, he declined."

The scene cut to Tracy Taggart wearing a headset in the left rear seat of a helicopter flying slowly over Beachside Avenue, the camera sweeping by each house and lingering meaningfully at the home of Angus McCarran.

"A dead girl, murdered and dismembered. Three associated deaths. And a piece of sea glass just like this one." She held it up for the camera. "Disparate facts being woven together tonight that could implicate someone perpetrating serial murder on

America's Gold Coast. Reporting from high above Long Island Sound, I'm Tracy Taggart, News 12 Connecticut."

The scene pulled back to the anchor desk as a carefully coifed Tracy Taggart wearing a blue dress looked right into the camera.

"We've been working this story all day and into the evening, and the one piece that's missing is an interview with State's Attorney Pers Mortensen. We are working on that and, of course, there will be lots of follow-up in the next few days. We are also examining an area near Beachside Avenue that shows an unusual abundance of sea glass. Lou?" she said, tossing back to the anchor.

"Great report, Tracy Taggart. As Tracy mentioned, we'll have more on the case of the headless woman in coming days. For now stay tuned for sports and weather. Winter's coming, folks. It's time to pull out those overcoats."

DeFranco watched her from offstage as she unwound from a hectic day. He liked the way the camera stayed on the McCarran compound without naming names. It might smoke out anyone associated with Kali's death. He knew there were risks associated with that, but if McCarran and his associates were clean, DeFranco was sure he'd hear great howls of protest. Silence meant potential complicity. It was a little backhanded but it would gel when he could get his search warrant. He hoped Dasha was right—but he knew anything she said or produced as evidence would be shot full of holes by competent defense counsel.

Tracy bundled up her papers and walked past Bob Bannon, lingering behind the scenes, and up to Chief DeFranco.

"What did you think?" she asked, confident with the answer.

"Masterful," said DeFranco.

"Couldn't have done it without you."

"Just sorry it took so long. But there's still a lot to do. An arrest would be nice."

"You going to beard the lion in his den?" asked Tracy.

"If you mean Mortensen, he'll be my first call in the morning. I want to present what we've got and go for search warrants of the McCarran premises. And I want to bring this guy Robert in.

I will need an arrest warrant for that. So it's Mortensen on the morrow."

"What's your timing?" asked Tracy. "Can I follow along with a camera?"

"Don't see why not," said DeFranco. "It's a free country. Not sure you'll get into his office, but you can try. How about after I darken his door? I'll confront him, and then we go for the search warrant. Mortensen needs to find me a judge."

"That means the guy and his friends are still out there," said Tracy. "Mind if I bunk with you?"

"Not at all. But is it because you like out-of-the-way boat slips or do you like hanging out with me? I have to know." He knew he sounded like an ass. Did she want him? Or did she want her story? Now that it had aired, would she choose to remain at his side?

"I think you know already, and it's the latter. I'm no floozy." He could tell she was hurt. It's the last thing he wanted.

He looked at her…hard. He saw an indefatigable reporter who, with an ex-Marine for a dad, knew how to stick up for herself. He saw the soft side that had nestled close through trying times. He saw a stalwart who didn't need to be with him, but chose to be with him anyway.

He saw a friend.

"Stupid question," said DeFranco. "*Paisano* tonight? Do you have your things?"

"I packed a bag in my car. Let's get out of here." They walked to the News 12 Connecticut parking lot, stopped at Tracy's car, and then found DeFranco's Crown Vic. "I guess I can call it my own now. Chief's privileges."

They pulled away from the station, failing to notice the white van that took up a position three cars back.

48

Whirlybird

Angus McCarran was dreaming that he was floating in one of those newfangled sensory deprivation chambers intended to block out all awareness of sight and sound. As usual he was working on a math problem, and it dominated his brain so completely that he fought with fury the wakefulness that taunted him just beyond the edge of sleep. A strange sound ultimately pried open first one eyelid, then another. It was a distant whine that grew into a crescendo, until it became a scream, filling the air beyond the double French doors leading to the balcony.

"What the hell is that?" he said aloud, hoisting himself out of bed and donning a terrycloth robe with the crest of the Duchy of Monaco over the left front pocket. He slipped into his velvet Brooks Brothers slippers and stepped lively to the floor-to-ceiling portal. He grabbed the brass handles and threw back the doors... to behold a Bell Jet Ranger helicopter hovering at eye level just yards over the seawall. Leaves, twigs, and sand were blowing in waves against the front of the house.

"Goddamn it!" he screamed at the helicopter, waving it away, until the sliding door on the hovering monster opened and a television camera protruded into his private space. The words *NBC 4 New York* were painted on the machine's flanks, and when he later saw himself that evening on the six o'clock news, he was appalled at his general state of dishevelment—wild hair, mouth agape, bathrobe barely able to conceal his pear-shaped girth.

The camera had apparently gotten its fill because the helicopter made a graceful pirouette and was gone, restoring Beachside Avenue to its usual tranquility with every retreating mile.

McCarran was shocked, amazed, disgusted...and he said only one word—"Robert!"—uttered at the very top of his panic-stricken lungs.

~

Dasha Petrov heard the helicopter too and, having seen the previous evening's eleven o'clock broadcast on News 12 Connecticut, knew precisely the reason for the shrieking roar coming across the hedge. She'd been absently stirring her coffee at the Scrabble table on this otherwise bleak day.

Someone just poked the beast, she thought. And then, after a pause to reflect, she said aloud, "Oh dear. Glennis."

Dasha had to protect her asset, and she didn't have any more books to return. She hated using Galina, but she had little choice.

"Time for a field expedient," she said.

She bundled into her Barbour coat and Wellington boots, placing her wool beret atop her gray head, latching it down with her Hermes scarf. She took a last sip of coffee and a bite of church cake, then set off into the wet. She took a deep breath, clutched her chestnut stick, and pressed firmly into the wind, toward the little door in the hedge. It was midmorning and she determined the principals would be occupied and Glennis would be busy in the scullery. She marched up to the McCarran service entrance and rapped on it with authority.

Glennis came to the door pulling dishwashing gloves off and wiping her hands on her apron.

"Glennis! Thank God you're here. I am so sorry, but I have an emergency. I've lost Galina and I need your help." Dasha was mad with worry—hair afright, eyes wide and pleading. She looked past Glennis into the vestibule. A dour Robert was observing the intrusion. He was tall and silently menacing. He was hardly threatened by the addlepated woman from across the hedge, especially after that morning's aerial assault.

"Glennis," Robert said. "Mr. McCarran will be needing us."

"But it's an emergency," said Glennis, turning on him, tired of his pushing and manipulations.

"She can call 911," said Robert. Glennis shot him a rebellious glare that Dasha swore she'd been storing up. She turned to Dasha and said, "Let me get my coat."

Dasha looked imploringly at Robert with a quivering lip, theatrics later recalled with satisfaction. He seemed to relent, but clearly despised this loss of control.

He had bigger problems.

Glennis got into a slicker and pulled a sou'wester rain hat off a hook, fastening it on her head as she rushed through the door. She followed Dasha toward the hedge, and Dasha thought through this critical inflection. She needed to get Glennis alone. She needed to protect DeFranco's principal witness to the night the girl in the dumpster met her fate. And she needed Glennis to collect more intelligence from inside the McCarran household.

She needed to send her asset back behind enemy lines.

Dasha rushed toward the door in the hedge with Glennis in tow, both of them leaning into the rain. Dasha breathed a little easier when she made it through—no Robert rushing in to hold Glennis back. They passed from the trim elegance of the McCarran side to the proudly downtrodden Petrov pile. Dasha closed the door and threw an ancient latch that Robert could defeat if he wanted to with three bangs of his mighty fists.

She turned in her tracks and confronted Glennis.

"I had to get you out of that house, dear. Galina is fine. But *you* are in grave danger."

Glennis burst into tears, a knot of conflict and torment.

"Let's get you into the cottage in front of the fire." Dasha led her to their little home in the garden and helped Glennis remove her wet things. She placed her on the couch in front of glowing pine logs and Galina smiled at her from the corner. Glennis was softly crying when Dasha got back from the kitchen.

"I just don't know what to do," said Glennis. "Mr. McCarran has been so good to me and my people. He put my nephew through college. The McCarrans gave me a job when I needed one."

Dasha analyzed the conundrum; she couldn't judge McCarran unfairly. Glennis would defend him. A wall would go up and

Dasha would lose her. Dasha remembered the interrogation rooms at the black sites on the Czech border, or in French Indochina, places where she'd won and lost the moment. Glennis needed time and quiet—an essential white space to surround and enfold the horrible images replaying in her mind.

What had Glennis said? *She was limp like a rag.*

Dasha rose to the delicacy the situation demanded, finding the brushstrokes to paint a new picture.

"Glennis, dear, your loyalty to your employer is admirable. It's who you are."

Dasha dissembled with ease, as the situation demanded.

"But Mr. McCarran needs help. This man Robert has done unspeakable things. I am sure Mr. McCarran didn't know." Dasha deftly expressed an alternative, one Glennis might embrace. She needed to assuage Glennis's guilt. She needed Glennis to feel like she was helping McCarran sort through the mess.

"Robert disposed of the girl, Glennis. He set up Mr. McCarran, and we need to help him. Mr. McCarran is a lovely, talented man but he's gotten in too deep with that scoundrel."

Glennis nodded and wiped the tears away. Dasha thrilled at her acquiescence.

As Glennis's handler, Dasha knew doing the right thing had always been the housekeeper's motivation. She shamelessly fed the woman's hunger for appreciation. She was providing the psychological scaffolding so Glennis could take the next tentative steps. Dasha had to reveal something of herself to weld the bonds of trust. "Glennis, I saw where Robert took the girl behind the garage. I can't describe it. He needs to be stopped."

"I don't know what to do," said Glennis.

"Darling, you are not alone," said Dasha. "I am here to help you."

Glennis squeezed her handkerchief and stared into the fire, tears streaming down her cheeks.

"Let's start at the beginning," said Dasha softly, an interrogator reeling in her subject, loyal only to the truth.

49

Morning Glory

They were beginning to enjoy their mornings aboard *Paisano*. The dawn crept through the curtains and found them entwined. DeFranco knew he needed to go slow, so pajamas were now the rule—and dare he hope one day that might change? He only knew he didn't want to drive her away with boyish ineptitude. He drank in the scent of her hair and luxuriated in the softness of her skin and the peaceful rhythms of her breathing. She was smart and beautiful—but they were also a team, and maybe that was more important.

She stirred, and he loved the way she just picked up the conversation from the previous evening. When they came aboard they'd made their way to the aft cabin for a lovely snooze, and before drifting off to sleep she'd wanted to know about DeFranco's father and grandfather and all the other DeFrancos.

Tracy stated flatly she knew she'd like them because she loved their Tony too.

She'd said love.

Now, dawn breaking, Tracy said quietly, "So your father was a cop?" as the light continued to fill their little space.

"And a good one," said DeFranco.

"Well, you're a good one too, Tony. He'd be proud."

DeFranco wasn't sure about that, but he *was* sure about the tasks before him. He was focused and determined, kind of like his dad, a man who loved life, his job, and his family.

He thought about Tracy and where things might lead. It was all happening fast, and he didn't want it to end. But he did wonder. If they weren't sharing this supreme test would she know he existed? He'd be chasing down fenced TV sets and setting up his summer softball league and taking illicit nips from his bottle of Jack Daniels hidden in his unkempt cubicle. She wouldn't know he was alive.

Kali had brought them together—just as Kali had led to the bitter end for Jones, Moriarty, and Talbot.

Kali had the power to make or break.

For now, they followed their little routine: jump into clothes, secure *Paisano*, breakfast at Penny's, then a watchful adjournment to Tracy's apartment for showers and to brace for the events of the day.

"I'll head directly for Mortensen's office and see if I can get him to cooperate. You wait a bit with Danny until I'm finished, then bust in and see if you can get an interview. My bet—he won't see me and I'll have to go around him. You can interview me in the parking lot after he throws you out. I might need to contact the chief state's attorney, maybe the Feds, get a cooperative judge to help. Westport town attorney might be my next stop."

"Does that guy have any juice?" asked Tracy.

"He's smart and he's got connections, so at least he can point the way. My police department has a corruption issue and that means potentially the Department of Justice."

DeFranco drove to Mortensen's office with Tracy trailing in the VW and Danny in the television truck behind. While Tracy and Danny waited, DeFranco walked into the building, his reputation hanging on the previous evening's TV interview. Uniformed security officers manning the metal detector insisted on a pat-down, and young lawyers in pin-striped livery eyed him with suspicion.

Mortensen has friends in the building, thought DeFranco, holding out little hope for a rapprochement.

He made it to Mortensen's office, identified himself, and asked a secretary to see the boss. He waited in hushed, paneled surroundings reflecting the intimidating majesty of the law. The secretary came back and said, "Mr. Mortensen is very busy this morning. He'll have one of his assistants help you."

DeFranco uttered his thanks and continued to wait. A young woman named Audrey finally made her way into the waiting room, introduced herself, and led DeFranco to an interview room.

Fresh out of law school, thought DeFranco. This will be a waste of my time.

Audrey apologized for the state's attorney, and, clearly prepped in advance, immediately went on offense.

"Mr. Mortensen is not happy with your grandstanding on television, Detective DeFranco. He has placed a call to the first selectman to protest your involvement in this case."

"Well, Audrey, the first selectman and the town attorney appointed me acting chief in the wake of Chief Talbot's so-called accident. And Tamara Moriarty is no longer on the case because she's dead. Mr. Mortensen has obstructed this investigation from the beginning, and if he wants a fight, my next call is to the chief state's attorney and to the Federal Department of Justice."

Audrey recoiled.

"And what basis do you have for that?" she asked. "You can be sanctioned."

"I can prove that Mortensen and the state's chief investigator have been promoting a false narrative regarding the Westport homicide of the headless girl: botched toxicity panels, failure to heed and secure crucial evidence, mishandling remains. There is a reason for all that, and I am going to find it."

Audrey started to fumble with her papers and looked at the exit. "These are details that you'll have to take up with the state's attorney personally, but you'll need to make an appointment."

"I need a search warrant and I need an arrest warrant. I have probable cause to arrest one, possibly four, subjects who could be armed and dangerous. At the very least they're a flight risk. I need a judge and I need the state's attorney's cooperation. Now."

"I told you he can't see you today. He has appointments, and court later this afternoon."

"I will add this malfeasance to my growing list of particulars. My next call will be to Mortensen's boss."

"I'm sure Mr. Mortensen will have an answer for you soon, Detective."

"My name is *Chief* DeFranco," he said, and walked out.

50

Mining the Truth

Dasha read the signs. Glennis was twisting her handkerchief and catching a sob in her throat with every other breath.

She was afraid.

"You're safe, dear," said Dasha, putting a hand on Glennis's shoulder. She knew she had to send her asset back into the dangers of the McCarran household. She needed to gauge the senior McCarran's complicity, assess the younger's culpability, ferret out any co-conspirators, and, most importantly, amass as much evidence against Robert as she could. The dead girl's hair and tissue samples from the back of the garage might suffice—as soon as DeFranco could rustle up a search warrant to legitimize her purloined evidence. But what about bank books or secret notes or computer discs? She needed eyes and ears inside. Sending Glennis back in—with a mission—was Dasha's only recourse. It was just like Prague and the penetration of the Wehrmacht.

Glennis needed to collect herself.

Dasha couldn't push.

"Tell me about the girl," said Dasha soothingly.

"She was very dark," said Glennis, normally blind to ethnicity. Still, Dasha noted, it was the first thing Glennis mentioned, likely as a reference point.

Glennis continued.

It wasn't clear the girl had been invited, and it was just luck that young John had been home to greet her. He'd extended the invitation, but was quite certain she'd never take him up on it. They'd had some kind of pleasurable encounter in Jaipur, and then John left for the States and that was that. They exchanged notes and letters, even a phone call. But John had moved on in the relationship, and the girl clearly hadn't.

The McCarrans were reluctant to show the poor girl the door. She'd come such a long way. John was in from school, his participation at college always haphazard or negligible. The young woman had joined the family for dinner the first night and they put her up in the guest chambers with en suite bath and a little fridge stocked with sparkling water and a sampling of comestibles. She and John spent time together and seemed to be reconnecting. Glennis heard them laughing as they sat in front of the TV. They took walks on the beach to collect the sea glass. They put their collection in a little velvet bag.

Dasha's mind worked the combinations.

But then John came to Glennis one day. He was in jeans with holes in the knees and a dirty T-shirt, his usual attire when he was home. The world was coming down on him, said Glennis, and he looked like that confused little boy she first knew when she'd arrived at the McCarran household those many years ago. He was a malingerer and a petty tyrant, but he was just trying to get by in the shadow of his father, the lion of Wall Street.

"He was just trying to find his own way," said Dasha, nodding in agreement.

She enabled him. All of them did, Dasha thought.

John was failing in school, and the Princeton administration was about to kick him out as a result of bad grades and marijuana and massive parties that ended with naked, unconscious girls.

"That's when he told me about his little friend from India," said Glennis. "She was in 'the family way.'"

"Oh my," said Dasha, feigning surprise. "And what was John's plan?" she asked, knowing the answer.

"He wanted me to talk to the girl to see if she wanted to continue it. He didn't want his parents to know, and he wasn't interested in being a father. He came to *me*," said Glennis. She seemed proud that young John felt comfortable enough in their relationship to seek her counsel. It meant she really was part of the family.

"So what did you do?" asked Dasha. Tears flooded Glennis's eyes as she twisted her kerchief.

"I talked to her and she seemed to make it clear she didn't want to continue it either. But she didn't know what to do. She was alone in a big house in a big country with people she barely knew with a young man whose affections were on-again, off-again. She didn't know where to turn. So she turned to me too." Glennis shuddered when she said it.

"But you didn't know her name?" queried Dasha.

"Nope. Didn't want to know it. I called her 'sweetie.'"

It was Glennis's mechanism for building in distance, thought Dasha. She didn't want to—couldn't—get too close.

"So you took her to your doctor," said Dasha.

"I know him from my church," Glennis gasped while shaking, the tears streaming down her black cheeks and falling onto her gray maid's smock. "All the ladies go to him. Poor lamb was so sick afterward."

Dasha reached out to her—then looked at the clock on the wall. She would need to reposition her asset soon. She knew she was being ruthless, but circumstances demanded it.

"Something went wrong," said Glennis. "She was bleeding and bleeding. I moved her to my apartment in the carriage house and put her in my bed and she soaked everything through. I got her some pads to stop it and fed her soup. She bled for two days and just lay there with the color drained. I thought she was going to die. John had gone back to school and the McCarrans weren't aware of what was happening. Mrs. McCarran had gone back to New York and Mr. McCarran was out and about."

"But what happened then?" asked Dasha quietly, feeling the seconds go by, knowing Robert and likely McCarran would be wondering what had happened to Glennis. Why was she gone so long?

"The bleeding stopped and she got better. I kept her in my apartment for four days and fed her and she was still pretty woozy but she even smiled once or twice, asking for John."

"But John was back at school and you had no idea when he'd be back," said Dasha.

"No. I knew nothing. I just had that poor lamb in my apartment. I did take her into town once, for a pedicure."

"And where was Robert through all this?" asked Dasha.

"He lives next to me in the carriage house. He was around, helping Mr. McCarran. I think he drove down to Princeton a couple of times to see about John. He knew the girl was with me. But he didn't say anything. He never says anything."

"Glennis, I need to know what happened the night of the party," said Dasha. "The party on the beach."

God...the time.

"John came back from school. He barely paid attention to that sweet girl. He just drank beer and called his friends and they all came over. They started drinking in the kitchen in front of the fireplace. They were talking and laughing. That sweet Indian girl came into the room. The color had returned to her cheeks. She was hungry, hadn't eaten a thing, but all she wanted was some nuts."

"Tell me about his friends," said Dasha soothingly, her mind raging at the clock.

"They were John's high school friends. Two girls. Four boys. His best friend from Green's Farms Academy. That Mortensen boy, Mikey. Mean little boy turned into a mean little man. Used to trap squirrels in the Audubon and torture them. I used to try to keep John away from him but it was no use."

"You said Mortensen?" asked Dasha. "His father is the attorney? A prosecutor?"

"I don't know what he is. I just know that Mikey Mortensen was no good. Half of John's problems were because of him if you ask me. But nobody ever asked me."

And that, thought Dasha, was the essence of Glennis's life on earth. A hard-working, God-fearing, churchgoing woman, ignored, trampled, disregarded.

She had lost her voice.

"What did they do, Glennis?"

"Somebody suggested they go down to the beach to light a fire. John got some blankets and towels and off they went. Left the mess in the kitchen for me."

"They took the girl with them?" asked Dasha.

"Yes, she went along too," said Glennis. "Last time I saw her alive. Two hours later John and the Mortensen boy were running back up the lawn with the girl. The other kids had left. She was naked. Her head was just hanging down. All that beautiful black hair wet and mangled."

Dasha looked at the clock. "Glennis, we have to find a way for young John and for all the McCarrans to finally separate from the bad people like Mikey and Robert. They are hurting them. You can be the critical link to a new life for them."

Dasha was making her pitch. She felt the old thrill of returning an asset to the field. She needed to make Glennis feel important, listened to.

"To help Mr. McCarran and young John you need to simply keep your eyes and ears open. And if you are not feeling safe, I want you to come through the hedge and come right inside." It was the best Dasha could do until she could create a communications link and a better defensive perimeter.

"Tell Robert and Mr. McCarran the truth. Tell them Galina hadn't gone too far at all and poor Dasha was upset and you spent some time trying to keep me calm."

Glennis nodded. It was something close to the truth.

Dasha couldn't ask Glennis to lie.

51

More to the Story

Tracy Taggart's second-day follow-up added new dimensions to the first. She wanted to draw the linkages between the various murders. She tried once again to interview State's Attorney Mortensen, and after a verbal scuffle with guards managed to speak with his spokesperson Audrey, who vowed the Westport murder was getting the full attention of the state's attorney.

Tracy and Danny found Chief DeFranco in the parking lot for a quick interview. He wouldn't antagonize the prosecutor, who was about to be overwhelmed by an avalanche of metropolitan area media. But he did express frustration.

"We should have had search and arrest warrants by now," said DeFranco, sending a message to the state's attorney via the airwaves.

Next, Tracy and Danny went to the medical examiner's office and found a very cooperative Dr. Goldberg, who showed her crime scene photos of identical footprints at the dumpster and also on Curtis's back. The doctor's treatise on supination of the arch added a certain texture to the reporting. It was the type of material you'd present to a grand jury or enter into evidence in a trial, not on a television screen—but it was information all reporters craved. Goldberg didn't seem to care, as if the wheels of justice stopped turning when he lost Curtis. She gave the doctor a minute to eulogize his colleague.

"Curtis was an extraordinarily gifted human being," the doctor closed solemnly.

"The Moriarty death was more of a puzzle," she told her viewers. "But we know of the chief investigator's involvement in the case of the headless corpse because of her falsified narrative.

There was no evidence of a heroin overdose, according to Dr. Goldberg." Tracy's tone raised suspicions regarding Moriarty's retrieval of the body from a Port Chester crematorium and transport back to Hartford.

"We have her signature on the receipt," she told the camera gravely. Curtis Jones had been in the process of rescreening the body for the possible presence of the date-rape drug Rohypnol when Moriarty had the remains removed. "Now Moriarty is dead," said Tracy, allowing the damning facts to state the case.

She'd leave the mysterious Westport police officers for another day. Better to tease it out, keep it running, because Hank and Jameson were beginning to see an uptick in ratings.

She and Danny walked along Long Lots Road, stopping at the breach in the guardrail where Chief Talbot's Cadillac had left the highway. "Paint marks on the chief's car showed he'd had a collision with a green vehicle right…here. The relatively light damage to the car would not have caused the chief's extensive head injuries, according to the medical examiner."

The scene cut to Dr. Goldberg explaining the murder weapon was likely nothing but a cheap hammer.

"Can we conclude that Chief Talbot probably knew too much?"

It was a classic cliché but important to her story's connective tissue.

Her reporting was penetrating the New York media markets, especially in light of the lingering, and as yet unfounded, McCarran link. The only thing that connected the billionaire to the dead girl was a piece of sea glass that might, or might not, have been found on the beach in front of his house. She wouldn't dwell on it. But the *New York Post* did, citing reports of drug- and alcohol-fueled binging at the McCarran's Gold Coast mansion. Someone was talking in Westport, Tracy and DeFranco concluded—someone who knew the young man, now the principal target of the investigation.

DeFranco was in the chief's glass-walled sanctum trying to get Mortensen's boss to take his call, while waiting for a call back from the New Haven office of the FBI. The US attorney was out there on the horizon and he was contemplating calling her too, when a DHL box arrived. Madge brought it in and placed it on his desk. It was from Jaipur.

He could trust no one with the contents except Dr. Goldberg, so he mounted up the Crown Vic for a trip to Stamford, box in hand. After a successful handoff—and a signed receipt—he drove over to News 12 Connecticut. Tracy had just finished her six o'clock stint, with another invitation to sit at the anchor desk to bring Fairfield County up to speed.

Her smile lit up the darkened corners of his heart.

"I'll be working through eleven tonight," she said.

"How about a little supper afterward. *Paisano* has a nice oven and you haven't tried my lasagna yet," said DeFranco.

"Love it. Can you pick me up?"

"No problem. Your chariot will await."

DeFranco was back on I-95 eastbound when a call came in on the radio. He needed to find a private landline to call the police station. He stopped at the service area in Darien and found a pay phone.

"A person named Dasha Petrov has been trying to reach you," said the supervisor in dispatch. "She says you'd know what it's about. She said it's urgent." DeFranco rang off and drove straight to Beachside Avenue, where he found Dasha in front of the fire with a glass of sherry. He took off his coat and joined her.

"We're in the endgame," said Dasha. "Here is where we find the most unpredictability, the most danger."

"We've got people talking, that's for sure," said DeFranco.

"Are the wheels turning on your warrants?" asked Dasha.

"Too slowly. I'm not getting any cooperation out of Mortensen. I'm trying to go around him."

"I'll come back to that," said Dasha. "My source on the inside told me about the dead girl, how she came to visit the McCarrans. A fling with young John while the lad was traveling in India. She followed him back. She was pregnant, and my source arranged for the pregnancy to be terminated. It didn't go well."

"Poor thing was tortured," said DeFranco. He thought of his own daughter.

"Well, she almost died," said Dasha. "But when she got a little better there was a party on the beach. Presumably Kali joined them. She was feeling better. One of the boys was Mikey Mortensen."

"No!" said DeFranco, legitimately surprised. Another puzzle piece. He'd found the reason the county's chief prosecutor wanted to shut down the case.

"He's a bad one, Chief," said Dasha. "My source knew him when he and young McCarran were schoolboys. Mean streak."

"Explains a lot."

"But trust me when I say this," said Dasha. "Now is the point of maximum instability. There will be irrational behavior now that the media is involved. You and Tracy are in danger."

"Hard to imagine they would hurt a reporter," said DeFranco. "But anyone who comes too close is vulnerable."

"They had no compunction about killing your Chief Talbot," said Dasha. "Why would they stop at a reporter? Happens all the time in some areas of the world. Regular practice in the Soviet Union and the East Bloc."

"Of course, you're right. Who is this guy?"

"We'll know more about Robert in coming days," said Dasha. "But I've seen his type. He's a mercenary. Doesn't care who he kills as long as it's in general line with his mission—and that mission is to protect his employer. Exchange Fairfield County for East Africa or Central America, even the American South during the Civil Rights campaigns. The powerful people sometimes eliminate the opposition—aid workers, rogue priests, even the press. They use people just like Robert. And they don't care who gets hurt."

"This is not the third world, Dasha."

"No, it most assuredly is not," she said. "But transplant an operator like Robert into this environment and you're seeing what can happen. He's been trained and paid to kill. So he kills. Just like surgeons are trained to cut."

"I don't think I can handle this alone," he said, staring into the embers. He'd been forced to wing it. Now he needed backup.

"You're doing fine so far, but no, you need reinforcements—especially now. You can't count on cooperation from the state's attorney. And we're seeing alliances and interdependencies. Mortensen's got the goods on McCarran. McCarran's got the goods on Robert. Robert's got the goods on those two corrupt police officers in your department. Glennis has the goods on McCarran, although she doesn't realize it yet."

"It's a snake pit," said DeFranco.

"Easy enough to unravel with a little time and energy. Don't get discouraged."

Dasha ran through her conversation with her spy. DeFranco viewed Dasha with a raised eye; she had exposed Glennis to danger. "She's an informant, Chief DeFranco. Nothing more or less. It's a tactic used by the very best police and intelligence agencies around the world. Don't look at me that way."

"Doesn't make it right," he said. He didn't want to find Glennis dead too.

"You can judge me if you like," said Dasha. "But I am a warrior. So are you, Chief. Circumstances have called on us to solve this case. Glennis is an intelligence asset."

"Dasha, that's pretty talk to make you feel good. She's a tool."

"You're finding your voice, Chief. Can't fault you for that. But in this business we all sup on information. Glennis will be protected. In my life I have moved mountains to protect my sources, and that will never change."

"I get it," said DeFranco. "But I don't have to like it."

"Suggestion," said Dasha. "You need to find the link between Mortensen and McCarran. Ferret out the collusion. And see if you can find anything on Mortensen's boy, Mikey."

52

Combing the Morgue

DeFranco left Dasha by the fire and went back to the station. He checked in with the handful of sergeants at his disposal and determined things were running reasonably well. More graffiti perpetrators at the high school and a spate of DUIs leaving the bar at the Westport Playhouse. There had been an escapee from the Hallbrook mental institution, and they'd found the poor guy in a bus station in Ohio. A domestic disturbance had escalated to the point where the husband of the union had required stitches. Then DeFranco had a brief conversation with his chief of maintenance and learned about the blown head gaskets and the skimpy brake pads and parted mufflers besetting his fleet of squad cars.

In short, everything was normal.

He went into Records and went straight for the M files, *Mc* to be precise, and found McBrides and McDonoughs but no McCarrans. There was an empty hanging file with *McC* typed on the tab. The manila folder within was missing. "No surprise," he muttered.

He braved the chill and walked across the square to the offices of the *Westport News*. He asked to speak to the editor and was soon closeted with the town crier's voluminous morgue wherein rested the life, the death, and the intervening goings-on of his little town. He browsed through the M's going back years and found nothing.

But then he heard Dasha's reprimand in the back of his mind to *use your imagination.*

He thought, they probably had the summer intern file these. What if he or she made a mistake?

He started in the A file looking for any reference to an Angus, then the C file to find anything coming close to a Carran without the *McC*. He was surprised to find an obscure brief describing the arrest of *Mrs.* Angus McCarran of Devon Road—perhaps before the gusher of cash that had funded Beachside Avenue—for driving while intoxicated and leaving the scene of an accident. Two other vehicles had been involved. There had been injuries and a fatality, a little girl. It was clearly drawn from an initial police report—big enough news in Westport to warrant a bigger headline, but relegated to the back pages. A payoff to the editor? No follow-ups. No interviews. The story died a natural death.

Now Mikey Mortensen was the one in trouble and McCarran and his man Robert were stepping in to help.

Payback?

Did he need an arrest warrant for the prosecutor's son?

53

Hearsay

Glennis knew Robert was an ascetic by nature—no pictures on the wall, basic furniture, a few books, and a small television. But she was still surprised when she walked past his apartment door in the carriage house and found the rooms more bare than usual, with two packed duffel bags ready to move out.

Robert was leaving?

She went up to the big house. Of course Mrs. McCarran was in the city and John was at Princeton. She, Mr. McCarran, and Robert were the only ones on the property. If Robert were leaving, it was good news as far she was concerned.

But then she heard voices—a heated exchange, not quite shouting. Dasha had told her she needed to be the eyes and ears if she were to help Mr. McCarran. She picked up a feather duster and went through the dining room, into the center hall, and then as far as the living room. Mr. McCarran's den was just beyond. She listened.

"You've gone too far," Glennis heard Angus McCarran say. "Your job was to deflect and contain, and now you've brought in more attention."

"I think I told you when I started. These things can be unpredictable," said Robert.

"That's not what you told me five years ago when you came here. You told me no job was too large. You could handle it all."

"This job *is* being handled," said Robert.

"Not when I have television news helicopters hovering in my front yard," said McCarran, raising his voice. "This was all to help Mortensen, who's had my marker for twenty years. It's too much."

"Fairly normal containment operation," said Robert.

"Maybe normal for that Congolese diamond mine where I found you. You can kill all you want over there and throw them in a ditch and that's that. But this is not the fucking Congo," yelled McCarran. Glennis was surprised by the vulgarity. Her employer never used bad language in her presence.

"It's like cutting out a cancer," said Robert. "You need to get at the heart of the problem, then cut away the margins so the cancer won't grow back."

"Stupid analogy, Robert," said Mr. McCarran. "These so-called 'margins' are blowing back in our face. The medical examiner. The new chief of police. The girl reporter. They're all coming after us."

Glennis moved closer to the den, dusting a picture frame and the top of a chest, trying to hear everything so she could tell Dasha.

"I can handle them too," said Robert.

"No," shouted McCarran. "Especially not the press. You'll bring the world down on me."

"Just another obstacle," insisted Robert.

"Right now it's Mortensen and his screwy kid Mikey in the line of fire. John and I aren't involved in any of it."

"Well..." said Robert. "You're a conspirator, but that's just a detail. Sure, they'd throw away the key for me. But you could do real time."

Glennis was surprised at how aggressive Robert sounded with their boss.

"I don't want to hear it," said Mr. McCarran.

"Of course you don't want to hear it. The boss never wants to hear bad news," said Robert. "I'm resigning. Effective midnight tonight."

"You can't resign. I still pay your salary and I pay your expenses. You have to clean this up!"

"That's what I'm doing, but you don't seem to like the way I'm doing it. You don't trust me."

"No, goddamnit. I don't trust you," said Mr. McCarran. Glennis had never heard him so angry.

"That's it," said Robert. "The end of the road. When the boss doesn't trust you, it's time to leave. Just one thing. My mission has just shifted from protecting you and your family to protecting myself. And I've got some margins to cut out."

Just then Glennis shifted her weight on the polished wood floor, emitting a slight creak. She coughed to make it sound like she wasn't eavesdropping.

"Glennis is that you?" said McCarran.

"Just dusting," she said. "Can I make anyone lunch?"

Robert looked at McCarran—eyes narrow, face red—and quickly left the room.

Glennis had an idea of what Robert meant by "margins." She wondered if she had just become one of them.

54

Closer

He found her more dazzling every day—especially when he stood offstage at the television studio and watched her work. She was steady, deliberate, grave when needed, light of heart when necessary. She shifted scenes with ease and took her viewers with her wherever she wanted to go. Her material was well composed and understated. She let the facts tell the story—and there were plenty of facts.

And he was utterly amazed she chose to be with him.

Who'da thunk it, he thought as she wrapped up for the evening. There was also an expanding timeline while the state's attorney dithered. Jameson, the TV general manager, didn't seem to mind. Each installment of the case of the headless corpse just improved ratings and drew attention to his down-market station, perpetually in the shadow of big media in nearby New York.

Tracy grabbed her duffel and followed DeFranco out to the Crown Vic. They failed once again to see the white panel van assume the position three cars back as they climbed the I-95 on-ramp. The van wasn't pushing to catch up. The driver knew where DeFranco and Tracy were headed. The pair chatted about her aunts and uncles from the land of the Taggarts—farmers, mechanics, Marines. Her father ran a farm-implement business.

"I want to take you out there," she said. "We can go swimming in the creek and dry ourselves on the grass. I love it."

"I'm there," said DeFranco. "But I want to introduce you to my kids. What do you think of a little trip to New London this weekend?"

"Not getting ahead of ourselves?" asked Tracy.

"Okay. Maybe a little."

"How about when things settle?" she said, and, a little deflated, he saw the wisdom in that.

They drove to the cove and unloaded Tracy's gear. DeFranco had a shopping bag. "True confessions. I got a take-out lasagna we just need to heat up. But trust me when I say, I make a really great lasagna."

"No worries. I'm starved and making a whole lasagna sounds like a big operation. Let's make one when we can relax."

The white van pulled into the marina and doused its headlights. It sat idling down by the Marine Travelift near the service department, with *Paisano* in the near distance, her cabin lights offering a warming glow against a biting chill.

55

Danger Time

Dasha was in her nightgown and robe with her eyeshade over her forehead. She was poking at the fire, and Glennis was pressing herself into a corner of the couch, trying to recede from the sudden horror that had become her life.

"I just don't understand it," said Glennis. "Mr. McCarran is so high-minded. He sounded like he knew what Robert was up to."

Better to have Glennis arrive at this painful conclusion herself, thought Dasha. Trying to convince her would only build in distance.

"It sounds like Robert is trying to pave over these troubles for his boss," said Dasha, stating the obvious to coax out more.

"Yes…but it's not just the girl. There have been others," Glennis said. Dasha would let her reflect, but now she needed to move Glennis from eavesdropper to functionary.

"Glennis," said Dasha softly. "They need to be stopped. We need to help that poor dead girl find justice."

"I still don't know how deeply involved Mr. McCarran is," said Glennis.

Careful, Dasha.

"You're right. I am sure it can be explained, but it's obvious Robert has been at the center of some terrible things. If we can stop him, I am sure McCarran will come out all right." Of course, Dasha had her doubts.

"What can I do?"

"You say Robert's bags are packed?" asked Dasha. "Let me get a friend of mine in the police department to come over and advise next steps. He's very discreet." Glennis softened to Dasha's wisdom. "Just put your feet up on the couch, Glennis, dear. I'll cover you up and you can get a nice rest."

She found Glennis a comforter and went back to her bedroom to get dressed and dial the police station. The chief wasn't there but she left a message for him to come to the cottage regardless of the hour.

Robert's bags were packed.

Dasha couldn't let him get away.

56

Hard to Get Good Help

Robert was none too pleased with his contractors from the beginning. Because of them he'd had to resort to the unfortunate expedient of putting the dead girl in the dumpster in the first place. His instructions were to get as far out of Westport as possible, a state park up in Redding, dig a big hole, and put her in. Bury the head and hands—deep—at least a mile away. But they came back to the garage with the body still in the trunk of a patrol car, wrapped in a blanket. Something about too many roots and rocks in the backwoods to dig a proper hole. They'd managed to bury the girl's extremities, but not the torso. The sun was coming up, and he'd had to think fast. He followed the patrol car over to the hardware store at Main and Canal, and created a deep pocket in the dumpster trash to put her in. Odds were she'd make it to the landfill without being detected.

Then there was the loss of the girl's trachea, the loss of the traceable Chevy, the botched recovery of the girl's body wearing easily identified Westport PD uniforms. He'd give both his contractors some points for their help on Long Lots Road. One patrol car behind to stop traffic coming from the west, one patrol car ahead to stop traffic coming from the east. Their little roadblock gave him time to do a thorough job on Talbot.

But after tonight, they'd have to go too. They knew far too much and besides, he could use the two packets of hundreds McCarran had given him to pass along.

Retirement in Panama wasn't cheap.

He looked at them huddled in the back of the van Shaquille had procured. Black jeans and athletic shoes. Black anoraks.

Black ski masks. Those beautiful H&K MP-5 9-millimeter semi-autos. Paid good McCarran money for those. FNH sidearms for close-in work. Night vision goggles. He would start things off from a distance with his suppressed H&K .308 sniper rifle, then let them go in to finish things off. As soon as the chief and the girl were done, he'd pick off the two nitwits and be on his way. Grab his bags and drive all night to the Canadian border. Then an Air Canada nonstop to Panama City. He could already taste the cold beer he was going to have in Casco Viejo.

Rich, out of work, looking for a new gig.

He liked the sound of it.

57

Threats and Opportunity

Dasha was dressed in her standard green overcoat and she stepped quietly through the living room, making her way toward the kitchen. Glennis was sleeping on the couch, mouth open and cheeks fluttering with each exhalation. The light from the waning fire was dancing across her peaceful countenance.

"Poor dear," said Dasha under her breath. For all her talents for manipulation, Dasha did care for her assets after all. But getting Glennis to unlock her heart and take meaningful steps was what espionage was all about. It wasn't just collecting information. It was doing something with it.

No use getting sentimental, especially at this critical stage.

She stepped into the crystal clarity of the cold fall evening, a bright moon casting shadows of the trees on her leaf-strewn lawn. She made her way to the little door in the hedge and passed through to the McCarran domain, feeling the old thrill that came with action and maneuver.

The big house to her left was dark. There was a single light in an upstairs dormer of the carriage house off to the right, where Robert and Glennis had their servants' quarters. She was taking a chance the carriage house alarm system was in the off position. Glennis had just come from there in a bit of a rush. Dasha assumed she hadn't taken the time to set it. There was no vehicle parked in front, so she also assumed Robert was out performing one grisly errand or another.

She tried the door.

The knob turned and she opened it just a crack. No alarms, flashing lights, barking dogs. All was well.

She got inside and noticed she was in some kind of common room. She found a stairway in the fleeting silvery light coming through the windows. She climbed to the top and found herself at the beginning of a long hallway with doors off to the left. She tried one and determined it must have been Glennis's apartment. Another door was open and sure enough she found Robert's two bags as Glennis had described, packed and ready.

Dasha went into his apartment and pulled a pair of rubber latex gloves from her pocket. She put them on to avoid mixing her own fingerprints with those of the occupant. The light was on so she needn't have bothered with the little flashlight she'd thought to bring, then found she needed it when she opened some of Robert's drawers. They were empty, of course, but she felt underneath each one to make sure no documents were taped in place. The bed was made and the closets were empty too.

"A neatnik," she said aloud.

She got down on her knees and unzipped the first duffel.

Male clothing. Nothing fancy. Standard issue L.L. Bean and Polo. A bathing suit right on top.

Going somewhere tropical, are we? thought Dasha.

Digging deeper she came across the handle of a gun. She pulled it out—a Fabrique Nationale. Belgian. Semi-automatic double-action with an open hammer.

"Old-school. Not striker-fired. Lovely," said Dasha. She would have liked to own it. It reminded her of the suppressed Browning Hi-Power she carried during her postwar years in Berlin. But she put it back.

Next came a notebook with names and addresses and payment figures. Then two bank books. The first one from the Royal Bank of Scotland in Grand Cayman showing a recent balance of 1.5 million dollars or thereabouts, then zero. Also a book from the Bank of Panama showing an inflow of a like amount.

"Damn it. My camera," Dasha quietly fumed. Her Minox camera, perfect for recording documents, was sitting in a drawer back home. "Foolish Dasha," she berated herself coldly. She put Robert's notebooks and bankbooks in the pocket of her Barbour coat and made her way softly down the stairs and out the carriage house toward the little door in the hedge.

58

A Gust of Wind

They were as ready as they were ever going to be, so Robert and his two contractors got out of the vehicle. Robert had thought to disable the dome light.

"I'll take up a position by that green electrical transformer," he told them. "On my signal, go in and finish things up. We'll meet back here."

He heard actions snapping open and closed and rounds being chambered. He set up on the box, extending the rifle's bipod legs for stability, and flicked on his night vision scope. He settled into position and trained the rifle down the dock. A quick adjustment of the reticle and the profile of the redheaded reporter came into focus.

"This will be quick," he said to himself, thinking through next steps for his contractors. Leave them dead on the dock or lug them off somewhere? Two schools of thought: dealing with them would just slow things down, but getting their bodies out of here would thwart the police, at least for a little while. Maybe the cops would assume they'd taken return fire from the boat? He was angry with himself that he hadn't brought his duffel bags, but that might have tipped off his contractors he was on his way out. Oh well. Quick trip back to Beachside Avenue and then he'd be gone. No, he'd drop the two assholes right here and let the cops sort it out.

He turned back to the primary target, reflecting on how pretty she looked as she brought a glass of red wine up to those cherry lips. He squeezed off a round as a gust of wind brushed his cheek.

"Damn it," Robert muttered under his breath.

59

Fusillade

DeFranco knew from experience that the sound of incoming bullets usually began with broken glass or splintered wood—long before you heard any gunfire.

So when a laughing, vibrant Tracy Taggart brought her wine glass to her lips—as *Paisano* rocked gently in the breeze—he wasn't completely shocked to see the glass shatter in her hand, and to see a huge hole erupt on the wooden bulkhead four inches to the right of her beautiful face.

They were under fire.

He expected it. From the time he took that blackjack to the side of his head on his kitchen porch, from the time Tracy's stalker assaulted him on the Stamford street, from the time he saw his home in flames at the hands of an arsonist bent on destroying every last vestige of the dead girl named Kali.

In truth, he'd been expecting return fire ever since his brutal success in the Delta, when that poor family lay dead at his feet.

Tracy looked at DeFranco, puzzled more than shocked. The only cut he could see was a nick along her hairline. But an instant later it produced a welter of blood that seized DeFranco by the heart.

"Get down!" he shouted.

Tracy complied, wiping blood from her eyes. DeFranco twisted around to kill the cabin lights on *Paisano's* master panel.

A second burst of gunfire came into the center salon of the trawler, blasting out windows, drilling through the wine bottles, riddling the dinner plates, and turning their salad and lasagna into an orange, atomized cloud. *Paisano* went dark as more bullets came into their space, pressing them into the teak-and-holly cabin sole.

He grabbed her by the waist and slid them both in a heap down the companionway steps to the aft cabin.

"You okay?" he asked her, knowing how stupid he sounded.

"Just a nick," said Tracy. He reached up into the aft head and grabbed a towel and started wiping up the blood, which streamed in a rivulet down the right side of her face.

"It'll stop in a second," she said. "I picked the glass out of it. Ideas?"

More bullets pocked and tinged into the main cabin just feet away—and Tracy and DeFranco were both coming to the same realization.

They would have to fight their way out.

"Got your Leatherman?" she asked as they lay huddled on the cabin sole.

"It's in my vest pocket. Hang on." He produced the tool and Tracy unfolded the knife blade to cut a bandage out of the towel. She folded over a washcloth to produce a dressing and tied the bandage around her head.

"That should stop it. At least I can see. So, my friend...a plan?"

"We've got the tools," said DeFranco. "Time to gear up. Can you get into your body armor?"

He had left their equipment on the aft cabin settee. Buckshot was in the bandoliers for the two Remington riot guns. Tracy had loaded magazines for her Kimber .45 in the offside pocket of her tactical vest, and she'd be able to stow her handgun, cocked and locked, on her strong side. DeFranco already had on his body armor, with shoulder holster and tactical vest over that. He stuffed two loaded magazines into the rig and chambered a round in his Glock 17 before he stowed it. He and Tracy accomplished their tasks on their knees in the half light coming through the ports while incoming fire continued unabated just over their heads.

He worried a little about the diesel tanks, but he worried a lot about the propane locker. One stray round and *Paisano* would get blown out of the water.

He also expected, with no return fire coming from *Paisano*, their attackers would venture down Dock C to finish what they'd started. They'd have to confirm their fusillade had ended the threat posed by the small-town detective and the beautiful young television reporter.

DeFranco crouched in the head and peeked through the curtain of the porthole. Dock C was bathed in moonlight on this chilly October evening. If they got off the boat, the shooters would see them before they'd see the shooters.

"How you doing there, Tracy Taggart?" he asked her, light of heart, suppressing that quaver in his voice. For an instant he allowed himself to enjoy the familiarity that came with their newly intimate life. But then more rifle fire intruded and his heart raced and his brain worked out the chess moves that just might save their lives.

"Just dandy, Chief DeFranco," said Tracy, trying to stop the shaking in her arms and shoulders.

"So here's my idea," said DeFranco. "I'll go up to the forward stateroom and undog the hatch. You stay down here until you hear them come to the finger pier to get aboard. When they slide open the cabin door, shoot the first one in, and shoot to kill. Center mass. Make sure he gets well inside before you drop him. I'll come out of the forward hatch and take down anybody else on the finger pier or on deck."

"I kind of like that idea," said Tracy. "But I really don't want to be separated."

"Divide and conquer, baby. We can't engage them on the dock."

"Agreed. So I guess we wait."

"Not for long," said DeFranco. "Kimber ready? Shot shells loaded? One in the pipe?"

"Yep. In all respects."

He reached for her. "You're shaking," said DeFranco.

"Just nerves. Let's do this."

"We're going to have a long, happy life. You'll see."

The last thing he felt as he moved forward on his belly into the bullet-riddled salon was Tracy Taggart touching his arm, his back, a leg—any part of DeFranco she could hold on to before the shooters came and they'd have to go down fighting.

60

Into the Breach

Dasha was feeling light-headed when she made it back to the cottage. She lay down on her bed with her clothes on and heard Glennis snoring on the couch in the other room, hoping the woman's caterwauling wouldn't wake Galina.

Robert's bankbooks were of passing interest. There was a steady infusion of money on a regular basis and very little outflow. She supposed legal authorities could go back and determine the source of the money. McCarran, she presumed.

But the notebook was more interesting.

Robert was a bit of a diarist, it seemed. He had a code worked up. Letters, dates, and, more importantly, locations. Notches in his belt, thought Dasha. Seventy-three entries, the most recent just this week: a letter, a date, and the words *LL Road*.

"Long Lots Road," said Dasha aloud. The scene of Chief Talbot's murder. "Busy boy."

She retrieved her miniature Minox, a requisition from her long-ago life, made sure there was film in it, and started snapping pictures of Robert's materials. Her goal was to get them all back into his duffel before he came back.

God, the *time*, she thought.

She took photos of the signature pages of the passports, the last four pages of the notebook, and the current balance figures, plus the account numbers. She put the camera back in a desk drawer and buttoned up her coat to go back to Robert's apartment and put things back where she'd found them.

Can't you just let it go? she asked herself.

But decades of tradecraft wouldn't permit that kind of sloppiness. Alerting the target by stealing these vital documents would send the subject off in unpredictable directions. No. She had to go back. It was a matter of discipline. She put her beret back on and stepped back into the cold. The arc of the moon had transformed the shadows on the ground, and she judged the time to be around 2:00 am. If Robert were back she'd have to abort. If not she'd press on, but go in with a solid plan for coming back out. Her training was kicking in.

She got to the carriage house. No cars out front, single light from the upstairs dormer unchanged. She opened the door and walked smartly up the stairs toward her objective. She got to Robert's apartment and slipped the materials back into his duffel.

Everything was quiet and she felt somewhat emboldened. She took out her flashlight and shined it under the bed, under the side table, around and behind the dresser. She went into Robert's closet. She got a chair and stood on it and felt her hand over the interior door molding, coming up with nothing but dust. But the ceiling of the closet had a camouflaged panel that appeared to lead up into the rafters. A bad day in Saigon in 1949 came to mind—an unfortunate tangle with a Viet Minh booby trap. Then she saw it—a human hair across a crack held in place with a smudge of Robert's saliva, his intruder alert.

Like everyone, Dasha was susceptible to the tug of human nature. Could she see the secrets behind the panel? Or wait for DeFranco's search warrant—which, by the way, was taking its own sweet time?

Bugger's a flight risk, she thought. He might need whatever's behind here, and if it's gone we might be able to slow him down.

She was talking herself into taking a risk a younger Dasha might happily assume. The Dasha of the present hour was more reserved, better able to calculate the odds.

61

Counterattack

DeFranco checked his gear, racked the slide of his shotgun, and peeked out of the companionway into the darkened salon. It was quiet, so he slithered forward through the broken glass and smeared food and red wine to the forward cabin. He got down into the forward V-berth and peeked out between the curtains of the starboard porthole. There was movement, a shape, nothing definite, at the head of the dock.

"They're coming Tracy," he called out to her. "It'll be okay. We'll handle it just like we planned."

"No problem," said Tracy weakly, still very much the Marine. She moved the safety switch of her shotgun to "fire."

DeFranco untwisted the two dogs for the overhead hatch and tested if he'd be able to open it when he wanted it to. He would have to stand on the V-berth, pop out of the hatch, and bring the shotgun into action on the target in one smooth move.

He went back down to the V-berth to look through the porthole. There were two of them on the dock, three slips away.

"Safeties off," said DeFranco.

"Ahead of you," said Tracy.

He could hear footfalls on the dock now. One black-clad figure with some kind of short carbine and a banana clip came first, followed by Number Two with a short rifle across his chest in a carry rig and a handgun thrust in front of him.

He ran through the possibilities. How many were there? Just these two? Or did they have a backup? If *he* were planning an ambush like this one he'd have a sniper in the wings with a nice view of the proceedings just in case things went a little south. He'd plan on it, then. Possible sniper was going to be the problem.

He heard Tracy position herself low and ready in the aft companionway. He felt *Paisano* move slightly as Shooter Number One stepped on deck. He winced as he heard breaking glass and then the sound of suppressed automatic fire filling the cabin. Of course, thought DeFranco. He's laying down fire before he goes in.

He wanted to switch places with Tracy right then and there. He hoped to God Shooter One didn't have a stun grenade or smoke.

But then he heard the door slide open and the first tentative step of Shooter One entering *Paisano's* salon—wait—then the beautiful, deafening roar of Tracy Taggart's riot gun filling the air with blasting light and deadly buckshot.

What? Another deafening, sharp bang came from her 12-gauge.

DeFranco came out of the forward hatch, pulled the butt of his shotgun up to his shoulder, and took aim at the human being standing on the dock. Shooter Two. He sighted down the rib of the barrel and placed the bead on the man's center mass.

He was about to take another human life.

He waited…a fraction of a second, then another, then more, while Shooter Two turned in his direction. DeFranco froze, swiveled to the right, and fired the shotgun past Shooter Two, buckshot scattering across the water and into the adjoining pier. Fire leapt from the muzzle of the shotgun as a riotous roar filled the night. Shooter Two didn't want any part of what was coming next. He ran limping back up the dock. DeFranco recognized that hobbling gait from the encounter with Tracy's stalker back in Stamford.

More rounds were smacking into *Paisano* in front of and behind him. DeFranco ducked down the hatch and came on his belly back through the salon. Shooter One was face down, half-in, half-out of the companionway.

"Tracy, it's me. I'm coming back."

He heard her sob, letting out the tension.

"It's okay. He's down. Are you all right?"

"Yes," she said softly. "Is he dead?" DeFranco saw her press herself back into a bulkhead, her Kimber drawn with the muzzle pointed down and away as he descended.

"I'll check in a second. The other guy is still out there. There might be others," he said.

He heard sirens in the distance.

Then…

"My God, Tony. Behind you!" screamed Tracy.

The giant, looming shape of Shooter One staggered into the doorframe of the aft companionway, struggling to get his compact rifle into a firing position. DeFranco turned and Tracy pushed him aside with her free hand, firing the .45—a gift from her dad—right into the man's neck just above his body armor. He fell backward into the salon. The smell of spent cordite and blue smoke filled the air. DeFranco crawled over to the shooter and shined his little flashlight into the man's face.

Hughes.

"Fucker," he said aloud. "I know the guy, Tracy. He's from my department."

They both heard the far-off sound of police sirens. He couldn't allow incoming cops to tangle with Shooter Two without a warning.

You've got to stop him, he screamed to himself.

"Wait for me. I'll be back," he told Tracy.

"You better," said Tracy. She huddled into the aft settee, knees up to her chest.

DeFranco stepped over Hughes and into the salon. At least this traitorous fellow officer wasn't going anywhere. DeFranco picked up the shooter's weapon—an H&K MP-5 with two extra magazines. Hughes also had a SIG pistol in his waistband, a compact Glock in an ankle holster. DeFranco removed them all, dropped the magazines, opened the chambers, and threw the guns onto the salon settee. He put the MP-5 magazines in his tactical vest.

He needed to focus.

He picked up Hughes's rifle and put the shotgun down. He needed better range and the rifle's low-light sights.

Shooter Two. Where was he? And was he the last one?

62

Field Expedient

"Assholes," said Robert, as he watched the fiasco unfold in front of him. Man down. His second shooter in full retreat. Success on the targets undetermined. Norwalk cops inbound. He'd been repositioning when the reporter and the cop had mounted their counterattack. When he set back up he couldn't get a clear shot at the cop.

Stay and shoot it out?

"Or boogie?" he said aloud. He played the odds. Cops might do his job on Shooter Two when they arrived. The detective and the girl *had* to be finished after all that firepower. No one could withstand that.

No. He needed to get moving. There would be some fallout. McCarran would have to deal with it. Robert knew when to fold his cards. He got back in the white van and rolled slowly toward the entrance of the marina, heading back to the carriage house, then into the night.

He was looking forward to a change of scenery.

63

Unmasked

DeFranco watched him go. White van off to his left. Maybe that was good news. Okay, he thought. Focus on the second shooter.

The sirens were getting louder.

He went up the ramp leading to shore and noted the state of the tide—an hour past low, but rising. Ahead of him was a forest of covered boats on their spindly poppet stands. He went down on his knees to scan underneath.

There. To his right. Something moved.

He crouched behind a RIB inflatable on a trailer and just watched. Someone was standing by a sailboat covered in white shrinkwrap up by the chandlery. DeFranco could see the shooter's breath, coming in gasps. He was wounded. DeFranco crouched and worked his way closer, staying off the roadway between the boats. He dropped down behind the sheet pile bulkhead and worked his way undetected along the shoreline of the marina, glad the tide was cooperating. He moved under the ramps leading to docks A and B. There was a break in the seawall and he climbed back up to the boatyard, now abreast of the chandlery building.

The lone figure, dressed in black, was standing in a breezeway leading out to the fuel dock. He had a second MP-5 aimed down the roadway separating the boats. He was wearing night vision goggles. DeFranco crawled toward the water side of the building, hoping to come around behind him. He was trying to stay low in the grass and dirt, hoping the guy's scan was zeroed in on his optics and not on him.

DeFranco moved around generators and propane tanks. He could see the empty fuel dock just behind the bulkhead. He

raised the H&K, telling himself to shoot if he saw even a fingernail of Shooter Two.

He worked his way to the opposite end of the same breezeway
where Shooter Two was standing. He paused to check his backside and his flanks. He was alone with the target. He moved
around a picnic table, stepped over a small hedge of boxwoods—
quickly, quietly, and relentlessly toward the man he would bring
himself to kill.

Shooter Two was scanning the road in front of him, leaning
against the doorway, clearly in pain.

DeFranco couldn't shoot.

He wanted to look the traitor in the eye.

He brought the MP-5 up to his shoulder, moved the safety to
fire.

He hoped to God he wouldn't have to.

"Drop your weapon and put your hands up," he said with
authority, not shouting, clearly not to be trifled with.

"Don't look around. Let me see your hands." Shooter Two was
breathing hard. He laid his weapon on the ground and put his
hands in the air. DeFranco took out his handcuffs and restrained
him. He spun him around, ripped off his ski mask and looked
into the pain-stricken eyes of Patrolman Wendell McKurdy.

"Figures it would be you, dipshit," said DeFranco. "How many
of you are there?"

"Three," said McKurdy, coming to the realization that his life
was about to change, and not for the better.

"Where's the third?" asked DeFranco.

"He left."

"White van? Was he your sniper?"

"Yes."

"I need a name."

"I just know him as Robert."

"Where is he headed?" asked DeFranco.

"I don't know. This wasn't our plan."

"No. His plan was to off you two jerks and head for the hills.
He kills people who get too close. Haven't you noticed that? I'll

deal with you later." Two squad cars from the Norwalk PD came into the boatyard with lights flashing. DeFranco put down his firearm, pulled out his badge, and forced McKurdy onto the ground. He had his hands up in the air when the first car pulled in. He explained the basic situation, described the mess aboard *Paisano*—one dead shooter adding to the general mayhem—and extricated himself from what was now a Norwalk police matter.

"Lock this fucker up and I'll come and interview him tomorrow," he said.

He needed to get Tracy.

Robert had gone rogue.

64

Loot

"Nothing ventured, Dasha," she said out loud.

She pushed on the panel in Robert's closet ceiling and it gave way easily. The chair brought her up high enough so she could just peer inside the aperture. She shined her light around and the beam hit upon a medium-sized duffel bag. She reached for it and couldn't quite touch the cloth handle. She needed to get higher.

She climbed down from her perch and searched for something to stand on. There was a yellow pages phone book underneath the rotary phone. She retrieved it and put it on the chair in the closet, once again climbing up to put her head inside the ceiling panel. This time she could reach the duffel bag and she dragged it closer to the opening. She got it the edge and worried it over the lip. It landed in her arms and she nearly fell backward.

"Hmmm. Heavy," said Dasha aloud, focused more on the contents of the bag than her own safety. She got it down on the floor and opened it. Cash. Lots of it. Plus small gold bars and white envelopes. She opened one of the envelopes and peered within. Diamonds. Heaps of them. Bearer bonds. And three passports—one US, one UK, listing a Grand Caymans address, and one Panamanian.

"Nice quality," she said, holding up one of the documents. "Looks officially sanctioned. Lovely little stash you have here in your bug-out bag, Robert. Keep it, Dasha? Or put it back?"

She stopped to consider the problem. There was the not insignificant issue of re-establishing the intruder alert. "Dasha, you've gotten ahead of yourself, haven't you?" she counseled gravely.

She decided to take the duffel on the theory it was hard to get too far without a passport. It would slow Robert down until DeFranco could get there. But she knew she was running an enormous risk. She went back to Robert's clothing duffel and extracted his semi-auto pistol. She put it the pocket of her Barbour coat.

As she turned to leave, she noticed headlights playing against the trees outside the carriage house and the sound of an out-of-tune engine.

Bad water-pump bearing, she thought for no particular reason, trying to distract herself from the sudden, unexpected danger about to come up the stairs.

65

Draw Down

DeFranco made his way back to Dock C with the MP-5 slung across his back. He made sure the police officers pointing their guns at him could see his hands. He held them up in the air, of course, and his badge was there for all to see.

"Police," said DeFranco loudly, with more than a hint of displeasure. After all, his own men had just tried to kill him. He had a brief exchange with the officers on the dock, then stepped aboard the god-awful squalor that had become poor *Paisano*, with a dead Hughes faceup in the salon.

"Tracy," he said quietly. "It's me. I took the second guy into custody. We're good. I'm going to try to turn on the lights and I'm coming down the companionway." No use adding friendly fire to the evening's festivities.

"Okay," she said, a bit shaky.

He made his way to the electrical panel and threw the master, then the cabin lights. The horror of the evening was there in full splendor—Hughes, a look of astonishment on his bloodied face, the bullet-riddled interior and broken glass, everywhere the ghastly stew of blood, gore, and lasagna. DeFranco looked down at his clothes and was stunned at the state of his attire. He came down the steps into their aft cabin, nearly slipping on one fluid or another.

Tracy was curled into the corner of the bunk, relatively unscathed except for the bloody towel still tied around her face. She had the Kimber in both hands, unable to relax her grip, although she did have the courtesy to control the muzzle down and away when DeFranco entered.

"You look like hell," she said.

"You too, sweetie," said DeFranco.

"We're a real pair, aren't we?"

Then they both laughed, delighted to be alive.

"Let's throw some clothes in a duffel and find a hotel. And I want to get you to an ER to look at that cut," he said.

"I'm sure it's not much. Stopped bleeding a while ago," she said.

"Let me see," said DeFranco. "My turn to play nurse." He pulled back the improvised dressing and the cut was small, just above her hairline on her right side and nicely stanched. He didn't think it would interfere with her television career, and it would be a good story to tell her dad.

"God, when he came in the doorway like that I just didn't know what to do," she said, crying, and looking at Tony with that supernatural blending of respect, admiration, and friendship—the longhand for love.

They hurried to pack some things and let the crime scene investigators aboard. He wanted to keep his Glock and his shotgun but he was sad to relinquish the MP-5. They picked their way through the mess and made it to the dock. DeFranco conferred with fellow officers and the police parted to let them through.

They made their way to the Crown Vic. "Let me duck into the shower by the service department," said DeFranco. "I've got to get out of these clothes. You good?"

"Just need to change my shirt and I'm back in business," said Tracy. They performed something of a cleanup and got back in DeFranco's cherished cruiser.

He radioed dispatch to check in. "You got a call from a woman named Petrov. She wants you to go to her residence as soon as possible, regardless of the hour. She said it's extremely urgent," said the supervisor on duty.

DeFranco looked at Tracy Taggart and wanted to find a bed somewhere.

"She used the word 'extremely'?" said DeFranco.

"Stressed 'extremely.'"

"Roger, 10-4," said DeFranco, putting the car in gear and aiming toward Beachside Avenue.

"Duty calls," he said.

"No worries here," said Tracy, not realizing that in twenty minutes she'd wish she could take it all back.

66

Familiar Territory

Dasha used to laugh at danger, adopting the tired British trope "a sticky wicket" when things weren't exactly going her way. Berlin was a nightly theater of treachery, of course, often with real shots fired. Then there was that awkward moment in Trieste when she was cornered by three KGB hitmen and managed to get out alive when her CIA cavalry arrived. The retreat to Formosa with the Kuomintang was no picnic. And of course there was the time she fell into the punji pit outside Hue and ran a sharpened bamboo skewer through her leg. The opposition had dosed the pit with human excrement to incite an infection, and the doctors insisted she had to have her leg removed. But then Constantine arrived and whisked her to Bangkok in a chartered plane to the king's own hospital where she could have the matter properly addressed.

No, she'd been out on the hairy fringes a time or two—but none of that compared with the sound of her own killer slamming the carriage house door, hacking up a knot of phlegm, and hurrying with heavy footfalls toward the staircase because, after all, he was in a bit of a rush.

Dasha left his room carrying the man's ill-gotten treasure and turned right toward the stairs, then right again into Glennis's quarters. She closed the door and managed to get it locked. She receded into the darkened room, guided by the pale light of a falling moon. She went to the double doors leading to a small balcony overlooking the car park. There was a copse of shrubbery off to the side and she heaved the duffel into the bushes. It was safely inaccessible for at least a little while.

The gun.

The last time she'd used a pistol was in the service more than a quarter-century ago, but she summoned the hurried training she'd received at an early clandestine base outside Munich. She extracted the pistol and found the magazine release. She dropped the magazine and stepped back over to the balcony door to see the bullets double stacked through the numbered holes in the side. Ten rounds of 9-millimeter Parabellum. She pulled the slide back, noted the empty chamber, then drove the magazine back home. She pressed the slide release, observing a round enter the chamber. The hammer was cocked and she was now ready to engage whatever came through the door.

She heard Robert pounding up the stairs and into the hallway. He was rummaging around in the apartment next door and in her mind's eye she envisioned him stage the duffels into the hall. She heard a chair scuffing along the floor under the panel in the closet. He wasn't worried about making any noise, slapping and banging away with urgent abandon. Dasha could feel his frustration when he discovered his riches gone.

Surprised, are we? she thought. You're so used to cold calculations, isn't it a shame when you start to lose control?

"God fucking damn it," he thundered in the next room, causing Dasha to flinch and bring the pistol up to eye level and aim it at the locked door.

Any minute now, she reflected.

"Glennis, you fucking goddamn bitch!" yelled Robert.

If shouts could kill I'd be dead, thought Dasha, who prepared for the giant Robert to come crashing through the door.

And then, in a night not without hubris, she thought she might be able to turn the man and bring him to heel. That's what you do in the field of intelligence. It was her calling. You always made a try for the bigger fish.

McCarran is at the heart of all this, she thought. Robert was just the help. She needed to go to the top.

"Come to Dasha," she whispered, not really believing what she was saying or thinking—only that she felt young, alive, and a central player on her own monumental stage.

Robert was banging on Glennis's door now and Dasha could tell he was putting his shoulder into it.

"It won't be long now," she said out loud, the doorframe cracking just as the words left her trembling lips.

"I'm going to kill you, you fucking bitch," said Robert as he came through the broken door and slapped on the switch to the overhead light. He was carrying an impressive bit of momentum, but he stopped short when he encountered his elderly neighbor aiming his own pistol at the center of his chest from across the room.

67

Surprise

DeFranco was calling in backup and Tracy was belted in, pressing herself into the big car's front seat as the chief wheeled the machine through the back streets of Westport. Dispatch was trying to explain they were lightly staffed on that particular evening and he'd do his best but he had two cars out on calls— one in the ER at Norwalk Hospital following an auto accident and one dealing with an infant turning blue.

They pulled into Dasha's driveway and ran toward the cottage, bursting inside to find a world-weary Glennis just coming to on the couch. Galina emerged from her chambers wearing both her robe and a puzzled expression. She looked around the room and didn't see her sister and started to moan.

"Where's Dasha?" DeFranco asked, reaching for his Glock.

"I don't know," said Glennis. "I must have fallen asleep."

"Who are you?" he asked her.

"I work for Mr. McCarran next door," she said. She pointed in the general direction of the little door in the hedge.

"Is Dasha over there now?" he asked.

"Could be," said Glennis.

"Can you stay here with Galina? I'll go look for Dasha," said DeFranco. He wanted to ask Tracy to stay behind too, but knew she wouldn't find it possible. She already had her Kimber out and, after this eventful evening, was quite prepared to use it.

68

Dilemma

"If you kill me now, Robert, you won't get your stash in the duffel bag. I know where it is. I can get it for you," said Dasha, confronting the man with the upraised arm holding what looked like a crude Irish shillelagh. "You club me with that thing and it will only slow you down. You'll never find it."

She was proceeding directly to the heart of Robert's immediate dilemma. This kind of negotiation didn't require arcane sophistry.

She had it.

He wanted it.

She'd open the conversation there.

"Bitch," said Robert.

"Oh, please," said Dasha. "You can do better than that. Let's figure out how we can get you your bag so you can be on your way. That's really the challenge isn't it?"

"Where is it?" he shouted, coming closer.

"I've got this nice gun of yours aimed right at your heart. On your way to Panama? Great likeness in that passport. Real professional job. Come any closer and you're done for all eternity. Let me repeat. How can we get you your bag? Time is wasting. Police will be here soon. I've called them. Your bag, Robert. I can get it for you. First I need some information."

Robert looked pained.

"How much does McCarran know about your various activities?" she asked quietly, her nerves made of the same steel that had belonged to that long-ago girl who'd defied the Gestapo. She didn't want to startle the poor man.

"He knows everything," said Robert.

"The death of the girl? The ME's assistant? The CID inspector? Chief Talbot? What did McCarran know and when did he know it?"

"He knew about the girl," said Robert. "The others had to go too. They were on the margins."

"So the others were your idea?"

"They had to go. A safety factor."

"Did young John McCarran kill the girl?"

"No."

"Who did?"

"Not for me to say."

"You want your bag, don't you?"

"Yes, you fucking bitch," he said, looking at her with those dead eyes.

He came six inches closer.

"Who killed her then?" asked Dasha.

"That little Mortensen kid. John told me the kid put a roofie in her Coke. He wanted to have sex with her on the beach. Ripped her clothes off. John couldn't stop him. He tried. The girl refused Mikey and he threw her in the water, then picked up some gravel and shoved it in her mouth. She choked on it."

"So it was the Mortensen boy, not John," said Dasha, the whole unseemly catastrophe now hurtling into view. "Why did McCarran want to protect the Mortensen boy?"

"A favor," said Robert. "Went a long way back." He stepped closer, the gun now just a foot away. She was within reach of his massive arms.

"Stay back," said Dasha. She was thinking, Why not just shoot him and be done with it? That's when Robert suddenly reached for the gun. He pushed the slide back and put his right index finger in front of the hammer as it came down, preventing the gun from firing. He held the gun in the vise of his huge right hand and twisted it away. Then he wheeled his left arm around and slapped her in the face. The air went out of her but she managed to remain upright. Robert put his huge left arm around

Dasha's throat and started to squeeze while he pointed the pistol at her head.

"Let's go find my bag," he said quietly, back in control.

69

Tables Turning

DeFranco and Tracy ran toward the hedge and only found the door because it was wide open and the moonlight shone through, revealing the opening. Pistols drawn and with probable cause, they entered the McCarran property. DeFranco immediately recognized the white van in front of the carriage house on his right. They approached and saw movement in the room behind the little balcony above. There was a duffel bag hanging on a bush just to the right of the entrance and Tracy picked it up. It was heavy.

And that was how they all came together.

Robert and Dasha appeared at the carriage house doorway. Robert was holding Dasha around the neck with the FN at her temple. DeFranco was aiming his Glock at Robert as he stepped across the threshold. Dasha was telling DeFranco, "Don't worry, dear. The situation is under control." And Tracy was left holding the bag, her Kimber still in her strong hand, cocked and locked and pointed at the head of the man who had very nearly murdered her earlier that evening.

"Drop your guns or she dies," said Robert calmly.

DeFranco knew Robert could—and would—pull the trigger. He couldn't jeopardize Dasha.

He needed time.

"Tracy, let's put our guns down."

It was a bad choice. Apparently the only choice.

"Give me my bag," said Robert. Tracy complied and he walked Dasha over to his van and put the bag through the open window on the passenger side.

"Where's Glennis?" asked Robert.

"Somewhere safe," replied Dasha. She didn't sound convincing.

"Your house?" Robert correctly surmised. "Let's all go together. You two lead. I'll take up the rear with the old woman. You flinch, try to run, anything…she's dead."

"You're the boss," said DeFranco, trying to work out their next moves. The problem was getting Dasha separated from Robert. They walked in a huddle toward the hedge and DeFranco was glad he still had his snubbie on his ankle.

Tonight of all nights, thought DeFranco. You've got to use it.

They made it through the door, Robert and Dasha trailing.

The garden cottage living room was lit up and they could see Glennis and Galina walking back and forth. Galina was stone-faced and Glennis was wringing her hands with worry. Glennis's face lit up when Tracy and DeFranco came through the door, but she let out a little scream when she saw Robert, the gun, and his hostage Dasha.

"Nice to see you, Glennis," said Robert.

DeFranco could see Robert start to relax. McCarran's mercenary had all his antagonists in one room: the small-town cop who wouldn't leave him alone, the crusading television reporter, the nosy housekeeper, the crazy neighbor lady. Robert also had his bag with his getaway goods safe in his van.

"Don't do this," said DeFranco. "Tie us up. Leave. Take my car. Tank is full. You'll have a nice head start." He was playing for time. He needed to distract Robert so he could get to his revolver.

"Thanks for the offer," said Robert. "But I'm going to finish the evening right here." He raised his pistol and swung it smoothly toward Tracy's head.

Later, DeFranco would look back on the next few seconds, trying to pull the time apart so he could analyze and filter the actions and reactions of everyone in the room. Glennis was helping the only way she could, by screaming at the top of her lungs. DeFranco could see Robert didn't care for that, and he swung the FN back in Glennis's direction. That's when DeFranco went down on a knee to get his faithful snubbie free of his ankle holster. At the same time, he watched Galina reach for Dasha's chestnut stick on the dining-room table. She used her one good hand to toss the stick to her sister. Robert turned his pistol back toward Galina while Dasha caught the stick in her right hand. Then, in one swift, smooth movement, Dasha extracted the blade with her left hand and plunged it deep into Robert's neck, giving it a good twist as it went in. Robert lowered his gun and started to choke and turn blue, his expression more curious than panicked. He put his hand up to his neck to stop the blood, which sprayed out over the great room in an impressive arc.

"Oh dear, not the Persian," said Dasha, eyeing with no small pity the rug she'd brought back from Tehran, where she'd helped install the Shah.

They all watched Robert gasping for breath, his face draining of color, blood rushing in a torrent. At last, their tormenter was felled like a tree. Galina smiled and walked over to hug her sister. Tracy moved Glennis toward the couch where they could sit and hold hands. DeFranco walked calmly to the phone to call headquarters, the state's attorney emergency nightline, and the medical examiner's office.

He was in no hurry.

Later, DeFranco would oversee the official gathering in the guesthouse while the scene was being processed and the body was removed. At one point, he noticed Dasha Petrov was missing. Several minutes went by and she returned through the greenhouse. He didn't think any more of it until two hectic weeks had passed and the chief, Tracy, and Dasha Petrov were out walking on the beach. She was trying to teach her new friends the difference between a redhead duck and a canvasback.

"The canvasback's head slopes toward the beak in a beautiful line," said Dasha. "And the male canvasback has those deep, rich colors. There is nothing prettier in nature."

Their conversation turned to that dreadful night when they'd almost become "margins" in Robert's logbook.

"We were zipping up the body bag, Dasha, and you had left the room," said DeFranco. "Where did you go?"

Dasha stopped and looked out across the still waters of Long Island Sound. It was a windless day, and sea and sky merged into a seamless gray. DeFranco and Tracy could tell Dasha was troubled, hesitant, trying to find some kind of inspiration to form the words.

"If only Constantine were here," Dasha said at last. "He'd know what to do."

"What's bothering you, dear?" asked Tracy at last, as Dasha brushed aside her tears.

"I trust you two with my life," she said. "You mustn't tell anyone. Agree?" The chief wasn't sure what he and Tracy were getting themselves into, but together they had looked into the abyss. They were now comrades in arms.

"Agreed," said DeFranco.

"Me too," said Tracy.

"That night, when they were picking up the body, I went back over to the McCarran carriage house and grabbed Robert's duffel bag off the right front seat of his van. I carried it across the hedge and put it inside the potting shed at the end of Constantine's greenhouse. I put some pesticide cans in front of it, and sprinkled it with peat moss. My accountant and I are still toting it all up."

Tracy Taggart laughed and gave Dasha a hug.

Chief Anthony DeFranco—Westport's own—looked into the old spy's eyes of blue. He hesitated, trying to assess what crimes had been committed, and finally said, "No one deserves it more, Mrs. Petrov. No one deserves it more."

Epilogue

Six months had gone by. A crisp fall had given way to a frigid winter and now a bountiful spring. Chief DeFranco was in his glass-walled office listening to the head of maintenance deliver a monotone of worn disc rotors and slipping transmissions and suspicious head gaskets when Madge entered with an envelope. Written in an elegant calligraphy, the presence of the chief of police and Miss Tracy Taggart was requested at the home of Mrs. Constantine Petrov. Cocktails at six, dinner at eight, this coming Saturday. DeFranco and Tracy had been living comfortably, peacefully, and often rapturously in Tracy's apartment on Long Ridge Road. DeFranco phoned Tracy at the television station and asked her to clear her calendar.

They had been invited back to the scene of their salvation. Of course, it could never be described as the scene of the crime, because the little cottage in the garden was where Dasha, with Galina's help, had saved them from certain annihilation. They were eager to check in with their friend, mentor, and now their savior.

The invitation carried the words *black tie*, so DeFranco rounded up a borrowed tux and Tracy squeezed into a sequined De La Renta, procured for the evening from a local dress shop she'd once featured on News 12 Connecticut. It was a bit of innocent baksheesh. Returning it intact the next day would not unduly interfere with her journalistic ethics.

DeFranco reflected as they chatted amiably before a mirror in Tracy's boudoir—he, knotting his bowtie, she applying mascara—that their relationship had survived the brute intensity of very nearly being killed. He worried she'd tire of him when they were off the case of the headless girl and back to their old routines. But he learned they could talk—and laugh—about anything under the sun, and their companionship was becoming rich and polished, something to hold up to the light and admire. Whether it was attending one of Sam's soccer matches in New London, or visiting Angelica's dorm in Storrs, or improving their accuracy at Lenny's pistol range, they enjoyed immensely the simple act of breathing the same air.

This night, they were a striking pair, and once a tuxedo-clad DeFranco had dispensed with the out-of-work maître d' jokes, they enjoyed playing dress-up for at least an evening.

The chief and his beautiful lady boarded the now ubiquitous Crown Vic and made their way to Beachside Avenue. They parked in front of the seven-bay garage, at once noticing a certain shine to the old place. The shingles on the garage had been scraped and painted, the hedges trimmed, the old cyclone fence extracted and removed, replaced by a handsome stone wall. Dasha had installed lighting down the drive, and DeFranco observed Constantine's budding lilacs in the crisp chill of an April evening. As they approached the little cottage, DeFranco and Tracy heard violins.

They knocked on the door and were greeted by a butler in a cutaway. They came through the tiny kitchen and bid greetings to a potbellied cook basting game hens and fashioning some kind of soufflé. The butler took their drink order and led them out to the greenhouse, filled with flowering plants and the abundant perfumes of nature. Dasha, Galina, and their trusted friend Glennis were seated in resplendent fan chairs, soaking up the warmth from the restored heating system.

"We turned it on and everything worked!" Dasha exclaimed. "Our bill has gone right through the roof!"

Galina laughed and wiggled her toes and, using her good hand, took another sip of champagne. Glennis had the weight of the world lifted from her shoulders and she beamed her delight as the butler passed the canapés.

"Tracy, darling," said Dasha. "We wanted to toast you at last. Your final piece on the case of the headless girl was brilliant, and we thought a party would be a fitting end. Nothing like near death to bring out our best."

DeFranco and Tracy stood hand in hand and beheld the scene in a kind of dazed wonder. Had Constantine's oil wells come back to life? Then the chief remembered Robert's duffel bag and smiled.

"Tell us, dear," said Dasha. "What was it like to put the final cap on the case?"

"I just told the story," said Tracy, accepting some beluga caviar on toast points with capers, onion, and lemon. "It was all of you who made the story happen. And it was you, Dasha, who helped us live to fight another day."

"Nonsense, dear," said Dasha. "We're a team."

Tracy's piece had opened with another helicopter fly-by. She and Danny occupied the back seat of the Bell Jet Ranger, which fluttered to a landing on the Petrovs' front lawn. They exited the machine and walked back to the little cottage, to the scene where Westport serial killer Robert William Altman—disgraced ex-Navy SEAL, former State Department security officer, and confirmed human rights violator—had threatened to kill five more individuals to cover his nefarious tracks.

As Tracy pointed out, Robert or his henchmen were already responsible for the deaths of Curtis Jones, Tamara Moriarty, and Gerald Talbot. His rampage had also resulted in the death of Evan Hughes, corrupt Westport police officer. And Robert was a central figure in the case of the headless corpse that had started it all.

Tracy's reporting and Danny's footage had already led to the arrest of Mikey Mortensen for the murder of Kali Patel. The defendant's fingerprints and the fingerprint from the sea glass were a match. Mikey had a scar from a bite mark on the knuckle of his right index finger. They also covered the arrest of a howling-mad Pers Mortensen, who was charged with conspiracy and obstruction. Tracy's reporting disclosed the role of turncoat police officer Wendell McKurdy—with accompanying interviews of the newly installed chief of police—in disposing of the first murder victim and also complicity in the murder of Tamara Moriarty. He was also charged with attempted murder for the raid on the boatyard.

Angus McCarran was charged with manslaughter, having hired, bankrolled, and conspired with Robert Altman. The tycoon was out on bail, but even the most confident legal observer couldn't see how McCarran could avoid at least twenty years in jail.

His father's rapid fall had a sobering effect on John McCarran, who was on the verge of passing his senior year on the dean's list. His application to Wharton had been accepted and he'd already taken up the slack in the executive suite at McCarran Holdings, representing his family's sprawling interests. He had looked into the abyss and stepped back. But the new state's attorney was not kindly disposed to giving the young man a free pass. After all, it was John's behavior leading up to the murder that had caused Robert's rampage. He had taken advantage of the young girl, and his inaction led to her death and the demise of others. After consulting with Westport's newly installed police chief, the state's attorney settled on the charge of conspiracy. Restitution: two thousand hours of community service under the watchful eye of Chief DeFranco. Wharton would have to be put on hold for a year, and that's how the billionaire's son found himself on most weekdays working in the police department garage, or cleaning the latrines, or helping Madge with the filing. He and DeFranco also spent some time in the gym together, talking about life and the pursuit of happiness. DeFranco noticed his clothes fitting better after a few workouts, and he also noticed a respectful attitude replace young McCarran's once loutish ways. One item the chief insisted on was that the McCarran family would agree to give Glennis lifetime employment, free accommodation, and a pair of assistant housekeepers to keep the McCarran place going while John settled into his new life of work and responsibility. Dasha asked the chief to make sure Angus McCarran established a twenty-million dollar relief fund for Robert Altman's victims on many continents. If that wasn't enough, McCarran would need to pledge more.

One thing Tracy didn't share with her viewers: DeFranco had been puzzled about the sea glass that had turned up loose inside the dumpster with the girl. Where had it come from? And why didn't Robert remove Kali's toe ring? It had been the Rosetta Stone that had unlocked the girl's identity.

McKurdy disclosed that on the night of the murder, young John had come around to the back of the garage where Robert was in the act of preparing the girl's body. He didn't want the boy to see her, so he quickly wrapped the corpse in a blanket and put it in the trunk of the blue sedan. John was convulsed with tears and he put the little bag of sea glass they'd collected together in the trunk with the body. Robert had sprinkled the sea glass into the dumpster when he'd deposited the girl, throwing in the little cloth sack that no doubt went into the compactor. The toe ring? He'd simply missed it.

After the medical examiner verified the identity of the girl with the help of her father's timely package, Dr. Patel came to the States to handle Kali's remains. McKurdy supplied the location of the makeshift grave on the outskirts of Meriden, and she was disinterred. Chief DeFranco wanted to be there, of course, but Kali's father waited in the Crown Vic until she was safely bundled into a body bag. That left the ghoulish task of finding all of Kali's remains, which DeFranco undertook privately with the help of a state police cadaver dog with handler. That's how the chief, an assistant medical examiner, and a bloodhound named Cindy came together one Saturday morning at the state park in Redding, with a map McKurdy penciled out in his jail cell. Cindy made short work of finding what was left of Kali Patel. The assistant medical examiner placed the remains in a bag and approached the chief, holding in his hands a dirty necklace with a locket. DeFranco opened the locket with a penknife and saw a picture of Dr. and Mrs. Patel on one side, and their daughter Kali on the other.

She had a name, and now she had a face.

It was her family's wish to have her cremated and the chief and Tracy accompanied Kali's father to execute this final task. There were tears, of course, which Tracy's final piece deftly skirted in deference to the family's privacy.

"Well, darling, it was a tour de force," said Dasha.

"We'd be nowhere without you," said Tracy. They tipped their glasses and drained their champagne and the butler poured more.

"And I have something for you, Chief DeFranco," said Dasha while Galina and Glennis looked on, enchanted. They were in on the secret.

Dasha reached behind her and pulled out a long roll of paper wrapped in a bow. DeFranco handed his champagne flute to Tracy, who shared his bewilderment. He undid the ribbon and unfurled the document and beheld architectural plans for a proud little house with a bowfront window and a cobblestone chimney. The caption in the box on the lower left said *Anthony DeFranco Family Home, High Gate Road, Westport, Connecticut.* There were side views and floor plans and details for a big kitchen with an island and a gas range.

This mighty man dropped the plans to the floor and put his hands over his face and wept. Tracy held him for all he was worth. And when his kids arrived the next day—swept up by Dasha's hired limousines—they stood on the front yard of their new home while workmen happily toiled.

DeFranco took Tracy Taggart, Sam, and Angelica into his broad embrace.

It was time to rebuild.

Acknowledgments

When one completes a novel, pushing the keyboard away to send the offspring out to face a cruel world, it's remarkable to think of all the people who contributed to the birthing. Eric Burns's early read sent *The Sea Glass Murders* off in a new and, I daresay, proper direction. Ken Bernhard, Esq., provided critical insight on criminal procedure, and Dr. Jim Bregman confirmed I hadn't gone too far astray when it came to medical matters. Special thanks to Jim's wonderful wife, Lisa, and fine son Justin for their interest and encouragement. Walter Smedley III and John Pfeiffer each gave *Sea Glass* a keen-eyed read and became early champions. Sam and Kathy Felix, avid crime and mystery book readers, gave the book their enthusiastic thumbs-up. Val Oakley, too, was an early enthusiastic reader. Stuart Horwitz of Book Architecture offered crucial perspective, and my dear friend Bonnie Barney took *Sea Glass* under her nurturing wing. My fastidious friend Doug Logan gave the final manuscript an uncompromising polish, and I will forever be indebted to Richard Armstrong, who, with Kent Sorsky, did so much to bring this book into the light. I can't forget my son Robert Andrew Cole, who has a particular gift for spotting his father's literary peccadillos, for which I am grateful. I am no less buoyed by Andrew's stalwart siblings Peter and Sasha, our daughter-in-law Leslie—and now of course our granddaughter Tula, whose love of puzzles already reveals a deeply inquiring mind.

My splendid wife Sarah patiently held my hand while I went through the trials of authorship, giving me the time and peace of mind at night, on the commuter rails, and on days off to tackle this project. Her unfailing grace and support extended to offering critical plot points, always thinking six moves down the chessboard.

It's an unusual experience to fall in love with a character you've created. Dasha is intelligent, brave, impassioned, insightful, and clever. While she doesn't shy from taking the fight to the enemy—often fatal to the opposition—she has a deep humanity. She's been molded from the malleable clay of one's imagination, but if there *is* an inspiration for this ardent soldier of democracy, it would have to be my dear departed friend Irina Zavoico, who fled a Europe destroyed by World War II and came to embrace America with unstinting patriotism. She and her sister Xenia Saparov were devoted to their adopted country, and loved America with the passion and commitment unique to an émigré community that had survived the dark heart of Nazi Germany and the soul-crushing machinery of the Soviet system. We miss them.

There are many pockets of plenty in this great country that lay claim to the legendary Gold Coast. But the Gold Coast that forms the principal backdrop for this novel rests along the shore of Long Island Sound in southwestern Connecticut. It's home to a broad diversity of ethnicities and cultures, and the driven strivers who have built and occupy this land of high achievement. They are the titans of Wall Street, the movers of markets, the creators of books and art, the masters of media. I am afraid I have trampled severely on their eminent domain, and I hope to be forgiven. But please know I have written a work of fiction—a simple entertainment—and intend no offense to the fine people of Westport and its environs. Be forewarned: In the next Gold Coast Mystery, Dasha Petrov confronts the KGB on her very doorstep.

Timothy Cole is the editorial director of Belvoir Media Group, publishers of health information products from Harvard Medical School, The Cleveland Clinic, Massachusetts General Hospital, and other health centers. In prior roles he served as an editor at leading marine magazines, and was the science/technology/aerospace editor of *Popular Mechanics*. Tim's editorial assignments have taken him aboard America's nuclear navy, to climate change studies at the South Pole, and to particle physics cyclotrons in Siberia. He is an instrument-rated private pilot, and holds a fifty-ton captain's license from the US Coast Guard. Tim and his wife, Sarah Smedley, live in Greenwich, Connecticut, and New York City. He just completed *Moscow Five*, the second book in the Gold Coast Mystery series, and is sending Dasha Petrov on more adventures in *Relentless*.

D' 1